ALSO BY HORTENSE CALISHER

In the
PALACE
of the
MOVIE
KING

RANDOM HOUSE ⌂ NEW YORK

Hortense Calisher

In the PALACE of the MOVIE KING

TO MY COUNTRY—*on the verge*

Library of Congress Cataloging-in-Publication Data
Calisher, Hortense.
In the palace of the movie king / Hortense Calisher.—1st ed.
p. cm.
I. Title. PS3553.A4I5 1993
813'.54—dc20   92-56807

Book designed by Gloria Tso

Manufactured in the United States of America

24689753

FIRST EDITION

CONTENTS

Part I

Part II

Contents

PART
I

You should know that by the last decade of the twentieth century, America—as we in the United States had for over two hundred grandiose if inaccurate years been calling ourselves—had become accustomed to taking to its heart or its bosom—sometimes both—a particular band of adopted heroes, tainted with foreign blood or even heavier radicalism but curiously homey in image once we got our hands on them. They were called dissidents.

The term itself, at first only to be found tucked in the newspapers and conversations of those sallow chumps called libertarians, had gradually wormed its way into the general pity. As everyone knows, this is the largest emotion in our essentially good-hearted country.

Soon the word "dissident" could be heard hissing gracefully even from the jaws of children in civics classes. The kid at a kid's elbow might even be the child of one of these heroes—on university campuses especially. There the father, if by any chance a noted scientist, scholar, or literary man, might well be occupying the special academic chair that some foundation had raised money for. It could happen, alas, that the chair was one usually awarded a native son. But since our hero had probably been saved from prison or worse by such swift empathy, who could begrudge it him?

Meanwhile, lesser lights of that same breed, or bachelor ones, might tour our college circuits, consoled for what they had left behind, or else found vulgar here, by comfortable fees and a round of affairs with those dazzling undergraduates who remain forever young.

Or so some of the more envious among us say. The rest—poets who in a country awash with careless freedom have no hope of speaking from behind iron bars, or painters whose nightmare visions are grounded only in Brooklyn or Illinois—know better what these heroes have done, and applaud them. When a man rejects martyrdom for America, that is the least one can do.

In the performing arts, matters go easier. Stars can twinkle there without reference to the "third world" or to any—almost like the scientists. Who wouldn't warm to the likes of a Baryshnikov or a Makarova, who vault an ocean to come to us, then dance us into that half-light where all are heroes, and meanwhile work like drovers to keep themselves on pointe? The playwrights have it harder, grumbling along in dirty cafés for years without being produced except in coffee-houses—just like our native counterparts. As for the journalists and novelists, they had better come to us already famous. Otherwise, what do you do when you lose your whole frame of reference? Or abandon it—the streets, the childhood, even the wonderful rottenness of hiding out? Exchanging it all for our Thruway mountains, with their poster restaurants, in which the spine sinks into the same chintz a thousand miles on into regions that, according to your cult of us, were once the whole savage's wilderness? What can you do with the new country except satirize it—once? And then?

One hears it goes more comfortably in Paris, traditional home to the political refugee, where dissidence in all matters except finance is a part of normal life. Or in London, where once you have been helped, with that lack of fanfare which is their pride, as long as you keep the peace you will be left to your own eccentricities, like everybody else. In either place, or in several other capital cities, you may well find a job, as well as the very bistro where your kind spends its evenings, and so sink into the mild freedoms and incontestable grievances that are every human's right. And for which you left home.

But if you want to continue being a hero, then you had better come to us.

Mind you, we can't always tell you why. Is it because in ancestry we were all once like you—thinned by important rages? The world wasn't small enough then to call us all by one hissed name. We were Puritans, Huguenots, steerage Swedenborgians—or prison offal who had served out our sentences for stealing a loaf of bread and still had enough muscle to ship on as deckhands bound for the land of the free. Or Spanish moneylenders and Polish chicken-slaughterers, each with a ghetto talent for ritual and a fierce need for their Ark. Plus of course a few lordly sprigs, with land grants for half of Maryland in their pockets; there are always these aristocrats. Almost all of us, though, spurred on toward equality by the fusillade of shots and death sentences aimed at our behinds.

Meanwhile, as the years mollify us, a taste for vicarious tragedy emerges, especially between wars. That's a time when the red in a flag may decline to an aesthetic pink—and our own bottom dogs no longer satisfy us. There are after all so many of them.

How much easier to pity and admire a person whose martyrdom comes from somewhere else! Indignation is good for the adrenaline. And after a hard day in the service of one's own country—as most of us consider ourselves to be—who among us doesn't enjoy a dram or two of holier-than-thou?

Anyway, here are men who have suffered for freedom's sake. Strange birds, some of them. Foreigners all. Pity them for that alone. As they come forward in our newspapers, with their guarded faces, or climb our podiums, or sink into small university towns, or rise to be international—or even so stuff themselves with our privileges that they must vomit these back at us—what is it that keeps them heroes? What's so familiar about them?

Is it that they resemble us—as we were, once?

· · ·

5

We Americans first met Paul Gonchev and his then wife-to-be, Vuksica, at a summer film festival in the great Roman atrium at Pula, Yugoslavia. At that time, Vuksica was one of their well-known film stars, and her twin brother, Danilo, a prominent journalist and sometime actor. But the crowd was both casual and amiable, and even those on the fringe were able to meet everybody.

Vuksica was pointed out to us as a captivating woman who infuriated men by her calm. In a film just seen, she had certainly been that. Nevertheless, up close, one saw how she could make intimates of any women present, by her assumption that they were all captivating in one way or another, with calm being a necessary virtue, if she and they were to manage in the wildwood of men. Which was what men were to her; she did not intellectualize us.

At first we didn't much notice Gonchev. He was that dark presence at her side, the man about to win her—lady film stars always being so equipped. He was a looker, too, in a chunky immovable way—though his cheeks already bore the saber scars of early middle age. Had he by then acquired that air of physical authority which so often surrounds a filmmaker—as if the world-at-hand could be upended by the turn of a wrist? If so, we didn't mark it. There were a number of well-favored men about, some with that very authority.

Later, when his own film was shown, he was identified as that Russian-born director who had just recently left his adopted Japan for one of those minor Balkan provinces whose existence people kept forgetting. There, he and Vuksica were to immure themselves, while he produced those unique travelogues for which the outer world would eventually beat its way to him. But at the moment, strolling those circular, segmented aisles in the sub-Roman dusk, we saw writers and reporters whose names we knew, beauties we yearned to know, and those were the ones we followed.

We all met again in an after-show crowd made up of a good portion of artistic Belgrade, at a long, white-naperied table in Pula's anciently classic hotel. We were very hungry and ordered expectantly from the menu, which, though written in purple bistro-script, was as extensive as those in any four-star hotel in Europe. As the waiter shook his head at each of our choices and we worked our way down the list, the table watching us bubbled with Serbo-Croat exchanges, finally bursting into uproarious laughter when, pleading limply "Coffee?," we were once again refused—and at last realized that the menu was a socialist farce. What could we have? The waiter pointed to what everyone else was having, and was all that the place served—matchstick pretzels and beer.

One golden-haired charmboy whose profile was as much a film star's as any present—that would have been Danilo—arose and, pointing down the table to each person's identical bottle and pretzel packet, said in excellent English: "He's having partridge. . . . She's having our national sausage. . . . I'm having *loup de mer*"—and as the waiter served us our packets and bottles: "He appears to have brought you chocolate mousse by mistake. But if I were you, I wouldn't send it back."

Was it at that moment, as all the smiling, punchinello faces begged our laughter, that we fell in love all over again with the Europe of our ancestors—and with life as lived by some of them?

And who were we?

Young buffs just out of school, abroad on our post-graduation grand tour. On which one traveled only to learn the differences between countries, in a dreamy poets-and-peasants overture. The steamships had all but gone, but the freighters lingered. Today's brute underworld of whole peoples embarking on rafts hadn't yet dirtied our screens. Travel could still be innocent.

While, back home, *Washington Crossing the Delaware* was now everybody's ancestor, regardless of race, color, or creed. Europe was half map, half particolored balloon, if with tangles of barbed wire in its shadows, and certain massed graves that must never be closed. But for us beginners, rough travel was a slalom on the record-breaking slopes, or an enviable fellow hanging by his cleats on Everest.

And movies—God bless them—were still movies. Not setups with one eye on art, the other on document.

Few around us saw—had Gonchev?—that we were all being led into that dark-bright realm where the movie would be us.

1

Director Gonchev

AFTER THE SCREENING of the film his student crew had been allowed to do, Director Gonchev was quite shaken. Could that have been Paris up there—the real Paris—and not the stage sets built by him years ago, which he had at last allowed to be used? Those thick-lipped curb-stones—surely he had never seen any like those before. Nor had he ever seen that street, penciled in so thin and gray, which had flitted the film throughout—a set more for some smart theorem of a ballet, to be danced on pogo sticks. Contrarily, that courtyard scene, in a Palais de Something turned into workers' flats and bordered on three sides with gesticulating heads, had been bigger than life, outsize for a budget documentary. And he would have sworn that the building itself was not on any of his maps of the Marais.

Counting his breaths as usual, it took him double the ritual—twenty deep ones, plus an extra that slipped out shallowly—before he rose from his preferred seat for viewings—tenth row off-center, the two rows ahead of him and behind him to remain empty—then swiveled to acknowledge the familiar committee faces with a smile that also noted the seat position each of them had felt up to this evening. So done, he swung up the aisle and out the summer studio door. The minute his foot touched grass the smile left him. Grass is so real.

Outside in the mountain air he is safe from approach for the usual half hour, while the committee in private session formally collects its thoughts, though more often waiting for him to tell them what those were. Before each viewing he had the time of sunset checked and the day's schedule adjusted accordingly, ostensibly because he was allergic to daytime pollen, but actually so that if any of the group ventured out to consult him on a point, his face could be in shadow or not, depending on where he chose to stand. So could theirs, but they could never hope to equal him at these small physical games, which had protected Gonchev's neutrality through several childhoods in as many adopted countries, and were now as chronic with him as anyone else's cough or trick knee. He thought of these dodges as his "arrangements." Those who saw through them interested him at once. They would have their own.

"Paul," the smartest student he had ever trained had said to him three months before, "you never sneeze."

"Stepan," Gonchev had replied, "you take a crew out, the next script."

Twelve weeks that louse Stepan was to have had for it, plus three days to get there, three to return, from the vast arena of studio lots that Gonchev had created on the location that had first wooed him—a plateau in the farthest range of the barrier ridges that crisscrossed and encircled this least known and farthest littoral of the Balkans. "No, take five days on the return trip," Gonchev had said generously, though he would have to fill out a form for it. "By that time it'll be autumn. There'll be snow."

No film crew from here has ever traveled outside the country's borders. In the sixteen years since its fiercely xenophobe government had hired Gonchev away from his adopted country, Japan, no crew had needed to. Reared in a nation where any ordinary citizen was a connoisseur of facsimile, Gonchev had been trained by men who had worked with the men around his own early god, Kurosawa. But the art of Japan, that exquisitely tiny area, was necessarily focused on achieving the infinite vistas possible in a box-room. And there he had felt himself still a Westerner.

Standing before the small but divinely floating panels in the Nijo Castle in Kyoto with the other boys of his lower school while the monk in charge pointed to the distances enshrined there, he had felt himself to be a Western dog, sniffing another kind of space. Not just travel space, for counting the time in his mother's womb, he was already in his third country and city. Nor mere adventure space, of which the émigré has more than enough. Space confined—to the grown man this was what had been adventure. As in this fierce backwater of a country that had made travel a sin—and was craving it. On film.

The essence of a good location was that you had to get to it; the more trouble this took the better. No one had warned him that the mountain range he had chosen had once been called the Accursed. Half the roadways here were off the horizontal anyway; he had merely set the studio lots as many versts away from the country's center as one could get, and on the longest hypotenuse. Dubbing his plateau Elsinore, not for *Hamlet,* as he allowed it to be believed, but for a once-glimpsed shot of an old location site in California's Santa Ana range, used long ago by the Hollywood he might now never see. Like his long-gone parents— and like them doomed to tiny countries—to the end he would dream of distance in versts.

What he'd been asked to do by this half-Muslim, semipeasant en- clave—whose thousand-year-old culture and leftover medieval blood- thirstiness had somehow got entangled in the logical brutalities of Karl Marx—was to give it travelogues. He had responded by offering to build them his movie-set cities, which were the only distances he knew. On the crabbed lots of Tokyo and Osaka he had been taught how to scissor, mirror-image, and holograph human burrows of any size, or even to create thriftily, with ever dreamier compounds, such wood and stone as might be needed. He would bring the art of the vista to their plateau.

And, with their oddly sub-rosa cooperation, so he had done, seeing only later what other use he was to them. For this country, which one left or entered only under threat, meant to keep fully abreast of things outside. It merely did not intend to let its citizens take part in them.

Tonight's footage hadn't run two minutes before the hair on his arms had risen in chill. No one else in the screening room seemed to have noticed what he had. Possibly only he was meant to. As Chief Director of Locales—a title that had amused him until he saw what could happen to the untitled—it was his job to keep those as tight in everybody's head—and camera—as they were in his own. It was a film crew's job to conform to whatever locales he sent them to film on that plateau, no matter how bemused their eyes might seem to be when they got back.

For though actual cities changed daily, and the major ones the most— buildings tumbling or burning, neighborhoods being rescued or vanishing, and the people along with them—his career existed precisely because of that, his archives containing reports and slides updated daily from all the sources, pictorial and written, official and contraband, that streamed in. Over which, after staff had gone, he himself charted and drew, played street sounds and collated directories, far into the night.

It was his joke that he could tell you the likely shape of a true Englishman's nose in any of the backwaters of London, or of a girl's leg from any one of the five boroughs of New York, including Richmond. To know the streets of those two cities, for instance, he had given himself the cabdrivers' licensing test for the one, and had scoured the tax rolls of the other, using a computer—a contraband gift that had one night appeared on his desk like an archangel—only to ratify what his own sense of urban plot and character had first told him. For fifty cities around the world he had now done this; the rest were not major, at least not at this studio.

In return, early on he had been allowed to "formalize" his dangerously foreign and "regime-ist" surname by the omission of two telltale syllables, had later been allotted a second, or "vacation," house, which he used in theory only (being well advised that such use might bring the syllables back), and as real advantages could have the car his wife drove, and send both his children, smart or not—the girl was—to be trained as scientists. Oh, what a lovely house of cards it had been. For now, he must manage to phone his wife.

He knew what she would say, had always said. That in the end there was nothing more dangerous than a departure from reality, either in a government temporarily surviving so, or in a man. If he would only take

11

up womanizing—until then she wouldn't feel safe. She could tease because she knew very well what the case was.

He was in love with a city. It remained in his head, as volatile as some woman with dozens of gowns and lovers she couldn't keep track of, its boulevards frozen into being centuries before that interloper Baron Haussmann had had his way with it, yet forever melting under its ever-present pillows of cloud. Since his own boyhood, when he had first contracted this love, Paris had been taken down a peg. In recent case, even Americanized. The world seeps in. But until today the thought of her, that she-city, had helped lighten his archive.

Now, whether or not this film was the real Paris, he had glimpsed what she might have lost in the minds of men. How could he feel this—a man whose trail of visas attested that he had never been farther west than Vienna? The trouble with Paris was that, in spite of the visas, he was convinced that he had been to it.

He would have been about seven. How come a boy of that age would be traveling alone in the Kyoto train? Yet he saw himself, neat as a pin in the shirt his mother had ironed for him, his hands folded over the ticket stub he would clutch until he got there. There was no train in the world that would carry a boy from Kyoto to the Gare de Lyon—a train on which one neither ate nor slept nor went to the toilet, but from which the boy alighted, the shirt still uncreased, lifting his face to the sky that was just as it should be, and made his way without asking to a concert at the Salle Pleyel. Yet he could still feel himself behind that face. The shirt had been his Sunday shirt.

At other times he knew himself to be merely the boy who had sat picking his nose and staring at the Chagall over his mother's dressing table, always Russianized with that picture, no matter where they were. In it a whole village was flying—and not where he wanted to go. But he had studied it like a lesson in levitation. And nightly had flown that art-pocketed sky the other way, on his own cirrus trail of cloud.

On Gonchev's plateau, the lot designated for that city, Lot Three, was ever being enlarged or torn down again, never complete. Only Gonchev himself had ever started a film there, and he had never finished it—though again, only his wife knew why. Publicly he had managed to keep his reasons professional: materials wanting, always an honest excuse here; or "Let's at least wait until they finish the Beaubourg." But it was the students who wondered. One could have one's idiosyncrasies here. But it was wiser to have the same as everybody's.

"Yes, Director," Stepan had said cheekily when assigned the new script. "Yes, Paul? And in the same series, I suppose?"

The series was one of whose theme—migrant workers around the world—Gonchev was perhaps too sneakily proud. Sidestepping the prescribed could become a talent all by itself here. All his work was more than merely geographical.

"You always suppose so well, Stepan."

"Thanks. And—what lot?"

He'd had the satisfaction of seeing the prodigy's eyes widen.

"Lot—Three?"

"There are whole gangs of Yugoslav migrants in the Marais, I'm told, Stepan. Artisans in the building trades." Danilo, Gonchev's brother-in-law and scourge, had suggested the script—"Since what with the casting possible here," he had said, meaning skin color, "Johannesburg is beyond you."

"Note the buildings and streets you'll use," Gonchev said, "all mapped." This was procedure. "And, Stepan, don't bother to get in touch. You're on your own." This was not procedure. Consultation was a way of life here. No one was exempt. After a team's fourth week out there, protocol required Gonchev to check. But even doing what he knew to be wise, there were limits. He would exempt himself from those streets.

"Lot *Three?*" Stepan had said again. His own reverent tone disgusting him, he had wiped his nose with the back of a hand. Still, he might have walked out of the room backward dazedly, as he had seemed about to do, if a boxed videotape of his own graduation-thesis film, on Gonchev's office shelf where Stepan always looked for it, hadn't once again wooed his eye. The thesis had won him a youth-class decoration, for which, dressing as all in his crowd did, he had no lapel. Government, always behind the times, should have given him an earring to match the one he wore. He stared at Gonchev's lapel, always bare of anything except his wife's bud-of-the-day. "No, Director," Stepan had said. "Don't worry. I won't get in touch."

Nor had he. Not a word from Stepan since, not even to ask for the two weeks' extra grace always granted, although it was autumn now, and there was snow in the passes. Lot Three was roofed where it mattered, like all of them. And open under the stars, where it had mattered to Gonchev. How else complete what should be real?

Tonight, the twelfth week, Gonchev had purposely come late, only in time to see the cans of extra rushes being deposited in the stockroom and the film to be run being handed the projectionist. "Edited?" the operator had said to a lanky form dimly seen. The answer had been sharp. "Edited."

Outside, the sun has gone down fast. Inside the studio building, whose walls are bathhouse thin, there is an expectant silence. After the first showing of a film, there always was. At any showing that followed—which would mean that Gonchev had tentatively accepted a student's film—he would remain present, and they would find out one more time, while he put aside his awesome specialty and modestly became one of them, how warm, practical, and even suggestible he could become. Often, by that stage, he actually was all those things. Even if last time, to help things along, he had resorted to a reassuring accident in which he had shaved off half his concealing mustache.

Only Danilo, Gonchev's wife's twin, had doubted it was accident. For facial hair was forbidden here. Let the Muslims explain that to the Marxists—and to the ghost of Stalin; Gonchev could not. Clean-shaven all his life, on his arrival he had immediately grown the mustache, intending to shave it at precisely midyear—halfway between assertion of his rights, and courtesy. Somehow, among all the cabals, it had been an advantage, and he now regretted his morning impulse. But one couldn't have kept half such an appendage. "Ah—" Danilo had said, on alighting from the Yugoslav plane that under special permit always flew him to an airport near the border. "Have you been missing yourself,

Paul? So have we." As for Danilo, for a part-time actor to veil a face so handsome would have been foolish. As the face said.

Because of Vuksica, Gonchev's wife, Danilo visited regularly, in order, he said, to watch the progress of this sixteen-year-long love affair, for which his twin sister had exchanged Yugoslavia for such a backward, if neighboring, country. And perhaps to reassure himself of the superiority of the civilization she had left behind.

Once a journalist in Belgrade, he had lost his right to publish because of an offending article. He had now turned to odd acting jobs, as in his youth, between which he managed the family forge, an ancient inheritance located not in Novi Sad, the university town where he and his sister had been born, but behind the street of the coppersmiths in Sarajevo. The forge lost money, recouped by Danilo's ownership of a small but excellent hotel on the outskirts, whose windows, he said, one could no longer open because of the yellow industrial smog from which that onetime provincial seat suffered.

"We are both mountebanks," he'd said, staring at Gonchev's still half-shaven lip, incurred that morning. "But at least I know." All three were very nervous during his visits, but the minute he left, Gonchev and his wife always wanted him back. Each time, when he was ready to be escorted on this side of the border to the Yugoslav plane—which could not land because there were no reciprocal flights—after kissing Vuksica and embracing Gonchev he always whispered loudly, grimacing like the devil with an earache: "Travel!"

Not a word to be said lightly in this country—even in English, which had displaced French as a second tongue all over Central Europe and was the language in which the three of them communicated best. Travel, even under permit, was akin to what fornication must have been in the old Franz Josef days. One scarcely left one town for another without a light or heavy sense of the illicit, and to receive a foreign visitor was a kind of adultery. Nowadays, in tune with the country's one remaining political alignment, only the Chinese would have been let in normally, but even they no longer came. On entering, Gonchev had stipulated that he and Vuksica and their family be allowed to leave at any time, but he was no longer sure this would be permitted.

"Was he kidding?" the mournful, comma-shaped man who always came to watch Danilo's plane take off said that time, ostensibly into the air, while following the plane's direction into the blue and making his usual notation on a pad. He never made any pretense of not listening but had never before admitted that he did. "Doesn't he know what Director Gonchev does?"

And what you do, Gonchev thought. That's why my impish brother-in-law's whisper was so loud. "A pun," he'd said, also into the air. "On the phrase *le traveling*. Which is French cinema slang for the dolly of a camera."

The man with the pad was cross-eyed, possibly from his job. After his elaborate explanation, Gonchev fancied he saw admiration in the one eye, respect in the other—and a trace of defeat at that angle of incidence, his curved neck. Pedantry was the national defense.

Danilo himself was in Paris right now. In Belgrade he and his wife still lived in the small apartment earned by her professorship of French drama at the university. His fall from grace had not dislodged them. It hadn't hurt that she came from a newspaper clan that had run famously with Tito in the old days. Even so, they now had a rathole in the Marais district, ostensibly so that she could keep up with her subject—though they were careful never to stay there too long. On their return, she always gave a public lecture, with slides.

Danilo was still in the Writers Union, though his name no longer appeared on their public lists. When he went to their meetings he was not much spoken to; as he had confided to Vuksica, "Ah, those in authority know how to pummel without a bruise showing." Still, he turned up every summer to report the annual film festival in the great Roman amphitheater at Pula, doing the one bit of journalism tossed him yearly. There people did speak to him, often not sure who he might be, for with his lean head, cat's eyes, and tanned tennis legs, he was often taken for an actor, though it was Vuksica who had been the star. In return for his winter of being ignored, he did not speak to them.

"*Enfin*, when I can't anymore breathe, I go to Paris. And when I can't anymore—*accommodate*."

The word had momentarily lowered the candle flames on the Gonchevs' outdoor dining table. A piece called "How We Accommodate in the Balkans" had been what Danilo had finally lost his place for. On the surface an account of a train journey to buy good iron ore for a foundry, it had documented how, going more or less eastward from Central Europe—"east" to be taken as much politically as geographically—he found each successive country solacing itself with the belief that in its next neighbor things were far worse.

In his own country, Danilo had written, where you could still travel freely, trade almost Western-style, and occasionally see women dressed like fashion plates from Italy, the authorities merely "blotted" you out of formal recognition. Whereas, in a seemingly even more fortunate neighbor country—not identified as Hungary—where things were much looser and better economically, on the disappearance of a colleague from the university, people were likely to say "Agnes? I believe she's in Switzerland. She wanted to go." And she would be.

Though surely that wasn't as bad, Danilo had written, as in the next country—not identified as Romania—where they were stupid enough to let the smashed synagogues of forty-odd years ago stay boarded up for foreigners to see, and to have two fancy stores in the capital, that former "Paris of the Balkans," whose windows were crammed with furs and delicacies, behind the plate glass polished every day for the tourists—and the populace—to see through, but whose doors were never opened. Where soldiers pointed their sabers at anyone who crossed the Grand Plaza to get to the national museum directly, instead of going around the periphery, since the dictator lived next door. And where, when bowling along their gentlest and most romantic countryside, one suddenly encountered a zone marked IMPASSIBLE. There, if you suddenly missed Agnes, it might be said, with a faint wink to tradition, "A vampire got her." Though meaning only that she had been locked up. Agnes would still be somewhere. If not in Bucharest.

Or, Danilo had continued, there was, flowering more or less in the center of all these, the country that, in homage to Hermann Hesse, he had dubbed The Country of the Glass Beads. Once famous for crystal and porcelain, and for the sardonic playwrights and storytellers who had multiplied like roaches among the vats of kaolin and fine sand, it was mentioned now only in aphorisms as crenellated as the turrets of its lovely capital—not identified as Prague. Now, only its writers were heard from. Occasionally, one of those spoke his mind. After which, as the tale went, if lucky, he was able to turn himself into a glass bead and have himself swallowed by an American publisher, ultimately to reappear, pale and translucent, on the faculty of some college in the West. But no one, positively no one, could know for sure what had happened to the populace.

Ah, but lastly, Danilo had concluded, there was the unidentified country Gonchev was now standing in, in a twilight much like yesterday's, in which the three of them had sat over their good-bye drinks at a table Gonchev's artisans had copied so faithfully that it had seemed to float like a Mies van der Rohe itself on the wheat-stroked air. A nation of such violent terrain—except for the hilly coastal strip where this studio was—that with one rude push it had been able to return itself to that age-old isolation which the others had had rethrust upon them.

As to the U.S.S.R., that hugely looming neighbor at Europe's easternmost who brooded over all of them so benevolently—the Great Stone Hen, as the teashop slang went—this fierce little nation's leaders simply no longer spoke to it. Why should they? They had their own language, on the Indo-European language table absolutely unique—and indeed Danilo never could learn to speak it. Plus many more old-fashioned peasants than most other nations had, and therefore more food. Last night's table had been loaded with their natural products. True, their capital, unlike others in the Balkans, hadn't much vestige of the fine manners, restaurants, and cloakrooms of the old Austro-Hungarian empire, under which "accommodation" had run on greased wheels. Though thanks to a man named Gonchev—Danilo had had the gall to mention—you would still have a sort of cinema.

Only—you could not go anywhere. For this was a country that had decided to swallow itself. You would not even have a tennis star.

Yet, as Danilo had last night reminded them, there were still considerations.

On those who fell into disfavor, the policy still fell short of that farthest neighbor's. Here, surely, they still did not—eradicate.

"And where *you* got the heaviest iron," Vuksica had said.

. . .

She was still so handsome, in the Ionic style. Other women let the designers put them in shiny black like a seal's flippers, or cut their hair to look like a mandrill's. She had met motherhood full on in chitons that seemed to change color hourly like freshwater pearls, and swept back her hair in a thick, burnished bun, instantly reminding one that for true beauty, a woman ought to be able to show her skull. The studs in her ears never changed. When she went anywhere she had only to change her sandals, for freshness, and choose one of the shaped pouches that always slung from her wrist, containing maybe a key, grocery money, and the coriander chewed here to keep the breath sweet—though once the pouch had carried a live rainbow trout caught that afternoon, as promised her hostess's little son.

The lusty noises she had made giving birth to their boy and girl were on a tape the two loved to hear. She always left the room when it was played, hissing "Collector" at Gonchev as she passed. Upstairs in the bedroom afterward, he would find her in giggles. She was saved from being an angel by thick ankles and a snort in her small-nostriled nose. Naked, they would survey each other. He was tall and sufficiently well made, with a face good enough for the official photographs. Her navel was long and deep, like a matching insignia within the long hips and buttocks, which sloped. She was like a spoon that cleaved to him. When they made love, the ear studs rode with her, and him.

But she would not act in this country. At the Pula festival a film of his had been exhibited, the last time before these borders had closed to him. Two films in which she had starred had been shown that same evening, one an original script made in the highlands of Montenegro, one a *Rosmersholm* done in Norway, with a heavy musical score that had tried to echo all of Ibsen's oeuvre, from the steamy, fjord-deep chords to the whistle of a wild duck.

Afterward, a crowd that seemed to represent the artistic life of the country had gathered at the Grand Hotel, a cavernous imperial relic where the menu went on for pages, though written in bistro indelible pencil. When he tried to order a meal, a ripple of embarrassment had gone down the long, white-naperied table. The waiter, a gaunt, melancholy type with a premier's profile, had said sadly that it was too late for the kitchen. Gonchev, laughing, had said that like other foreigners, he had yet to get a meal there at any hour. For a minute the fine Serbian sparkle all down the dinner table had dimmed.

"I'll order for you," she said, next to him, laughing too. He had never seen anything like the gaiety of the women of Central Europe, compounded of some warm yet brittle irony. When his order came it was the same as had been set before them all, the tiny pretzel sticks you could get at any of their railway stations or bars, and beer. He had understood then that the menu was a relic too.

"See," she'd said, "I have influence."

His professional insight on the Montenegro film had made her pinken. "Yes, cinema verité is what I do best."

In the Ibsen, as she herself volunteered, she had been too stiff and ladylike, too nice. He had responded only that he had disliked the score. Giggling, she explained that she had been married to the composer, pointing out a harlequin with deep facial lines, three seats down. At the time the film was made she had been leaving him. "I'll wash you under with fake Sibelius," he had said to her vengefully, and had nearly sunk himself also, professionally. Now he and she were again friends. Everyone in their world had to be friends these days, she said.

She'd said little about his own film, the set for which—London, for a film on the period of Karl Marx's residence there—was still one of his best. Although at Pula they were at the moment despising such sets as too Hollywood and in general too American, they had been delicate with him, knowing how hard it had been for him to get permission from his new country to come to Pula at all. Later, he had guessed that his film had been shown as an example of what they meant to avoid. They intended to stick to the real, at all costs. So did he, though he had his own version of real.

"If we here do a certain number of local films"—she'd not said official ones but he thought she meant that—"we are let do other things." For instance, the director who had done her other films—"that blond madman down there"—would shortly be doing a comedy known privately among the Belgrade film crowd as "Upside Down in Ljubljana," in which she would be one of those stately women who still carried baskets on their heads. "A comic version of a documentary; he's quite excited about it." She sobered. "It's best to be." But after that he hoped to be allowed to do a film in Canada.

Would she be going too? No, it had a male star—the new trend. When the blond director made a point of coming down the table to greet her, and incidentally to stare at her neighbor, Gonchev was made to see that these two must have had an affair, probably a long one.

"And who's that other fellow down at the very end?" he asked. "Who's he?"

Danilo, the star conversationalist, so soon to be silenced, was this night in his element, though Gonchev suspected that to be in one's element every night was characteristic of many men here. "Is he one of your madmen too?" Gonchev had already guessed what attracted her, wondering if he could qualify.

Her eyes were hazel. No contact-lens peacock-blue for her. The smudgy dark brows knitted. "You don't see—a resemblance?"

Then of course he did. At a distance, with one's mouth thinned by speaking and the other's softly quirked, the twinship had not been so marked. Later he would see that their resemblance, powerful as it was, very much depended on light. The red-and-black forge-light that Danilo loved and courted anywhere had in the end baked in him a different spirit, no matter the skin. The two looked most alike when quiet, and in shadow.

"Oh. Your brother, of course. He looks like you. If anybody could. But you know—you don't look much like him."

He couldn't have said anything more welcome to a twin. When she found he hadn't eaten since noon, they left the crowd—as noted by all—and she drove him to the cottage where she was staying. Her car, like most in this part of the world, had elderly lines and sounded strained. It was the same with the car he had just been assigned in the new country. "Your car makes me feel at ease. It grinds just like the ones I'm returning to." This was the first time he had spoken of his new place. He was to notice that every time he mentioned it she opened her eyes wide, but asked nothing.

The cottage, one of a row of them situated near a small lake and vacated for festival guests, was scarcely the dacha he would have assumed a star would have, but it had a blunt bathhouse charm. At four in the morning she caught him one of the rainbow fish for his supper, then another. While they sat over the fishline he said: "Sibelius. During World War Two, my mother said, there was an international fund raised among musicians to keep the poor fellow in cigars. My parents were long since out of touch with him by then. We couldn't contribute. Not that my father would have in any case."

Smiling, she had put a finger to her lips, and caught the first fish. "Why not?" By the time she caught the second one he had answered that, and much more.

"No, I never saw St. Petersburg. Petrograd." His family had fled from there to Vladivostok, where, supposedly, he was born. Though his mother always insisted upon it, he was not sure of it, nor of the year. "The Japanese only held it, you know, until 1922." But there had still been some there long afterward. Both his maternal grandfather and his father had been concert pianists. The Japanese ex-commandant, enchanted by their music, had helped them to move on—first to Harbin, where Gonchev was half-convinced he had been born, though his Russian mother couldn't bear to admit it—"Harbin is all I remember"—and from there to Kyoto, where Gonchev grew up, wanting Europe. "My grandfather heard his friend Tchaikovsky conduct the opening concert of Carnegie Hall, in '91. My father first heard Serge Rachmaninoff, also a family friend, when he was four. Later my father was a pupil of Scriabin. Sibelius made them laugh. They said his tone poems were only day-boat outings, on some Lutheran lake."

Busy reeling in her line, she'd murmured a wish that her composer "ex" could have heard that. Gonchev suspected that she had never heard of Scriabin. He wondered how many ex-husbands she had. The answer was four; she had married and divorced two men twice. Alternately. "Oh, you tend to be faithful," Gonchev said. She hadn't replied. He wasn't surprised to hear that the blond director had been the other spouse.

The two fish, with their small snouts and rounded backs fringed with fin, seemed to him like a fat pair of eyes. Idly he put them snout to snout on the sand, and under the flashlight pebbled in a nose, tufted in a weedy peruke, and in one swift ideograph, there was a face.

"A samurai!" She clapped her hands, just missing the fishhook.

"No, a wrestler. But here." He thumbed the sand, making a passable warrior, head only. And shield.

Could he make a geisha?

Ah no, there were limits, he said, meanwhile carefully putting aside the hook.

He must have a Japanese eye for such things, she said; it must be good for his job.

No, it was the jobs that had saved him, he said, for he couldn't stop seeing the external world in arrangements, from a soup plate to a landscape. Without the work to allay that, the urge might have driven him mad.

They ate the fish, which had been cleaned in the inlet and roasted over alder twigs, washing it down with a slivovitz whose flowery essence, she said, had come from a special orchard. But afterward nothing ever seemed to him more special than that when they went in to make love it had already grown light.

In the dark he would never have told her.

"I think I heard Rachmaninoff too," he said, taking off his sweatshirt. "A tall, gaunt man with Slav cheeks and a shaved head. He hummed along deep, the whole time. Like an organ stop. I would have been about seven." Of course he had heard his father tell ten times over how the tickets and the air fare had been sent to them in Kyoto, in order for them to hear their family friend again, at the Salle Pleyel. "Fourth row center," his father always said. "And there is a particular organ stop that Serge's humming along sounds like. It is called the *vox humana*. Ah, God—to hear it again."

The tickets and the fare had been a tactful way of helping them to get from Kyoto to Paris, to join the other émigrés and remain there. No return fare had been included.

"But we went anyway, didn't we?" the boy Gonchev always cried. "I remember it." His mother, sewing for their living in the prescribed way of refugee wives married to uncertainty, said, biting off a thread: "In

Asia, it is not hard to remember Europe, is it Paul? Don't ever stop hungering for it. But remember too, we always pay our own way."

In those times, it would have been a miracle if they had gone. But also odd if they hadn't? Proud as they and all their acquaintances were, they would sometimes accept help from one of themselves. His mother might not have wanted to go, he could suspect now, because she was too proud to let their friends abroad know that his father was by then musically past it—since, once in Paris, what else could he have done for a living, if they had gone and remained? Yet perhaps they had gone—and had had to return, so ignominiously that it must never again be referred to? In Kyoto, true, they'd had a home by then, and his father still got engagements. But once away, even in bad circumstances, would they ever have come back? As Gonchev the grown man dropped his pants, he said: "I keep thinking I heard him. I remember it."

Already lying on the bed, she took this as the gift it was.

When she was asleep, he rose and went to the kitchenette. Unlike the way most couples were said to be, he would prove to be the wakeful one after sex, she the sleeper. The cottage kitchen was provided with the same red, blue, and green long-handled pipkins that hung in every grocery commissariat he had seen here, and on the counter were the same slabs of state cheese and state ham. All the state stores in Yugoslavia offered exactly the same merchandise, as was the case in his new country also, to which his mother, by then a widow, had accompanied him for the few months before she died, so at last attaining Europe for good, if only its rim. To the end she had been scornful of the slabs. Those here were different only in shape.

Opening the small but precious refrigerator—the owner-tenant who had vacated for Vuksica was a professor high in the bureaucracy—he saw newly how strange it was that butter sweet from the dairy should be stamped so as to remind you of civil law. The stamp here of course was again slightly different. Only the precious gill of ground coffee in its twisted envelope was the same.

His mother, in spite of her hedgings, had always yearned for them to press on eventually to Vienna, saying that she would go there for the coffee alone, and the winter Gonchev was ten they had actually spent some weeks of the concert season there looking for engagements, only to have to return to Japan, where, during the American occupation at least, his father's talents had sufficed. For his father, even Vladivostok had perhaps been musically too late. As for vintage slivovitz, he would first have sneered at it, as he had once at sake, and then become its slave.

Gonchev took out the bottle, musing on how domestic matters, tight as they were here, were looser than in his new home. There, if apples were being sold by the peck, one would never be able to buy only two, as he had done yesterday. He poured a shot from the bottle into one of the minute triangular glasses, like a coolie hat on pointe, that one saw everywhere here, and let this essence flower through his nose.

He always liked to leaf through a woman's kitchen, though often they mistook this as a sign that he wanted to live with them. He had never done that, even under the rapid wind of an affair. None of them had ever moved him to it, though much that he saw was endearing. When women lived by themselves, or in the leftovers of households once shared by a man, the life-areas where they catered to themselves were the softer ones, rather like the winking fontanel in a child's head. Not that he had ever committed the stupidity of thinking them children. They were equals, whose bones might not grow together quite at a man's rate or strength but would outlast his own.

He felt at home too in vacation cottages and bathhouses, so often minimalized almost to Kyoto scale. He opened the small kitchen cabinet. Inside, on the summer-bare wood, there were only a few spices. No sweetmeats. In his new country if a woman had chocolate, that foreign delicacy, this meant she had certain connections. To be fair, the same was true with a man, though not on quite the same terms. His own servant got chocolate for him when she could, never saying where. She wore a hat to and from work and whenever she served coffee to his committee, because she was not a servant but labor force, and he would never dream of asking where she had procured this surely forbidden Swiss import, only mentioning casually, now and then, that he didn't much care for chocolate. But given his status, which redounded to hers only if it was properly provided for, chocolate must nonetheless appear in the cupboard, and had.

Not long ago he had opened a new flame's commissary and found Italian rice in it. The round grains had interested him; he hadn't known their origin and had thought them perhaps local to his new abode. There was no place on earth where there wasn't a black market, she'd retorted; then why did he deplore? He hadn't; it was merely that if you lived in a place, weren't you wiser for your own sake to go along with its daily limitations of a minor sort—not lie abed in them, but make do?

She had been an actress, a nonnational, about to be asked to leave the country after some years' residence, possibly because of the strict sexual code she had too openly violated—as she was doing with him. His mention of a bed had been tactless, if unintentional. Possibly she had hoped that his influence might help her stay.

"Why—y—you—" she'd said, "you're their black market supreme, Gonchev—what you do for your masters here. Don't you know that?" Triumphantly, for he hadn't answered, she had cooked her risotto, which he'd eaten—with some disappointment. For though she did well, as she did in bed, a grain that was both unfamiliar and a sin as well should taste more distinctive than it had. He hadn't minded what she'd said. The new would always interest him, even about himself. But anger wasn't what he wanted in a woman, or triumph, or connivance either. The shape of what he did want eluded him.

He fingered the Hungarian paprika that Vuksica had cooked the fish with, bright orange and fresh, not officially embargoed on his home market, as far as he knew, but simply never there. How his cook would exclaim at it! Should he steal it or ask for it? In the small cabinet his fingers looked huge and threatening. He had to smile, dropping the tin. Behind it he saw a box that had been opened. Raisins of local origin, by the imprint. Hungry again, he had a few. They were yellow muscats, long and oval. He took some into the bedroom with him, carrying also a tray he had found, on which he had placed a glass of water and a slivovitz, for her.

She was awake. He stopped short. The sex had been blinding, but that could happen. Settings could do that to him—but not this. Maybe it was his age, somewhere near forty then, as far as he knew. Now that her eyes were open, it seemed to him he had never seen a woman so properly naked before. Yet they had made love in the light. When she saw the tray she gave a pleased cry.

He wouldn't let her rise, but fed her. There were tears in her eyes. He had to say something frivolous. "I almost stole your paprika." But in what a voice it came out! He tried again. "I like it with my eggs."

Her mouth quirked. No one had to tell him how his new country was scorned by its neighbors. "Oh? You—have eggs?"

He saw what her irony was—as in all this part of the world, it was the same as the men's. He wanted to brim too with that gaiety, one that his countries so far had not taught him. No wonder her body made him feel as he now understood he did.

"When we don't," he said with a grin, "we make them. Or I can."

"Oh? You have a cook?"

He nodded.

"And what shape is she?"

It was clear what she was asking.

"No amphora. And wears a brown felt hat." He put down the tray and turned her over, that long spoon, then rolled her back again, flicking her buttock. "And you—do you fish for anyone regularly?"

She wasn't angry. She would vie—he could see that. Or else say nothing.

"I've never been married," he said distinctly. "Before."

"You're—you are mad."

Yes, approve of me, he prayed. Approve of me. He looked down. His eyes were brimming. But surely that long, oval navel was—yes, just so. Unclosing his clenched hand, he dropped the raisin in.

It fitted exactly—the biggest arrangement of his life.

So it is past sunset now, and nobody need see anything except what he wants them to. The mournful man who had been at the airport, who maybe was shaped like a comma because he had so many supernumerary jobs of the first importance, comes hurrying out of the studio building, built by Gonchev to resemble the Avala Studios outside Belgrade, half in the hope that this would persuade her to act again, possibly even in one of his scripts. No, she had said, acting was everywhere these days—look at Danilo. It was up to her, and to whoever could, just to live a life. It so happened that she wanted to live hers with him.

He had asked her of course, on which side—the acting or the life— she included him.

"You do what you have to do," she'd said. "If ever I saw it." Then she had put her hands on him, first at his temples, then at his thighs.

In his moments of depression, which for all he knew might be moments of clarity as well, he told himself that like many a missionary before her, she had chosen him and his new country because she thought they were the worst.

"Director Gonchev," the man says, "it's been close to an hour. They're getting restive in there."

Gonchev holds up his hand for a pause. Both he and the messenger— who has expected this—take deep breaths. Just at this part of the day, in this season, the dark-leaved grove in which they stand gives off an odor as arresting as a sound. Like eucalyptus, though it is not eucalyptus. To enhance this, Gonchev had shifted a waterfall and removed a portion of hill. There was nothing wrong with nature, he always felt, except that it had not been built. Both he and the man stand there, inhaling. Then Gonchev releases them both with a little salute, as if to say: This too is living.

"An hour? Indeed." He always said that. The man expected it. Having said what his job required, he must be rewarded in kind. No harm in rituals that soothe the unavoidable facts.

The studio lights come on, calibrated to a photo-cell. They would indeed be restless by now, steaming along in their usual dogmatic positions. He had long thought mischievously of recording a film to be called "Committee"—it would be a challenge to hang any secret video on such a crowd. Or possibly he might get them to act as themselves. He would have to persuade each man that he himself was a unique locale—but that would be easy. Who didn't secretly think that he was one?

"And how do they feel about the film?"

The man straightens, as much as he is able. "Oh, oh. Very pro. Only they want to—go home." He always said it that way, haiku-style. He had perfected it.

"So do I," Gonchev says. "So do I." On the instant he feels that routine has carried him too far. But at some point it always did. The only solution he had found was to go on with it. "I tell you what. This is Tuesday." It always was. "Why not gather all the committee family-style on, say, Sunday. Isn't that the fall festival?" Or the spring one, as the case might be. "Everybody to relax. Apple-bobbings for the children. By then we'll know our minds for sure."

And he would have delayed long enough to know theirs.

Vuksica, who dealt with the wives, always did so very fairly, both to them and to him. They would come to her at once, telling her what their men had told them to—plus a bit more. Such as how old So-and-so had misplaced his false teeth, which with him meant pique at some fancied slight, and so had had cramps all night—which would be transferred to his argument. Or how young So-and-so, who should know he had no claim to a political title in capital letters as yet, had however decided to apply for it.

"You don't feel that you compromise yourself, doing this for me?" Gonchev always asked, mainly because he loved hearing how she would phrase her reply. "Oh no," she'd said—only a month ago, for he often had two films on location at the same time—"I'm just . . . the siphon. They look up to me—a little. And of course I look up to you." She'd said this with such a quirk that he'd given her a playful punch in the ribs—"for not knowing how a siphon works"—and they'd gone off to bed. Even with all modern precautions—Danilo at first bringing the pills in as he could, until Vuksica had found that the women here had a more regular illegal supply—it was amazing that the Gonchevs had only the two hostages to fortune that they had allowed themselves.

The messenger is truly remarkable. He is writing down Gonchev's instructions as tediously—and as copiously—as if these were new to him.

How I enjoy my children, Gonchev is thinking. The two would be coming home shortly. The girl from the youth farm where she was working off her atonement for being smart enough to qualify for university instead of labor force; the boy, who probably would not have to serve out such a term, from the youth camp required for boys of all ages. Lucky heir to the physique of Gonchev's maternal great-grandfather, who had been a serf, he was on the champion junior decathlon team, and already "training for the Olympics"—as the local phrase went—"just as seriously as if we could go." The girl, departing for her stint, had said: "Wish I could go to the farm merely as if I were going." She had inherited the irony.

The man is now waiting for Gonchev to extend his hand, which his hand will meet halfway, for two enthusiastic shakes. Then the "interview," as it will be called on the man's worksheet, will be over, allowing him time to get to his motorcycle, ready to fall in behind Gonchev for the other half of his duty, reported daily merely as "road check."

Gonchev's hand goes out the prescribed distance, which it knows as well as any nearsighted seamstress knows her tape measure, but absently holds on, without the one-two shake. The man does it for both of them—one . . . two . . . then disengages, staring indignantly.

"Sorry. I was thinking of my children. Got any?"

The man stands mute, but aggrieved.

"Oh, come on." How long have Gonchev and his personal spy known each other by now, at airports and interviews directly, and at the discreet distance never to be acknowledged, even in headshake?

Five years at least, since the man's predecessor had died, and from the beginning it had seemed to Gonchev that he and his present follower each ungrudgingly admired the other's stamina.

The fellow before this one had been a burden, so slow that one had always to wait for him to catch up. Nevertheless Vuksica, who knew that one's wife slightly, had urged that they attend the funeral. Which they had done, at a distance delicately judged as proper. This action had moved many, though word had later come down that such gestures were not prescribed. Well—apparently he was going to commit another such one.

"You could answer that you don't know how many you have." Gonchev waits. "That's a joke."

What does the fellow have to look like that for? Like Gonchev's chum at the school dispensary in Kyoto, offered castor oil on an orange, which fruit he had never before had the luck to taste.

"I'm not supposed to."

"Not supposed to what?" Gonchev says sharply. "Not to know? Not to say? Or not to see a joke?" He knows he is taking advantage, but can't stop.

That face, his daily vis-à-vis, slowly lengthens to a gargoyle's—a Notre Dame one, seen through rain. Then to a wizened balloon, losing air.

"It's my job not to," the other says softly. He looks behind him at the studio window. "Or was."

True, they have breached the distance to be held between them. Or bent it, the way you bend a ray of light with, what was it, a prism? Even if they could conceal the fact, would the relationship become unbearable?

"I tell you what," Gonchev says. "From now on I'll wear dark glasses. You do the same."

"They've seen us," the other says. Though he was already standing apart.

At the two broad windows the blinds, rolled down to the sill, are indeed shifting. In the golden light behind them, pointed black shadows flicker and spread—silly, frustrated goblins, waiting to make somebody a nightmare. It was hard to take a committee's shadows seriously. "No, they're still backbiting in there. I'll go in. You go on." He turns around, calling out to the man, who has already melted into the grove. "And mind you—keep your spirits up."

Inside, the twelve men return Gonchev's salute—all of them seated as he would expect: the old musclemen here, the modern benevolents there, and the honest admirers always too far in the rear.

The team who have done the film are in a cluster by themselves. A crew just off a film is like the cast of a play after closing night; there's still a lingering allegiance. No telling yet whether this crew is further joined, in secret mutiny. Though at his entry they glance up in a body—like those who have collectively done you wrong?

31

"Where's—the fellow?" the oldest committeeman quavers. He means the supernumerary, by custom due in for a final salute. The other elders shift uneasily. Bad form to notice any defection outright. Because then one might tend to note the punishment as explicitly. Yes, the old man dodders. But if so—what of themselves? Gonchev meanwhile can't help noticing, as always, the hard black-and-white chiaroscuro that human flesh falls into under the influence of fear.

"The man's onto his second shift, don't you suppose, Director Gonchev?" The head crewman stares down from his height, his nose, and his ambition at his former teacher. He is still high on camera-ego. His stance says he'll say anything. And film anything?

"Ah, Stepan," Gonchev says. "Been somewhere?"

Everybody laughs, relaxes. The boss's dirty travel-joke. Gonchev can afford to apologize now. "I've held you late. You must all realize why." Keep the eyes lowered. Discipline is built on nonrecognition, as everyone here knows. Once it gives way, the recognitions scatter like mice.

He can hear them shift in their seats. Now, after expressing polite admiration for Stepan's film in toto, he will proceed in the same mild mood toward a certain section of it. There may be one burst of enthusiasm—out of line, out of order—which he cannot contain, leaving all of them apricot-cheeked, feeling their own spontaneity, via his. Then one gets down to it. Little by little, gaps will emerge. Between what was achieved, and what intended. The process is known as Analytical Review.

At its finish, all a film's successes will be seen to be the result of the great research environment in which they live: the country's vigilance, the committee's, Gonchev's, and the team and its coordinator's, in that order. All the film's troubles will be assigned to the well-known frailty of art. After which the necessary revisions can begin.

He hasn't sat down yet. This means he isn't as ready as usual to be cosy. Although no project getting this far has ever been totally rejected, there are these ups and downs, actually looked forward to. What more satisfying to a committee than the existence of enormous differences that, on peril of one's future, will have to be adamantly resolved—in a way everybody can predict. Now the dialogue can begin.

32

He rocks on his heels, fiddling with his sunglasses. Do the returned crew members look any different?

They're all dressed according to the proper excesses of today's avant-garde, or yesterday's—those worldwide declarations of boots and hair. Research keeps them au courant. Stepan wears those lankiform jeans which testify that he is a man who speaks as much from the crotch as from the heart. Plus a musty singlet he might have inherited from his butcher forebears, although there's no visible blood on it. He and his crew would have blended in fine abroad—if abroad they have somehow been, though if they've been hobnobbing with airports, wouldn't it show in their eyes?

Many people here have convinced themselves that such sins show up Lombroso-style in the physique, like the drooping lids of thieves, or the lack of lobes in a murderer's ears. Gonchev can't quite go that route. Yet it's always seemed to him that people freshly back from far places do have a rhythm, slowed or interrupted, that you might spot, and a glaze of perspective in the irises.

No, they look as usual, when a team is this young and this good— smug with desire accomplished, and hostile to whatever has gone before. As if, in the far reaches of a country so rich in secret ravines, they might well have built their own replica city—as youth always yearns to? And put all their rebellion where he himself at their age had known it should be—into the work?

Protocol demands that Gonchev now go round the team, shaking each hand, which he does, looking into each face. After Japan, the Balkan hodgepodge, admixed with half of Europe, still amazes him. Here's a short, plump, dark Turk, as bowlegged as a Phoenician sailor might once have been, with a swatch of ebony hair just an edge too shiny to be Mongolian, and Hitler holes for eyes. There a gaunt North Italian fellow with great cavernous cheeks, the thin mouth of a pre-Renaissance por-trait, and the sunniest of smiles.

The three youngest cameramen, who often work together as a trio, are pink and white as girls, but don't let that deceive you, Director. When busy under the old klieg lights in the back of the studio, those three faces emerge so zinc-white and black, as if daubed with the old makeup of the early films they have studied, that he half expects a Chaplin to jump from behind the dollies, or a Dr. Caligari to take over the box. At which moment he loves the three like a father, for what he is sure they are planning: to run through all film history as swiftly as they can—and then do it in. And because he knows they can't do it here.

"So now a moment of silence," Gonchev says. "To reflect." He always says this—into a silence already weighing like the snow felt tonight in the air. "Let us go over your film scene by scene. I will enumerate them."

After a pause, he intones: "Inside the Palais de Justice at Chaillot. The courtyard. The Beaubourg. Montmartre. And—the Jeu de Paume," and rests his chin on his folded hands. Once a student had murmured, "Does he think he's a priest?" and Gonchev, hearing, had answered, "No. But this is worship."

Most of the committee here knows only cursorily the sets Gonchev had built; but two are in the habit of checking them out devotedly, using his own archives at Elsinore.

The old Palais? A fine take he should praise—copied as it was from old clips of the interior at a performance of *Murder in the Cathedral* in 1952. He might demur at all the footage devoted to the courtyard, since none of that size existed in the Marais, so far as he knew.

The Beaubourg—a necessary cliché these days—but was it already so dirty? He himself hadn't checked on the real one lately, and would take their word for it. While Montmartre—well, that lovely hill is always the same, give or take what sneaks up on any city—or on a small-scale model of one. In this case more than a few hairline fractures in the church and a mushroom clobber of huts—workers' flats?—downstage. As for what some call the "air" in a film, which in his own films is almost that—"petroleum jelly" is more like it.

Only last month he had used the lenses from some cheap sunglasses of the nineteen-thirties to get a proper effect. "How can you verify all this?" the state curator had asked suspiciously. Gonchev might as well know he was suspected of having spies in the West, in fact, all over the world. The man had stared grumpily at the model of the Jeu de Paume, in which new lighting had been installed, as in the original. Gonchev had found all the specifics in a highly critical article that had complained for some forty pages in the *Nouvelle Revue.* "A network?" Gonchev had laughed. "You think taking care like I do is like taking drugs? Come, come. Your government allows me the best clipping service on the globe." He still makes a point of saying "your." "But I should never have succumbed to the temptation of showing the Orangerie at dusk, Curator. Any city may look unreal at that hour—but a model has an obligation." Talking over these people's heads, he sometimes told himself the truth. "You've a point though, Curator. Maybe I sniff a little art powder now and then."

In his early days here he had cautioned against just that. "We will be the true documentary. Of the age. Not because we have everything here. Because we don't." He had made a lot of people happy, not excluding the government. It had been a xenophobia of which anyone could be proud.

Stepan isn't chafing under this delay—but isn't grinning either. "Something always comes out of Papa's cataplexy," he had said once— in Gonchev's hearing. Explaining what that was: "The hypnotic state animals get into when they are shamming dead." His brother is a veterinarian.

"Warm in here," the plump crewman says. "My frostbite's giving me hell."

"Shut up, Osman," Stepan says. "Or put snow on it."

Is it possible, Gonchev asks himself, that this fellow has my interest at heart?

The committeemen are exchanging murmurs and covert notes. How is it that men with their heads inclined sideways always remind him of monks? In particular the monks leaning over the deathbed of Saint Francis in the Giotto in the basilica of Santa Croce in Firenze.

Well, I'm not Saint Francis, Gonchev thinks. But neither am I on my deathbed as a director. Put a Giotto lens on the cameras, and I'll paint this.

The crewmen are now sitting on the floor, back of the elders, there being no seats for them. Never are, for the young. Some clasp their knees tight, some sprawl. The whole room is a monk's-hood color, Capuchin. Spotlights of golden gesso on the bent heads. The Middle

Ages, fighting the many-sidedness of life. In a Commie studio. Near the beginning of the new millennium.

If anyone should have a tonsure, it's Stepan. For his documentary thesis he had opted out of the usual topics—Our Holiday, or Our Family Tree—doing a short on his vet brother's clinic instead, with a little griffon as heroine. Eighteenth-century elegant—the last thing one would expect. But not quite a trifle. He had then done an extra film, already famous—the Documentary of a Hayrick.

Hay here is stored throughout the pastureland in house-high fretted wooden frames whose peaked and carved pediments, luminous by moonlight or dotting the heavy green afternoons, spoke for a still-Gothic countryside. No one had ever noticed before how, alongside them, ordinary human faces became human dolmens, totems gone back to nature in the stone, as a member of the board of examiners had said. "Not totems," Stepan had interrupted, having listened rigidly until then, as required of candidates. "That's fashion. Leave that to the magazines of the West." In a way he was accusing these petty moguls. With their feverish imitations, what had they done but leave the country in everything but name?

They gave him his degree. Couldn't have done otherwise. The word "Hayrick!," used to counter any idea held to be of false quantity, had since become a student cry. Secretly, Gonchev is proud of him. How do you best teach them? You make rivals of them.

Into these two silences, the old dodderer chuckles. "You should see the pumpkin my wife has grown. It is certainly going to win at the fall festival. She should cut it from the vine now, or a frost could do it in. But she won't. I told her, 'What do you think you're growing, a moon?' " He chuckles again. Can't he smell the *en garde!* atmosphere here? No. He has the impenetrability of the healthy old. That pink leather face with its tight gray Neptune curls will live for years yet. He has given up the drama of expectation, that's why. The men in their middle years smile at him. The young men around Stepan shift closer to each other, in disgust.

As for teacher and pupil—we've already crossed recognitions— *ping*—like swords. Stepan knows I'm going to push him into kingdom come. He knows I know he'll work his way back.

He's had to build his own Paris—and has done it here.

"Ah, Stepan," the Director at last says.

Stepan raises his head. The posy of young heads around him does the same, their chins lifted to him. Yes, he's the ultimate patriot. He'll rebuild all the locations if he can.

He expects me to stop him. Tell him I'm doing that for his own good, and the country's—for us not to be the laughingstock of the world. He won't believe me. His son, the next generation, will; he'll be the one to travel out. But I can't wait for it.

No, he'll think I've done this to win time for myself, and there's a bit of truth in that, else why did I send him there?

"This film is unacceptable," the Director says. "If the committee cares to send a committee—to wherever it was filmed—they'll see why. Let them measure the curbstones and compare with the data in our archives. The courtyard as well—under the arrondissement where it is supposed to be." He is about to add that if they blame the pupil they must also blame the master, but sees they are already on the way.

"Lot Three is unfinished," a voice says from the rear. "We always wondered why."

The commissioner of weights and measures often expresses the first opinion. He is an admirer of sorts—the kind who comes slow to the judgment and quick to the doubts. "And why assign it to students?"

Stepan is now smiling at his crew, and they're smiling back, if some of them miserably. They won't speak up, daren't. But by now they know the answers. What's still unfinished is still dreamable. And dangerous.

Gonchev lifts his chin at all of them. A beard might dignify it. Bone structure, refined over many years of thrust, will have to do. His battle jacket, a sixth or seventh edition of the one he had entered this country in, sits on him as easy as the garments of a man's own era usually do. "You can film forty-nine major cities from archives," Gonchev says. "The fiftieth—it is better to have seen."

He'd have risen from his seat but sees with interest that he had not sat in it.

"Next Sunday is the fall festival, yes? The studio will be undergoing some alterations." He has just decided this. "So Vuksica and I invite all of you, and your ladies, to our house instead." He smiles at the old man. "Bring the moon."

Then he starts down the aisle, not counting his breaths.

"Gonchev?"

Turning, he sees the old man has risen from his seat, his gnarled hand raised like a preacher's.

"Gonchev—the committee has never had a case like this. What shall we do with the film?"

The old man looks pleased to be onstage, but his hand is beginning to shake. He hides it in his vest. Altogether a natural arrangement.

Although, when you tend to approve so of the old boys, aren't you yourself becoming one of them?

He sees that Stepan isn't going to say a thing, not even to ask what changes are to occur in the studio.

"Burn it," Gonchev says. "Or study it."

2

Under the Valonias

OUTSIDE, GONCHEV GOT on his motorcycle, waiting a moment before he kicked off. His parents had never departed on any moving vehicle without first folding their arms and bending their heads in brief meditation—or, as they called it, Sitting Down in the Road. Always, before leaving a house for good, or a country, they had done so. He never knew what God or gods they had invoked to bless the journey, since nothing was ever said aloud. According to his father, the other Russians who had been with them in Vladivostok had scorned this habit as the custom of serfs, but the Japanese whom the Gonchevs had managed to meet in Kyoto had taken kindly to it, as they did to all formality. Later, a Japanese schoolmate had told Gonchev, "We would rather you people had customs than not," and he had understood—this reassured them that he and his sort were not merely white barbarians.

The motorcycle, a rarity in this country when he first came, had been his since Kyoto, from which it had arrived by sea and overland, with an attached blessing—in Japanese but of unknown origin—that had been carefully translated by each country along the way; he still kept the tattered list of the various versions in the machine's kit bag. He is superstitious enough never to supplant the old cycle with a car, although Vuksica drives the one allotted him as director. Besides, having only a cycle means that no one rides home with him from the studio, an advantage if he wants to stop off to relax at some obscure wayside bar, and no one ever comes home with him.

He and his wife never have official company, those dinner parties of favored intimates in which all those of rank are pressed to indulge. Instead, hordes of the Gonchev children's friends are welcome to run through the house, and there is also a constant traffic of Vuksica's women friends—each of whom thinks of herself as Vuksica's closest, although all are treated equally.

At first Vuksica had formed her alliances with ordinary women met in the household way, from shopkeepers' wives to the women on the farms that neighbor their own, not only the head farmer's wife but those of the laborers, and even the single girls who were conscripted as maids. Gradually the lure of her company, and her very lack of a social sense, which here meant a lack of the wish to rise, had drawn in others from above. The wife of the president of the Assembly, who has a country house near their house, had herself said to Gonchev: "We thought Vuksica standoffish at first"—which meant politically uncooperative— "but she's not, is she. Nor shy."

He'd replied, "No, but what is she?," really wanting the answer. He always wants to hear what is said of her.

"When I find out, I will tell you," the president's wife had said, not quite laughing. So—they too want to find Vuksica out.

Meanwhile, if on the way home he does stop at a bar, it is one toward which the agricultural laborers straggle at end of day, slowly filtering through the low door, hunchbacked and swollen with the land, to sit in muscle-bound talk, their drinks paced not by their pocketbooks alone but by the rhythms from which they come. Workmen of that sort, even the crafty or foolish ones, have a cropped stare, a terse honesty of the joints. He likes to watch them, seeing the bar and its patrons as linked to all such the world over, through the dark archive of the physical.

He can never be too certain of his motives, though, and knows how this worries Vuksica. When you grow up in your own country, as she had, you inherit your arguments, even if you later depart from them. In contrast, how can he be so sure, for instance, that his love of orderliness derives only from those compartmented lunchboxes at his first day school in Kyoto, their tidy lacquer always dotted with the same fishy pink and gray? Or that Kyoto's temples, whose high, warped wood had outwardly seemed to him dullish, and their plazas, bare and scrabbled and not even square, have nevertheless imprinted on him—in his love of long silences—the wordlessness of the passing monks, an occasional one of whom had now and then bent inquisitively to survey the Western child's shaggy head. To that child's mind the shorter monks had been the more affectionate, if only from not having to bend so far. Yet even they, from their grave silence, had seemed to demand of him the same response his teachers there had: not so much a conscience as a history.

What worries Gonchev is that his motives, obscure to him as they may be, so often work out well. Why, for instance, does he prefer to invite the committee to the house in that unorthodox, spontaneously Western style? Where had he, Gonchev, never in the West, got that style from? From films he had seen in the past, of course, as they themselves would have recognized, and out of such old ones from abroad as were permissible here. Or from the contraband they might have seen once or twice in their lives, but must never admit they have seen. Whereas he, in pursuance of his trade, can admit even to that. If he keeps cautious enough—and daring enough—his film work will excuse him almost anything. And this too worries him.

Why ask the committee home at all, this time of all times? Only because a minute before he had decided to remodel the studio—and why that? Why can't he know his motives, like other people? They all accept these invitations, of course, each man individually flattered by Gonchev's intelligent choice of him as one of those to be asked to that house *en famille*. Once there, the women will yearn for more of Vuksica than she is likely to grant, and the men may go so far as to warn him or twit him privately, on certain of his intransigences. He has never given them the opportunity to do this publicly. Yet by the time the news of his break with routine—always a serious matter—gets further upstairs, all may ameliorate. Up there his action may even begin to make sense to them—more so than it has to him. The top proles like to think of themselves as capable of wider comprehensions than those below; it is their substitute for not being allowed to be gentlemen. All this has happened before. He has broken some rules, often unthinkingly. They have been intrigued, and eventually have followed after, maybe with excuses altogether off base. But he, the émigré, has shown them how a rule can be bent.

Then—would all be as usual again in the house of cards he is approaching?

In Kyoto, when his father bought for him this same motorcycle, the American teacher who had been selling off his goods had sealed the bargain with a Suntory whiskey that had sent the senior Gonchev, already sodden with the sake that was all he could afford, into one of his harangues. "Always leaving!" he had declaimed. "Humanity is divided between those who leave and those who stay. My wife is of your persuasion, sir—a leaver. She's the one who's really buying the son your machine." And then with a whine into his emptied glass, "Pity you don't have a musical instrument for me. Then we could bargain again."

The American's wife, one of their nice goose girls, had been sorry for the young Gonchev, who was ashamedly studying the books for sale, one of them in his hand, although he hadn't yet opened it. "Take it. Go on—do." He had. On the way out to the car the Gonchevs had borrowed to get the motorcycle home—the American helping young Gonchev load the machine he didn't yet know how to ride, the girl-wife hovering—his father had said grandly: "Don't bother with a receipt, my dear fellow. I can see you are honest as the day. But, Paul, what are you doing with that book? Put it back immediately."

The book, hung on to, had proved to be a nineteenth-century Byron, full of steel engravings prophetic of the very landscape through which the old cycle now rumbled and spat. Here are the same high, craggy roadsides, thin white cataracts, and heavy arborvitae. And a promise of ruined romances to come—if one will but turn the page.

But it is too dark to do that even in memory. He may just as well drive in circles, imagining this badly lit countryside as he has so many others, until morning can verify it. He has enough gasoline to indulge himself, a privilege of few. No doubt the shadowy functionary has seen to that. In a way he welcomes the man's company, as one might relish that of an old enemy. In the event of the man's death, Gonchev will certainly go to his funeral, too. Gritting his teeth at the tappet of another motorcycle behind him—how does the man manage to mute it like that, only a cheap local product?—Gonchev drives on.

Under his wheel, the land itself woos him, wanting to be his—white road unfurling, patches of hairy fern uncoiling as if from the point of a pen. The only way to escape from whatever he is escaping is to think of his cities. One after the other, he imagines all forty-nine of them. The fiftieth he will save.

When he drives up to his house it is almost dawn. The door, framed in cobblestones set in mortar and interspersed with lath, is as neat as a new handkerchief. On the garden side of the house Vuksica has stenciled the whitewashed wall with trellised flowers in bright colors, as was the custom in that Danube town of her grandfather, where she was born, and to which she returned for her first wedding. In that wedding photograph she looked as hardy as any fresh young shoot ready to branch out in its native ground—and there remain.

"We might be in Novi Sad now, eh?" Gonchev, taking tea in the garden at the table under the flowered wall, sometimes said knowingly. Danilo, if present, would laugh. But Vuksica always answered seriously. "No, not without the university. That I can't draw." Or "No. There would also be the flour mills."

Inside, the quiet house is all cool wood-brown and white. She has a serene talent for keeping it uncluttered yet warming. But something else he hasn't noticed before. How—permanent. Perhaps it doesn't do to enter one's house at dawn.

On a table there is mail. A telegram, or rather this country's handwritten—ergo, censored—version. For Danilo, from Gonchev's sister-in-law, who is leaving Paris for home. Where he must join her at once; she is giving a professional reception, with slides. What this means is that he has to show himself in order to erase the taint of living too much outside Yugoslavia. The telegram, such as are allowed over the border, is without envelope and would have come by runner—the local ones on foot, like messengers in some ancient drama still going on.

Letters from the children, too. The lad hasn't won the decathlon but doesn't seem downhearted, and is going off on a bicycle trip with another fellow and two girls. The latitude allowed non-Muslim girls and boys here is in inverse proportion to their lack of other scope. Gonchev's son goes on about one of the girls, who had won a mathematics prize. "She's as smart as Sister." And therefore must be smarter than he.

The letter from Gonchev's girl at the farm is the surprise. "I love it here. There are some wonderful people. And some foolish. A sow ate its own children. Those in charge of the pigsty didn't get to it in time. There is an arboretum from the old days, with many foreign trees. Three other girls and I have formed a club—we stand for five minutes under each tree that is strange to us. It is wonderful." Those last three words had been stamped out by the censor but are still readable; the worn rubber used by the postal authorities is an undercover joke. "Better than ballet," Laura had added. Which she had long ago rejected, because no matter how many *tours levés* one attained to, the feet—and the body— were required to return to Position One.

An oddly childish letter for a girl on the way to being a woman. But all letters sound adolescent here, thanks to the rubber stamp.

In spite of which his boy and girl are already drumming up their prospectuses. Always too soon, as parents are warned. Yet he wouldn't like to have children who had no theories. So he must hope that theirs won't be painful to watch. He picks up the boy's letter again. Klement and his pals are going to the west border, and back. "It isn't far," he had written stiltedly. They would go only to its nearest point, a distance suitable for beginners. In time, as Gonchev knew, they might journey to and from all the country's limits, reaching the farthest only with maturity—and always returning.

Border-bumping, this sport is popularly called—a premarital rite of passage expected of most citizens, and well regulated and exploited by the authorities. Men here often continue the practice, in male groups only. In later life, perhaps at some crisis, a man might make a pilgrimage singly, to some holy border point of his choice. Stepan, while still Gonchev's student, had done a documentary on such a man. Women by and large give up the practice just before marriage; half the population is Muslim still.

In fact, if Gonchev ever bows to Danilo's urging and makes a contra-band film on this strange republic whose isolation is stricter than any even the Kremlin dreamed, he hopes to photograph, quite matter-of-factly, how the hammer and sickle has got itself entangled in the Koran's web—all the way from his own committee's impassive politics, a harem of men, to the land's Garden of Allah plainsmen, and Oriental penances. Meanwhile, slang to do with border-bumping has entered the language of loafers and group leaders both. And has sprouted its insignia on his son's bike.

Vuksica is lying asleep on the big bed, in a welter of books. This means that she too has had insomnia, although she refuses to name any sleeplessness of hers that detrimentally, saying rather that it is nature's rush of adrenaline toward problems often best confronted in the silence of night. Her blue nightdress flows over the books. She likes snuggling in lots of material—making herself hard to find, as he sometimes teases. But in a woman so rightfully nude when she is bare, this one coyness is surely to be ceded her.

The bed, her choice, is huge. Those few outsiders who have seen it—her women cronies, and an occasional student who crosses through the house the wrong way from Gonchev's study, perhaps intention-ally—gasp when they see it. And feel free to make remarks. Everybody here is invasive as to private property. Taste, the most private of all, must expect to run the socialist gauntlet. "So if I have quintuplets," Vuksica answers, "there'll be room to feed all of them." He suddenly recalls what Stepan, slouching at the bedroom door, had replied to her: "From five breasts?"

Gonchev had wanted to be annoyed at that, but she had merely screwed up her eyes at the young man and said: "Half the world has the visual stance these days. Without the taste to refine it." But added to Gonchev later: "That young man—he means to do you in."

"So do all one's best students," Gonchev had said.

She will already have heard what happened at the viewing. The committee will have gone home and informed their wives. He wonders if he can tell how many of those had promptly phoned Vuksica by counting the number of books she has pulled from the shelves—one after each call—and then discarded. He loves finding her asleep in any style. It is when he can count his blessings. And with all he has to be thankful for, she can giggle too.

Her eyes open wide. Whenever this happens he says to himself, "There they are."

He picked up one of the books. She reads cookbooks for solace, this woman who has played Ibsen. In a bomb shelter she would probably bury herself deep in recipes for blanquette de veau, and read those aloud to the children. Even in a country that had no veal. Perhaps especially so in that case. It still took his breath away—that she had come with him across a border from behind which she might never return.

For he is no longer under any illusion that this country will honor the agreement made sixteen years ago—that he would always be free to leave. Nor is she, although he has never brought himself to ask her point-blank. As she too must see, he is serving this tight little fastness too well.

In his first five years here he was too delirious with building his sets to want to travel, even for research. During his second five years he began to ask to leave temporarily. Once in order to check on the ravages of that great flood in Venice, which might have ruined buildings still standing in his Elsinore in perfect replica. And once in excited conviction that his own files, amateurish and secondhand though they might be, indicated measurements for an underground midden that Mexican archeologists had never recorded.

The grounds for refusing him have always been reasonable enough. The first two times he had been needed in his projects, irreplaceable. A man likes to feel so—and they know it. Even the third request had been plausibly denied. He had asked that he be allowed to travel to interview the descendants of three gypsy families from this very countryside, who, brought to the World's Fair of 1881 in St. Louis, Missouri, had later settled there, founding farmsites, still preserved, whose buildings and artifacts were said to be identical with those indigenous here at that era. By this time his interest was more in the travel release than in the project, though he would have returned. A library such as his at Elsinore is hostage indeed.

But he had erred in making his project too fervently historic. Socialism prefers its national prides to be run-of-the-mill modern. He was told that it was not in his mandate to film this country's past. And not his business to. Further, the country was in deepest mourning at the time for the mother-in-law of its dictator. To contaminate any border by crossing it, even if you were a nonnational, would have been disrespect. And still furthermore—in case he had a documentary in mind—honest gypsies did not settle, much less farm. And finally: the city of St. Louis was not on his list.

During his and Vuksica's third and most recent five years, he has half amused, half solaced himself by proposing projects ever more cannily worthy from the government's point of view—so forcing the authorities into excuses ever more agile and varied. A mutual admiration has developed. They applaud his patriotic sense. While he has begun to comprehend—and, yes, even to clap in a grisly way—the high art of excuse. But to admire is almost to tolerate. "If you don't watch out," Vuksica said during the fifteenth year, "they will become the artists. You will become the government."

During this last year she has said nothing. When he agreed to come, already obsessed by his cities, he had thought that he and this little Balkan jumping-off place were merely exchanging opportunities, and that he would do better for them than they had dreamed. He had even been excited by the forest of religious myth—a tiny country as much islanded by its own metaphor as his Japan. Like some savage feudal bird—the kind that glared from the old Japanese prints—that had got a lump of modern concrete stuck in its crop. And the marvelous terrain—he had romanticized that too. It was virgin. He would bring it cities—but without harm.

He had been the naïf. How long it has taken him to see that travel—first negated and then surmounted—is the real national myth. With his help, how cleverly this semi-peasant enclave has managed itself—and him. Nobody can get out? Make a virtue of that, and vicariousness a sport. Meanwhile offer the rest of the world the same sport at a price. Except through Gonchev's films, almost nobody can get in.

Is it his fault or human nature's that to the West this sub-Balkan enclave has become one of the last Edens of the imagination. The films he in the end was pressed to do of the country itself were as dull as national socialism could make them, even with scenery and faces out of the Old Testament. All his own imaginations had gone into his cities. Who could have foreseen that the artificial cosmopolis would become the hobby of a few film buffs, then a cultist rage? Underground, of course, like most of his sources. But even that titillated the world abroad. "Surely they come to laugh," he told Danilo. "Granted," Danilo said. "And stay to groan."

What the committee understands of his réclame is minimal—only enough to look the other way at his avenues of research, and his ever-growing mail. But counting up the receipts, who among them hadn't a forefinger to rub circularly against the ball of a thumb? So of course they hadn't acceded to any of his sardonic requests. Not letting him loose, say, to take plaster impressions of the Olympic City, even though it was to be in Moscow. Or to do an anti-papist film à la *Frankenstein,* in which the black mummy-nun of Assisi—who would have to be preliminarily photographed *in situ*—would attempt to vampirize that sacred mauve masterpiece the corpse of Lenin. They will never let him go—anywhere. He is their rate of exchange.

Recently these humoresques of his have flagged. After sixteen years, his great plateau, under need of repair, is in the throes of a Plan. One so costly, yet so approved, that he should be transported with creative energy. The mail from abroad, increasingly permitted, is chock-full of respectful inquiries he can't respond to, plus Festschrifts for celebrations in his honor that he can't attend.

Instead, spending each morning among his blueprints, or surrounded by his ruddy-cheeked film crews, and going in a trice—which means by golf cart—from his Bombay to his Budapest, he has sunk deeper into what any Zen monk of Kyoto, accosted in his own dun meditations, would recognize: You cannot build your Elsinore and keep it too. The golf cart, an excellent replica proudly built by a properties crew in a country that has never seen a golf course, is an example. Or consider it in another way, as Gonchev is always willing to: Build an Elsinore too faithfully, and it will disappear.

To Vuksica, to whom he grumbles in the ordinary husbandly way about a host of things, he has said nothing of this, nor to Danilo, whose pragmatic *tut-tut* he doesn't want to hear. What he needs is a monkish ear. To listen, and then be off, without reply. Sometimes he thinks of the spy.

The women Vuksica talks to may not be her confidantes, but they are a release. Those on her inner list are all bright, if not as widely educated as she. All are impressive, the short ones as plump as kernels, the tall ones as majestic as queens. All have the sophistication common in border territories; no contraband of any sort would surprise them. Or perhaps all women are smugglers inborn. Yet in the Muslim way, these serve without question the men who physically serve them. "Your friends," he'd said once to Vuksica. "Here a woman's independence is only what? Cracks in the calico?"

She had known he was asking about her. "Cotton doesn't crack. Only silk."

She will answer him solely from her reality. Yet lies in wait for his homecomings, like a field where he might plant his fantasies and so rid himself of them. It's his dreams she wants. He is lucky in that. Or has been, up to now.

He indicates the books. "You heard."

She answers him with the crooked smile she always brings away from her seraglio. "Two told me that you had turned down the film. Two told me about the studio. One told me both."

"Five." The books strewn around her are double that. "And five breasts—remember that young man's remark. Well, you were right about him."

She is never particularly concerned with being right. "You rode far?"

She knows he rides in circles on these occasions. She means "How long?"

"I left at ten."

In the light now filtering in, her eyes widen. He has indeed ridden far. But she will wait for him to say why.

"He built his own Paris. I can't believe they actually went, that is. Got out, the whole team of them. And back."

"No." She sits up, unhurriedly. "That is what he would do. Build it here." She brushes the books off the bed, finished with that episode of weakness. "That is what all of them will do."

He nods. "Students." His mouth twists. "His curbstones were terrible. Like swollen lips."

She begins to laugh. Once upon a time his eccentricities of vision had merely charmed her; now they amuse as well.

I'm all right though, he thinks, until the day when what I am makes her cry.

She clasps her knees. "And the studio?"

She never likes to go near it. She still fears he wants her in those films.

"At first I thought, knock it down. What's it doing here? Then, no: Let nature level it. Let it go back to grass." Under the intense foliage here, and the pressure of crag and rivulet, any buildings left to themselves, on his mountain, for instance, don't stay intact long.

She claps her hands. "Then—it could become a memory."

Copy of the Avala Studios, Belgrade. He sees it, vined and derelict yet elegant, like those fallen colonnades and ruined follies in his Byron. He and she would sit on its steps and talk there, ruined too.

"And the locations—I'm going to have them all smashed in. I'll do it this time, I swear. 'To modernize,' I'll say. Secretly they love the word, though they'll ask me to use another. 'Of course, Minister,' I'll say. 'To revise.'" He turns to her, eyes alight. "Then I won't. I won't, do you hear? That'll be the Plan."

She doesn't ask what he and she will do then. She never has. With a sigh, she takes his hand. "It was a long ride, eh."

"If I'd come upon a hayrick, I'd have asked it to turn me to stone."

She cups his cheek. "It's not the road for them. The one you always take."

And these days, his is not the right face? She doesn't say that, but he hears it. He rubs his face in the palm of her hand, kissing.

Suddenly he hears the silence in the room. The room presents itself in all its power, as a room suddenly will. Nothing to be done about it, or with it. It is. It stays. Up against such clarity people shift furniture, acquire new wardrobes, take trips or new lovers, even move away.

He must mention the letters from the children. Who are no longer children.

"I see Klement has gone border-bumping."

She blushes with a mother's defensiveness. "Only to the nearest one."

Accompanying Danilo to the airport, she and he often pass such beginners, clustered at the border there. The younger boys ride alongside the barbed wire on their bikes, dismounting here and there to stand nudging and gawking, clustered as if for body heat. Or they walk the boundary dreamily in pairs, side-glancing the way yokels in ordinary countries pass a cathouse. When older, the young men whiz back and forth on their parents' trucks, ending up in village pothouses, with now and then a rampage, boasted of ever after.

All the country's other exits are highland passes through its natural barrier, a mountain system near his plateau so rugged that few such sportsmen are ever seen there. Even the most foolhardy mountaineering daredevils more often confine themselves to the broken or fused ridges that descend from the central plain. Those who are successful are met at checkpoints by cheering border guards, photographers, huge campfire dinners at which blue ribbons are distributed—and by an escort to bear them proudly back.

White-water enthusiasts sometimes try the rivers, which are unnavigable, but more important to the myth, flow from east to west. The river region's hospital, welcoming the injured, is almost tropical in its delights.

Altogether, border-bumping is like that most daring of sports, the military maneuver. At any moment it might become real.

Klement, left to himself, would have been content with the plainer pleasure of the athletic games. But the tide is bearing him out. For a simple boy, but a greedy one, it is not a good tide.

"I could do a home documentary then, on the border-bumping," Gonchev says bitterly. "For that, one need build nothing."

"You'd copy that Stepan? Your own pupil?"

"One comes to it."

Not you—she usually said. The nightdress has bunched up around her knees. She draws it tighter.

"But for Laura to have to . . ." To him, young women his daughter's age are still unfocused animal-vegetables. Wand-slim sillies, with their sharp hound's-teeth stuck with sugar, and tits that will surely never be more than pimples. Or the pansy-faced ones, with meal sacks below, and feet like churns. They run through the houses with his girl at the head; he had been proud. But for his fine, crooked-smiling girl, with eyes as black as ditches when she is sulky, and a mind hung like a Maltese cross around her neck, what tide could there be? "To have to stand under foreign trees. For the smell of them."

"It was the sow maybe sent her off. She's never seen such a thing."

"No. You don't eat your children. Nor me." He searches for her foot, finds it, and squeezes. The foot does not respond as usual. Yes, we are a loving foursome, he thinks, even if Klement loves only himself. But can such a nucleole be enough? And love can grow conservative.

He puts his head on her belly, to hide what he would never ask, although he mouths it. But do I eat you, the three of you—by what I do? "I talked with our man tonight," he says.

"Our man?" But she knows.

"You know. You see him at the airport."

"You *talked* with him?" She half sits up.

"It's a beginning." He knows he's said that before, in other connections. But the vision persists.

At times it is only the two children they thrust onto the plane with Danilo, he and Vuksica trailing away casually, without even a wave, as if the kids belonged to Danilo now. Or Vuksica waving them off on her own, while Gonchev engages the lazy border guards in talk. The guards are used to this routine flight and sometimes don't even emerge from the guardhouse. But if they were to alert, and had their guns with them, he could always say he had wanted the children to see the inside of a plane. Or perhaps he could get the guards used to that, and one day the pilot, that kidnapper, would take off. Or sometimes, it is only Vuksica and the girl who go, leaving Gonchev and Klement behind.

He can never quite see all four of them going, except in the version hardest to fantasize, in which he has persuaded his follower, the man, to go with them. Persuaded only. He has a feeling that the man can't be bribed. Also, that unlike the man they had before, this one is almost certainly a bachelor. That day, like the four Gonchevs the man would be carrying little with him beyond his usual notepad, in order to clock this Sunday-afternoon departure. Or excursion. *To find a new location,* Gonchev would have said to him earlier. *As you may have noticed, I don't build them anymore.* He has the strongest sense that the man can be wooed, is even one of his fans. Or does one always feel that after a while about a spy?

And if the man wasn't to be persuaded? Whether Danilo or Gonchev would be the one to use a pistol is moot—perhaps both of them. On the other side of the border the foreign plane would be waiting. The pilot would have walked toward the guardhouse on some pretext. And both Danilo and Gonchev can fly a plane.

Yes, that is the most difficult version, and the one with the most holes in it. But the best.

"But after what happened last time," she says in a whisper. "After you talked with—his predecessor."

He raises himself up. "The other man's funeral, you mean? Unnatural? No, come on. They wouldn't need to go that far. Men wear out quickly in such jobs. And that one wasn't young. No, maybe they do that sort of thing over the border. Over Border Four. Or Border Five. But not here."

"You used to name the countries right out," she says. "And the borders. Not number them."

As they do here—not traveling even with the tongue.

Gonchev sits up fully. "One comes to it."

The starchy scent of her nightdress is still in his nostrils. A blue smell, with baked-in hints of the iron. He fingers the stuff. "Not silk?"

"Cotton."

"Then it won't crack, eh? What does it do?"

There's an old cat-scratch scar at one corner of her mouth, long since healed to a hairline. The scratch lifts, in a millimeter smile. "Wears thin."

They exchange that look which, between couples, is the sounding of the drum. The books still on the bed, one after another swept to the floor, rattle and spit their injury at him, then shut up. She does not help. Her face has that droll, sad quirk that comes on old lovers who know they are making love to their whole history together, and to their mortality as well. The same look must be on him—which could be why she had asked him, not long ago, to shave his mustache unaccidentally, and keep it so. I want to be able to see what's happening to us, she had said. A thrill had shot through him, as if they had exchanged heads, in an act that had become simple for people like them. What's happening to us, she had said. Not just—to him.

He begins to unwrap the yardage in which she sits, a child on a beach, its torso half under a rampart of sand. Part of the fabric is rumpled, like any much-used garment, part still lies in severe, starched cones that, if enlarged by a lens, might remind the eye of a desert. He knows from his mail that there are now landscape artists who wrap whole deserts with borders of nylon string, using guy-wires, and teams of aerialists. Arrogant men, those are, or cowardly, not to dare instead that human terrain the body, which shifts in sympathy with the onlooker; which a little assists.

There she is.

So many manipulations of space are open to people nowadays—and they take to these so indiscriminately. Or are subjected to them in hordes, as he and his parents had been. In the exercise of his profession he himself has learned how to move crowds about, to manipulate them. Maybe that was why he chose it? Later taking his revenge by locking himself up in a country more fiercely resolved against migration than others of its political ilk? Danilo had once accused him of that.

"The fanatics find each other," Danilo had said. So—this country. So—Director Gonchev. Who sings of the world like a countertenor, like an angel—in exchange for not being a man?

But the Stepans here—will they do the same?

The white plateau of body beside his has gradually changed over the years. He glances up at the windows. The dawns can not be held back. But in nature's great going down, the artistry is age. He is too weak to promise either himself or her to give up his wild evening rides. Indeed she hasn't asked him to, remarking over the years how these frightened the children but also alerted them. And perhaps his rides are the very madness that still holds her to him.

Every man has his own sexual metaphor, and every woman too. He cherishes the idea that *in extremis* his and hers blend. So, now the night is over.

He put his warming arms around her warm core, spread his legs, and ascended, over the border. When he reached the top he thought there might be answering tears in her eyes, although she kept them closed. He was where he wanted to be. Here.

The blue nightdress, once an extravaganza, lies on the floor, so worn that one can see the carpet through it.

These days he sleeps on heavily afterwards. Vaksica wakes at once, feeling that she must follow the progress of his dreams as if they were her own. Some she has seen on actual film—his films. Others he has told her of. If he twitches or groans now, it could be to one of those, the unfilmed ones. Such as that nightmare ride in which all the foliage is reversed, the leaves straight out like street-sign arrows, the tender tips of the ferns uncurling to points, and even the big valonia oaks, which no other plain in Central Europe now has many of, streaming out like one-armed coastal cypresses, black with a horizontal rain that never falls. In another ride, he vainly tries to urge his motorcycle, running in dead heat with the wind, yet stationary, toward the national peak here—one of the highest summits in Central Europe—around whose crest groups of pilgrims, arranged in rosettes, are gathered, ready to cross over into what can only be air.

By his own report, in each of these dreams that one phrase, *Central Europe,* runs alongside him, always attached to some natural object or phenomenon—a tree, a wind direction, a peak—but in the dream he never notices. He tells her these things only in the first vulnerable moments after waking, ashamed of their obviousness, and she too tries not to honor them with recall. Wanting no inroads on her well-acted life.

55

Among his real films there are two sequences she likes best and tries to "run" at times like this, in the hope that he too, pillowed on her shoulder, is somehow attending them.

One is of a blundering-voiced North Sea port in which the fogged-in hulls of freighters and their brass-buttoned deck personnel are seen in constant séance. Above them, a gull out of Dürer is flying south. In the second sequence, one saw the mineral-water-toned London estuary at dusk, spotted chrome-yellow with the lights of dockside pubs. Off in a perspective "as angularly impossible as those between governments," Gonchev had said, one saw the tricorne hats of all the Thames's bridges, lighted too, stringing the air. "As if just awarded the Order of the Garter."

He had worked for days to get that gull where it was. "To have one know that it is flying south." For both sequences he had pored over Turner's Thames paintings and had used a lantern-slide technique. His best locations are painterly—the ones with no obligation to be real. Only the heart of the watcher, profoundly beating, wanted them so.

"Abroad, there's a growing market for such curiosities," Danilo had said on the patio yesterday, just before leaving. He was in the act of trying to swat a big fly. "Paul could never do so well outside. Over there, how they love watching us Central Europeans hurl ourselves against our fences. Our brave allegories, how they rejoice at them. Our famous irony, how it relieves them. An American magazine wants to publish my old essay, the one that got me into trouble. They suggest that if granting them permission would be too risky for me, they might arrange to steal it."

She can see herself in Danilo's mirror. "And what will they send you in exchange? Cigars?"

"Or get contraband books to me, they said. Anything that will make me more 'comfortable.' "

"Well, you have cigars."

"Straight from the Cuban source. Better than theirs."

And the books he can get in Paris—if he wants them.

"So they think Paul's films are satirical?"

"What else?" He stares at her, the flyswatter across his knee. "You don't think they are showing his New York film in the Palais de Chaillot this very moment because they need to see New York?"

She shook her head mutely. Even after so many years she couldn't think that.

"Then what?"

"That . . ." For sixteen years she has thought of nothing else. Of how, no matter what compromises Gonchev's title and function might indicate to them out there, he does them a bitter service, which she in turn serves. "That . . . the world would want to see how the world looks from here."

A fly, the biggest yet, was crawling over the bowl of fruit, slowly traversing a big globe of plum, the swollen ravines of some figs just arrived from the south, and a mountainous pear.

Danilo put his head in his hands, groaning softly. His fishscale-cut hair was still dressed like a romantic lead's. "My God, my God, the Balkans." His headshake died between his shoulders. Both brother and sister shrugged. His hand came out at her like a bargaining shopkeeper's, palm out, fingers crooked. "This strip of rock-dwellers. A few plains, a crease of sea. That was never quite Turkey. That will never be Greece. Savages—who turn their backs even on Italy. They want the world to know what they think of it? They think the world wants to know? *Merde.*" In the middle of his tirade he stopped short and said in a dead voice, "No, it's your idea, isn't it? *Aie.*" He fell back in his chair.

She turns her head aside, as if there were somewhere to turn. Having one profile as good as the other makes it no easier. His are the same— the only way in which he and she are truly identical. So, like a couple of coins in a pocket, each already knows the other's other side.

Elsewhere, what a mixture Danilo is, the hands wrinkled from the forge, the nails shining from the most recent hotel manicurist. Meanwhile she, keeping herself so spotless, going from dress to similar dress straight as a compass needle, wrapping her life in dead-on focus from day to day—what is she? In a spasm of love for her brother, for his very mixture, she leaned forward to him.

The hand with the swatter flashed by her. Plum blood spurted all over the white cloth. The fly lay dead in the center of the plum. Sometimes, when tapped lightly, they dropped like bits of muzzled black lace, but this one's mandible was smashed to cream.

"Sorry." Danilo, who had stood up to do it, sat down, heavily for him. "You have such ripe fruit here."

She threw the plum overhand into the sumac grove and went to get another cloth from the huge cupboard full of home-woven linen. Let it seem boastful, the linen was there. Old stuff, hung with lace and beveled by the needle, and still obtainable at any local fair. At Christmas, she used to send some by Danilo to her sister-in-law in Belgrade. Until once, the note of thanks said: "I took the cloth you sent to Paris with me. How our neighbors on Bellechasse admire it." Coarse, stupid woman, with her slide shows. At the close of which she no longer served cake or coffee, or even bread and cold cuts, on a cloth which would have been identifiable to all their Belgrade friends as from Vuksica. "More professional not to serve anything," she had written. After that, Vuksica sent no more linen.

Although bushel baskets of fruit, brought up by a laborer every day of the season, were ranged on the house steps, she did not refill the bowl. It is past that hour now. The sky behind Danilo's head is orange. He is smoking a cigarette. Any cigars he brings in are for Gonchev, who passes them on to the president of the Assembly "for comparison." Although tobacco grows here, the country's once active if primitive industry is only now reviving, along with the charcoal-burning from the valonia oaks. Far across the fields there are sheds where the bile-colored tobacco leaves are hung, but the wooden cigar forms were crude, Danilo had once told her, and the workers who wrapped the leaves too fat-fingered, even the women. "Takes some little Cuban," he'd said. Gonchev, who, in order to build his two Chinese cities, Shanghai and Beijing, had commanded and got handiwork fit for a mandarin, hadn't commented.

"How pure the air is," Danilo says. He and she had exhausted any Belgrade gossip day before yesterday. But ordinarily before leaving he would have been collecting her greetings to those at home, dwindling and outdated though her messages have become.

Yes, it is a privilege to breathe here. Trees frame the place like a proscenium arch, but the house and ground give no feeling of having been especially chosen for that sequestered purity. Rather, there is a sense that the same natural order stretches on for endless miles. From the domestic view, all the borders of this universe are far enough.

"How fat—that poison-sumac," he says. "They really cultivate it?"

Those furry, purple-brown cones branch like candelabra; she's become fond of them. "In the old days, they used to export the leaves to the tanneries in Trieste. Now of course, they use only the tanneries here. Children have to learn not to touch the branches."

He tamps out his cigarette carefully, in a dish. The ground is so rich with bark and leaves. "Nature. Here one could almost begin to believe in it again." As the time to go draws near he always becomes gassy with compliments. Though she isn't fooled, he can't help himself.

A serving-maid brings coffee, brewed in brass pipkins Vuksica had carried in from Belgrade. They use the same here, but his sister hadn't known. One has serving-maids here, too. Swept away for a brief time, they had returned to their natural niches as soon as the dust of equality had settled. In his own country these pawns of economic theory now get better pay, and a man can't fuck them or hit them unless they want one to. He wouldn't be surprised if in this feudal country, which has merely switched its military hats, as it has been doing since the Middle Ages, even the *droit de seigneur* existed somewhere—maybe in one of those dread mountain arêtes his plane had once been blown into, where a young girl couldn't run far. And where the hereditary overlord, for all one knew, may still own even that sanctuary the church. People often have no idea how attractive the combination of socialism and ancient custom can be.

No use seeking such information from Paul. Who has never made love-dramas. And laughs at how the French filmmakers cling to adultery as to a last aphrodisiac. Such cleaving to one woman as his brother-in-law has done can make a man strangely innocent. Although since the woman is Danilo's own sister he certainly would not wish her deceived. And, Vuksica being both who she had been and what she remarkably still is, the world would well understand Paul's adoration.

"Ah, God," he says as usual, at his first sip of the coffee, "real Turkish."

"We're closer," she says. "Some seeps."

He laughs. "Over the border?" A phrase only he can say naturally in this place. "Sewn into a hemline? Or in a *cache-sexe?*" Because he suspects where she must get the coffee beans. From one or the other of her dear women friends, who would know how to smuggle, and where. So Paul can remain pure, and still have his fiercely craved morning cup. Danilo refills his own. "At home we're getting third-rate pebbles, from some African bloc we have to be friends with."

She looks uneasy. His sister wants everything back home to remain as it had always been. So do most émigrés, even in Paris, moaning in the cafés over some wretched little hogtown on its faraway mudflats—only let its name end in *ursk,* or *ania,* or *bach*—while at the very same moment the light from the Seine might be making all the cocottes look like marquises. Or even when they themselves have fancy girl students from America in tow. Yet her own husband, though born an émigré, has no one country at heart; that is part of his talent. And living with Paul is now her talent.

Danilo is listening to a clangor in the fields. "What is that?"

"Stone-breaking."

"So late? Real peasants."

"You don't have them anymore?" she cries, aghast in spite of herself.

His brows go up. Her use of that "you" affronts him. "Ours have tasted the apple."

The welkin strains down, brewing its blue. Her brother's head has lost its bright halo. In an hour he would be up in space. Here one can hear every pine needle drop. Some people give off an air of perfecting themselves in plane travel; her brother, Danilo, is one of those. In such travel he hones to a fine point what he is on land.

She had once done that for herself, in her films. An air of completion, of being literally in her element, was said to have been what had helped to make her a star. That is why she hasn't dared act since coming here. For her, terra firma must enter the spirit the way the old earth-dyes once entered the woven cloth. So instead, she will impose her sandaled foot on the land, her food on the table, spread a serenity like gold dust through the house, and watch the bodies of her children shedding their fine cell-light. These are her boundaries, and the daily interchange between all these granaries her travel. While Paul spreads his unique wings for all of them.

Even Danilo, while pecking and criticizing, keeps a pair of sandals in her house. Paul and she and he are one another's vital audience, none of the three at another's expense. Until now.

The gossip from home is getting frailer. Not because events, good and bad, would ever stop slamming in on Belgrade, that brilliant, never heartbroken city, where she had once shone, but because her own clues as to who and what are politically or professionally au courant are ever lessening. A juicy brawl at the Writers' restaurant, and Danilo has to spend an hour, if for her a delicious one, explaining why. A newly reigning cabal at the Pula festival, and she knows none of the protagonists. While Danilo now has had two small parts on television, both much noticed. "They said I looked like that new British actor, the one who never changes his face? I did that on purpose, of course," he'd told her, his mobile face flickering merrily. "He's all the rage just now." She had never heard of that actor, nor had Paul.

"He's not in films yet," Danilo had said, staring off into the greenery surrounding them. Jumping up then, he had plucked a flower and loudly admired it. He still looks youthful enough to play male leads; she and he both started young. Although these days no one would joke, as they had then, that Danilo photographed like Vuksica in curls—the joke being that she has never worn curls. Fewer and fewer would recall this now. Or even who she was.

But what's itching her brother? One minute all bouquets to her and Paul's idyllic life here. The next minute sitting himself down in the chair closest to her, to tell her, with the same bent knee and sweep of the thigh with which he had once played Laertes, but also with the crumpled family look that always comes over him when he talks of the forge: "I'm thinking of selling it."

What's he saying? The forge has been part of his needed life-space, as anyone who notes those hands can see. Will the television, in which, he is saying, he thinks he can go far, take the place of his beloved hours with his ironworkers—cherished even though the forge no longer produces the Neanderthal-style ware that had been its pride?

"Selling might bring me life-space enough to be sent to America," he's saying. "Not to stay. But to be sent." Meanwhile, such a new life will disassociate him from his always dangerous desk—not that it would ever woo him away permanently. But political rehabilitation, all the stages of that contre-danse—he doesn't have to remind her of those, does he? It won't hurt if some of the same out-of-favor stalwarts who had applauded his daring article now deplore: "Danilo's gone over to television—that fluff."

All this he chatters, meanwhile picking at the thick scallops of the tablecloth, as he used to pick at the corners of the playscripts they rehearsed for one another. Often at the forge—as much the sign of their family as any farmer's farm. To be thrown on the scrap? This he hasn't said for sure.

Instead, he has swatted flies, though already dressed in his flight jacket and leather shoes. He is staring at that farthest dell, where Gonchev, in the first flush of his and her arrival and the charmed infancy of their children, treated by the peasants as if they were royal, had erected a playhouse for them. And, as everybody had teased, for himself?—although Gonchev has never done more than gaze approvingly at its tiny eaves, flipped up in Oriental style.

The little ten-foot-square house, made cunningly of old barn siding, had been set far enough from the house for her to use it as the focus for a line of hedges and shrubs she has gradually caused to be set around their entire haven here. The enclosure's wandering green line is so varied, yet so accessible through openings the ground staff well knows must be kept clipped, that only a landscape gardener intent on the same effect might guess what she has done.

How wise she has been, Vuksica thinks. When one has an enclosure one has built oneself, one can tolerate the larger one. Here, inside her green line, the permission is all hers, to go or come. Or to effect change. As with Paul and his distant plateau. But she will never name this precinct of hers.

The name Elsinore, seen routinely on a master builder's contract on Paul's desk or heard on the lips of a servant reporting Paul's call from there, makes her shiver. When one runs a household, seeing the artfully construed meals succeed one another, and the curtains meld with the seasons, one comes to know that one is only imposing a routine on the dream that is life. This hard-won routine is honestly hers, to vanish forever when she does. But she knows better than to impose any notions of property on the dream.

"Tell me more about the television," Vuksica says.

Danilo turns around, dramatically full-square. "I thought you might never ask."

She rolls her eyes in their old comedy response: Stop spouting script—but he ignores that.

"As for the parts I'm getting now—I'll just do them. They're nothing much to talk about. Or do you mean—about Paul?"

"Paul? What's Paul got to do with television?"

"Nothing." Danilo picks up the ashtray and sets it down again, *lento, lento.* "Nothing," he says deeper. A third "Nothing," meant to be *basso,* is only breath; he's out of practice. "But television may have everything to do with Paul."

Oh, come off it, Brother, she thinks, in English, British English. Don't give me these balanced sentences. Do your job only on the job. She often thinks in English these days. She had been a dubber for foreign language films for three years in Rome, before getting her first good part. Aloud she says: "If you mean he's the only television this country has, then, sure. But we all know that."

"I don't mean."

"Oh?" She raises her head. Far off there is the throbbing of a motorcycle—Gonchev's.

"Your profile is still so good," Danilo says with satisfaction.

"You offering me a job?" This wouldn't be the first time he had tried wooing her away, although that hasn't happened in some years. Now he is too fond of Gonchev, of them all. While they, suspended in what he may mock as their warped Eden but always comes back to, are part of his needed living-space.

He laughs. "No. Just self-congratulation. But my wife"—he drops his voice—"my wife heard something in Paris."

Oh, poor Rémy. It has done her no good to Frenchify her name. Every time Danilo starts a new affair he begins referring to her, in her presence or out of it, as "my wife." It comes like clockwork. As everything does with Danilo.

So she won't stoop to ask him what Rémy has heard.

"What are you looking so hard at?" he says, waiting for her to ask. "The playhouse?"

"No. Maybe I'm thinking of how—I might plant some foreign trees around it." Though Paul could get them, maybe, she never will.

"Vuksica. For God's sake." He has read the children's letters. Will his sister also stand under trees?

The stone-breaking has stopped. A furl of smoke plumes out of the tobacco shed, straight up in the still air. Some workmen must still be there to tend it; the rest will be walking home. Few have wheels.

"Pity," he says, "that Klement can't be trained for the forge. To inherit it. He would be perfect."

She doesn't answer, not even to say "Hush." Everything is already hushed. The hair rises on the backs of one's hands.

"I will never forget this afternoon," he says. "Look at it. Smell it. What is politics?"

Far off still, they hear the motorcycle. Then, at a decent interval, a second one.

"He talked to him," she says.

Her brother understands her at once. "What? Again? To the shadow?"

"He believed in that other one's funeral."

"That—it was natural?"

She doesn't even nod. His sister never wastes gesture.

"He'll believe in any funeral but his own," Danilo says.

She's listening. The road curves on for some miles before it reaches this house.

On the table some pastries are arranged in one of those lacy serviettes that unfold to a circle, with a niche for each small cake. The maids are very proud of the serviette, which Danilo had brought from France.

Vuksica twists one of its folds to a sharper point. "Perhaps you'll stay longer one of these days. Or even come to stay. Since you like our afternoons so much."

Gonchev has often teased that he is sometimes two steps behind the twin-jumps in his wife and brother-in-law's talk. To Danilo the sequence is quite clear. "It's true then. What Rémy heard."

"Television, yes. We are going to have it here."

"You're mad. They would never. They could never. Or they don't yet understand what it is. What it does."

"That it makes anyone connected with it say the same thing three times over? Perhaps not. Though I have noticed this."

He stands up, stretching his arms toward this extraordinary fief he hadn't known he was so fond of. Such lurking fairy-tale dangers, such miles of gullible green. "But Gonchev is the country's television."

"No. Not yet. They know the difference. But he will be. They are considering how to break it to him."

"He doesn't yet know?"

"His night riding has been bad."

He nods. One was never sure what Paul let himself know. "How did you hear?"

"Have one of these." Vuksica points to the pastries. "That plain one. Bitter almond in it, from Italy. We don't get those almonds."

"Ah. I often amuse myself, wondering which of your girlfriends gets you your contraband. My guess is the big corseted one. With the behind like a pendulum."

Vuksica smiles. That was the president's wife.

"But—television!" The word flutters on the air like a brand-new butterfly. "That will amount to opening the borders," he says, hushed. And suddenly he spreads his arms to her, to Klement, that bully-boy who sometimes gives him the creeps, to his sad niece of the trees—who is really a young woman now—to Gonchev himself, whose madness has brought them to a land for which, Danilo now sees, he might quickly forget his fondness. "And so—you can all come back."

The wrinkles of irony on either side of her mouth are deeper than any of his. "Not real television, don't you understand? Gonchev's kind."

"You don't mean—you mean—like his films?"

She takes one of the recommended cakes and chews, as if to taste fully what she'd said. She rarely ate cake. "Yes, don't you see. They think he can do anything."

"So he has, almost. But this time they can't know what they're asking." Maybe she doesn't either, sequestered here so long. He thinks of the television studio at home, ultimately tranquillized, as it daily is, by human woe. His friend Popic, the announcer, for hours on end calmly describing the utterly indescribable.

Though maybe they aren't planning to have real news? Maybe only transcriptions of the classics, like the lighter Chekhov, some of which had just been done in Belgrade. Or de Maupassant's *Pierre et Jean*, the story of two brothers and their mother's adultery—and either a set piece of nineteenth-century mores or a brilliant forerunner of modern incest studies—in which he had just played Jean, and has had his first Paris review. No, they are too straitlaced for that here. But perhaps cartoons—miles of happy cartoons? Or artistic ones? Would Paul, the "dazzling international trickster," as some abroad are calling him, settle for that?

"Oh no, they do know," Vuksica is saying. "They can be quite sophisticated at times. Or their young people . . . are finding out. But the old guard—they know Paul. They are going to tell him that they know they're asking the impossible."

And that's why Paul came, why he stays. To have a whole country think you can do the impossible. To do it—and have the world see.

"But television is international. Is Paul going to create a plateau, an Elsinore, of the world?"

"He has thousands of slides." She says it sadly. "Don't all the—what do you call them?—networks?—use those?"

"Canned stuff? On occasion." On lots of occasions, he has to admit. Pretty-pretty stuff, with the oddly provincial air of respectability that comes from being prepared in advance. "But what about the news, my dear sister? Would they want him to fake it? Would he try?"

They hear a motorcycle, a heavy, old model, sputter to a stop up above the terraced hill behind them, at the house. Farther off, if one knows to listen for it, a second machine veers off and away, signing off like a clerk's pencil at end of day.

If he does, Danilo thinks, if he does that, then will I have to go back to writing articles? To save the family name?

They wait. Paul does not come down to them. He'll be standing about up there, overlooking the whole estate maybe, mulling how he could make a replica of it somewhere else if ever needed. Those are his happiest moments.

"Would he?" Danilo says. "Go along with it?"

"Paul has always said he would choose nature every time. Even a second-best nature. Even a fake one. Over what he calls the phony melancholia of events."

Yes, I will remember this afternoon, Danilo thinks, the boulders cool under his feet with that numb, blue chill of ancient stone, which penetrates even the thick-soled American running shoes his wife had bought for him.

Though Paul's phrase makes Danilo shiver, no Central European would have to ask what Paul means by it.

Events that had once been almost too large to be dreadful—and now, under state regimen, are too small to notice. National events too phonily mixed with the personal. Days spent under petty bureaucracies that perform like actors' stand-ins for the heroics of life. Poetry, mocked now as never before for not being in a major language—derided even by the poets themselves. Newspapers and even television scripts that report in self-mockery too. A sense of parades participated in that are never quite one's own. And all the while, in spite of the marvellous minor-key humors invented to describe one's path, and the amber-colored cafés in which one pursued women, a sense that all one's days are being spent on what one knows to be—a plateau.

Where even one's melancholy is not quite one's own.

Paul's cities are his irony. Does he think he can do the same with the news?

All irony is based on unfairness, Danilo thinks. Hence my own country's celebrated versions of it—which we export. And why not? It's not as if we haven't had our agonies. Maybe even a secondhand melancholy is better than those.

But the trouble with Paul is—what is the trouble with Paul?

"Elsinore," Danilo says. "I saw the new map of it. In his study. And a copy in your bedroom as well."

"He sometimes maps at night. When he can't sleep—even after his ride. Things are getting very sticky now. About the security out there. Bad as the terrain is, No Exit is not what it was. Or rather, No Entry. People from outside are suddenly mad to see it." She smiles at him through the fading light. Even at dusk her facial expression warms the air, as if larger than other people's. Or does this happen only with him, her twin, lazily catching what his own features might be forming? And, in taking such cues, passing on to her very thoughts? That's what twinship is—cues. Often in Belgrade, looking at himself in a mirror, one of her hints, delivered to him here, blossoms into meaning.

She is looking at his shoes.

"Rémy got them for my birthday. Nikes, they're called in the States. One can buy French copies in any Paris fleamarket. But these are the real thing. Even my size. I must say, every now and then Rémy pulls off something."

Indeed, Vuksica's face is supposed to reply, she pulled off you. But this time it doesn't. "Our birthday," she says. "So could you do me a great favor? Leave those shoes here?"

She has surprised him utterly.

"But why? They won't fit Paul." Who in summer wore only tabi, on large feet whose perfect lack of corns shamed Westerners, and in rough weather wore boots, made by one of his workmen, that one would swear had belonged to a Hapsburg.

Nor would Danilo's shoes fit his sister. She might be more or less "identical" with him, but a woman's domestic life enlarges the hands and feet.

"To copy."

"Ah." The national disease. Or Paul's. "But would Paul wear them? Not at all his style."

She bends to them in just the way that, when they were children, she'd sometimes appropriated a portion of his food, for though almost from the first she had been larger than he, they had always been served the same amount. "Nike." She gives it the full Greek pronunciation. "That means victory, doesn't it? Yes, maybe he'll wear them. When the time comes."

He doesn't want to leave his pair. So chic, their gray-and-blue wings, and in Belgrade unique, as yet. Already smelling of himself in the nicest way. And of what he had done while wearing them. Not that Danilo needed such stylish props to help him annex that little actress whom he'd taken along for a farewell visit to the forge.

"I'll miss them," he says, giving her the same rueful pout with which he had once shared his food.

"Not like you'll miss your recent weekends in Sarajevo."

He acknowledges this, a shrugging. "I am maybe stretching out the farewells to the forge," he says with a laugh. Changing the woman, of course.

"And maybe Rémy will pull off another pair of shoes," she says. "In between her slide shows."

"Sister," he says. Always a reproof—as when she said "Brother." "So far, those shows keep us safe. And able to be in Paris. Where she misses your linen, by the way."

"Everybody misses something," she says, at the same time looking over her shoulder, so that for a moment he thinks that what she misses stands there. But it is only a car up above, drawing up to the house door with the slow rumble and cough of a very old vehicle. A tall woman climbs out of it, backwards.

"Ah, I recognize that bottom," Danilo says. "She bringing you bitter almonds?"

"She's an expert in handicraft. Sometimes she helps Paul out—at Elsinore."

"Ah."

"No, nothing like that."

"I didn't really think so."

"It's Elsinore she's interested in. Very."

"Chuh." He had always disliked the place, seen once. He watches the woman enter the house door. "I see now, hers is merely the backside of an embroiderer."

"Who walks the ramparts out there." Her voice is muffled. "You may remember them."

He shudders. "Those crags. That white light. And thousand-foot drops. And no wall. So she walks them, does she? I retract what I said."

"She also has a brother. He's now on the outside."

"I see. Family affection—and those almonds. And did I see chocolate?"

"Oh, that's common here—if one is discreet. After all, we do have a coastline with Italy. But birth control pills are not so easy. Or Greek cigarettes. For a Macedonia Oro, some people here would—"

"And cigars maybe, for comparison?" Danilo the cigar-bringer says. "Does her husband know about this?"

"Who knows what a president knows. Or wants to know." She delivers that like a line from a Molnár play, in her old style, or one of them. "But the brother is small-time. He wants a larger connection. And our money is no good to him."

"On the international exchange? I'll say not." Although now and then, when he finds himself with a piece of pocket change, it can go to a girl as a lucky piece, the silver content being so high.

"So the brother has a possible partner, from Greece. Who is not small-time. If, say, she had something more important than handicraft to sell."

"From here?" Danilo sweeps a glance across the green. The fields are almost black now, waiting for stars, the nut-brown house up above showing a pale-voltage light. One can breathe the air down to one's diaphragm, as an inalienable right. But this was nothing to sell. "My shoes! Surely those are important enough?"

She doesn't laugh at his sallies anymore—hasn't for how long? "This partner—a shipper—he has connections with the U.S."

Aha. So that's what the lady wants. Or the husband does? Everybody wants what they sell—the Americans. Though they're no worse than the French, whose military gear is even chic, the bombs with that darning-needle shape, and those saber-thin planes. Maybe war is the ultimate connection. Craved even by a place like this, which claims to want none.

But why Vuksica? For whom the stake would never be a mere pill. "Ah, the partner? What nationality is he?"

A slight hesitation. "Half Greek, the other half—one of us."

"Yugoslav?"

Does she wrinkle their fine Serbian nose? Inhaling, as he does when visiting a certain woman in Ljubljana, his nostrils pinken with that choice irritant and aphrodisiac, a half-enemy's perfume? "Croat."

He sees that the president's wife, Mrs. Trim, as he has been told she is popularly called, after her husband's own nickname, Trim, is advancing down the hill toward them, at a skating pace that shifts her various majestic bulks, from the minaret hair to the porte cochère skirts. Suggesting the schooling of many political receptions. Or else she is actually on wheels?

"How does she do that?" he exclaims. "Like on roller-skates."

"Quite celebrated for it," his sister murmurs. "Her gait. Her feet give her a lot of trouble though." Vuksica is red. She can't show it but he can tell she is laughing—ah, how good to see. "Don't stare, whatever you do," she says between her teeth. In a minute or two, holding his own breath, he feels the red in his cheeks; they haven't done this since she and Paul came here; it's like old times.

"She won't want to meet you head on," she says in her normal voice. "She's very Muslim." Adding, "but she knows all about you, of course," as if he must be satisfied with that.

Of course. And has seen him—and his shoes—from afar? With the handicrafter's greedy, acquisitive eye?

"Don't worry," he says, still watching what was commonly called an Etruscan beauty in these parts, from the high-coifed hair to the deeply stamped eyes, whose thick frame of brow and lash make them appear to stare frontally only. Impressive, like all Vuksica's pal's, but not his sort. He goes for small, sly, well-bred women with whom he can play hooky—not, God knows, from their husbands or other lovers, but from the strenuous ethical dance that consumes his country's days. Women with a physical shimmer, often not otherwise attached to their moral conduct, which the old-fashioned used to call "ruinous." There's no sight quite so relaxing to him as that square of afternoon sky which hangs reassuringly at the windows of all convenience hotels, as if hired too for the afternoon only.

Not that the game of undercover love isn't played everywhere, even in this greeny paradise of stumpy peasants, no doubt faithful until death, some of them, and of boundaries, to breach which might be more libidinous than any garment's slow fall. The pursuit of illegal love would be operatic. With everyone in the cast showing that form of valor he has been told is most revered locally—that mute courage under which one may be drawn and quartered but must say nothing. The national name for this endowment being: *trim*.

How can anyone imagine television here? And there are surely no convenience hotels.

Mrs. Trim has stopped to chat with an ancient groundsman, apparently waiting for Danilo to leave.

"We'll go to the airport as soon as she goes," Vuksica says. "You'll find your sandals where they always are."

Under cover of their cheek-to-cheek farewell he whispers: "Why does she smuggle?"

"For her brother. For her husband. For the birth control pills, even. And . . ."

"And . . . ?" She is still in his embrace.

"And because this is how women are friends."

When she and he stare like this, he feels they have two eyes between them, not four. Sister, what is it you have to sell? Or buy?

She isn't going to tell him.

"Silently, eh?" Danilo says. "Women are so silent about these things. A matter of *trim*?"

Voices carry here. Both the gardener and the lady raise their heads.

Danilo bows, and turns his back, pulling his sister to face him. Behind them, out of the corner of his eye, he sees Paul coming down the hill toward them at his own peculiar gait, sturdy of pin, yet vague. That's useful with students, Vuksica has told him; they are never sure of how much Gonchev sees. But actually, she'd said, Gonchev's manner comes of an émigré unsureness as to what he may safely show.

To Danilo, his brother-in-law, when moody, looks like a tree out of Grimm—a tree that has been tranced.

"Sister," Danilo says, "what do you miss?"

But she has seen who is coming. And knows too how the voice carried here. So he hadn't been sure of her intonation, though the one word was intense enough.

"Paul."

Back in the room they called his, on the shelf where he kept the sandals, handwoven leather ones much like those one could no longer find in Belgrade, he found that his worn pair had been replaced by a new pair, of the correct size. This too gave him pause.

At the edge of the airport, going through a routine so familiar to both sides that Danilo often had to repress a generous urge to caution this side's border guards not to be so bored, the Yugoslav pilot, released from his interrogation in the windowless hut of quarried stone, is walking back across the field to his plane.

Next door to the hut a modern pavilion bristles with gun emplacements and a revolving turret, but also contains domestic amenities—cots for sleeping between shifts, tables for card-playing, family snapshots, and totem stuffed-animal toys, all of which the two guards are very proud of; the job is a state honor as well as one with bonus pay. Ordinarily they swap jokes directed at the departing pilot in his own language—"See that patch on his pants; that's where they keep their tails, these people"—or loudly envy his boots—"Built to walk the devil's own territory, don't you see?"—swatting each other when the pilot waved acknowledgment. Today they lounge in the old hut's doorway, looking glum.

Danilo had taken an initial step toward the guardrail—in any such encounter his generation has been taught to move slowly. His brother-in-law and sister are standing well back, as they always do, ready to wave the plane off into the blue—or, today, into a low dirty-white vault about to snow—when he hears a shout behind him.

He has never before heard Paul shout. A strange guttural cry, like a

Kabuki actor's. The border guards half rise to attention, but without shouldering their guns.

"Where's my man?" Gonchev says in Serbo-Croat, then in their language. "My follower."

The man with the notepad isn't there—and, as Danilo now realizes, hadn't been behind them, lagging at his usual deferential gap.

The guards look at one another. "Maybe did he phone in sick?" one says.

"Yeh, maybe did he phone in sick?" said the other.

Gonchev strides up to them. "I have to be checked." He points to Danilo. "He has to be. Phone in."

"*Toom* who?" one says. Or so it sounds. The other man echoes him. "And why should you care about him?" they say in chorus.

"Care about him?" the woodlands sang. Even here, at this fenced-in landing strip, echoing crags surround them.

Just then they hear a familiar, stuttering obbligato—how had they ignored the lack of it along the way? A few seconds later its maker comes into sight. The cycle's forewheel is wavering. The man is driving very incautiously, with the aid of one gloved hand. When he dismounts, they see that this man, of whom Gonchev likes to say, "My shadow has almost no profile, these days; I'm hard on him," has a broader outline than usual, the right arm being in a bloodied sling. The left arm also seems at an odd angle.

Head modestly bent, he pays no attention to any of them, either to Gonchev or Vuksica, who has moved to her husband's side, or to Danilo at the rail, or to the pilot, frozen there in the field. Least of all to the border guards. This is as usual, and in proportion. But when he comes to take out his pad, which he does with the aid of the hand in the sling, the pencil proves to be still in its slot at the side. To remove it with the angled left hand, in order to write—no, he cannot manage it.

Gonchev steps forward. At his side, Vuksica puts out a hand to stop him but fails.

"Allow me," Gonchev says. He writes on the pad what must be the proper details, or must stand for them, in whatever penmanship. Then he returns the pad to the man's breast pocket.

Vuksica, during this process, has turned the color of whey.

But no paler than the follower, who now says, in the general direction of the guardhouse but without turning his head, "Report ambush at side of road. Three men in our own uniform." He squares his shoulders. "I return by the same road."

Mounting his machine, rounding it past Vuksica and Gonchev, who stand in his path, he holds his pace long enough to say: "My family thanks you," and drives off again, still steering with the left hand, the arm of which Danilo judges to be broken but not set.

From the plane, rising higher and higher, Danilo watched his sister and Gonchev, waving as they always did, Gonchev with one fisted arm as usual, but Vuksica wildly waving two. "Good God," Danilo said to the pilot, who in the noise of takeoff wouldn't hear, "is something wrong?" Were those two being aimed at from the guardhouse? The guards have disappeared.

But no, Vuksica's hands are still twinkling. Gonchev's arm sinks to his side, but one of hers remains up until Danilo can no longer see her, except for the sticklike arm and a long flutter of garment being closed in by snow.

"What wheatfields they have here," the pilot says, when they have reached altitude. "The snow will nip them just right." The plane can take four passengers, but Danilo is always the only one.

"What snow!" the pilot says, shortly after.

And finally, "What crags."

He is Danilo's friend, or he wouldn't have come at all. After this, he is silent, Danilo also. Friendship between men can be silent too.

So would smuggling be—for man and woman both. Especially if done for love. Or sex. But clueing-in can disturb things. He must not think of it.

Up here, in this chugging steel fly, the vast arêtes and snowy ridges on either side fall away into each other in a panorama of selflessness. As always, he feels the hot glee of being alive, breath by breath, and thinks, as his favorite philosopher, the British bishop, Berkeley, might, Where does this great snowy room go to, when he, Danilo, goes out of it? And what is politics at home, when he is here?

But he and his pilot always make it. After all, Belgrade is so near.

As he descends the steps there, he always has the same thought. That there may be no drama more subtle than a nontragedy, unmarked even by accident. Is Vuksica, back there in Eden, thinking that of her life?

There is a roast-nuts stall just inside the terminal, and as the humdrum air of his country assaults him, he wishes she could smell it with him. What is patriotism, other than the familiar brown odor of one's own branch of anthropophagi, cooking up what one had always known them to cook? And she was, after all, so near. As he walked on, to make his connection to Paris in spite of his wife's telegram to return to Belgrade, it struck him that Gonchev, who had never been to Paris, nor to almost any of the places in his own vast lexicon of Elsinore, is nevertheless a person of whom he, Danilo, even when he sees the man at his sister's elbow, thinks of as—far from things. Rather than near. Was Vuksica thinking that too?

Yet one ought never count up the cities one had been to. He, Danilo, never did. It tempted the gods somehow. It wasn't safe.

In the tiny, empty Paris flat next morning, rehearsing in front of the shaving mirror for his first appearance in a French television series, he thought he saw Rémy, there over his shoulder for a moment, behind him. Not the absent Rémy, ticking over her teaching slides at Belgrade University, her head working like a metronome—and her heart as well. A young Rémy, careless and soft, and not afraid yet, with nothing sharp about her except the wind-blown points of her bob. The Rémy he had married. Their drama is a belated one now, though he knows all the lines. Why this vision, then, so long discarded?

After the television show—whose director had liked him, promising to enlarge what had been a small role for a good-looking Slav—he is at the mirror, shaving again, this time before going to report his arrival at the café where, either to hear gossip or to allay it, any Serb must now and then appear. He would prefer not to, by now, but has never resisted. If he becomes a success here, will he sever that connection? He doesn't need the café sessions, half steambath, half dream, to remind him that what is emigrated toward or from colors all a man's life afterward. Or a woman's. Although he fancies his wife would join him here for good at his least word, no further vision of her returns to the mirror, in any version, past or present. Or indeed in any future one.

Instead, he sees his sister, whom every mirror must evoke, although this hasn't happened so intensely for years. He finishes shaving. Actually he's hearing her more than seeing her, with those half-muscular responses that are an actor's memory, and for them both a teamwork in which he and she are still in tune. She is feeding him his clues?

On their drive to the airport, for instance. Her car had been out of service, waiting for a part that a factory on the other side of the range must fabricate. So the three of them had been jogging along in a sturdy wagon, half-filled with sheaves that enclosed their musing. "Would you ever emigrate again—you two?" he had dared.

"A true émigré is pushed," his brother-in-law answered. "As I was. Beginning young. Or else does it like your sister." Seated next to the wagon driver, he had swiveled on the wooden seat in front of them to look at her. "For love. If I can still call it that?" A man's laugh to his wife on such a subject; ought it to have had that edge of triumph in it? "Mrs. Trim is always telling me that Vuksica could almost be a Muslim wife."

Gonchev had picked up a wheatstalk and was stripping it. "An artist must go anywhere, 'nilo—like I came here. But only for art."

A vibration had passed along the smooth lath of Danilo and Vuksica's common seat. Not for love?

Had his sister actually said that. No, she'd said nothing. But he had heard.

Plus that one word, heard now as both answer and warning. What did she miss. Paul.

Paul—as he used to be.

Was it possible that, as with himself and Rémy, his twin was missing what had never been there?

No, from the first he has admired his brother-in-law for his exaggerations, which have not ceased. Vuksica loves Gonchev for them. And maybe even cherishes the fact that he is not in touch with them.

The Americans who swarm to the intellectual cafés in Paris, and often talk as if their function is to explain Europe to Europeans, would soon spot Gonchev as a man who, as they like to say, isn't yet "fully in touch with himself."

A process that most Europeans regarded as requiring a lifetime. If completion comes to Americans that early, what do they do with their old age? Indeed Danilo, like many men he approves of, is proud of being a walking abyss. From which that fine creature, his own very self, might someday reach up and wallop him. With a stinging surprise.

He sat down on one of the few chairs in the flat in order to change his shoes, then remembered he had no extra pair here. The flat, passed on from another Serb, is neat, and in a better arrondissement than they deserve, but he and Rémy keep little in it, never knowing for sure when they can return. Also they suspect that in their absence the resident owner of the building now and then rents it out.

No matter about the sandals. At the studio, two French technicians, one male and one female, had admired them, inquiring as to the source. But that clinches it, against the café. He can't wear them there, where, though they know of his sister's circumstances, and in their vague, insular way of Gonchev's professional post, they know nothing of Danilo's trips to see them. Nor does anyone in Belgrade, except Rémy, always so afraid that Gonchev would get himself and them into trouble, if for nothing more than being too conspicuous. "He's a genius," Danilo had defended, and Rémy had spat, "Those are the kind."

For a long time back all the greetings brought to his sister from home have actually had to be made up. He isn't quite sure why he'd done that. It's the sort of thing that a man can do to a woman without offending his own ethical sense—a way of dealing with their intently frivolous pastimes. After all, he has always lied to women. It was almost gallant of him, in this case—and borne up by a funny sense, more than a hope, that Vuksica knew it was a game.

Bothers him though, to have kept up the charade so long. Charades are for journalism, where one can keep one's imagination in safe tow. Not to be carried on with one's closest, who, if she has caught on, now won't dare to tell him what she is going to do. As their face in the mirror is now telling him, she is surely going to do something.

What had he himself meant when he had replied to those admiring technicians, "No, one can't get these in the ordinary way of things. These are my last pair."

What does that place mean to him? That held-in world he walks toward through a guardhouse, brought by the smallest real plane obtainable, to that green fief of immensely swattable flies? Where, when you wanted something otherwise unprocurable—like a table, or an idea— you manufactured it yourself? Why would he miss a country where you could not have affairs?

This miserable flat has no view. In Paris, given such an alley-flat, you are presented your views in most other respects. But also your rooftop.

Climbing up there, he sees that the landlord, an elderly widower who resides thriftily in one of his rear apartments, is taking his lunch hour away from his duties as his own concierge. The iron chair he sits in is chained to the stonework of the one corner of the roof free of vents or pipes. There has never been a second chair. Since last seen he seems to have slipped into dotage, plainly not sure which tenant Danilo is, but with the classic hostile French nod ceding him the right to be there. Then he returns aloofly to his share of the view.

Paris rooftops babble, even when they are quiet. They will furnish inaudible converse to any who give a good hard look, yet keep what is said to themselves. A safe place to say good-bye to what Danilo hadn't known he was leaving. To what, in his bones and his mirror he is sure he will not see again. The French have such good words with which to say what can't be said; occasionally they even confuse their good-byes with their helloes. What is "Au revoir" except "Good-bye, hello—I see now what you are to me?"

The owner is staring straight ahead in the fixed way people do in front of television screens, old folks especially. As if they are blankly looking on at a present time that is going on for too long. The landlord's flat mutters all day, in the morning crackling with weather and politics or an occasional bombing, gay with voices in primary colors in the afternoons, when the daughter and grandchildren come. Television screens must be made of unreflecting glass; perhaps they are the mirrors of the future? Or are going to be his, Danilo's, from now on? In which one would see nothing of one's past, nothing at all? For the past, one would have to go, pulled in spite of oneself, to a musty old café, mirrored in the style of too many successive empires, and back-street even for Paris.

But inside him, fusing like a hurt of which one suddenly becomes aware, a crystal is forming. In it he sees his sister, not as he had last seen her but in the garden enclosure she had made for herself—and alone. The image is fixed, as people are in photographs. Or as memory is. He has a foreboding that this image will remain with him, that she will persevere in this crystal of his as might the image of some old possession. He will never again be able to clock her outer change, even in some actual mirror of his own. But around her are all the green arrangements, near to fairy tale, as he now sees them, of her far fief.

Is she going to defect?

Straining, he tries to see her slipping through some secret buttonhole in those borders, known only to those sibylline smugglers who would push her through. But he sees nothing.

Is it he himself who is going to defect—from his own country? And from Rémy as well?

Always before, even the thought of Vuksica would have advised him what he was going to do—and what to think about it. He sees that now. His defection has begun with the forge.

Now he feels only this new abyss. "Ah well, you were always the younger twin"—can he hear her say that? No, nothing. Twinship without clues, what a heartsick feeling.

As for Paul, if one thinks of him only second, or even last, that is because he is not a person who needs to be thought of first-off. He is an émigré before he is anything else. He will always be taken care of. History will manage it.

But I—Danilo thinks—isn't it my obligation now to be more myself than ever before? Paris, that haven for expatriates, is certainly the place for it. Where even the burden of all the political evenings one has left behind, which no one from his part of Europe can ever escape, can be taken care of by a café. As Danilo the actor only, perhaps he could escape even that.

What one has to do nowadays is exempt oneself from places altogether, and from the categories that go with them. As he has already all but done in the matter of his birthplace, now full of yellow smog anyway. The hotel they own there is in Rémy's name, being mostly her idea. And a family forge was, understandably, baggage too heavy to carry anywhere.

What one had best say farewell to is the places, not the people. In whatever words one finds at hand. Otherwise, that core of ice forming within can poke too dangerously at one's vitals; even the soles of one's feet feel skinned.

Just then the landlord scraped back his chair and got to his feet, peering at Danilo from eyes sunken in bloodless lids. "Why, I know you, didn't I say so to my daughter last night? Adèle, I said, regard the man there on the screen—isn't he our third-floor rear? The one playing the foreigner?" He bowed to Danilo's assent. "Of course, you don't have to try too hard at that, *hein?* But it pays well, *non?* See here, I'm just going down below again. Take my chair." He bowed again. *"À bientôt."*

Paris is certainly a good place from which to say the good-bye that is hello. The corners of nearby rooftops, daubed with some glistening stuff, waver in greeting, almost like hands, but not receding ones. Over there somewhere is Orly Airport, from which he had come, and from which one can go almost anywhere. He will go back at times, if only as far as Belgrade. Perhaps all this is merely a weaning from that twinned closeness so souring to Rémy, who, each time he returns from a visit, rages at him for not having outgrown it.

Paul has never been jealous; indeed he had fostered their triumvirate. In some peculiar way he lacks jealousy, though not passively. Maybe because he is a genius, and therefore not like anybody else? He denies both these accusations. "Nonsense, a genius is more like other people than anybody else going. Though people may not see it at the time. And I am not that." Vuksica, laughing, had asked: "What are you, then?" As if in all their years together she hadn't sufficiently learned. "Outside the borders—of wherever I am at the time," Gonchev had answered somberly. "By a matter of birth." Was that why he was so comfortable locked up where he was? Danilo had been going to ask but had been stopped by a look from Vuksica—one of those hintings more often exchanged with a spouse.

Those two can take care of themselves, even if not joined. It's he, Danilo, who is alone, even when with Rémy. If so, with TV he has a chance now to be so, while crossing all the borders of the world. First in screen image, then in reality, he can and will go anywhere. While oldsters all over the world, and youngsters too, would peer at him, confirming him. "It's you—isn't it?" He would be more like himself than most people are.

Maybe he would even appear, if only in image, in that comic-opera country he has just left. Perhaps Paul would be able to splice him in. Into what would surely be the last of those grand charades by means of which Paul too, now that one thinks of it, keeps himself himself. Even while he chafes—for which of us wants to be only what he or she is?

Except my sister. Who wants only to be with a man who—chafes? No matter where?

Enough. In Paris the very air is analytical. Whether or not its citizens swallow the results. Every little flower, even, is either a little Catholic or a Huguenot. And blooms the better for the argument. As do the cheeks of all the cheeky girls with their pouting backsides, girls who, even when scarcely grown, are still of ambivalent outline—half matron, half cocotte.

Enough that, with all his premonitions, he is here.

In spite of that, a sob escapes him. Over east, a ghost of a cloud airbrushes a Channel sky, which autumn has turned lawn-green. The cloud becomes the very shape of an afternoon-tea table, its linen glinting like the white soul of handicraft, and in its center—that black speck— magnified almost to tragedy in a place so far from the world's bourses and pleasure circuits—a mashed fly.

He scarcely knows how to pronounce the name of the place. In a place so remote, where *le traveling* was a camera, the name had seldom been necessary. He and Gonchev always used the English form of the country's name, in the language that is their common one. And Vuksica had followed suit.

The cloud has disappeared. The name chooses itself out of the possibles. So far?

"Adieu. Adieu—Albania."

3

American Express

"Good God," Gonchev says, staring at the prospect before him. Seated in a tiled niche, the wet mosaic slippery under his naked buttocks, he seems to have just awakened. The environs before him, lightly steaming, are almost too vast to be a room, even a public one, and there is no proper floor. Instead, pools of varying size—and temperature, according to the air above them—are interspersed between ramps of gentle outline. Groups of nude men are standing about, talking. Others recline, solitary on some craggy outpost. In the largest pool they are immersed to their waists, slapping their chests. In what must be the hottest, only the heads appear, on each face a look of agonized submission.

The place has a ceiling, though. Why shouldn't purgatory have a ceiling? Whether the group just passing should appear to be almost enjoying themselves is more moot. Or perhaps is the key. Isn't that what would happen? A kind of eternal "almost" that never gets to term?

Or perhaps all here are in committee. Doesn't he recognize that laxly passive boardroom look even on those who are speaking to one another tête-à-tête, that idle swing of the hands? For as far as his eye can penetrate the humid ozone here he sees many faces with that same half-hangdog smile. Perhaps purgatory is all committee. Say what one will, there was ever a certain enjoyment in sitting on the most tedious, as judger rather than judged. And while comfortably certain of never getting to any too permanent conclusion.

Opposite him on one of the crags—which Gonchev now sees are not of stone but a man-made composition he recognizes but can't yet name—an impressive-looking man of robust middle age reclines. He's wearing a pince-nez, attached by a black ribbon, such as men of Gonchev's grandfather's day had worn. Is he really wearing it—or would reminiscence styled to the eye of the beholder be the rule here? A similar pair of spectacles had once reposed in a drawer of one of the bureaus— in what house of Gonchev's youth, what land?

Or is the man merely some eccentric loner? He is also wearing what appear to be black swimming trunks—the only man here doing so.

Gonchev looks down at his own body. Still familiar, if a trifle thinner. There is that mole. Less belly than when he must have left his real body—that's nice. If he has left it? A pinch given to his thigh leaves him in doubt. Does one bring one's body along to the afterlife, remembering no hint of how one came? Feeling no pain—in fact some relief—at what was left behind? Yet an irremediable sadness—over whom? Plus an almost guilty gusto—as always—for any new place.

Yes, this could be his purgatory, tailored to him, as for everyone, in accordance with what he had accomplished yet hadn't achieved in life. Since in that life he had never been a formal Christian, it would be about par for him to be remanded to a setup in whose actual existence he doesn't quite believe. Well, that too is justice. He has spent most of his life in such places. Or in creating them.

In fact, apply his mind to it now, his almost blank mind, and he is almost on the point of recalling the commercial name of that stage-set stuff they may have used for the ground surface here. In that wonderful film of Gorki's *The Lower Depths* they had used a similar substance, but that was long ago. Is there a period, an era, to this place? Or is the idea to be disoriented eternally?

Gonchev puts his head in his hands. A blinding ache is assaulting him. He's sweating too, must be 85 degrees here, Fahrenheit. Not hot enough for hell, no flames. Not cool enough for—what's that other fashionable religious state? Millionaires get it, from a surfeit of satisfactions. But also not quite martyred saints. Anomie? No, he feels too roused for that. Even hungry.

Grunting, he plumbs toward the depths of himself—ah, thank God, or whoever the big Who, his innerness still has some fathom to it—and tries to pull up the name of that substance he's sitting on. He can see it on the faded labels of the vats that Kurosawa himself had used, still then preserved in the studio where Gonchev had first worked. . . . The studio's head designer, new there, at first cursed the stuff for its perform-ance, because he had misread the instructions on the American label, then overused it with such partisanship that he had almost lost his job, for having constructed, in a studio where the sets were constantly shifted and quarters small, a set of chairs strong enough for baby hippopotami to sit in them, and stuck immoveably to the floor.

In front of Gonchev now pass visions of all the many compounds he has used in his professional duties. Cold tea that actors can drink like whisky. The exquisite rubber fried eggs and plastic pastry elegances of other mock foods, Oriental or Western, that his first adopted country had made with such catholic devotion. Varnishes that silk a patina onto wood that isn't wood. A villainous slag, formidable enough to make whole ravines, yet light enough for two dollies to move.

He recalls that intractable glue composed of two elements which, when blended, bond for life—at least the lifetime of the user. And how in his apprentice days the young artisan next to him had used it to glue a fiberboard tabletop to a borrowed majolica pedestal, property of the German embassy in Tokyo, whose quarters the studio had rented for a day's filming.

It had been apprentice Gonchev's sad duty to warn the crew chief, via his own off-hour researches in Tokyo's art archives, that the pedestal, purloined from Italy during World War II and dating from the Renais-sance, was one of the artifacts still being searched for. *Epoxy.* The glue whose components the Japanese had even improved on, as they had the fiberboard—which after thirty years may be still in situ. And might be until that millennium in which all bodies and souls, and maybe objects too, rise up in their original forms.

But that's not the compound he is searching for.

Opposite him, the solitary recliner now takes out a cigarette from a pocket in his trunks—ah, that's the reason for them—and a holder whose era matches his pince-nez. The smoke that rises from him is real. This is no dream; Gonchev well knows the difference. Those man-made dreams which preoccupy the waking hours have a poetic looseness that avoids the harsh detail. The symbols in which one actually dreams transcend even that, wrapping the feet in clouds of vapor or lead, on which the dreamer stands, feeling emotions vaguer than human, hungers one does not state, terrors of travel without destination—or the comfort of talking with the dead. Who, though one knows better, are still alive.

Gonchev stands up. Reality is more tenacious, more niggling. And, whether or not horrible, blessed with interest. He sees that the pool between him and the smoker must be the coolest. An ancient man is entering it leisurely. He's as skinny as an armature, yet somehow an image of hope. He is real—and observable. In reality, on being challenged, one knows one's name, and those of all loved, and the remembered look of their faces. As Gonchev painfully does. Also the look of one's house. And motorbike. On which one knows too well one didn't arrive here. In the nondream one knows everything except how one came to be there—and when.

One even can summon—as he now has—the name of that composition on whose protuberance the smoker is stubbing out his cigarette. Gonchev sees once again the bags of it in its dry state, as it came in the old days, and may still. Dear old all-weather substance, for want of which his whole plateau had had to be built on bedrock instead. Trusty compound, which, when correctly mixed with liquid, made hills and dales that would have cost God a deal more trouble. The substance whose black-and-orange-labeled name he can still hear the workmen trace in their light Nipponese voices.

"Prastiklon!" he cries in their English. "Made in Amellica." It comes out a bleat. A garble, to anyone else. Like many a memory. But enough to convince him he is painfully alive. And in possession of most of his wits. Or at least a man who, even when waking from whatever ambush into pleasanter consciousness, does not assign himself too quickly to Paradise.

"At last!" a hearty voice is saying to the left of him. No genie. That's a real voice. Someone in the niche beside his, or down the line? How come he hasn't noticed? He finds he can't turn his head. He's been staring straight ahead the whole time.

Slowly he turns his upper body.

"Turkey feathers," the tall man seated a few feet down on the wet banquette says to him. "I was thinking of burning some under your nose. Infallible." Like all the exceptionally tall, he has that air of condescension, maybe unintended, that comes from looking down. His features don't endorse it. Eyes comically wide above a quizzical proboscis, in a large, cocked head that moves with each sentence in a premature lurch. "But we were advised to let you come to naturally. After that second bump from yesterday. Rough flight. Got a touch of it myself." He indicated a badly swollen ankle. The rest of his perhaps fifty-year-old length is tanned, except for the white swimming trunks made of the man's own skin.

"Besides"—again that lurch, like an ingratiating dog, one of the bigger breeds—"burnt feathers would be bad for that voice box of yours. Sorry about that. No accident there. We were told you wished to make it appear that you were taken in duress. And you certainly were. Afraid they overdid. Those border boys can surely bludge." His eyelids blink, while the head cocks sideways. "Short for bludgeon. My own boys would have been better at the snatch." He half rises, his big hands swaying at random, or in canny syncopation—then sits down again. An incarnation of the one actor of whom Gonchev has never tired, perhaps because he almost never spoke. Except in those marvelously incomplete gestures, calculated to a hair.

This man too is no mere actor. He gives orders, rather than taking them. Maybe he's been a director. A great pulse jumps between Gonchev's temples. He hasn't met a fellow director since Japan. This one sent to welcome him professionally maybe? So that I may at least know that I'm not in limbo. I wonder who he is, in life. For this place isn't quite dream—but is it life?

Gonchev has never corresponded with directors; they're a private lot, and jealous of each other. But he knows who most of them are. And apparently the man knows him. He is relieved to be known. In a new place he always dislikes explaining who he is—it's as if you're labeling what your life is to you. His head certainly aches, profoundly. And there's an odd flutter to his tongue, which feels lax too, as when one has been slugged—as he had been once at the gates of Elsinore by a crazed peasant woman who had thought it the devil's residence. Or as if he's been drugged? He'd smoked opium once in Harbin, the time he'd gone back. A great feeling. But he hadn't worked for three bruise-colored days afterward.

A potbellied man covered with body fur hurries by, strapping on a watch. Perhaps everyone here has been a director. Or—how shall he ask it?—could this be the stage set itself?

"Are you—were you ever in the theater?" Gonchev says.

The man slaps his knee. Awkwardly, as if he's had to aim and has nearly missed. "Everyone asks. Or used to. No, I'm not Jacques Tati. And he was never me."

"You could be his understudy."

"Ah, but that's what I do do," the man says merrily, as if he has just discovered this. "Understudy. In several theaters. But never in front of the footlights. Tell you about it, later. But right now, how're you feeling?"

"I could say better if—if I could remember how I felt—before." Now that he is speaking, he is ashamed to say what he does feel. His grown body surprises him. It ought to be a child's. "My tongue—is there something wrong with it?"

The man soothes his left forefinger on two upper front teeth. "Not at all, considering. You've responded to a doctor. To a waiter, even. I'd say—it's doing remarkably well. Only—we'd assumed you'd be speaking Russian. Your native language."

"No. Only my first—native language." My body is Russian though, Gonchev thinks. That's what's wrong with it. It doesn't match my tongue. "I had only kitchen vocabulary." His voice is hoarse. "Household. What the cook said to the child in the kitchen." When they'd still had a cook. Bright windows, a wooden table. Vegetables being peeled. To him vegetables would always be Russian. And soup. "Then we moved. And moved."

"We may have been misinformed, Pavel."

By whom? Somehow he knows better than to ask.

"We don't always know the full identity of our sources."

"I am christened Paul." Again he is a child, his feet freed into tabi after the last of the outgrown leather bluchers, his face raised to the monks like an earnest little cup of European culture. "After the painter."

"Ah, yes, Gauguin."

"Klee." Who had once given his grandfather a drawing, in exchange for their musical soirees. How we clung to it. Called *Eyes in the Landscape*, that drawing, and sold long before Gonchev was born, but mentioned in the family history every week of his young life.

"Ah, yes, Paul Klee."

He feels sorry for this teachery man. Teachers should not make mistakes. "Later on we spoke Russian again, of course. In the family."

"What had you spoken in between?"

What else but the language of whatever country they were in?

"Day or evening?" Gonchev said.

How the man stares.

This man knows only culture, not people. Why confide in him? But Gonchev's tongue runs on of its own. "Evenings, we chose which of our other languages to speak. While my mother sewed. She sewed for our living, you see. And she claimed to be bored. Or sometimes she joked that a certain language went with a certain dress. 'I am going to botch this dress,' she once said. 'It requires Czech—and I don't know Czech.' But they were really educating me, you see. In the only way they could."

He has never said this to anyone. Not even to Vuksica. In those early years, how he had longed to, a little tramp carrying his bundle of bemused gratitude at the end of a long stick his parents never saw.

"No wonder you went for pictures."

He could cry, from the mercy of that. No, this man is not bad. And Gonchev's headache is ebbing, if leaving an emptiness. "Why am I telling you this? You're not a monk?"

"Ah," the man says. "Wow, did we go wrong. And, no, I'm not a monk." He leans forward, speaking slowly. "But—I have been to Edo. Luckily for both of us."

The old name for Tokyo—why say it with such emphasis? "Kyoto, it was," Gonchev says irritably. I am dreaming all wrong. "And how do you know my work?" I am only ten years old.

"Take it easy, Paul. Concussion's a ticklish affair. And you've had two. Next plane's not until tomorrow. We can spend the day here. Growing you up."

When he smiles his teeth are modern film teeth, Gonchev sees. Very natural, yet too good to be true. Too expensive. Those are business teeth.

"According to the records, Paul—or the absence of them—you're either an accomplished fifty-three, or a onetime prodigy, now forty-eight. Lucky man. All your life you'll have the option to choose." The man reaches behind the hump he's sitting on and snags an object he points like a gun. Not a gun. A bottle. "Russian Leather Cologne. At times our department is very literal. Put some on your forehead, Paul. A present from our government."

Ah. So, that kind of gun. He's awake.

So. What kind of spy is this? From where?

When one is used to having a personal spy, and in a country that has only a single bourgeois brand of them, one loses touch with the fast spy scene he and his parents had been convinced they knew as well as the street maps of wherever they found themselves. Back then he had learned to sense spies visually, also to classify. Something of such a life often comes out in the skin. Warts, or else an excessive smoothness, waxiness, or oiliness. Some spies were bulkier than the bulky, others thinner than the thin. Or, if average, the very essence of averageness. From some inner excess or lack that wouldn't stay hidden.

But this man's integument, pink and white, well fed and watered, looks as if it exists only to hide the long, almost contradictorily powerful bones. Serious bones, in a pleasure-loving skin—what nationality is that?

"Had to study Russian myself of course," the man says. "To keep abreast."

Gonchev studies him, the inquiring nose, the lifted chin, the eyes veiled in fake sleepiness. "Abreast?"

"Of what they don't know. Don't know they don't."

"Do you?"

There those teeth come again. "Ha. Have some more cologne." He twirls the bottle. "Wonderful language of course—Russian. The only other one equal to English, would you say?" When Gonchev doesn't say, he puts the bottle down, twiddles his fingers on his naked hip, where a pocket would be. The eyes are empty. It's his body that is the soul of inquiry. "Know Nabokov?"

"Who?"

When this man sighs he is all courtly disappointment. That's the resemblance to Tati. Whatever his mood, real or assumed, it absorbs all of him. "Exile par excellence. A tongue on a string, attached at the other end to its lost home. You Russians make the greatest exiles, you know. You're the professionals." He sighs again. "Used to carry him everywhere. Every yacht should have him."

Ah. This man works internationally, then. "As crew?"

The stranger leans back on his crag. His long body gives off the air of having preselected its couch. "Satirist. And just the right size, for my money. The big ones are eaten up by love-hate for mankind. Equally divided. An exile's love goes only one way—back."

What's he driving at? I am being tested. But how?

"Lucky man," Gonchev says. "To have just the one place—for either."

The tall man brings his hand down on the crag, without apparent hurt, the pink-and-white palm absorbing like a mollusc the substance to which it clings. "For you picture people, isn't it the same?"

No, thank God. If Gonchev had had to be encumbered with this love-hate each time he moved, what then? "Pictures love most what they haven't yet seen. That's what pictures are."

His questioner opens his eyes wide, as when men wish to be caught thinking. Or is he getting ready to spit out some hook—and catch me? Though I am already caught. Which is what is meant by interrogation, foolish Gonchev—have you forgotten?

"And yet you're such a linguist."

Gonchev feels he has closed his mouth just in time. "I speak a few," he mutters, keeping his head low. When he does that he sees the steam rising all around them from the heated pools dotted with faces, and from the crags. These are heated too, as his backside now feels. Makes one want to piss. Where does one piss in hell—anywhere? Or does one never?

Answer: he and this man aren't in hell. But he's already known that, maybe from the beginning. Émigrés are thrifty, mister; we tend to be our own satirists. This is a real place. A kind of nonplace, actually. But even those, so rapidly growing around the globe, have their characteristics. National ones, even. So get out the mental atlas, Gonchev, and calculate where you are. Your pride will be—not to ask.

"How many languages d'ya know, Gonchariev?"

Keep your head down, Gonchev. He's given you the name you haven't had fully since you left Japan. "About seven or eight. Enough to speak." Russian, Japanese, English, a little French, some German, some Serbo-Croat. A smatter of Romanian. Plus a fair command of the language of the country he has come from.

The blood must be creeping back into his brain, in its constant underground language. His studio, his brown-and-white house appear to him, as primary clear as in an illustration in a child's book, which can happen to the places left behind, and, whenever his parents and he had moved on, had so happened to him. Has he been moved on, as when a child? There's the house, Gonchev—must you turn the page? "Horse feathers," as they say in America—the States—in that film, which could be seen in Tirana, the capital, until his own committee had denounced it as agit-prop. That's the house from which, slugged and drugged probably, you have been raped. Find your way back.

He raises his head. "But street signs I know. Undergrounds, subway ads—all the language of transport. In all the languages there are. And the names of materials." He fondles his crag, staring meanwhile at his own thigh. Ordinary skin for a well-nourished man of middle age. Nothing unique about it. Not a spy's. And where we are, this man and I, is a place I should know of. Not ordinary, but still a place, a worldly one. You've known of its like for years, Gonchev, even though you may never have been to one.

Pictures of Baden-Baden, of Montecatini, flood a channel through his brain, sparkling with fountains, spouting waters to swallow. Bath: and the eighteenth-century affectations of the British—lace at the throats of men showing off their calves. Roman nakedness: Caracalla. And more muscular outposts in Osaka, Karachi, Tabriz, where philosophy vies with vanity, and the steambath takes a backseat to shrieks of religious valor and the clash of rehearsing steel. But they're all the same place. Hell may be such a place too, in its way, but this isn't hell or purgatory. This is a spa.

And the man in front of me? Spy or not, I know the country that skin is native to.

"Ah—but what we don't yet know—that's the most interesting of all, isn't it, Gonchev?"

"Not to me. Whatever I do know—is my—"

"Pride? Goal?"

"Hoard." Gonchev stares. No, he's not a Tati, although there may be Scandinavian here—Low Country phlegm. Pink, well-tended skin, taut with adventure. "For instance, your name? I would be pleased to know that."

"In what language?" the man says lazily.

Gonchev laughs—near to a bray—and chokes to a stop.

Across a crag the man with the ribboned eyeglass looks at them in disapproval. Where has Gonchev seen just that inflated nostril, just that curve of lip, like in that famous sofa shaped like a mouth?

Just then, three other men bow to the eyeglassed man from neighboring seats; two make their way toward him, in between the fake rocks. Diplomats, he would swear, by their posture alone. He watches the three confer, each with the slightest gravitation of the ear toward an imaginary center, speaking sibilantly from a stiff upper lip. Clothe them in any formal public costume from the last five hundred years of European history, insert them in those yard-long paintings in which the signing of treaties was once commemorated, and those three would fit right in.

This place is still in Europe. More Austrian than French, but not Austria, Slav, rather than German? For certain, not Italy. Not Russia, not with those eyeglasses. Slav, yes, but not the pug-nosed kind—or not most of the faces here. And the arrogance? Gay rather than stolid; this is Central Europe, not East. These men are used to beauty in their women—how do I know? And to pepper in their food. Not black pepper—what kind?

An orange haze floats in front of his nose. Does he actually smell from some kitchen below a waft of chicken mulled in—paprikash? Smells are the absolutes of memory; they never change a molecule—but the brain can misidentify. Yet those men, by the gymnastic of their mouths, aren't speaking Romanian, a language more Romance than not.

How assured those men are, and sleek. Yet they have suffered. Or their country has. In each skin and eye there is that sad European ochre, that residue.

The man next to him has no such tinge. In only one country can people still have skins like his, brutally pink from wars not on their own territory, yet plump with innocence. Gonchev remembers a motorcycle bought, a Suntory whiskey offered, and a girl thrusting a book into his hands. When these people sell you something there is still guilt; they have to act as if they were really giving you something.

This long boat of a man—what's his guilt? What's he giving me? What does he think he is giving me? That's what he so wants to tell me; he's full of it. Like those ice-cream-cart men in his country, who benevolently proffer children the sweet for which they must pay. In their films it always seems as if this man's country would have no smell. And neither does he. Yes, that's where.

But first I must know where I am. Where he and I are. Come, my archives—gather. Open all your doors, my Aladdins. Light me your lamps.

Gonchev rises to his feet on his crag, snouting the air. He's a tapir, sniffing for leaves. An elephant's trunk, probing a landscape. A monkey bustling up a tree to chatter clues with his crowd. He's any sentient animal, scouting where it has never been before, by means of the images in its head. That he has tens of thousands of such pictures and sensories is what makes him a man. As well as the particular man he is.

"Sit down, Gonchariev. Please. Gonchev—which I see you prefer."

Seizing the cologne bottle he sits, splashing the stuff onto his cheeks and brow. Its cool tonal odor of barbers and boudoirs after sex can't confuse him now. He sees his fact-granary at Elsinore. A barn-size structure, open to all visitors willing to make the safari, or to those government servitors required to do so. He can see his private office, where he used to feel he was sitting in the center of his own brain, watching the world's information flow down its ventricles, to become his brand of fact. As the afternoon sun falls on oak cabinets, turning edges of drawers to gold, spotlighting a clutch of file cards retrieved, he reaches in, godlike, to pick a city, to make it rise from its cardboard womb. What matter if he himself cannot get out? The world comes to him; he is a cobbler of cities.

But now he is outside. And the clues won't come to him. He'll pretend to be asleep. Give it time.

In the end he locates this place—in some antique files long since deactivated. For the city in which this place is located is no longer a major city. Or not anymore. In the thick old photo he resurrects, these crags are tan. What he has found in the file is actually a brochure, the sort that such places send on request, with little maps of their facilities, designed to show one their elegances, and at what price. This place is intended to be a sort of heaven, not a hell.

As for the men here, in much of Central Europe this would be the hour when the ministers of state and other upper civil servants were accustomed to come. Good place for talk, casual or criminal.

Or to hide a hijacked man.

And a woman?

Vuksica. He starts up, forcibly holds himself down. The women would have their own side here, in the old-fashioned way. Nereids, a little fat for his taste—if this is where he thinks it is. Merry widows, shorn of their hide-and-seek lace. But will she be among them?

He remembers now. He was off for one of his rides, farther than usual. "Don't worry if I don't come in until morning. Or even noon tomorrow," he'd said to her. "I'm hungry for the sea."

Usually when he said this, once or twice a year at the most, she came to him to be in his arms, pressing herself against him belly to breast, in that farewell by which wives voice all the cautions at once. This time she hadn't done so, instead sitting where she was, great-eyed, her hands in her lap. So he had gone over to her and knelt, rubbing his face in her lap. "Playing the silent part?" he'd muttered. One of their jokes—meaning that at times he could detect a staginess still in her, directed back at that other life she had left. But this time she had stood up, as she did when impatient with a child. "Where does your lap go, Mummy, when you stand up?" their daughter once said.

So he'd got his feet too, rubbing his face with his own palms. She must be displeased again at his carelessness. The sea back there had a significance that other boundaries did not. Hunger in that direction wasn't wise to display.

"In the old days," he'd said, "you liked me to—"

"To what, Gonchev?" she'd flashed.

She'd called him Gonchev—not her habit. And he hadn't noticed. "To risk."

"In the old days?" Repeating was not her habit either.

"You liked your men to risk."

Bad taste. He'd never teased, compared.

Now he sees that flush rise in her neck, to her face, almost seeming to pitch her forward. "That's risk?" had she said almost inaudibly?

When he'd gone to mount his old trusty she hadn't walked to the window in the painted garden wall, where she always watched him off. As he rounded the screened front door on his wheel, he'd seen her seated on the bench just inside, rocking over her clasped belly, as if with gripe. He would have dismounted but the machine, no longer easy to start, had been well away.

He groans. A minute ago he was congratulating himself on his retentive powers of mind.

"Still in pain, Paul?"

Does he half want me to be? Is that the way they'll work it, warming in. "Was I?"

Turn the question. Keep that instinct, no matter what. Where possible, give no answers.

Apparently the stranger knows that code also. "You sleepy again? After concussion, have to watch that. Your head still ache?"

"My mind aches," Gonchev says, in spite of his resolve. "Ever hate your mind, mister?"

"For what it can't do? Sure thing."

"No. For what it can." Gonchev points. "Look over there, those three. They love their minds—they're bathing in them. That's why they come here. Ministers of state, aren't they? Upper civil servants." Gonchev breathes deeper. "Spies, Mister X. Or men who are both. In the old Austro-Hungarian Empire, I'm told, one came even to such places as this only by protocol. Separate hours for the businessmen. Accountants even later. And we theater people last of all." Gonchev folds his arms and surveys around him, an explorer on a promontory long since in his dossier. "Who says that old empire's gone?—just because a hydrofoil can take us from Venice to London over the surface of the sea."

Or from London to Paris—is there a schedule for that? He'd had all the schedules in his office, for the one vehicle more than any other on which he'd yearned to ride. That would be the way to sail toward Paris. Just workaday for all the commercial travelers, and the housewives banded together for a day's butter-and-cheese shopping in Dieppe—but not for him.

Mister X is faintly smiling. "Your researches are . . . just as we've heard. And, yes, the manners here are still Imperial. So perhaps—not quite so loud please? They're unlikely to understand you. But it does attract attention."

Has he spoken too loud? His ears have the blocked quiet that can occur after a flight, in which one's voice seems wee. "I didn't realize." He shakes his head, wanting to flap his ears like a dog. Instantly wishing that he hadn't admitted anything.

How can he wipe that grin off X's face? That's the trouble with this man's nationals. They don't know the subtle distance between a smile and a grin.

"I have to make water," Gonchev says, and stops short. From language to language, bathroom terms are the shiftiest. Going to the john or the loo one declares a national distinction. Going from the men's or to the head, a social one. As from the ladies' to the powder room. And the salle de bain is not the bathroom. "Toilet" is the safest in English; he has always preferred its thump. But even as a boy it was his pride to know all the necessary ins and outs.

Right now, his ear holds an odd echo. Had he said "make water"? Or "urinate"? Or maybe "piss"? The echo didn't seem to offer any such syllables. Would concussion do that? More likely a drug.

When he calls me Paul, too—the way he says it. With that same echo, from long back. And my tongue does feel different. Even my mouth. Not, thank God, my sight. Which actually seems sharper, with that aching outline I never thought to see again.

"Must be somewhere near," X says. "I'll ask."

"Don't bother," Gonchev says. "I'll find it."

"Shouldn't ask, if I were you. They mightn't understand you."

He's leaning back, insolent ass, eyes veiled with some advantage he holds. Should I hit him?

No, I can do better than that. "So this place is new to you?" Gonchev says.

"Never been in the country before, until last night. You slept like the dead, by the way."

"I was dead." But not now. "And you?"

"Me? Oh, I never sleep. Not if I can help it. Anyway, when you began really coming to, our medical adviser recommended bringing you downstairs here for a spell."

"You travel with a doctor?"

"There are phones. . . . You really have snapped back, haven't you, Paul. At last. Very exciting. For me."

And for me. Gonchev stretches, slowly. Ouch. Yes, he has certainly been hit. If not beaten. "So you've never been in this country, sir? Neither have I." As ten to one you already know. In case you don't, you may have that for free. "But probably you too need to . . ." He pauses. Let the word come of itself. "Urinate. So do I. So let us go along. But first, let me brief you, on our whereabouts." Gonchev thrusts out his chin. Ouch again. But one must strut at these times, take every postural advantage. Body language they call it in this man's country, even making documentaries on the subject, in their best proprietary style.

"We're in Hungary, then?" Gonchev says. He sees a flicker. "Ah, so we are. And the city—Budapest of course. This would be the Buda side." Although there's not a window down here at which one can see out. "Across the river is the city's other half. A superb trolley system will get you everywhere, in either. The new Hilton—better than most Hiltons, they claim—is just across the street. The authorities have made them conform architecturally. The Fortuny—is it?—is the restaurant. Gypsy music."

Or would it be Magyar? He's not quite sure of the distinction, in casual music, that is. Otherwise "gypsy" is a common Central European insult. Certainly so to those men over there on that hillock. Not quite Austrian, not quite Slav, no. As Hungarian as their handsome or sly eyes and their noses, high-bridged or not, can make them. Plus that orange pepper in the air and—one's told—in the temper.

Gonchev finds himself bowing. No more ouches; ah, that's better. "In short, this is the famous Gellert Hotel. And this is its spa." He blinks. "One of the best for its price in Europe, I'm told. The pedicures especially. Or so they boast." Shutting his eyes, he summons the floor plan in the brochure, shuttling along its arrowed angles like a mouse. Opening his eyes, he gets to his feet, rubbing his backside. Prastiklon makes marks. "Just down there it'll be—the locker room. And other facilities. Will you come along?"

After a second, the lounger beside him rearticulates his long figure and gets to his feet. "After you."

They set off, Gonchev in the lead. The hair rises on Gonchev's nape, but he makes himself saunter. These lazy-talking ones, mere copies of Joseph Cotten in the Orson Welles movie. But sinister is sinister, Gonchev thinks. Give me a tidy little guy on a cheap homemade motorcycle, anytime.

At the locker-room stalls he and the man pee side by side. What is intimacy?

"When you're ready to tell me your plans—and mine—let me know," Gonchev says.

"Right."

Nothing more is said until they reach the attendant's desk, where Gonchev's hand goes vainly to the empty pocket of his trunks. No money. Or locker key. No pocket. No trunks. He is a child.

"Allow me," his keeper says. He murmurs a number.

When they are handed their clothes in exchange for keys and coins produced from a wallet the stranger must all this time have been sitting on, he feels better. Above the attendant is that neat little sign often displayed: ON PARLE FRANÇAIS, WE SPEAK ENGLISH, MAN SPRICHT DEUTSCH.

"May I have the time?" Gonchev asks, indicating that he wishes to set his watch. "And the date here?" His good old watch doesn't show the dates, but the man won't know that.

The attendant spreads his hands; he doesn't understand.

"Ah, you don't understand English after all?"

No, he doesn't.

"How about French?" Gonchev repeats his request.

Sorry.

"German, then."

No.

The attendant's hands, spread wide, are manicured, gold-ringed, and very expressive.

"Must be the swing shift," Gonchev says. "Or standards have gone down. He only understands Hungarian after all, eh?"

"No, Gonchev—san."

The stranger's nod is suddenly familiar—quick, light-voiced, vertical. Gonchev compresses his lips, holding in some bleat of his own.

"I warned you. That they wouldn't understand you."

"What do you mean?"

"What language do you think you and I have been speaking?"

"What else but yours?" English, that is. Although his accent is not very American.

"But you're not. Speaking it."

He looks down at his watch. Swiss. Does it have an enigmatic smile, acquired in the murk of a Bergman scenario?

From time to time he has been asked to conferences, symposiums. Or even to collaborate on a film. He has always had to refuse. But his colleagues would be resourceful. Magisters of the scene change, from *Dr. Caligari's Cabinet* on. Could he have been kidnapped here? By consent?

"Is this a—a movie?" Gonchev quavers. Immediately he feels ashamed. For him to say a thing like that. As if he'd given up a piece of his heart. Like somebody in a street crowd the dolly cameras have crept up on.

The stranger—the spy, or is he some rival director?—sees his shame. "I'm sorry. We didn't intend this. Let's dress and go to your room, Paul, and I'll explain as I can."

"I—have a room?"

"Suitable to the status you'll have with us, I assure you."

"Aha. A hijack. Some movie."

The spy reddens. "If so, one in which Gonchev himself has collaborated. Or his agent."

Behind them several gentlemen are waiting; one of them is the skeletal ancient. Who smiles now, as one naked man to another.

"Let's go, Gonchev. I think you rate a drink. It's safe now."

Safe. That's what they want a child to be.

"And I'll explain."

The old boy behind Gonchev has a smile much like Gonchev's watch.

"In what language, mister?"

Yes, the man's real enough. Guilty, triumphant. And apologetic, exalted, charitable, sly. Pink with the health of his good intentions and his plausible needs. American.

"The one we're speaking. The one you've been talking in since we picked you up. Since you got clonked, that is. The only language you seem able to speak. Which is why I've been your little godsend up to now, since I happen to speak it too."

"And which language is that?" But he already knows. How could he not, with his *l*s and *r*s interchanging, from glottis to tongue-tip.

"Japanese."

The little old skeleton behind them wants Gonchev to move on; he's chilly. "Okay?" he says, grinning over the international word. "Okay?"

He moves on.

They've given him a suite, clearly one of the best. Brown-paneled walls extend like a stage set, yet close in with the cozy stuffiness of Central

Europe; the alcoved bed is a mock emperor's. Sent to find his way up here alone, he'd half hoped that this might be from tact, that when he opened the door he would find her here, dispatched to him from the women's side of the spa—a white-robed odalisque floated up stairwell and elevator just in time to greet him from such a bed, chin on elbow, reclining. But the broad bed is bare.

From the suite's tall windows he can see across the river to the other half of the city. Down below, people are traversing what is obviously the main avenue, in those rhythms of which, seen from above, they always seem to be pitiably unaware—here a risky saunter into target-land, there a dangerous ricochet. Yet they manage. Off to the left he can see trolley cars, and their queues. In every direction he looks there's a sense of access—out. Or the possibility. How long since he's had such a view?

It's then that he sees the phone.

To call home is not possible. Calls to another country don't exist there on the personal level, or at all without lengthy preamble. Even the president, rumor has it, if compelled to speak internationally, purifies himself afterward, in one of the communal baths.

But Danilo. Who has two numbers, one in Paris, one in Belgrade. Both known by heart to everyone in the Gonchev family, as a kind of talisman.

Paris, city of talk. Where any arrondissement must ring with multicolored chat. Where he has—as anyone might—a brother-in-law. The simple family term calms him. His temples pounding, he picks up the phone, dials for the outside line—and is answered. By what must be the Hungarian for "Number, please." And he cannot say the numbers in any language except one. He tries.

He is still sitting by the phone when his keeper enters, in a fresh change of clothes, a bottle of whiskey under his arm. "Conference. And drinks." He stops short. "Ha. Can I be of use there?"

"I wanted to phone my brother-in-law."

"Why not? Can I assist you with the number?"

Gonchev sits, wordless.

"Hmm. I get it. Your brother-in-law, he doesn't—?"

"Our common language was English."

"Hai." He shakes his long head. "Pity." He sets the bottle down. "Been wanting to ask you—" He leans across the phone, his mouth emitting syllables.

"What is this game?"

"Just testing. I simply asked you whether you understood what I was saying and could respond in English. Let's try again."

It's like an echo, Gonchev thinks. Of what I do understand. But far off. Or like Zen. Which you must strive toward with your whole reception, not just the ears. But be cautious, Gonchev. Admit little.

"I do and I don't."

"Oy. Oy."

"What is," Gonchev says with effort, "aw-ee?"

The heel of a freckled hand hits the forehead, now dashingly covered by a wet-combed forelock. The fresh clothes are white, from sweatshirt to blunt rubber-soled shoes. The head gives a fast side-to-side shake. "Oy—is Oy." But his eyes are sharp. "Wait-ait a minute." He runs to the door, outside of which a big cardboard box is upended. He runs back, opening it on the way. In it are a shirt, pants, and shoes exactly like his own.

Gonchev gazes down at himself. This is too much. Where's my floppy linen beach hat to match, Nanny, with the brim that buttons on? And my colored tin shovel and pail?

"Even the shoes will fit," his companion is gloating. "We got the size. And the style you prefer."

"I prefer? Not me." He gestures toward the phone, where his brother-in-law's voice waits to be unlocked. "Maybe Danilo."

"Come on. All that dossier we were sent. All your model answers. You must remember, Paul."

He's heard of these forcings—who hasn't? Psychiatric ultimatums. Used on artists and intellectuals especially. Or these temptings toward uniform. That little lizard insignia, for instance, on the pockets of both shirts, the one worn and the one offered. Join us.

He won't snivel. He can't cry. But he feels his beatings now. The only path to dignity is to remain sincere. "It's bliss to speak Japanese again.

I don't deny that." And horror to have to be told that I was—but this I won't say. "It makes me feel like a child. But I'll be damned if I'll be shown off like one." He stares at the insignia on the man's pocket.

A laugh. "Our middle-aged man's hippie uniform? Comfortable though. Each to his taste." He's twirling the cap off the whiskey, pouring it. "Whiskey's impartial, fortunately. My name's Pfize, by the way. *Pee, eff, ai, zed, ee.*" He translates. "The *P* is silent. Perkins Pfize."

"Fi-ss." He has almost no trouble with it.

"Some call me Perks."

His mouth feels full. In Kyoto prefecture the Japanese students taking English would complain of this in their spare voices: *It make lee mow so foor.*

"Pelks," Gonchev says. "Pelks."

"Mmm." In English Pfize murmurs a favorite oath that Gonchev would later, much later, identify as "tough tit." "But you can see why I didn't name myself right off. Well"—he pushes a glass at Gonchev, raises his own. "To our sins."

He isn't fool enough not to drink from that bottle, by the shape a famous one. It will help him call his own tune. "Mind telling me what my sins are supposed to be?"

"Manner of speaking. Here's health."

"A captive has no health."

Pfize sits up. Leans back. Slaps his temple. Leans forward. He is always leaning. "You were not captured, Gonchev-san. You were rescued. By your own request."

"I—signed something?"

"We don't require that. Not under the circumstances we have to— meet. With most in your category. But in your case we happened to have the fullest reports—and cooperation."

"From who?"

"Your"—Pfize smiles discreetly—"intermediary."

"My . . . ?" Vuksica was right, one should never talk to them. My follower. Who dogged me the way movie stars are followed in Pfize's country? My fan? "Our little spy."

"The one-armed bandit?"

"Only one arm, yes." Because of me.

"No, not him. Actually, he wanted to come along. But we couldn't have that."

"He wanted to come, then?" Gonchev says, tranced. He would have come with us? "Then—I was right. He followed me for so long."

"We let him go."

"You let him go?" To lose the other arm—at best.

"Can't afford to bungle. He might have wanted to kill you."

"He wanted to come," Gonchev says. "God rest him. So—who did turn me in?"

"I wouldn't put it that way." Pfize has that fool smile on him again. "She has the highest references."

So for a minute or two—Gonchev will say to himself later—a few betraying minutes, he let himself believe it. A woman—not waving good-bye.

"She wanted to be there, you know. Even though she herself got us the crew. She doesn't trust any man, that lady."

Not me? Maybe not for some time.

"But we couldn't trust her. In view of her other relationship. Though she was able to convince us. That the country would never have let you go. Too valuable."

"Her—other—relationship?"

"Quite a person." Pfize smoothes the indented whiskey bottle as if it's a cat. "The lady Trim."

He need never explain to Pfize why he wept.

He discovers Kleenex again. And how much else is to come? "What will you do with me?" he says, when he can.

"Put you to work. What do you think we do with you people? Put you on an island?"

"Maybe," Gonchev says bitterly. "Maybe to your Alcatraz." Where the journey—the journey of being Gonchev—will finally stop.

"The Rock? That's been shut up, for a generation."

So have I, Gonchev thinks, as Pfize, leading him to a desk, sets before him all the paperwork that has helped to bring him here.

Document after document, each speaking to the other in an officialese whose swing carries over as Pfize translates. All resulting in the ordinary green card that must accompany Gonchev everywhere. As will the one label he spots on page after page of this biographical lore on him. The English word glints at him through a mist. Now and then a word has turned right side up into meaning. But not this one.

"What's this one word?" He points to it. There. And there.

"We've never yet had one of you from the films before," Pfize says. "One of those."

A word to fill the mouth. That will be hung around his neck like a cat's bell. Or a sheep's.

Pfize teaches it to him. It hangs lighter on the tongue than one might think—his first word in American.

"Dis-sident."

His companion's full name, John Perkins Pfize, is used only by that holy entity "the Department." Somewhere out in the normal world, he implies, there lives a simple John Pfize. Gonchev will be hearing from him from there—from time to time. "I keep an eye on my protégés."

Once he convinces himself that Gonchev isn't shamming, he begins contrarily interlarding his Japanese talk with English: "Too much of a strain, otherwise. I'm a troubleshooter, not an operative."

Meanwhile, Gonchev's English does not return to him, but it is his pride never to give any inkling of how far at sea he actually is. Those informed of his state will still not have any idea of the true scenario. Living among freedoms constantly touted to him, he is like any prisoner seized at night, on unknown instigation. That he is an honored one, and expected to respond according to attitudes already taken for granted by everybody he meets, he discovers almost at once.

Luckily, a new country always sharpens the wits. As of old, he retains hints, phrases, glances, events, like shells picked up at the shore for later identification. Better still, Pfize is a happy recorder, who avails himself of all the means with which his nation is abuzz. Although his own aims in life may be, as he says, "voluminously vague," he tapes every inch of his progress toward them. Even offering, once they get "home," to send Gonchev copies dating from what he fondly calls "the snatch."

On the planes from Budapest to Berlin and from Berlin to London, Gonchev learns on his own:

ON PFIZE:

That the Perkinses, Pfize's mother's family, had either given their name to a noted variety of rose, or else had taken the rose's.

That Pfize's father, a pioneer in something pharmaceutical not specified—"Not Kotex, but still the wrong kind of escutcheon for a school kid to carry"—had brought up his son all over the globe, on an itinerary that far exceeded Gonchev's: "I've spent more time between trains, caravans, safaris, you name it." And that though Pfize's young experiences were surely more benign than Gonchev's, and included the best hotels, he seems to think that he and Paul are kinsfolk adventurers. "Like most of my clientele."

That Pfize, although "a dollar-a-year man," is enormously proud of belonging to a country that "knows how to use its wealth"—meaning, how wealth should be excused. "When you grow up bringing like penicillin to poor buggers who never heard of even aspirin, you have a head start on humanity."

As a youth Pfize had thought himself doomed to go into art—"the well-known second generation track"—because products like Argyrol and Little Liver Pills—"both invented by friends of my father's"—had brought forth museums and music. But he had realized in time that yachts didn't translate easily into Bohemia—"not on the active side"— and that he didn't want to end up, like a Hirschhorn or a Rockefeller, "only on the collecting end."

That he now "collected" for human rights. "Lobbying is for the birds. I go and get you people."

And that, yes, in Gonchev's case, he had used the yacht.

And finally: "Knocked me over with a feather" when he'd first heard Gonchev's moaned responses to the medic, and first semiconscious speech. "You don't much hear Japanese that pure. Not from us foreigners." But the year Pfize had been in Tokyo—his fifteenth—his tutor had been a teacher from the Peers School.

ON GONCHEV'S PART:

It seems to be assumed that Gonchev knows why he has been "snatched" and to what prospect he is going, on which, Pfize says, he is merely "filling you in." Give him his due, when he uses an English phrase and sees no reaction, he is immediately contrite.

Language is their irritable cameraderie. Gonchev, never word-crazy, can't get used to what comes to seem a constant picking of one's own pimples. And Pfize's Japanese, like his finicky changes of shirt and other hygienes, is too blanched; there are no mean streets in it.

Inside Gonchev, Vuksica's name whirs and is swallowed. He drinks liquor, but refuses further medication. He eats well, moodily reflecting on the wiles of self-preservation. Throughout Pfize's long recitation he has scarcely said anything. Reaction seems to be expected.

"What are these feathers you keep talking about?"

In London they stay at a cheap hotel off the Edgware Road because Pfize wishes to avoid reporters for the nonce. Adding whimsically, "And because I like dives. Or, no, I really don't—but they're good for me." He's so self-conscious about his insides. How the man goes on and on about why he does things—is it because he's rich? Or do they all do it, where he's from? Because interest in them is worldwide? Except for a tourist or two Gonchev had helped with directions in Kyoto, or the girl who had given him the Byron, he has never before conversed with anyone of Pfize's nationality.

He and Pfize share a room because of the tape recorder, which sits on a rickety table between the two beds, thirding them constantly. "Want to go to a teahouse?" Pfize says. Does he mean tea shop? No. From his eyebrows, sex is what he has in mind.

Gonchev, now that he knows the hotel's address, knows pretty much where he is and could even tour London issuing taxi instructions, plus certain other curiosa, such as that a particular pavement in the West End—in front of the Arts Theatre Club—is believed to cover the bear pit where bodies were flung during the plague. But there is no place he wants to go, except to where he can't. That's what limbo is. The room has no phone. He is glad.

On the runway to their final plane, which is Air India, because Pfize likes the food, Gonchev at last balks. Up to then he had been having little "blackouts," only not black—cinnamon brown rather, or an electric yellow charged with minor thunderbolts. But for a day now his head has been clear. He plants his feet, unmindful of the swirl around him. "We're not in first class, no," Pfize says. "A hangover of mine from the old DC-10 days. In case of crash, the smart money always sat in the tail. I still do."

A steward trips up the access to the plane, carrying his little bag. Airline staff have a special nimbleness; over sixteen years Gonchev had forgotten this. And they carry their flight bags as if these contained extra body parts. An odor of foreignness suddenly plies him. Tentacles of travel. Images of streets not yet seen. Rain forests of crowds.

"Come along, Gonchev." Pfize's tone is like his own to Klement once, when his son stood squalling, after a parade's end in the capital, because he couldn't ride a tank. "I promise you everything will go first class once we arrive."

When you get to be of an age to ride a tank, you won't want to, Klement, Gonchev had told his son. . . .

As for me now, I can't arrive; I mustn't.

"Take me back," Gonchev says. He wishes to God he could say it in English. Or any European language. "Take me back."

Ah—belated stage fright? Pfize isn't surprised. But they can't go back, doesn't Gonchev see? Getting him out of that country required arrangements. And personnel that could never be re-recruited to get him back in. "Personnel's too grand a word for them. Fishermen. Thugs. Smugglers, actually. Tough as pirates. Who don't even speak to one another, normally. And got paid in three currencies." Whenever Pfize mentions money his eyes deepen. "You can never go over the top again in these matters, Gonchev. The very documents took us three quarters of a year.

And I'm not sure I could ever get back in." His eyes crease. "Maybe. Who knows? But not now." He plants his hands on Gonchev's shoulders, using his superior height for the first time. "Could you?"

Pfize will have an arsenal of persuasions. And packs a gun? Not that he'll need one: This poor man, Paul Gonchev, well-known film producer, isn't well; I can vouch for him. With documents. Errand of mercy. Been too much for him. Here's his green card.

And I, Gonchev, haven't a sou. Or a yen. Or a ruble. Or a zloty. Or a country.

An Indian family scrambles by them, the man in strict Western-functionary suit, with good tie pin and attaché case, the heavy-armed woman in sari, two boys in short pants trotting ahead on stick legs, and a small girl in a frilled jumper lugging a canvas satchel much too big for her. When the woman has almost reached the two smiling stewardesses at the plane's doorway, she stops, presses her palms together, bends to kiss the ground, and walks on, her cow-eyes brimming as she passes him and Pfize.

Or a family, Gonchev. You don't have that.

"Three quarters of a year, Pfize? Arranging with whom?"

Three quarters of a year ago he had been away from home, in the capital. Arranging for supplies at Elsinore. Mending his fences. Bringing the President some of Danilo's cigars.

Pfize says sadly, "And we'd been thinking you were recovering so well. Come along, chum."

Who is "we"? Gonchev hasn't yet seen any of the implied team except Pfize, who may be in the grand tradition of such romancers—alone, and bluffing it. Not that governments don't use such people from time to time, especially if they can fund themselves. Although in Gonchev's childhood the petty informers and "arrangers" whom refugees like the Gonchevs had had to be wary of had more often been conning the governments. And if poor enough—and in the Harbin of those days Russian enough—could even be such a family's "friend."

His parents had had such a hanger-on, a dessicated demi-nobleman who brought them cadged sugar cubes to suck with their tea and in the end helped them get a piano. "Who cares how the poor man arranged it?" Gonchev's mother felt. "A piano belongs to no one but God." In return she mended the old man's underwear, and in between sorties to the keyboard, Gonchev senior and he were able to toast Glinka again, calling the composer Mikhail Ivanovich when they were in the money enough to be in their cups. So the informer got his gossip. "What harm," Gonchev senior said, "if we feed a compatriot a little warmth? We're never going to give him any gossip newer than what really went on between Chopin and George Sand. And everybody's a little happier."

It's true, Gonchev thinks. There is a pure happiness to be found only in the nightfests of émigrés. Mornings belong to the host country. To the borrowing—from one another—in order to canvas the sweatshops. And to the child who keeps his soul truant from the kindliest school.

Ah, that was another world, people of any sort will say of forty years ago. Whether they remember the songfest or the sweat. Or the monk's school. But a grown man seasoned early in such wandering will have an advantage. He won't wait for the world to be different. He knows it for the same anywhere, anytime.

"I don't feel dizzy," Gonchev says. "Not anymore."

"Will you come along then, like a good fellow."

"I'm coming. But I warn you. I have my autobiography back."

"You poor guy. We all know what that means. Second thoughts. Sobs in the stilly night, over those left behind."

But Pfize's "*T-t-t-*" is wary. There's a subtle rhythm between the followed and the follower. When next they talk he will look Gonchev straight in the eye.

In the packed plane, between curry, musk, scarves floating down the aisle, an army of children (of whom Pfize says, "Note the lips, all curving in or up, not down—Buddha to the life"), curt Indian husbands ("Have you ever seen men more profoundly paterfamilias?"), packages tumbling out of nowhere ("Indian travelers are a delight; it's always a party"), and toilets increasingly malodorous, Gonchev is briefed.

Requests for his release—"We don't call it sanctuary"—had been coming in all the previous year, the most influential via an Italian director famously Communist. Pfize can't mention names. Gonchev, who thinks he knows who, doesn't bother to ask. "We met him once, in Belgrade."

Pfize is aggrieved. If Gonchev knows that much, then will he admit that all subsequent applications, testimonials, were submitted with Gonchev's acquiescence? Plus the necessary photographs of him. "Dozens of those."

Gonchev laughs. It is his first. "I did not take them."

Pfize has his limits. Gonchev had better understand that as a dissident he's not of the first importance. "Nowhere near A-one." Although they will faithfully take care of him. Pfize himself had never heard of him, though aware that more than a few had. Pfize is not as embarrassed as he should be. "Not my dish, you see."

Then why did he do it? Gonchev won't ask it, doesn't have to.

It's that tight little backwater Gonchev's been in. "Getting anyone out is quite a coup." And there are signs that the place may be opening up. Diplomatic reciprocity, even. "We Americans will be the pariahs for yet a while." But exchange trade may soon be possible. Some already—"Bootleg television."

"So I heard," Gonchev says in spite of himself. In a declivity of his plateau, twiddling an old Italian black-and-white set, he and Mrs. Trim had spent an otherwise blameless night.

"Hai?" Pfize is not as surprised as he should be.

"I have never seen the color kind."

Pfize stares. "Oh boy. What human rights await you."

Pfize can't believe that although Gonchev understands the concept of those rights, he has never heard that phrase.

"So I drink," Gonchev's father used to say. "An international pawn must have some rights." But had no obligation to politics. Gonchev's mother too always denied that political pressure had forced their wanderings, or later, their poverty. "You couldn't stand the winter there; your poor little nose was all chilblains," she'd said of Vladivostok. Of Harbin, "I always wanted to see China." And of Vienna, and his father's ultimately vain search for work there once, when they were on their uppers, "Did you know your mother has a friend there? On—on the Oberstrasse, I think, she lives. Or near. All these years she has kept for me my dowry chest, in which are all my school certificates. I think we must go for it." The data of these stories spun from her like her stitching. Once they were in Vienna, the friend hadn't been further mentioned.

Gonchev had never been able to find the street on any map. "If your mother had been sentenced to the Treblinka prison," his father grumbled, "she would have vowed she had to meet a cousin there." Paul hadn't understood her need for autonomy as anything more than the artistically preserved gracefulness with which she had adorned their rooms in the lowest boarding-houses.

He understands her now. He too is being sent.

The flight movie is just coming on. For the first time in his life Gonchev ignores a screen. Who? Who would bother to get him out? Some who would—the committee—didn't have the wits. Those who had the wits—his young rivals—didn't have the means. While the country itself wanted to keep him. Who—with the wits and the means—would that have bothered most?

"My late wife scarcely ever made a move without the tube," Pfize is saying. "She even managed to date the Weather Channel."

"Your wife"—Gonchev chokes on the word—"is dead?"

"Oh, no—sorry. Just my last one. Third. Two kids by each. Wives all very good friends. When I'm in Washington I date them all, sometimes together. Like geishas."

He's only Japanese for the time being, Gonchev thinks. Whoever he "rescues" he takes virtue from—and style. While keeping his home haircut. And the yacht. I am only a bonus to him—from his fifteenth year.

But why shoot the rescuer?—if I had a gun. Or strangle him? He's not to blame. And what good is an outcry on a plane?

If I'm ever taken prisoner, Paul, Gonchev senior had said, I will drink with my executioners if so offered. Wherever you find yourself in dangerous company, Paul, be sure to order the national wine.

The stewardesses are now lowering the blinds.

"A little late," Pfize says. "That too is India."

At times Pfize is so much not quite what he should be that Gonchev can't help liking him. Instead of seizing Pfize by the lapels, which has crossed his mind, he touches the suede-patched elbow on the armrest between them. "Pfize—where is my wife?" He cannot help quavering.

The elbow twitches. Pfize remains dumb.

"Is she safe?" Gonchev says roughly. "Have you had dealings with her? Will she join me?"

That elbow knows something. It is going to lie. But how? The man's an amateur. He messes up all the conventions. That's why nobody's yet managed to kill him.

Pfize turns. "Why, Gonchev-san." His voice is as tender as when he first stanched Gonchev's bruises with a styptic pencil and applied circles of adhesive to the worst. His own face is kept down to the nude by means of a small electric mower he hoards in a pocket and whips out at any opportunity, even in the hallway of a hotel. Gonchev's face is stubbled between the patches.

"Why, Director Gonchev." Pfize has the bow down pat too, whoever it may belong to—perhaps to a butler being careful not to patronize the scruffy visitor his master has foisted on the household. "We were given ab-so-lutely no suggestion. We had no idea you had a family."

The plane hasn't lurched. Only that small personal terrain one keeps under one's feet on one's own has shifted—that little platform meant to be proof against all outside treachery.

Just then a girl in the middle of their row of seats gets up to go to the aisle. "Bitte schön." A thick, yellow-haired silhouette is all he can see. Although she is surely nothing like any woman he has ever had, he can smell all European womanhood in her white-bloused underarm. He stumbles behind her, into the aisle.

In the washroom he communes with his splotched image. When he had asked Pfize those uncomfortable questions Pfize hadn't blamed the concussion. Pfize expected those questions. Did he even lead me on?

Don't let yourself know the answer, Gonchev. If you had a twin, your twin could know, without your having to do so, although in time both of you would. I have seen that happen many times. But you don't have that convenience. In our cozy triangle you were always the molly, the third. I never felt so before, he thinks. Nor needed to. But now I do. So close your mind, Gonchev. It's your human right. You'll need your little platform to be as it was. You can't risk—

The toilet door is pressed impatiently. Before he leaves he manages to peel off two of the plastic circles on his chin.

When he returns Pfize appears to be asleep. In the flickering light Gonchev can see that many passengers are dozing, while the screen natters on. Those of his neighbors who are watching appear to be staring through the screen at the future, at what awaits when they land. On what will appear to be safe ground.

Pfize is watching him through his lashes. "Want me to tell you about the snatch? I can do that."

Getting no answer, he proceeds. "We'd been hanging about for days, offshore. Word got to us you were riding toward the sea. We'd been thinking we'd have to send a posse inland. But there you were, cycling toward us under your own steam. You walked right into it. The little guy on your heels caught on at once what we were up to; he'd been ambushed before. But you? My own guys can deliver a polar bear unmarked. But, Jesus God, those pirates? Only tickle their chin-dimple with a fingernail, and they want to draw and quarter you. And tickle you did, Paul, once you did catch on. You challenged the biggest man there. Actually he was standing offside. Their big boy, more ways than one. A really fine-looking specimen. He gave you a bit of his lip. In his own language. And by God, you answered him in it. That's what sent you to the ship's hospital. Such as we had."

A passing stewardess waggles a finger at Pfize—*shh.* He waggles a finger back, ignoring her. "Languages, Paul," he hisses. "What a pity. Our local man, the one we deal with, pissed us off later. 'Your cargo,' he said—that's you, Paul—'your cargo called the big Greek a gypsy; what did he expect?' "

After a while Pfize whispers: "You asleep, Paul?"

"No."

The movie being screened is old and faded. Even when new its colors would not have been true. In it somebody is chasing somebody. To avoid finding out who is after whom he stares down at that faithful moonface his watch.

"Paul?" The elbow patch shifts. "Remember any of it?"

Across the face of the watch the ferns stream like arrows. Pointing back? He tries to add a clump of shadows, his overturned machine. Nothing. What he sees is a woman in a window, not waving good-bye.

Confusions cross the face of the watch—and perfumes. No, that's the German girl wanting out again, her heavy jaw brushing past him.

"Paul? You don't remember any of it?"

A man's cleft chin. Touch it with the fist of memory. That chin-dimple; that's worth saving.

Gonchev hides his watch under his cuff. "Not yet."

It will depend on how long he is to stay where he's going. He sees now that his life has always inflected not merely to a new country but to that country as crosshatched by time. So that Vladivostok, maybe the worst wrench to his parents, meant only a kitchen-loss to him, the preschool child. So that Harbin, those dragged-out years of over-the-shoulder terrors, of scuttling past police who were not police and squeezing pennies to make broth, was only an interim, compared with Japan, that long swaddling-time. Which now has risen, has it, like one of its ghost-witches, in apology for the last sixteen years of him? Inserting the staid little syllables of his first moral language in a throat that would prefer to be silent, stunned with loss.

Orange juice is being served, the last breakfast. Some of the Indians are being served their native equivalent, others, eating Western, are not. That will be the difference between them. The first lot will be merely travelers eventually returning to India, after having visited. The others, maybe with sisters and brothers scattered as far as London—or is America farther still to them?—are now returning to New York, in or near which they now live. Once that would have been called staying behind. Or not going back. What did they term their residence now? We live here? The verbs for an émigré are constantly changing.

Pfize is filling out the landing cards. His gray pen is like him, long, special, svelte, trying not to be noticed. "My good-luck charm," he says, seeing Gonchev note it. "But just to be sure, I have dozens of them."

What has he written on Gonchev's card?

" 'Nothing to declare.' You don't, do you?"

He has been lost; he has been found. He has been ambushed, hijacked. He has been sent. Just short of turning to stone, he has been snatched. Bloodied free of family—rescued, they call it—and bandaged. He is carrying all his lifework on his back, out of the darkroom of the past, and he hasn't one slide to show for it. And he has been defined. Without his consent.

Nothing?

"On the contrary," Gonchev says. "I declare everything."

4

Geography

"GEOGRAPHY," GONCHEV SHOUTS over his shoulder in answer to the pack of reporters behind him in the stern of the tugboat just casting off again from South Ferry, this time for Bedloe's Island.

"What's been the main influence in your life, sir?" a young turtleneck with his cap on backward has just asked him.

You want to talk straight to a cap like that—the more so when the answer to that impossible question has just come to you. They think the tug has just now brought him in straight from Europe—off one of those freighters lying at anchor mid-river. But the wind is too strong to say more. The man from the mayor's office who is in charge of the welcoming ceremony is already snugged up in the cabin with his bodyguard. Even here, authority travels with its echo. A deckhand has just pulled Gonchev back from the prow. On any of the small boats in his life he has always made for there.

From a prow, or leaning over the side, you see a great city's façade unrolling like a balance sheet. Huddled here in the stern you see a city's waterline. Docks with underpoles fringed with what could be nineteenth-century weed. Water the color of sadness, or squid. Or, in the rays of a sun not yet setting on a great harbor, the color the word "Buddha" takes on in the mind.

At dawn Gonchev and the young Japanese acting as his interpreter, boarding at the pier as the tug's sole passengers, had circled around Manhattan Island under the care of that same deckhand, who moved like a footpad, spoke only to show them where the head was, and brought them mugs of sweet tea. In calm, the shoreline had unfolded itself for him alone, as maritime cities do.

Returned to the South Ferry landing for the tug to pick up this crowd, he is sea-dreamy, as if actually arriving in America in the old way, by water. No sooner had the anchor been taken up again and that question asked than an answer had come to him straight up from the sea, and through the hold of this doughty little vessel. On whose deck he and this wedge of questioners—some capped like that turtlenecked fresh-face, some bareheaded, and one hooded black figure in the rear who may be a woman—are standing on the orb of the world.

The chop of the boat makes him seem to be jouncing for joy. He is half listening to the neglected news that comes through the soles of feet ordinarily nulled by the use of the wheel. Or of the air.

"Your first public statement," the shivering interpreter manages, his stiff hair blowing straight up. Borrowed from a local college, he has a voice so soft that Gonchev has to bend to hear him, and a jacket too thin. He's a poet, and not very quick at this work, but Gonchev is glad to be out from under the thumb of the too-amiable man who had replaced Pfize at the airport.

"Name's Smith," that man had said, following this with a guffaw. "Not much easier for you to say than Pfize, is it?" He spoke serviceable Japanese. Gonchev had been whisked through Customs by signals as hard to spot as those between bidder and seller at a horse auction, then ushered into a long car with smoked windows. "Keeping you under wraps for a couple of days. At a hotel. They want to bring you in by boat. Like in your movie. First sight of the U.S. from the old Statue herself, eh? Maybe make the front page." Clearly Smith, only doing his duty, doubted that. "But it's not a bad hotel."

Their route could only be sensed: the tires purring on a highway, the air-shock and grind of a tunnel. One backing-up, many turns. Dark rides, with an underling at his side—Gonchev might as well be at home. Secretly he scratched the window with a fingernail. The glass was the safety kind he'd read about; he even knew the wholesale price. "Cheaper here." His guide was surprised. "All your products," Gonchev said. Including the propaganda.

The hotel they drew up to was elegant in country-inn style, even floodlit. "You'll be free as a bird in this one," his guide said—and this he clearly believed. "We'll take walks."

A man abashed by the sound of his own name is almost certain to be dull company. Smith, by his own boast "a late-marriage nut," was forever on the phone to Washington, either chatting to the much younger wife, when he leaned romantically on the hotel sofa, a cigarette drooping, or talking to the babies, when he sat on the floor, making animal noises. As an avowed sufferer from "Foreign Service amoebic dysentery," he was also much on the toilet. Gonchev spent the days at the handsome pool, which had large blowups of Tai Chi exercises he imitated energetically, and the evenings lingering on the edge of soirees he assumed were geisha entertainments aimed at male guests by jazz hostesses, until he was advised that these were wedding receptions, overstocked with healthy bridesmaids dressed in gowns scattered with brilliants and bravely slashed.

He had no idea where he was—and was damned if he would ask. Instead he amused himself with the possibility that this suave establishment, bright with primary colors and bathrooms wooing one with little packets—of which his guide had murmured, "Your first greeting on American soil, freebies"—might actually be an elite sector of that historic port of entry through which millions had once had to pass.

On his and Smith's one walk, they went by identical brick villas that might well be compounds, their sidewalks in first-class military repair. One roadside sign repeated itself. "Smith-san, what's that word there?" Informed that it was "Island," he swept his arms wide. "Ah, El-lis Island?" Causing a middle-aged pair tending garden in identical white hats to stare, unamiably. "No, Gonchev," Smith said, gurgling. "Long Island. Gar-den Ci-tee, Long Island. Just a nice place to live."

Driven in at dawn this morning, he had had his first daylight look at a skyline seen only in night glitter from the plane just before landing, all the East Indian passengers crowding to the windows, despite warnings. "Beelt by men with un-lee one *di*-men-*shun* in their heads," he and Pfize had heard a man singsong to another: "Up." A fat wife had interpolated gaily, her gold neckbands shimmering. "Wel-l then, you two weel have to look shah-arp." To his wonder, he had partially understood them on his own, with the help of mime. Asian mime.

This morning, Smith had been driving his new convertible with the top down. "El-lis Island," he said with a snigger, waving at the Chrysler Building and the Empire State. But Gonchev isn't going to smart over his own gaffes. He remembers that a newcomer to anywhere will be both humiliated and enlightened. And that this will likely never stop, even for a man about to be made a kinsman in one blow, by a kind of swearing-in at a Statue of Liberty. "Human rights people," Smith had said. "Don't expect too many. In this town you have to be the biggest." He'd made one of his noises—*woof.* "But they'll give you a little flag."

Once he'd left, the young translator had pitched in. "How do you hear the English, Gonchev-san—as a blur?"

"No," he'd said, glad to get it clearer to himself. "Like I heard Japanese when I was still a Russian-speaking kid. Clickings—quite separate." Later, in that gray Kyoto of early childhood, the words had become fish-shadows he had swum to catch. "You see, to me words had become like objects." Whereas to draw—which every child there had seemed able to do—was like breathing. "Like inspiration—in the medical sense. And the camera? Like a lung." He broke off, embarrassed. But the young man, Saito, was a poet after all. "What did Smith-san whisper in your ear, Saito? When he left." Saito cracked a smile. "He said, 'The man's an innocent.' But Gonchev-san, I do not believe you are."

"Here, take this," Gonchev says to him now, pulling a bold tartan scarf from a pocket. This wind was nothing to the blasts on his mountain. "I only bought it at the hotel. For something to do."

It feels good to give something. He has money now, cash, and government checks of pinkly feminine hue. Plus a temporary billet for an "efficiency apartment" in a dormitory for internationals, where Smith had deposited him in Saito's care, in time for breakfast at a pancake house before they caught this boat.

Over his "hashed brown and egg," a phrase he memorized, finding the food delicious, he'd confided to Saito: "People happen off so quickly here. Even if you don't like them." For the past years he'd been used to such stasis, in people and in time. Here the present was almost at once the past, as well as the future. "It's like tourist trouble. Was the Taj Mahal yesterday or is it tomorrow? I was never that kind of foreigner before." Gonchev swallowed the eggs.

"Oh, we're all like that," he was told. "That's our way." Saito's parents still had similar trouble, but he had been born here. "And it's super for poetry." Gonchev wiped his mouth. "Su-per." He had been able to say it because he had never heard it before. It was neat on the tongue. And the egg warm in the gullet.

"Hey-y-y," a big guy in the forefront of the pack on the deck behind him is now saying.

The reporters want in. They disapprove of the private confab. He already knows them—faces out of Daumier's newspaper court-trials, bitten red now by the outdoors. Sour-merry, whatever their ages, and with cynical lips. Their irony should make them his natural friends. The wind jostles their words. He yearns for there to be no barrier between them and him.

Waving Gonchev's muffler, Saito begins to chatter in dovetailed English-Japanese. "He bought it at the hotel. For something to do." He's a poet who leaves nothing out. Of a sudden, though, Saito turns green and vomits toward the tug's rocking side. The deckhand, reaching casually with a long arm that seems to grow like rope, hauls him off and down a hatch.

The reporters smile meanly, Gonchev too. Seasickness is such a caricature of real mortal woe. And the cure's so certain. Then—as they press around him, pushing their smiles at him, shambling with the deck, all talking at once—it hits them, and him: He can't speak. And for him it is always the same, as in any language he can't speak. They are the jury. He's the criminal.

"Ho-ho." The big man's laugh rides the wind. His thatch is as thick as a cap. He reaches through his colleagues to pull forward the hooded figure. The two of them stand in front of Gonchev, rising and sinking with the swell, feet planted wide.

The hooded figure is a woman. Asian. Young. In standard international freak-black. The leather jacket sleeves balloon. The sticklike legs end in unisex brute boots whose splayed flanges quiver. The handsome shoulder bag swings like a semaphore. Gauntlets cuffed halfway up the arms hold all together, clasping at the chest. Black points of hair on the pale cheeks. It's a performance.

When the big guy claps her shoulder she nods, twitching off a glove, the slender hand sliding back the knitted hood from one naked ear. Humble, yet controlled. He recognizes that humility, waving its fan at him from the days of his young manhood in Tokyo. Demanding nothing—yet demanding it always.

Inclining slightly, she says to Gonchev in unsmiling, perfect Japanese, then to the rest in English, "He says to tell you he brought a spare. Me."

Everybody grins except Gonchev and the girl. The boat, heeling slowly, swings southwest in a wide arc and is out of the wind.

"Flaherty here," the big man is saying. "As in flah-ers. Even if my beat is the pavements of New York. And you, sir—do you know where you are?" He points. They are cruising almost opposite an island in the near distance, with strangely hybrid buildings. "Roman towers on top. Parochial school down below. You'd think the pope had ordered it. As for that Ellis, who gave it its name—?" He shrugs. "Who he?"

The girl is quick-speaking, deft—and not quite neutral? Gonchev even gets the flavor of this man.

As for the island over there, it's nothing like the hotel. Nor yet like those lagooned civic ruins in Italy, where for a fee one can piss in a Roman aedile's latrine. Only a checkpoint, that's all it ever was. A montage of shadows, moving along, along. But those in charge here still keep it up. They don't have many ruins, yet.

"Yesterday—I thought I was over there. At a hotel," Gonchev says to her. "And explain who is this man, please. He doesn't have a microphone."

A man laughs. "Flaherty gets you in the kidneys, not with the mouth. He's a columnist."

Another says: "This Gonchev—he came in yesterday? Dopesheet said today."

"Came in by freighter. Like in his movie."

"Saw it. Even had the World Trade Building in it. Or you would've sworn."

"You trust this guy?" a third says. He wears a checkered brimmed hat.

And bless the girl—she translates everything.

Mikes are pushed at Gonchev. Names spark; credentials fly.

"CBS . . . ABC . . . NPR . . ." the girl says languidly, as if chewing soup.

"Tell them I already know their alphabet." Being on water always makes him cheeky, the way hunting turns some men into samurai. A couple of rough syllables escape him.

"What's that?" the girl says, startled.

Good. He wants those slim eyes not to be neutral. Takes doing, but he's done it before. "Cyrillic. My first alphabet." Like a few old rye-bread crumbs still in the mouth. "I taught it to the monks."

"Monks? You are—monk?"

"No, no. At school. In Kyoto."

"Ah, Kyoto—" she says.

"KAM-AHN BEH-EEB," the men chuff.

"What's that mean?"

" 'Come on, baby.' Slang. Not nice."

"BEH-E-EEB! Kam-AHN."

"The name is Roko," she says to them. And to him.

Flaherty is watching them both. "Shove it, boys. Our paper is paying her umpteen an hour. And cheap at the price."

Translating that, she is as flip as a pancake turner in a window. And glad he's not a monk?

"She working for you, Flaherty? Or for him?"

"Can it, pals—she's just out of Wellesley."

"My college," she says to Gonchev. "But the other's not true. I support myself for three years."

For the first time Gonchev can take pleasure in this cul-de-sac in which a man and his interpreter are locked up together.

The boat has meanwhile nearly stopped, its engines grinding. Nudging its passengers to the view.

"Big Mama," Flaherty says.

The Statue. Fisting at the sky as if that still can be done. It's a shock. This is a country. Not just a border.

A chorus issues behind him, the voices as thin as hallucinations. "Climbed it, I was a kid. Up, up that iron spiral, thought I'd die . . . Used to let you in the crown even, the forehead. Not now . . . Yes they do again now—only not in the arm." All the voices are hallowed, the girl's too, translating: "She looks so small from here . . . So small . . . small."

He feels the intimacy peculiar to travelers met by chance on a monument. Standing in the parlor of a continent. Looking at its prize piece.

A piece of copper-bronze, greened by weather, of whose structure he knows every detail. In his film the modern harbor was seen through an old brown-etched rendering, *View from Castle Garden, East River, Brooklyn*, in which the minute boat, lacily drawn behind the huge statue, was either paddle wheel or sail, the lithographer's pen millimeter-fine, the perspective infinite. On a five-inch page.

"Help me to tell the truth," he says to the girl. And she does not translate.

Flaherty is watching them. "Tell him to give us some of that geography of his."

The boat, trudging on again, must be mid-channel. If they asked him to parse the streets of the city, he might be in trouble, after so long. But rivers and inlets stay the same.

And the girl wants him to show them. She's on his side.

"That must be Staten Island. The Borough of Richmond." He points. "There the Kill Van Kull—Jersey . . . Out there, Lower New York Bay. Then other bays; I am not sure of the order. Then the ocean." He drops his hand. "We would leave by the Narrows. If we were leaving."

Their mikes are listless. Who leaves? That's Europe. Or pieces of Asia.

"But how did you know?" the girl says.

"I had once a library." *I had once*—the past tense of the émigré. His mother could tally every one of her vanished wedding presents, whether sold, stolen, or left behind—including two dray horses whose markings, if ever met again, the young Gonchev had been convinced he would recognize.

"And the river is salt," he says. A great river always has salt in it, his mother had said. Salt and tears. Exiles like us understand this, Paul. That's what keeps us different from the citizens.

He turns his back on the Statue to view that long façade, as at some point all immigrants must. Later, on small streets one will come to know, one walks in cooking smells, hears staircase laughter. The young whores seem like girls in white stockings, out shopping for the family dinner. Even the beggars are out of the rain somewhere, with a palmful. Then it is that the hunkering shapes of a city—any city—will seem to enclose all its inhabitants with warm bruin arms. Where one can dream that no one is starving, no cheek is slapped. And even the dead are warm in the minds of those who knew them.

But for that one needs to be walking, old-style.

The reporter who doesn't trust him sidles up to him, hat cocked. This sandy-haired chap has a chin-tuft—always a sign of vanity. It wags for him. "How does it feel?" he says, like a doctor sliding cold steel up your ass. "How does it feel to be a citizen of the free world?"

"But I am not free. I was brought." Speak the facts, his father always advised when they went to register as foreigners, but smile easy; they may not recognize them. "Citizen of the world will do."

"Like everyone else," the young one with the pencil says. "And what about outer space?"

"The camera doesn't see it as that. Only we do."

The pencil is nibbled. "That's—profound."

The others groan.

"Come on, Gonchev. Give us a statement." Sandy-hair swings like an orator, pointing toward the shoreline they've left. The nails of his right hand are manicured, flat and shiny; those of his left are dirty gray. "What's this mean to you. To people who come here like you. Like they tell us you came." The voice conspires. All stories will be undercover to him. All lives. He wants to be the joker in the pack.

The rest are looking at Gonchev as if he's an innocent, yes. But one who might possibly know something they don't.

He can never see any city he's worked on as a mere city. "It's—a vision." They like that, but he can see they've heard it before. "But in broad daylight, like now, do even your clouds seem to you made of brick? Even rectangular? That happened to me yesterday too."

"Yes-ter-day." His questioner cocks back his hat. "And didn't he drop something about a hotel, fellas? No wonder they wouldn't let us come up the harbor with him, only meet him at the pier. Like he was just in. Out of the storm."

The translator keeps translating.

"Oh no, they staged this," Gonchev says. "Perhaps they thought I expected it. They thought you did."

Flaherty is smiling. "How did you come over, boyo?"

"What does 'boyo' mean?" Gonchev whispers to her.

"Irish. I think—friend."

"I came on Air India," Gonchev says to him. "Very comfortable."

The crowd roars.

"You may be going to be our best dissident," Flaherty says.

"But I am not sure I am one. What does it mean?"

Flaherty blinks. "Say that again, Roko."

She does.

Flaherty thumbs an ear. "Jesus."

"Very canny," the joker says. "Who's he left, back home? Or is he scouting for funds? These movie guys always are."

The girl is staring at Gonchev. Hard to catch almond eyes widening. Hers have.

"A dissident?" Flaherty says. "Somebody who doesn't believe every-thing he's told."

"Not even that?" Gonchev shoots back. The habit of authority, the manner, is returning on him. Maybe the effect of the boat.

But is it authority, when they laugh so much?

Half a dozen mouths are now calling out the same thing.

"They want more about their city," the girl says.

Theirs? Isn't it hers?

That's what a city is. It always wants more about itself. Some demand it harder than others. No—he hasn't lost his library. History is here with him, heavy in his eye. Only the truth will discharge it.

"Is it—too much?" he says, staring over east, at that marvelous bric-a-brac. "Maybe only at first sight," he adds out of politeness. "But—someone will want to move it away."

They are silent. The boat is nearing Bedloe's.

Somebody says: "Tell us more—about our famous skyline."

"About your—sky-line," Gonchev says, attempting that word in its own syllables, for which a few salute him.

He takes his time. At home, in the blue dioramas sent him, the city had looked romantic, futurist. Here the edges of that long façade seem as threatening as assassins' knives. On a harbor street he knows to be one of its earliest, the one called State, a building fronted entirely in curved metal extends like a bladder clapped on its old neighbors—money extruding from history. The expanse he and they are sailing past has more thicknesses than any slide can show. It knows it's real. This city knows itself so hard it makes the sky above seem papery. It would draw you with an electric suction.

"New Yo-l-ke," he hears himself say in his childish lilt, and forces his teeth together more adultly. "It's an ugly woman. That you want to fuck."

Flaherty slaps a knee. "Absolutely the best. Depend on him."

They are at Bedloe's now. The flat white ferry marked CIRCLE LINE that brings passengers to and from the other slip is disembarking some, taking on others. It's a homey boat; it has no responsibilities except to them. The teeming millions are already here.

Nearer, the Statue looks not much larger yet. You don't really feel its height, it's said, until you're inside. That's as it should be.

The man from the mayor's office comes out on deck, yawning; Saito emerges, still shaky. Gonchev walks toward the prow. Behind him is his own entourage. Klement, who often suffered the vomits as a child, had had those same whitened chaps and pale lips afterward. Laura and her girlfriends continually thought up headgear, either comic or stunning; that band of spikes up there on the Statue's brow might well be what they'd wear. Her flowing skirt might be Vuksica's.

At a nod from the mayor's man, cameras click. "Something to send home to the family," he says. The mikes press around Gonchev like matchsticks. "Say something. To the country that brought you."

"Such a short distance to liberty," Gonchev said.

. . .

Flaherty believes: that when men like Gonchev are let loose in the United States, notes should be taken on them—to show what "the system" does to them. At the same time, a man in Gonchev's position hadn't a chance of understanding Americans without the help of Flaherty himself. Ideally every last immigrant who had ever come here, whether via the steerage or the Concorde, should have had monitoring, in a universal census that could have given us both our democracy and our history all on one plate. "With all our problems in one flaming carbuncle in the middle. For Congress to blow out once a year, like a birthday cake."

At sixteen Flaherty had fled a city school—"the Jesuits wouldn't take me"—under a profound need to serve the country he loved in any way but the army. "I was saved by me family escutcheon—flat feet. So what do you do if your heart flows with love of the nation and fear of what its fools will for sure get it into? And when, though you're short on money, your generosity wants to be as great as your rhetoric? You combine the two."

He is one of those Irishmen with a head twice as big as most and a boy's features gone to beef. In his father's day he would have been the glory of a neighborhood bar. Instead, he had taken his always-wetted-down tongue into the newspapers, and now works the city like a beetle, leaving behind him a trail of print. "My forte is to make people feel the importance of indignation—for at least ten minutes." He brings his subway readers the same fine smell of corruption that comes through the windows as they ride, while his richer fans enjoy the genial way he makes book on how the poor live. "I'm the stock character on which they both depend." He doesn't disdain the Irish accent. "Both my parents were born in Queens but their fathers were fresh in from the green." One of those had become a trolley-car conductor. "Ah, the grandeur and clang of that. He took me on his farewell ride."

Flaherty is so local he's international. A type who drags one into his own grandiosity, he intentionally misquotes famous credos, mixing these in with his own outsize phrases. After the welcoming speeches—delivered in an outbuilding by the mayor's man and an island functionary—he approaches the dais where Gonchev is still flanked by the mayor's man and a wilted Saito. The tug has gone on, not waiting for them. The reporters had scrambled in a body for the every-hour-on-the-hour departing ferry, not waiting for the speeches. The audience of Human Rights people consisted of a few passengers formally shunted into the hall from the just-docked ferry, augmented by a parcel of boys who picked at the bunting on the side walls, and a toddler who danced in duet with her own hairbows throughout.

The three on the platform would have to wait for the ferry's return. "But there'll be a limo waiting at the other end," the mayor's man says. "All a question of wait," Saito giggles miserably, to Gonchev.

The dais is attached to the ceiling by worn red and white crepe-paper streamers that revive in Flaherty's breeze. "Well, that was a ceremony, eh? But take heart, Gonchev. When the gods depart, we men arrive."

"Scram, Flaherty," the mayor's man says. "You've had your chance with this gentleman."

"Oh, I don't interview those." Crooking a finger he hauls Gonchev and Saito off to the toilet. At the latrines he stands between them. "Powerful," he says, watching Gonchev's stream. "I won't contest it."

To a Saito wearily translating all, he says: "Ask him will he and Miss Roko come with me to my bar?" Watching Saito urinate, he says: "Hmm. We'll send this poor undernourished lad home in a cab." And slips Saito a bill.

Boarding the ferry, Gonchev feels at home. In Europe ferries were a seasoned traveler's small change, though much gayer than this one. The inside of this boat is like the saloon of a turn-of-the-century provincial hotel, stripped of its piano. "An oldie," Flaherty says. "I was a kid, they were paddle wheelers. Painted scarlet. There was an Italian played the violin and handed round the hat. We took picnics and rode back and forth. Sarsaparilla, and a dozen hard-boiled eggs."

Saito feels sick again. Roko gives him Kleenex out of her black pouch but shows no ethnic sympathy—rather the reverse. Flaherty and Gonchev take him outside, Roko following. The mayor's man remains inside.

"But there should be a limo," Flaherty says. "He's from the Department of Motor Vehicles."

Rivers and their traffic always affect Gonchev, even this one so neglected in husbandry and expertise. The ferry treads the fouled water like an old draft horse. "I would like to hibernate on water. To live on it. Like in a village."

"Why not?" Flaherty points upriver. "The Seventy-ninth Street Boat Basin. People do." He knows some folk there. Two women sailors who rent a houseboat. "They don't get many berths. But sometimes they get a chance to ship out. I'll check."

At the slip again, there is the limo. Gray this time, with a pebbled top. "Like dragons, those cars are," Gonchev says.

"No, only the dragons' tails," Flaherty says. "But you must be a big fish yourself, Gonchev. Or know one. This town, people only bob for whales."

Gonchev refuses the limo, insisting that only Saito be taken home in it, stretched on the backseat. Finally, after some protest, it snaps away.

And Saito vanishes, as people do so casually here. Off the screen.

"Good of you," Flaherty says. "But we're glad of your company."

Those big funeral wagons make him uneasy, Gonchev says. "I came from the airport in one."

"On your way to Hollywood, eh?" Flaherty peers up the hill. "May take a while from here. But there'll be a cab."

The dockside is all but deserted now except for the ferry office's dim lamps and the long bazaar-window of a snack shop that offers everything one could wish for, even if it is closed. He feels the peaceful hilarity of exhaustion. The girl's fluid voice and Flaherty's rich one are like two separate waterfalls. In the small park between where one boarded the ferry and the curbstone where the three of them wait, a big carved eagle on a pedestal spreads its guardian wings. Up above, on streets in his maps called by their old names, State and Union, that façade is dark now except for the occasional hazel eye of a window. The arms of the city are about to enclose him. In the possibility of being known. Once again.

"Starlight Pier," Flaherty says, sniffing air more like leftover douche than sea. "Only the rats are out. Wait long enough and you'll see one. Or become one."

Some cities are proud of their rats, even eat them. Most seaports live with them. Once upon a time they and the fleas brought the plague; now men can do that for themselves. Gonchev doesn't want to say any of that, or even think it. The first hours in a great city where one is to live are a gloss that will never come again.

Twenty minutes go by. "Cabs'll come," Flaherty says. "At least two or three. The last ferry to Staten Island's not been yet. But what do you bet, any driver who bothers with these pickings will be a dinge. And a recent arrival."

He has a special laugh reserved for himself—for the Flaherty persona. "Thirty years ago my obsession with the black-and-tans would have been for the troubles they cause, not those they suffer. Now I'm as anti-white as a white Irishman can be." He flicks the epaulet of Roko's jacket, with a remark.

"I am a recent arrival," Gonchev says stiffly. And what did he say to you, Roko?

Flaherty shoots him an answer before she can say.

"He says you are not an arrival, you're an ikon."

And to you, what? Gonchev says.

That I and my people are like the Jews. That we can take care of ourselves.

We're not this guy's captives, Gonchev says to her. You want out, I can manage it.

No, she says. Listen to him.

"And by God, he is black," Flaherty is shouting. "A Nigerian by the look of him. Probably with some watches to sell, on the front seat."

They get into the beat-up cab. The young driver's starched collar gleams like an altarcloth. He has to be coached on where to go, repeating the directions in high, lilting English. The driver's seat shows its stuffing at the top. He has put one of those wooden-bead seatcovers over it. A turkey-feather duster hangs at the front window. Before they sat, he dusted. The rear cushions are tattered too. There are no watches, front or back. "He's underage," Flaherty whispers. "And the cab's a gypsy. Not to worry. They all drive like Mercury."

"Wings on his ankles?"

Gonchev is getting his second wind. In the family pictures brought to Harbin, one salon had shown a bronze of the god, so equipped. Part of the unseen baggage we carry, he thinks now: The classics, made into sitting-room lamps. In Kyoto his inner eye had had to shift again, bowing to the dogma of a four-mat room, and in due time a six. And now will have to shift again. Here they have eagles. And the huge eyries to which their own psyches fly. In a country where even children maybe live on the thirtieth floor?

Flaherty settles his big haunches between Roko and Gonchev. "Sometimes wish a limo was my style. . . . Did you know that kid, Saito, has a Ph.D. oral exam tomorrow, the poor sod? And all next week. You won't see much of him, Gonchev."

"No." The bill Flaherty passed Saito had been large. "But how did you know?"

"My business. To know everything. And have people know I do."

Our Balkan servants did that, Gonchev thinks. And got paid accordingly—not much. But this is the United States.

"You could use Miss Roko here. I happen to know she is free."

You don't have to, she whispers. I did not arrange with him. I work through an agency. I never see this man before today.

Of course, Gonchev says to her. But I'm hoping you will.

Flaherty's now monitoring the meter. "Why, it's honest—poor slob. He'll learn." At a red light he taps the driver. "You don't have a meter-jumper? Under your seat? Or in the dash? Not to double the fare, understand. Just to put an edge on it. Like we expect. Raise your margin, boy. Like the rest of us." The driver doesn't reply.

Leaning back into the silent cab, Flaherty says: "Penny for Gonchev's thoughts, Roko. Or no, make it a dollar."

Gonchev ponders. "I am counting my baggage."

Flaherty laughs. "Have to do that. Even in a democracy."

At the next red light the driver says without turning his head, "Do not call me boy."

"Oy." Flaherty punches himself in the gut. "Right. Otherwise—just get us there, eh?"

Gonchev lowers the window. They are reaching what must be the Village—Green-wich Village. His mind is running smoothly over his maps. A delicious sensation, akin to the extra sense-of-being that is the preamble to sex.

"I have two bars I go to," Flaherty's saying. "One where they can always find me. One where nobody can. We're going to the first."

"Who is—'they'?"

"Uh?" Flaherty's sweat is clean-smelling and laundered, if constant. He relaxes in it, rarely surprised. "What's he say?"

Zipped in neatly, her batwings folded, Roko is scarcely a dimension between them. "Gonchev-san says—in his world the word 'they' can have a special meaning." This is the first time she's used his name that way.

"Get it. Government? No-o, nothing like that. Just a Village hangout. Maybe once people went there to find the intellectuals. Now they find me. . . . Of course the Village means nothing to him."

Gonchev peers out the window. "Eighth Street? Not so wild as when I used it. There was that shop someone sent me slides of. Gorilla rugs, with the heads still on. And one rug—like made out of a man. And that street with the lonely name. Bethune."

"Get it," Flaherty says sullenly. "Geography."

The bar is in a cul-de-sac Gonchev has never heard of. He feels as one does when with a guide, agreeably lost and about to be enlightened. Flaherty pays, tips, nods, and waves democracy away in its cab.

At the rabbit-hole entrance he wheels. "You been up since dawn, Gonchev—long day, worn out, lot of people in there—want to call it quits?" His eyes are cold. Is he afraid his protégé won't do him proud? Or sick of doing him justice?

"I am tired. But only in the back of my body." Desperately tired of talking. But from now on, he must. "I could eat."

"Easy. They don't just do cheeseburgers here. You can get a very decent hashed brown and egg."

Inside, the place is not as smoky as its equivalent in Europe. People take the cigarette seriously here, Pfize had said—or the upper class does. Yet the long room has the brown fug of a true bar, managing this somehow from talking mouths, old beer, and back-kitchen smoke. A quiet corner or two, but most of the crowd are moving between three large tables Flaherty points to. "Ballet and theater. Literature. Art."

Shortly, in the oozing of bar intelligence, everybody knows who Gonchev is. Roko, her hood pushed back, owl-size sunglasses jutting from her small sickle-moon face, keeps slipping him the biographies people are exchanging behind one another's back. Gonchev finds his own responses accelerated. She and he are talking privately more.

Once he stops dead, to say, "We've found a rhythm." After a circumspect pause she replies, "We've lost Flaherty." But she too is using the "we." Gonchev, watching the man at the distance the room affords, is thrilled to find himself still a director. Seeing how, from table to table to table, Flaherty is stage-managing him—and the crowd.

If the columnist is using the newcomer, so are these people. To enlarge themselves. Or to answer their own inner questions. A fleshy young man from the painters' table leans over Gonchev. He looks like Balzac, or like the famous statue of him in his blowing iron cape, but is a collagist, as someone whispers: Pebbles and plush, and many times a millionaire. "What's it like for you to be in a king country?" Asked what that means, his long coiffure moves ahead of his oracle. "A country that is king of them all."

Gonchev reminds himself that he hasn't yet seen the subway here. Collecting data on Moscow's, the Paris Metro, Hampstead Underground, Montreal, had been an early passion his Kyoto teachers were amused by. He quotes them, feeding Roko the haiku slowly.

" 'In the world's packed subway / the lion roars / and is seated.' " Gonchev pauses. " 'But is it a lion?' "

The man sits down, in squeals of approval for Gonchev.

But it wasn't me who did it; it was the Zen, he says to Roko. And they are only glad to see him pricked because he is a millionaire.

If he's to go on saying he's no dissident, will such people believe him?

At the theater table a balletomane is describing his own "relationship" with "Mischa." How he saw the calf of his ballet idol's leg from backstage at the Paris Opéra. "I was beneath the stage slightly. And there it was, a foot or so above and six inches in front of my eyes—the great muscled leg. It was rehearsing." Later, the devotee had seen Baryshnikov in the Green Room at Lincoln Center. "So small, he looked. Saying nothing, sitting next to his gross American girl. And I am just then telling someone about my Paris experience. 'Like Chartres,' I say. 'That great leg.' And I see him—looking at me. *Him*—looking at *me*." The narrator is now looking over at Gonchev. "That divine calf muscle— who cares about its politics?"

Sometimes, will I wish to be a performer only? Am I already wishing it? Gonchev says half-aloud.

But Roko is already speaking for an American woman, a correspondent for a leading magazine, who has joined their table. "We cover fashion in everything." She herself is sweet-mannered, sly. Blond hair cut like a British child's, a face to match, ravaged by what? Many of the women here have that air.

He recalls the women of his part of Europe. Their scarves, their noses, impishly blunted or elegantly curved, little scimitars. Their esprit. The ones with passionate hair. Their talent for conversation with a man.

This woman is so very well dressed. She notices him noticing. "If you spend time on how you look it drains half your energy, doesn't it?" she says to Roko as to an accomplice. Addressing Gonchev, she says brightly, "We seem to have either movie-star types or wives. Of course, domesticity is a rock—we believe in it. The other half of the time."

He sees a tablecloth, a tender light—back there. And Roko here, staring at him.

"Mr. Gonchev is just now severed from home," she says. "Perhaps he can't yet answer you." He wants to cover Roko's hand with his, but the woman is between them.

She persists. "Europe's movies. They all use women to symbolize. Over and over. Their women are either crushed or mixed up." She coughs; she's smoking hard. "Even the books. When your artist type or your political type is suffering for the world, what does he do? He flops in bed with his symbolical girl—preferably an inarticulate one. To think it out."

Roko says to him sotto voce, "I want to stop talking this. Please—"

Flaherty leans into their triangle. "Is there some drama I should know about going on here? Frances, you spouting your line?"

"Our women . . ." Gonchev sees them. Next door to government, or in government's bed. "Our women are—smugglers."

Flaherty says, " 'Scuse us, Frances. Haven't yet polled Table Three."

"These tables are numbered, eh?" Gonchev says as they are on the way over there. A beer has cheered him. "Like my movie lots."

No one must quip but Flaherty. "Bottoms up, boys and girls. Meet a movie king who's read *Hamlet.* Give him a chair."

"Nobody reads *Hamlet,*" a man says, appropriating the chair. "Except English actors. All the quotes have been used. Though not by me." He is young-middle-aged, with a face going saturnine. He has brought his soda water with him, and his silent woman.

"What are you doing here?" Flaherty says. "I wrote you up last year. I said you had your pen on the pulse of the nation—drinking its blood."

"And this is Paul Gonchev?" The man thrusts forward his hand. "Honored."

"This guy wants to be shot for what he writes," Flaherty says to Gonchev when they are all seated. "Or at least put in pokey. Like all of them do, these days. But he's so entertaining, nobody will. And he'll empathize with anybody—even a pit bull."

The man hunched in the chair resembles one, ready to spring. "Are you against literature, Paul?"

Gonchev shakes his head, muttering.

"What did he say?"

Roko glances at Gonchev, for permission. He shrugs.

"He said, 'Boil a language long enough and you get a syrup.' "

"It's true, he's never transcribed from books," the man says. "Is he against, like, *David Copperfield, War and Peace?* Great books made into film?"

Those aren't films; they are marionette shows, Gonchev growls. No, don't say that, Roko. Probably he's written a great book.

"I have nothing against them," he says.

"Ha, I suspect you're more for painters, maybe."

"Ah, they're my brothers. My silent brothers. I learn from them. But they don't move." His Japanese is clicking along now like one of their fans, mechanized. "And they are like me. Neither for nor against."

The table is crowded now. In the peering faces he sees that this may be wrong of him.

"He's starving, Gonchev is." Flaherty has been drinking whiskey. "And I better eat."

Bars are bad places to begin a new life, Gonchev tells himself. Nothing happens in them, essentially. That's why people come. Before he can stand up the other man scuttles around the table to kiss him on both cheeks. "I could help." His voice ruptures with emotion.

He wants to write Gonchev's new film.

Gonchev stands up, thumbing backward the man's chest. "A writer is a committee of one, no? So am I."

To Roko he says, I had the same trouble over there, with the government.

More faces have pushed in, hanging on his and her words. Some nod. One man claps.

"Ah, watch out for applause," his male embracer says. "It'll teach you its tune."

"Not in bars," Gonchev says, grinning. "Just because I'm new here, sir, doesn't mean I'm innocent." To Roko Gonchev says, Let's get out of here. But quietly. Order us something to eat—then let's scram. I'll be going to the toilet. After a minute, follow. Toilets are just inside the door. Meet me outside.

As he makes his way around the table Flaherty says, slurred, "He's right, you know. We baby them."

The other man says, "Well, we all have to go to the men's room. But his films lack agony. I could put it there."

Roko, ticking this off, eyes to the ceiling, right hand at her ear, is summoning the floating waitress with her left.

Outside, he says to her: "Better to listen only, in a bar. And forget what you hear. And always know where the toilets are. May I take you to dinner, please? I have money. Some place you know."

They scrabble for a cab and are lucky. He is careful not to sit too close. "What did you order for us, back there?"

"Only for you. Hashed brown."

After his laugh is explained she is still solemn. She won't translate her own reactions.

"Listen, Roko," he says, "I'm not going to have an artificial life here. No matter how they try."

She inclines her head—almost a bow.

The place she takes him to is a storefront, not far from the International House, where he's quartered. Its window is a lens through which one can see undergraduate life. The three-page menu card is a joke, she tells him inside; they serve only chowder, a long sandwich called a hero, pastry, and coffee or tea. He orders every item except the tea. "I was in a hotel once, where the menu was pages long, but they served only matchstick pretzels and beer. But it wasn't a joke." She doesn't react. "Yugoslavia," he is compelled to add. He resolves to suppress any further urges to say "once"—and not only to the young here. He can already feel how his past will be taken from him.

In the frank light he can study her. With the hood off again and the sharp attire mostly under the table or hung on her chair, she is a rather pretty person who can afford to make herself ugly for style's sake. Hair cut in low points curves under the thin jawline, sliding to a V at the nape. A single earring dangles a disc of onyx on a silver chain. The hair is eely black, the nose only slightly snub.

In Japan he had several times slept with a woman into whose pouted nostrils he could see straight up. She had been a scholar of the theater, and he had begun to feel that he could descry all her learning nestling there. Some human orifices the body itself kept modest. He has a flash of that oval dimple the abdomen carries like the hub of a shield.

Roko is known here. A couple of boys hail her, a clutch of girls leaving say, "Hi, how's your brother?" He and they are at the Juilliard, the music school—which is full of Orientals, she says. "They tell us we Orientals will soon own everything. First the violins. Then the silver. Then the land."

Is she smiling, or not, in the old dream that still gets lip service from

a country's citizens—and refreshment from its emigrants? The Gonchevs had never had the disease as hard as some. They were artists,
wanting that world above all.

"You're not Japanese," he says suddenly. "You're Korean."

She blinks in assent.

"But you studied Japanese. More than well. Where?"

"Waseda University. You know that college? My parents grew up in
Tokyo. My father sent me back."

"Ah, the fancy girls' school." He knows what the father would want.
What all the oppressed want of their conquerors. To be them.

"But I came back here after a year."

"Why?"

"I was born here," she says almost sullenly.

"And Korea? Would you go back there ever?"

"Seoul? Why? We're all here."

"Ah. All here." The phrase is a love potion—seductive, dangerous.
Sent out by this country itself?

"Saito too," she says. "His family."

"He doesn't do as well as you. I saw you didn't—think much of him."

"Not much, no." She permits herself a shrug. All her gestures are
minimal. "He's a weak one."

"And women—like the conqueror to be strong."

The minute a man talks about women to a woman, the level of
acquaintance changes. At first she won't answer, then says softly, "I like
Americans to be that."

He's astonished. "Why?"

When she is insulted she does smile. Nibbling at it. "Because I am
one."

Her voice carries. Several at other tables glance up, return to their talk.
Many of the faces are like hers, more or less. And yes, there's something
American about the faces, the body posture. At almost every table
there's a musical instrument case at somebody's side, or stashed against
the wall. Or open. Those faces, those instruments; it's a documentary.

"So are those instruments—American," he says. An alto sax, lying on
its side on a bistro bench. He can almost hear it bleat "Born here." And

that trombone, maybe. "Not the violins. But they're trying—I see that." His voice shakes.

"You must be ready to go," she says. He has eaten everything, she little. "You've been up since dawn, somebody said."

Only Saito could have. She doesn't want to mention him.

"Since dawn." The words have a trumpet sound. "But I'm not tired, me. The first day, when you change countries, is always the longest day in your life."

She accepts that, with her chop-chop business nod.

"That cello case, though. Look at that opulent thing. It wasn't born here." His chin is trembling, his eyes damp. Fool—is he going to declare everything?

"I watched you on the boat," she says. "And on the ferry. On the shore, too, while we waited. Even in the bar. While a person talks, you are seeing the shape of him, yes?"

He can only nod. It is exactly what he does. Exactly.

"Is there nothing visual you hate?" She presses her hand to her mouth, speaking through it. "Nothing—you hate?"

He dares to touch the tip of her nose. "Nothing you need worry about."

She shies away from him and back into her chair, a wary girl, American. "I do not worry outside my job."

That gets through to him—to where he is. In the present. Forever.

"Let us go there," Gonchev said. "Outside your job."

In a houseboat, water fractures light. The outlines of one's cup and chair have an omnipresence. Whether the boat moves or not, one gets used to the illusion that it is moving. Just so, one grows accustomed to the shifting of the other body in the bunk, as the waves of sleep wash. The house smell is a musk of heater oil chased by breeze, and blanket-damp with a hint of salt. If there are rats, the master of the Basin keeps them at bay. Rules are strict—an invisible picket fence around this flowing habitat. People are secret bedouins, rocking, holding still. Some here go every morning to the job—only so far. Others live for the scenery of a port now only halfheartedly warehousing the sea. Twice a year, maybe, a battleship may slide itself in front of your mug of tea. Now and then a nearby tenant ships out.

Dare he get used to the country behind all this? There's a forest of learning to be entered; he won't resist. He'll walk it as he would an arboretum, noting the tags. A visitor, vowing to remain one in spite of the role laid on him. Can he? Even from offshore, there's such a strong potpourri of "freedoms" blowing—their word for "laissez-faire." Buying an apple or two, not a kilo, or a loaf not of state weight, is so simple here, even if the loaf isn't quite wheat. Only his house lies at anchor. On shore, crossing the dreamy, dangerous parkside and uphill to the vigor of Broadway, he steps at once into that cloudy magic the planet America, which the whole globe must sometimes wish to be as when first discovered.

Down here on the boat, he's still a bigamist, faithful at heart to his other home. His family are already at risk of becoming saints, safe on their pedestals—even Danilo, his sometime gargoyle. At night, tossing in stertorous presleep next to his already dead-away companion, he keeps them alive, naming them.

One doesn't really hibernate on water, but enters a whole other household of connectives. The two women for whom he's been allowed to hold down the place have stipulated that the phone be kept under their names. Whenever it rings, even if it's for them, he feels as if the whole country is ringing him.

This time it is.

"Smith here. Busy week. Hope you're ready to go. All's set here. Showed the films around—wow." The onrush stops short. "Smith—remember? Sorry about that. How was your welcome by the way, Director?"

Nobody's yet addressed him as that here. The word braces him. He answers in the director's dry voice. "They didn't give me a flag."

.   .   .

"America's green," Pfize says, stretching his weight carefully on the houseboat's shaky chair. He's just back from abroad. "Green for all the empty land we've still got and haven't stunk up yet, no matter what they say. And for our innocent intentions."

He's smoking what he says is his one cigarette of the day, a Gaulois Bleu. When he can't get them he has them faked, down to the wrappers. He watches the curling smoke; the wind off the Hudson is bland. "Europe's blue. Blue with bad dreams—mostly about us. Blue moods they set to our music. And those blue hours they put out on their own. Tail of the afternoon, spur of the evening—and the women perfumed to the roots of their hair. Wherever the hair may be." The chair creaks. He laughs. "Will this chair hold me, with what I'm thinking?" He hums. "Am I blue? . . . Aaam I blue?" Tamping out the "cig," he's about to flick it overboard. But this boat isn't quite at sea. Others ride in close. Anchorage is at a premium here.

Across the river the apartment towers on the Jersey side are sparking up. One nearby sloop has had lights strung along its rigging since Christmas.

"Looks like a candy shop." But Pfize likes it. All those oddities that people who live on water come up with have his approval. He's only stopped off in New York "because of this crate we heard you were living on. Right in the big ci-tee. This I had to see."

Of course they kept tabs on Gonchev. Whether or not connected with that, Pfize has already been down to chum with the marina's master and any other park employees at the gate. "Sailor's courtesy," he says, also going over the weathered little craft stem to stern. "Not ba-ad. Sure could do worse than that galley. Couple of dames lived here? Sailors? What do you know." He asks their names but doesn't know them. "Had a woman sailor on the *Cynara* once. She was okay. From Marseilles. And one from Hamburg. They have a hard time with the unions." He laughs. "So do we." The *Cynara* is his boat.

"You don't recall being on it? Hmmm. We never bring her over here." But he's brought Gonchev a gift from her. "I was really moved, you know. That you'd elected to live—where you have."

The gift is an ancient bead-fringed pillow in the shape of a small boot.

"Kind the sailors used to sew, long voyages. To send home to their mothers. Or their home girls. As a guarantee they'd meet again." He's said nothing yet about the clear evidence that a woman is living aboard. Instead he calls for a hammer and nails and hangs the boot himself, then says: "And now my news. Good and bad." He always says it that way. "Bad news is—we think you're ready to work."

The neurologists up at Columbia Presbyterian who evaluated Gonchev's difficulty in a weeklong series of testings—some folk in Washington had thought it might be bogus—have given him a clean bill of health. "Matter of fact, they're damned excited. Shouldn't be surprised if they ask you to leave your brain to the Smithsonian." He coughs. "All in good time, of course. Do I detect you're still not really sure of us?"

But Gonchev himself is grinning—at the sheer gymnastic looseness of exchanging freely with a male roughly coeval in age and experience. Instead of always having to translate the translator's feelings—on sleeping with the boss. Though he thinks he in no way acts that way, he sometimes suspects Roko would prefer it—to sleeping with a child?

"So—they think I'm ready, eh." He will miss this glimmering cradle of a landscape. The plan is for him to start with local appearances, then go on a cross-country tour attached to various groups plying the far-reaching circuits the government has accumulated in order to show off people like him. Real ones.

"You'll be an attraction."

The medical exams hadn't just kept to his synapses. Doctors here envelope one in a haze of psychology, their own sometimes included as a bonus—and of course for that approach his ailment is prime. To one young guy who'd seemed more straightforward he'd said: "But I am not a dissident, I tell you. I'm a filmist." How that nice redhead had laughed. "You'll get around to it here, in time. Now just tell me what you see after I put these drops in your eyes." The top examiners had had their own interpreter, a biologist, Czech by birth but reared in Japan, whom he often caught studying him with her large, luminous eyes. Her son knew Gonchev's films and wanted his autograph. "On what—a potato?" Gonchev had said bitterly. "A potato?" the doctor readying him for a CAT-scan had said. "Now that's interesting. Why?"

Because I sometimes feel like one, ready for the peeling, Gonchev had said to the translator, adding: "You were born in a martyr country. Tell me. Wonderful, what's done here—to support us heroes. And to snag them." His mentors have begun introducing him to some. "But to exhibit us, circus-style—what do you say?"

To the waiting doctor she'd said swiftly, "The subject can't say why." To him she'd said, "The stuff of heroes—we can't make it in the lab." And in afterthought, with that sidelong quirk which brought her kind back to him with piercing force, "Of course not all the martyrs' biologicals would be the same."

He remembers the chill morning of his final "psychological workup," in a hospital so cogent that one could scarcely risk subjecting any doctor there to the same. "Cold out," he'd said to the receptionist. Even she had looked at him speculatively. Answering, after a pause: "Maybe."

At the outset he had told his interviewers, "I don't know Japanese. I am merely speaking it." And those who write him up talk of his neutral eye, "As if the man's not speaking really but merely seeing—and able to tell us so."

He hadn't understood their surprise. In their country, where the merest scrawls by new painters are regarded with awe, and "collage" is a common game, even sometimes present in what they call a "commercial," he feels at home. It's they, the psychologists, who are still depending on words, in a country gone visual. Just like his former place of employment, except that there they had done it for a purpose. Here visuality has just grown—enormous weeds, only waiting for someone to master them.

What they say of him as "the dissident Paul Gonchev"—should it worry him? "Mr. Gonchev is comfortable enough with the world to work at reinventing it—and actually lives nowhere."

Is Pfize now asleep, or pretending to be? Since last seen he's lost much of his likeness to the actor Tati. Maybe the resemblance always lay in that, wherever he is, he brings farce with him. Today he's wearing heavy lace-up boots and a lumberjacket, toned up by a Londonish knitted tie, under which he's eased open the white shirt. He blinks his eyes. "Don't you want to hear the good news?"

"Heard it before."

"You sure, Gonchev?"

"Permission from you to shoot a film for you on the country I've just left?"

"*Because* you left it."

They still believe the documents they have on him. If he isn't careful, they'll convince him. In the kindest way, do they brainwash too?

"To exchange one officialdom for another?"

"But that's why you people come. Freedom brings its own razz-matazz. You expect it."

"No. You people do."

Pfize is quiet for a second. "Know something, Gonchev? You're a dissident born. Even over the phone I can hear you shaking your head." He gets up from the chair to stretch. One sees the implied space he is used to. "I tell them—someday he could turn out one of the best we've got. He's only suffering from absentia. Like they do." He wheels, secret-agent style, his eyes screwed. Their latent cruelty could be natural. "You could fake such a film—isn't that what you do? Maybe use shots of the Montenegro terrain? We could import you the slides, the artifacts."

"You people. Importers in the blood."

"We imported you."

"I don't forget it."

"*And* your pictures."

Is this the enemy? With that edgy smile which seems to belong innately to this nation—as the bearer of both good and bad news?

"I won't be doing those anymore."

"No films? What'll you do with your time?"

"None like those." He walks to the rail. Not all these boats have them. From this vantage he can see in every direction—the city to the east and south, the western shore; he's the point of the *V*. Under him, the river flows north. When you're right in a city, you don't film it. When you're in a new country—what's he always done? You wait for the new news. On what to do with your time on earth.

"What's wrong with your old films?"

"Nothing. Not at the time."

"People loved them."

Nod, Gonchev. And nod again.

"So you won't say." Pfize is rooting in a breast pocket. "We all get depressed. I was—way down. What with one thing and another in the U.S. Before I hit on you."

Every man should have such an enemy. Who else to tell it to?

"My pictures lack agony," Gonchev says. "And only I can put it there. Now that I know."

There's Roko, coming up the dockside. Gonchev has tried to persuade her to wear colors, surprised at her offbeat choice of them in the scarves she sews for others, in the continual exchange of gifts that occupies Koreans. She herself will go only so far as today's white. With one slash of color—magenta, copper-green, or today's royal purple—on the eyelids. She's taken to painting those.

"Hah," Pfize says, loud enough for her to hear, "your little dish."

Once aboard, she'll slink past them into the cabin and stay there. Gonchev runs to meet her and escort her on deck, introducing her in Pfize's terms. "Wellesley—out of Waseda."

Pfize sweeps her hand to his lips, very grandee, but absentmindedly. In his left hand he has a snapshot he holds out to Gonchev. "Recognize her?"

He does, with a jump of the heart.

"Just wanted to be sure. She picked up a visa in Rome. We got on to it in London. Don't have the details yet." He puts the snapshot in Gonchev's limp hand.

"And—?" Gonchev asks with his eyes—the other one?

Pfize shakes his head silently. No sign of her. "Well, I'll be off." He bows again over Roko, this time with the cocked stance of a kindly uncle not above a spot of rape, then claps Gonchev on the shoulder, bends to his ear, and is gone. Leaving Roko to stare at Gonchev hunching over the photograph, with Pfize's whisper in his ear: "So remember, Gonchev. Go for the green, eh?"

And think blue.

.   .   .

The three bags revolve endlessly on the airport carousel. A watcher waiting for their owner to appear could assign them any metaphor he cared to: *Time Passing, Rotation Exemplified.* In the end, which comes every two minutes or so, they return to being three bags revolving: a cloth one whose double straps and soft sides shriek its Balkan origin, under a smeared label with only a large red *T* remaining; a mahogany leather satchel as smooth as a newborn piglet, tagged ROMA; and a suave black ostrich attaché case, tagless but surely British—a portable that only the carefree would have left unguarded. Whether its owner has grown more so these past months or merely oversophisticated from travel, the sole watcher, who is Gonchev, can't decide. But mulling this puzzle—and the hope that seeing her will solve it—keeps him sane.

He has been there for two hours, parked by the airline's liaison hostess, who'd indicated a bench close to the wall. He is still standing. He'd come alone, as fitting climax to the solitary public outings he has learned the habit of. All his American identities bulge in his wallet; he thinks of the rest of him as himself. And hopes he isn't wrong.

One other clump of baggage is on the far side of the carousel—a pair of skis and a pair of oars, bound together, and a gray knapsack—a neat biography. Its subject shortly comes down the ramp, a gaunt young fellow with hair shaved to the bone, in jeans and slung with carryalls. He is angrily petting a camera, which he now hangs carefully on a shoulder in the last space possible to him. Seeing Gonchev he smiles, shakes a fist at invisible authority, and goes for his oars and skis.

It is a relief to change problems. How the devil will the boy manage? But slowly hunching, sliding an arm up and over, a hand appearing here, there—surely he has three of them—he rises almost erect, grins at Gonchev, and totters off.

So Gonchev doesn't note the couple coming down the ramp until they are almost upon him—a red-lipped girl in sloshy khaki with hair tufted like a chickadee, and a sleek black-haired young man. Italian, maybe. He hasn't been watching for couples.

"Papa."

Holding her to his breast he parted the hair to show the white scar where the eight-year-old Laura had cut her scalp open in a sled spill, and pressed his lips to it.

149

. . .

To be a father again. To adore. To be adored. All in the sweet rhythms of the games of toss you and she used to play, you always stunting the energy of your ball. Now it's she who does that, you who plead for one more game. She's as feckless as she is self-confident, and with a competence to match. She is the carousel, and all her baggage hasn't yet been identified. Yet he has a daughter again.

When he last drove her off to business school in Tirana, she was a giggler, prancing after what "all the girls" said, or did, or wore. Now she is a womanly creature who loves him like a mother, a stage mother of the kind a director who has to use a child actor fears most—not a harridan, even pretty, and determined to make her boy a star. If Laura pushes him as smartly as she expects to wheel herself through the "contacts" that she predicts will bring her, first, a job in Wall Street, then a flat in the South Street Seaport development, from which she will take courses at "the Cooper Union," he may well have to resist.

Yet—she won't talk of home. Not of her mother, or of Klement above all. Not even at the airport, when she raised her gosling's head from his chest, rubbed her cheek on his stubble, which she has always loved to do, and clung to him, but in answer to his hoarse "Vuksica, your mother. For God's sake, say"—hacked out in their common language, a jumbled local patois mixed with Serbo-Croat, which he hadn't yet realized he was speaking—would only say in a glassy voice, "She's going on. She promised to."

In the taxi from the airport she lay back on the seat in her bright, broad-striped shirt, saying, "No, I'm not sick," just as she had done when the blood from the sled's runner trailed down her forehead. There is no blood on her this time. The imagined escapes are so different from the real ones.

The taxi whines on. They hold hands. She isn't looking at the city yet; of course it would be her third major one. Still, at her age he'd thought of the world as a great jumble of significant peaks, only waiting for his call. To have a child who's already had such privilege excites him. Yet he doesn't even know the details of how she has got here—this last year's nestling. He is sounding that abyss of parenthood into which all are said to fall, sooner or later. She sees him staring at her broad stripes. "It's a Rugby shirt," she says, half hoot, half sob. She casts him a wild look, but a ripe one. "I'm out of my depth, Papa. Forgive."

Dismissing the cab on the upper Drive, he walks her down the hill and along the low-walled ramparts that overlook the Boat Basin. He has to tell her about Roko. He hasn't dared dream she wouldn't be hostile, or at least aggrieved, but she nods and nods, even eagerly, saying, "Later, I'll explain too. Maybe everything."

He leads her forward as if the day itself is his protégé. Certain days in this town are like none he has seen anywhere. Ugly or beautiful, they have three seasons in them. Maybe the great mixed crowds here, tussling with the weather, invoke their own native atmospheres. And for him the river is fast becoming what trees had once been to her, but he is too shy to tell her so.

At the dock she stretched her arms to the village of houseboats and tethered small craft, even a sloop. The sun was setting behind a moody, industrial veil. Yet the water shimmied back and forth, talking to itself. You could never trust a river not to be lyric. "Imagine. Imagine," she said. "The new world." And turning: "Is it that for you?"

He took her hand. "I'm not out of my depth. But sometimes—I wish I were."

She's wearing rings unfamiliar to him, modest twists of gold, but unlike those she and her girlfriends had worn—all of the same few designs carried by the state stores. Since he last saw her there have been men in her life—maybe even before. A father doesn't like to scrutinize a daughter's body as he would a stranger's, but she is almost that now. And there are such signs of openness, and bloom. Touching the new rings, he lets her see that he's aware—and she responds, she will talk, indeed needs to. It's a little like a flirtation. Naming no names, she's informing him that he now has rivals.

As for the young man at the airport, who disappeared before he could be introduced, he's no lover—a word she uses without blush—nor yet just a seatmate. An Iranian princeling, cousin to a girlfriend at school with her in Tirana, whose family had given Laura a ticket to Rome—a first-class one that she'd managed to turn in for a coach ticket in Belgrade, using the surplus otherwise. He had helped her to sell a couple of heirlooms ("Which I will repay later," she said fiercely), had himself bought her the fancy attaché case ("It will help me get the job interview, he said"), and indeed wanted to marry her, if only because he was on his lonely way to be a student, in San Diego. Actually to hide, for there is a price on his head. "Like on my girlfriend's."

The family had left Tirana and was fortifying a remote Italian island, but he won't go. He carries a cane with a knife in it instead. "Fool. They would shoot." He's not as smart as his cousin the girlfriend, but he looks just like her.

"Like two otters," Laura says. "That hair, and the profile—who could marry it?" By this time she is laughing immoderately. A sober minute later: "But he is like me." How? "A refugee." And with that she fell mute.

Gonchev knows what the heirlooms must have been—a reliquary and a vestment, both from an archbishop ancestor of her mother's, on the Novy Sad side. Had Laura nicked them or been given them, and when? Nor has she said at what date she left the capital.

"It's getting chilly for anyone from Rome," he says. "No, that's right—you've come from London." Again he has that sense of abyss. "Anyway, the sun has set. Roko will be waiting. Let's go in." He stumbles over the patois they have been using, which is too peasant-rough for here. It helps to pick up her two big bags. In his left hand is "the capital," in his right hand that other edge of empire, Rome. Laura carries the "interview" case.

He remembers what his father was carrying when they entered Harbin—a patent-leather dressing case tied with a rope and a soiled oilcloth bundle—and his mother's disbelief when her aristocratic Russian lisp met blankness—"My tongue feels dead." No matter in what style, the crossover is always the same.

Laura has heard about that. She says, "I'm glad it's a boat."

Later, inside the houseboat, the three of them sit at table. Roko has made "a food celebration." There reigns that combined lull, of food still to be picked over and evening light from the windows, which Gonchev remembers as the haven hour for refugees anywhere. To this the houseboat adds a faint suggestion of motion, if only a trick of water and eye. The two girls have been shyly estimating each other, his daughter's Slavic lids almost as narrow as Roko's—but the two have clicked.

Now, wanting her friendship as well as her filial love, he says, "I too am a refugee"—and sees her puzzlement. He says it again, as he just had—in Japanese. Suddenly—once again, this is all he can speak.

Roko sorts it out for them. "No, it's not a mess," she says to Gonchev, who is hitting his head with his fist. "To her you'll speak the daughter language—you soon will again. And to me the Japanese. Until you can do both, I will translate." Fluttering her fingers at Laura's neck—the first time she has touched her—she says, "A translator hears only the words." And to both of them, in quick reprise, "Between us, the English may come back to him." And finally: "I know about words." The only boast he has ever heard from her.

Laura says in a rush, "I'll set about learning Japanese at once. I'm quick at languages." And to him: "I feel better already."

"She always does," he says, half-choked, to Roko, "soon as she sets about something."

Laura says in their patois, "How tired she must get—of the translating," and to his surprise, he can tell Roko in Japanese what Laura has said. And they all burst out laughing.

"It's nothing," Laura says. "At my business school there were three or four languages going, what with the new visitors—even Chinese," and is silent again.

"So it's opening up—the capital?" He sees again those raw, semiantique byways that smelled of beetroot and peddlar's steamy stalls and boot-dirt and regally ironed linen all at once—but never of argument.

Laura spat something.

"And closing in, she said," Roko says.

As darkness fell Laura was enchanted. "You can almost touch it," she says, reaching out. "I am touching it. New York." When she yawned, blinking, Roko led her to the third bunk, which was behind a partition. He could hear Roko's murmur and Laura's cadence; Roko must be showing her how to dispose of her clothes and shoes boat-style.

When he tiptoed in to say goodnight, Laura was already asleep. The bunk had been aired and the bedclothes were sweet-smelling. The lamp on the wall shook slightly. It's like a manger here, this light. But who is giving birth? And turning off the lamp shining full on Laura's face, he thinks: Vuksica.

In the night they hear sobbing. Roko goes to her, tactfully, with tea. Then back to bed. "She was repeating a name," Roko whispers. "The name of the girl on the island, maybe?" Gonchev, on elbow, staring at his clenched fists, doesn't answer. His flashlight casts a weird glow on his knuckles. The relationship between hand and eye is to him the most important one of the body. What is happening to that unity over here? Maybe Laura's right to dub herself a refugee from the beginning. He has always before moved himself onward in terms of what those knuckles did with what he saw, forming no other allegiance. Sloughing off the countries one by one.

Laura has fled something. She will embrace her new status as she will a career.

And Roko? He can't judge—except domestically. In bed, an American girl with the same geisha manners she has at table, serving him. In his ear, a professional voice, sans either criticism or humor, serving him. It's improbable that at bottom she has any further mystery. Yet as a man he is committed to the cliché that any woman has some. Roko functions like a clear glass prism, positioned so that the white light transmitted through it is always the same. Yet all prisms hold refractions of color, which appear when you turn them. He prefers not to mention his wife's name to her, and never has.

In the night they lie without thought of sex; the presence of a third makes them circumspect.

"She is daughterly," Roko says, as if he has asked her. "She will make money here. As a daughter should." The gap between him and this other person in the bunk suddenly yawns.

"And she is sisterly," Roko says. "She was grateful for the tea." The voice is a metronome but the person behind it can be wounded.

"We are three," he says, gathering her in, if only to hold. Waters away, another voice sounds—a buoy swung by its own currents. It did not say "Four."

The boat, washed by the entry of some craft, rocks now and then, reminding him of all the currents there are.

Laura wants to see and taste everything but remain a riddle to everyone except herself. Why?

"When you're a woman and smart, that's the best way."

"You learned that from your mother," Gonchev says. "So tell me, do you know the answer?"

"To what, Papa?"

"Her riddle. Did she tell you?"

"Oh, Papa, if you are a riddle it's because you cannot give the answer to people."

"So—" Gonchev says. "You'll have no trouble gaining your ambition, eh? What about trees—do you still stand under them?"

"No, they don't count here—the distances here do without them. But if I can't tell you what Mother is, I can tell you what she does, how she acts . . ."

Yes, Gonchev thinks, that's all you can do with an enigma.

"She sent you away, you know," Laura says. "She did that."

He doesn't answer.

"I don't know for sure why," Laura says, "but . . ."

"So you do know, Daughter—so say." He looks at his daughter. She's the only other one I'll accept that from.

"Because she knew you had to find your city," Laura says.

It's a shock to know that he himself is no riddle. "But sending is not finding."

Laura stares. "Papa. You were always sent, no? All your life."

True. He thinks of Harbin, his parents' trek, his whole career. "The pictures sent me. Or beckoned me."

She looks hostile enough now. "I don't understand art. It's only an excuse."

"For what?"

"I don't know," she says sullenly. "But I know it is one."

"Your mother—you never learned that from her."

"She can't know everything."

"And that's what you want?"

Laura is at the height of her beauty. Her smile is all healthy pearl and lip curve. "For now."

"What will your mother do?"

Laura looks at him as if he is an idiot. "When you send a loved person away—then you wait."

"For what?"

"I don't know. Maybe it makes you young again."

"Young," Gonchev says in a terrible voice. "So she's found a man."

"Oh, they find her."

That was true.

"But that's not what I meant." She is troubled. "When I was sent to the youth farm, when I came back I found Mother standing under trees. She said she was just practicing how it is to be me, her daughter, Papa—but I wasn't sure of it. And the next day she was careful to let me find her practicing a shotput. 'I'm being your brother today,' she said. But I didn't believe her. She doesn't like him very much."

"No," Gonchev says. How hard when that is the case with a child.

"It's all right, Papa," Laura says knowingly. "We don't have to like my brother. He's the kind that a country adores. And right now, we'll have to hope he's protecting her."

He could see the boy strutting that.

"Until she embarrasses him," Laura says. "And you know she will somehow."

"Then what?"

"Then what," Laura says. They stare at each other.

"Prison?" Gonchev says. But they often didn't bother with that over there. He puts his hand on his throat—at last acknowledging what they did do.

"No, not to his mother," Laura says. "My brother is just a—big muscle. Not a murderer."

"Not yet," his father says.

Laura accepts that. "No."

"So?"

"A kind of nursing home, that's what. Where one would kindly place one's mother. And sister, if I'd let him." She is pale.

"How did you get out, Laura? The American wouldn't tell me."

"Because he didn't know." She narrows her eyes at him. "He doesn't tell you everything."

He feels the innocence of a father before a daughter who has swollen into a woman maybe riper than he.

"I learned to fly," she says. That dimple on her left cheek—she has learned to suck in her smile so that the dimple smoothes.

"How—where did you find a machine?"

"At the airport."

Gonchev is proud. "Ah, my God, Laura. Better than a motorcycle, eh?" His fists tighten on its old handlebars, whose trek is now over forever. "But how did you get the extra fuel?"

Her head droops. "Not that kind of a machine." She goes to the rail of the boat and stares into the water.

"What other kind is there, that place?" No tractors, and, anyway, too slow. The guard's car? Barely possible. He sees it like a flash incident on film: the one guard asleep or dawdling inside the guardhouse, the other unmanned, a swift kick in the balls by a determined girl, who in one whirling motion sheds her skirt, whips it in the air like a bolo, knots it over the guard's head—and flees. But where? How?

"The pilot," she says. "I found—him." The tone she uses, she might be telling her father she is engaged.

Across the Hudson, oily black on a night like this, a thousand condominium apartments glimmer their hints of lives, helping even the stars here to join the bourgeoisie. He finds a voice, as fathers do. "The best kind."

She doesn't reply. He remembers that pilot—the merry squinch of his eyes. Where would he have taken her? Not to Belgrade. Some border-town provincial inn, dirty courtyard, but the sheets clean. He sees Vuksica's linen, blinding white in the sun, cool blue in the bedroom shade.

"Ah God, what it is to be émigrés. Pillar to post, pillar to post. And no logic to what you do."

Laura shook her head. "No, Papa. The best sort. My logic is—to be an émigré."

"They'll love you here," Gonchev said.

5

Night Letter

Vuksica. Ah, God, Vuksica. How long is it now? You must come. You imperial slut. It matters, what you've done. We always trusted that you would do something of the sort, didn't we? And I? So I have a woman. Yet in dreams I break all your bones with kisses, nightly here—and the one little bone "for real," as they say—the one that never goes crack.

Laura is always saying those two English words now. I hear her—the way one sees the light behind the pattern in the kaleidoscope—but I cannot yet reply. "Oh, Papa," she says, "you're not for real. Come down off Elsinore."

Your daughter—ours—is smart like a bourgeoise. She will never understand our medium—yours and mine. She pays lip service to the theater, of course—which she thinks of as "the stage." Film she used to hate, and of course we both knew why; it bound her young life. But now she is already more American than her friends, whom she calls her "group," and when they go to the "double features" she faithfully attends. She laughs at that rubbery word "yuppie," which means a young conformer who will go down all the approved money-paths, but her cheeks are as pink with that social delight as any of theirs, and contact lenses have turned her eyes blue. She has already informed me that "popcorn," a loud stuff they can crunch while watching film because the actors can't hear you even if your neighbors can, is good for the bowel.

Laura is good for me. She'll keep me on the path they've made for me here, until I can make my own—which I will, you'll see. But she's one of those blessed who will never see the light at the end of the tunnel. Not the light you and I are fated to see. Or even as her brother does. Who hasn't her shrewdness, but after a fashion does see his light. Which I fear—no, I know—will be an evil one. From which even you will not be safe.

Laura will be the safe one. She has found already a stock-market lover, whom she will assist at his operations while she learns them, and on the weekends they "backpack," a word I can't stop to explain, except to myself. I can hear most English words now, but not say them yet. Nobody knows how much I understand, even so, and I am not going to tell them.

So—each of our children has only the one dimension without the other. Our girl, the brain without the goal, and our boy, the appetite for never-never land, and a mind like a serf's. It's natural. They come from people like us. European parents admit such things. Not in this country. They defer to their genes.

You are what you are because of your beauty, which acts for you like an extra sense. I am what I am—well, you know why. My parents went from one small stepping-stone of reality to another, daily. One day starvation, next day in funds—and every day the minor humiliations, but the wonders, too. In each country they gathered the marvels, yet suffered those tender side-issues a native scarcely sees. What kept them going financially was their craftsmanship—my mother, her sewing, my father, only a mechanic at the piano, but he could supply showers of notes, like bundles of the grapes we couldn't afford. But what sustained them most was that they weren't musers. They had no time to brood. They were émigrés par excellence, of that kind. And given my serf grandfather perhaps—if one does credit the genes—almost bound to produce me? How do I know? I don't. You are the only one who understands that I don't know things—I see them.

For me—I had to find the hidden niches where our family music didn't go. My mother's sewing constructions were useful for that. Within the jiggings of the stitch and the loop, or her long wool thread winding its landscape, I could watch how scale makes space. Add to that all the languages that roughed and tickled my ears, and anyone would see how I had to escape beyond.

Oh, Vuksica, did we marry because we both saw that you would push me here? I think of that each day I wake. Not like a nagging. Like a hope. There's one love potion that you and I never brewed between us: guilt. That's why I think you will come—or that I must manage it. Maybe through that silly genius who thinks he alone got me out. Tomorrow, or one day, when I am maybe looking over the rail into the water at night, or sitting in one of those museum haunts which keep one close to film, the answer will come, the picture. Even though I have no crew to command, I will effect it. You will arrive. And I will speak English. How could I speak it now, when it is the only full tongue you and I shared?

Listen, Vuksica. My hidden niche—I've found it. I'm in it. Here. This country is an open secret that only I know. Which I can tell you, because you don't need to get it from words. God, at times how I hate languages. No old Lambretta—or even one of the new Hondas I sometimes seek out in a shop and then walk away from—will get me past those. Didn't I see that even on my wildest rides? But I'll do it yet. Again. As I always did.

Listen, my navel—this country is a palace the natives don't see. Falling apart, but with such grandeur. That's why I let them take me into every last corner of it. The West they call wool-ly—I will have to see why. The Christendoms where they worship snakes, they tell me. The faces that come by the thousands—and the streets. Those streets alone will be my salvation—but first, my studio. And how else would I study, except with that traveling box camera I was born with? It's not for nothing, you always said, that I came into the world with one farsighted eye, the other nearsighted, plus a little astigmatism to blend.

That's why I won't let them link me to their Hollywood. Who needs it? as they say here, or Laura does in quite another connection. Who needs it, Papa, what you did over there? If I'll go to Hollywood their way, she says, she'll go too, and show me what to do "moneywise." Maybe there's no Japanese word for that, Papa, she says, but we'll still make out. And my interpreter giggles. She and Laura get along well.

I broke into Serbo-Croat when Laura came—I thought she was your messenger. Then it stopped.

But I will be on keel again if you come. When you come. If I have to ask the silly genius—who knows I call him that—to shanghai you here too. Ah, that's a word I begin to love. *The Shanghai Gesture.* What films there were, when there could be titles like those. Some of the titles that are turning up now can be wonderful, but they exhaust the film before you get to it, like the circus barkers in those one-ringers we saw once over the Yugoslav border in that small Italian town—I don't remember the name.

Ah, borders—that's the gist of what goes on here—underground. They've lived without them, more than any of us. But they don't admit that, not at all. Or that the wilderness is the people, not the land. So they have a kind of double truth that they can solve only by pictures. They are like me—Americans. Only pictures satisfy.

Vuksica. This country is the palace of the moviemakers. Come. Follow me. Be my beloved spy.

And none of this could he write, did he write, except in his mind's eye.

6

On Tour

"Everybody's so angry here," Gonchev says to Roko after two months as a practicing dissident. "So little gaiety, really. Although according to the newspapers, thousands are dining out all across the continent."

Yet this simultaneity enchants him. Though not exclusive to the States, it has reached its apogee in them surely—everywhere restaurants and theaters swarming, and the money flowing like sweat. Gold seen everywhere on the women, but never, as in Europe, on the front teeth. At first much of the food tastes like brass to him. He is always being told that a freshness has gone from the fields, due to chemicals, but he is privately convinced that more likely this is because of the hot, anxious breath of the people, always worrying about what now might be above them in the clouds, or in the waters below. It is sometimes hard to find a tree in all its mature if naïve glory—or an unselfconscious woman, or a ripe old man. He still seeks out such men. In other times, of course, he had hoped to become one.

"Your air's full of newspaper breath," he told one crowd, not pleasing the reporters. "Helicopter stutter. Airplane chorale. And your language is going back to the alphabet." He chanted a list, although Roko had persuaded him to omit the accompanying pow-wow shuffle. Initials for everything in life that was big-time to them, "Government. USA. Museums. MoMA. Terrorists. IRA, PLO. The B.O."

As for the small things in life—he is told over and over that they are hoarding those; so much has disappeared. But that people are clinging on bravely, maybe to a child's fist, which, if pried open, can still display maybe a minute red top shaped like a planet or a pear.

What it comes down to is that they really want him to tell them about their lives—while they are unwittingly telling him just that.

At the end of his speeches, clicking his heels for their attention, he always tells them the same thing. "It's not me who's dissident."

And no matter what, there is always a round of applause.

A number of museums took him up with gusto, billing him as the expert on cities-by-picture, or lumping him in with the architects, which guaranteed more respect. By which they mean response. Those societies that focused on the word—authors and poets—tended to ignore him altogether, as not their brand of dissident. Organizations concerned with freedom had him appear once, as a curiosity. Theater wings and dramatists' guilds were friendly but frankly waiting on performance to come, before they booked. A girl in one of those offices, a programs director, was very helpful to Laura, who had dragged him there. "His act—people do better around town if they've been in prison. Or have maybe a manifesto in their credits. You should get him on one of those." Probably he would do best in the universities, she added. "Where people are still uninformed."

Newspaper reporters are still the most familiar with his situation as a government-sponsored dissident-at-large. On the museum circuit he now and then sees Flaherty, who has been transferred to his paper's cultural desk. "Born in Hell's Kitchen, went to church to the Jesuits, and to a college of chiropractery—and my mom is half Jewish," he said. "I'm the most all-around cultivated guy they got." He nodded at Roko. "So how's he doing? As a professional émigré. Bet they never seen one like him before."

"I am like a dog on show," Gonchev said. "They mistake my howls for speech."

"Nice work if you can get it" Flaherty crooned, about to fly.

"But my daily stint has nothing to do with my reflections."

Flaherty stopped dead. "Welcome to the common lot." Then: "I'll report that to the other dogs."

A curator intervened, twitching his bow tie at Flaherty, who was tieless and in a sweater the very color of anonymity. After their confab, Flaherty turned to Gonchev. "He seems to think you're being misunderstood, um—but, ah, very fertilely. In plain talk, you're a wow, Gonchie. What you been saying lately? Still on the city, I hear."

Flaherty hadn't waited for reply but had peered into the projection room, where a film of Gonchev's was mounted around-the-clock, then at some of the prose placarded on the walls. Some statements were Gonchev's own answers to questions at appearances, others were the museum's, all in a robust lettering styled like clenched fists. "Gives you confidence, wish they'd print my stuff like that," Flaherty said, humping off with a good-bye wave. Roko ran after him with Gonchev's question. "He wants to know where to get a sweater that dog-khaki color."

Flaherty gave him the finger. "Won't ask which end of the dog. Tell him to try two nights out in Mexico City, then the wrong cycle at the launderette."

At the museum appearances, where either slides from Gonchev's films or full showings are arranged for him, on themes attuned to the arranger's sympathies, he has merely to appear afterward with the canapés and engage in his brand of nontalk. He grows adroit at this, and, according to Laura, at appearing sincere.

"I am sincere!" To her he can shout.

"All right, then. At appearing as sincere as you are. Not everybody can do that."

When first introduced, suave and frowning, and in his suede jacket now so rubbed that it might be sincerity's skin, he is fine. Later, he may have to restrain himself from pinching the buttock, saucy or huge, of any female who finally turns from his unproductive lack of talk. Sometimes he wonders what Roko is saying to them.

Buttocks, articulate in any lingo, are what get to him. Maybe a mauve velvet, round as a pillow, or a slim black-trousered pedestal to a jacket and a white stock. What Laura, applied to, defined as braid, a new-old fancy scrawling itself these days on women's clothing anywhere from tits to back pockets, sets him wild. It's my kind of writing, he thinks. What the other kinds are he has never considered. Meanwhile, faces can be avoided for this convenient symphony of backsides. Faces talk. And have to be talked back to.

When he does so of an evening, or a dusky artistic afternoon, it's with an anarchy that has come to be expected of him. Maybe they don't know that in European men, sexual energy is often allied to political anarchy, sometimes interchangeably. In Middle and Eastern Europeans especially. Look at Danilo.

In New York what he can talk to people about, if really pressed, is their city. Which has, after all, so welcomed a man sent them spuriously. A city about which he seems to know more and more because of not being normally articulate, and in the lazy fopdom of having no steady work.

He speaks in a rush that exhausts and maddens any interpreters substituting for Roko. She is used to it, and by now could probably deliver his tirades herself; instead, she reports them in a pearly calm, her voice a white musical noise.

"A great city has to be mysterious," he tells them one night. "Must continue to be. Only do that, and you will keep the balance." Whereas every newspaper in town blasts the city's corruptions, until even the cowed subway riders grow sick of them, though fewer enter the parks except under the protection of a dog. "And your charity," he says wickedly, "so impersonal. Even when it doesn't work." Any government agency called spews recordings requiring more phone calls. "A soup kitchen talks." In his heart he might only be making the cry of an artist out of touch with his own magic and itching with fear that it might not return.

"Your city's getting easier and easier to understand," he tells them. "Even by its dolts." And so is their country? This he can't yet say. "But for any city great in its day, that's always been the end. Such cities always die. Leaving large phrases behind them. Like . . . that they weren't built in a day." Or that you need only to see them, then die.

Once, early on here, in an outlying suburb, he said something of the sort. A cloud of unease settled over the camp chairs, as if all in the hall had been struck by earache. Here and there eyes squinted but no one spoke. Back in the car, his well-meaning escort, a volunteer from the UN, explained that "these people out here" were socially on the rise. To them rising was patriotism itself. He had bad-mouthed what there was to rise to. "A city might be to hate, yes. But not by a foreigner." To a born alien like him this is the oldest lesson; how could he have lapsed from that bitter inculcation? And so soon?

She had patted his knee and accepted his muttered "I forgot" with the abstract ease of a woman in the driver's seat. "Feeling your freedom?"

So clinching for him what had been exposed to him in his first days; their freedom here carries a strong dose of cant. "Cheap at the price," he said, and was rewarded with a smile.

But in New York itself he can be laughed at, or quarreled with. One night a man did shout from the back row, "Rome's still on the map!" Gonchev half hoped for someone to add, "And Paris!" In which case would he have said, "I have never been?" Or "Yes, I heard Rachmaninoff there?" For it has occurred to him that here, absolved of his childhood, he might find out for sure. But no one spoke.

They waited for him to answer the heckler. "Oh yes," he said, meaning only that maybe his own logic is wrong—for the short run. "But this city isn't built to be ancient, is it? Maybe cities no longer are." In spirit he meant, not in materials. He couldn't be sure how Roko translated. But no one else heckled.

When she and he were home he said: "I'd forgotten. How a city like this gives every citizen his own castle. Even the bum in the alley, squeezing out his sleep. How imperial they all are here. Everyone an emperor, Roko. *Hai.*"

She could lie on the waterbed without causing a crinkle in the water. And had the translator's lack of intonation. "And empress."

He could not really talk to her, he thought.

"Ah, I am only getting back at them," he told Laura later. "Not just that audience. All of them. Want to know why?"

"Why?" Laura had a new manicure. Pinker. But must she scan it?

167

"I am being swallowed up by observation." He shouted it—what he should have shouted to those faces in the Citicorp church, whose pale, nonsectarian wood was like this country, open to anything. "By having to observe." Foolishly or not. And by being observed also. He is losing his personality to these audiences. But how explain this, in the gibberish she and he have to talk?

"Oh, Paul," his daughter said, untroubled. "But that *is* you."

And here was a tone he recognized. His heart skipped. Whom had she been talking to? Or corresponding with? "She won't ever give you the satisfaction," Vuksica's women friends had said of her. "The satisfaction of—satisfaction. But you learn to love her for that as well." But Laura won't talk of her mother these days.

"So it's 'Paul' now," he managed to grumble. "No more 'Papa.' "

Laura's shrug reminded him that it was time. "And we are émigrés, after all. Derek says it is our duty to observe. Or did he say 'destiny'?"

"Not duty, if I know Derek."

She grinned. They were father and daughter again.

"Maybe every émigré is a—half a dissident. Tell that to your mother." To keep the possibility of messages he will say anything. Even if now that he has said this, it begins to be true.

His daughter kissed him good-bye. "Oh no, Paul—Papa. I'm not. Not me."

But the very next evening she came running, to say that a lecture agency wanted to handle all his nongovernment bookings at much-increased fees. He would have enough money to live on for years. "Years and years."

This is an English phrase he already knows well—and dreads. "And where will I be living?" he said, in the jargon they now always spoke together. "And with who?"

" 'Where' is no problem for you," she said, steely-eyed. "Or never was—since I hear about you." For she was afraid even now that he wouldn't settle down—that somehow he would again escape. "As for 'who'—you are living with someone."

When he makes the gesture a man might make under such circumstances, she is furious with him. For Roko is in the room.

"She doesn't know Serbo-Croat," he says. At least she never interrupted when he and his daughter conversed.

"Women are natural linguists," his daughter said.

But Roko knows her place even so. She might well have her own mystery, even if one not to his taste. Her passion for that college of hers, for instance—because it has made her more Western. A woman can be made ridiculous by such leftover school spirit, if kept too long. Often at colleges he meets these middle-aged sweethearts of some brick-and-lawn Eden where they had passed their angel time. "At night," he teases Roko, "do they stand up in bed after prayers to cheer university?"

His only confidantes these days are women. Laura, Roko, even the agent in California, who now and then phones. That is not the same as confiding in the one woman of one's choice. What he needs is a man in his life. Or a man outside it? All the men on his circuit are in the same boat as he, or else are organizers for some cause. Causes. One cause makes a hero. Several make a circuit.

What he needs is a spy. Not a Pfize. A paid one. To whom he, Gonchev, would still be a rebel, even a madman. To whom he would still be a man on his own.

Oh, Gonchev, remember? Those deferently veiled glances, that *put-put* of attention, yards behind? That speaking silence, like gunfire withheld?

What an anchorage was a spy.

He does better when traveling. And best in the provinces. There, away from the purity of planes, that international cleanliness, a European can salve his wounds with the sight of that amazing slovenliness which mass transportation had brought to the West. In Europe he'd already glimpsed such sights in what they call pop art here, and had even been sent slides of the actual disorder of the American landscape. At the time he had been at some loss as to how to make use of what had seemed random blight, or else a weird unraveling of the domestic urge.

Now, in a car or a train, he can glide by within yards of these landslides of dead machines turned to bronze by the fingering sun, and watch that gold orb go down behind umber hills of crusted garbage, while at the train window the mournful back ends of towns slip by in moleskin light. Followed by the shantytowns.

Surely these cannot be American habitations—these dim sheds huddled so near the fortress tanks of industry? Yet as one draws away one catches telltale flecks of humanity, laundry, red and white as flags, blue as the ocean, and virtuous white. What a witty country, to have touted this as its art. Or what a brave one, to make a civilization up-front of what foundered here. For a civilization it is, rushing by him without compromise.

Whether the show is valiant or depraved, against it the neat station-masters' plots of his railway youth seem child's play. Or the sleazy train dirt of Russia, with its noncarbolic stinks. Or slums in the Asia he knows. Or has only heard of. India's flesh-rubble. Manila's sunny sores. None had made such a proud philosophy out of its underside—or not without invoking religion as excuse. Or had gone even further, into this cool, nonsectarian rationale of waste?

Repetition's the key, he thinks, jolting along. To how a nation deals with its numbers, and its space. So—my Japan, doomed to neatness, even in the psyche. So—China, teetering along on feet still bound by the thongs of population, saving every pebble, whether rich or poor, and in the most rigorous domestic enclave the world has seen, every twelve hours offering its nightsoil to the stars.

What he sees nibbling everywhere at the trackside rear end of America are the movers, the moving companies, the blanked-up warehouses with lines of vans waiting, and on the roadways, their rolling stock. In a kind of kinship he begins to learn the names of these aliens who have made good. This is his first American spoken in public. "Sullivan Movers, Roseland, Luttenberg, Midland, Mayflower," he chants at his delighted audiences, changing the names as the thruways change with his itinerary, sometimes even hitting on a local van company—"Santino" (a man shouts: "My father-in-law works for them!"). Gonchev instructs Roko to say for him: "This is my Indian chant," while he makes a pow-wow noise on his mouth, with the cup of his hand. "Clown," Laura said when she heard. Roko, waiting neutrally, said nothing.

As he and she drive in hired cars from city to city—for in the middle of the country the college towns grew close enough to do that—it seems to him more and more that these trucks, silent at the side of their headquarters, or groaning past his car, are what is moving, not him.

What he looks for are the ignored marshlands that fringe the railway sidings. Thin gray hedges and spindly trees drawn with chalk, surely, mud, and gravel soil, traces of snow or black scum swapping the seasons in an oil pool, and the sky noncommittal above. The lost parts of Europe were like this too: cheap, melancholy wastes that no one ever pointed to.

Repetition. As all visual technicians agreed: What the eye had, the mind grew to accept. Accept it then, Gonchev: this telephone-pole no-man's-land your boyhood was always kind of a sucker for—because the phone calls, like you, are only passing through. Hope to accept—but not to love.

The lost parts of Europe. Isn't a man like him one of them? Asleep, he can't dream. Wide awake, he sees a house and its enclosure run before him, not as a continuity but as a succession of stills, replacing each other in the flickering way that first imitated what goes on in a man's eye and brain. The house is all brown and white now, as it had been before a hand painted trellises on its south wall. The garden would be sepia; all that improbable green must be frozen now. Vuksica herself is nowhere to be seen. The facade of the house, curved in front like a breast, still presents the housewifery behind which she had hid—a woman who would no longer act for him on film but at last had acted, from her house?

Driving at Roko's side when it is her turn at the wheel, he watches the two landscapes unroll, the one where he is and the one that will not let itself be dreamt.

"What?" Roko says.

"Nothing."

They turn to the left, into a motel.

That night he dreams about the house. It is only a setting now. All sets not in use look abandoned by the craft that has made them. They wait to be vitalized. It would not be easy to film from such a distance, and with no camera of any known make. But if any director could plot a film literally with his own flesh and intents, wasn't it he? Hadn't his life to date been a rehearsal for this, only running the takes over and over? Examine the house, its exits and entrances. A set is made a certain way, for manifold uses. Or his always were, not counting the costs.

In the middle of the night, in a Holiday Inn in a town called Delaware, although it is in Ohio—or is it Illinois?—Gonchev sits straight up in bed. "All your dreams are scripts, Paul," he hears his wife say. "Now recognize your real sensations."

One slept without a pajama top in this warm cage of a room that comes to meet one no matter how many miles on, in faithful rendezvous. The linen is of a certain same texture, the pillows reachable; all lamps and glass-topped tables are in their appointed places. There is that odor of slightly disinfectant almond, as if a woman grown familiar to you only by her overstrong scent has just left. You envision meeting her some-day, if only to ask her to change it, but you are aware that this may not occur. Such irritants often lodged in one's own home; when the wind blew from a certain direction over the wood being burned in the tobacco-curing, his and Vuksica's house smelled heavily of tar. But there these samenesses became part of the hominess of home.

At his side Roko sleeps like the amahs he used to see in Asia, cast down on a doorsill into a depth that repaired their working-hours humility. It is the most Oriental thing about this Western-educated girl. She never snores, but she never awakens either, to succor his night terrors or be succored for her own, as Vuksica would have done. And this recumbent figure—not blamable, simply there—is now part of the script.

Can a motel room become home merely because it is familiar, because it reappears? Bringing sensations one twitches to, has a fund of knowl-edge on?

Could a country?

He has been by turns subjugated by the countries of his past and energized by them, afterward even assaulted by memories of special qualities he might at times even miss. But it has never occurred to him to love them out of duty or need. Or thrall. They have been, one after the other, like dragons he has had to meet, not to kill but to tame. A home was meanwhile elected by circumstance, or by the woman one lived with. Or by a mild interest: Sa-ay, what about a houseboat?

From birth he has been taught to inhabit a country through work, and to escape any binding emotional injury.

But here he is vulnerable. Like a man on the dole, fattening on those needs he can afford. Idle hands to feel up the girls at the pub, tongue to train to talk—he who has never had time for language. Hours to meditate. And a tour laid on, with mail following him like a moveable Barmecide's feast: Dear Mr. G., Want to document how our whales spew up springtime? Look in on our outfit when you get to the Coast. . . . Sir, We at a newly endowed laboratory are interested in your aphasia and offer all our resources. Will you be our guest guinea pig, when you get back? . . .

Consider hard offers only, Laura warned. Roko translates them all equally and when pressed for "American advice," shrugs: "It's like coupons. Tear up. Use." Derek advised "Settle for the scenery," and gave him a tip on discount sunglasses.

Can't they understand that he is awash in their freedoms, which are scattered like itching powder everywhere? As for tax deductions, traffic violations, leashing your dog, and cleaning up after it with what the hardware stores list as a "poodie-pan"—yes, they can be fractious about those. And about murder, if it is sufficiently public. Or thievery, if sufficiently large. But in the decision realms of the spirit, he has a suspicion, both he and they are afloat in the anonymity of the self-governed. Buoyed up by that life-belt dogma: Be Happy.

As for manners, no universal code except perhaps that a man can't pee discreetly anywhere in the open—even in the boondocks, Derek had warned. Laura, giggling "That's to help make them not the boondocks," had been for a moment so painfully like her mother that he almost can tolerate her American office garb of wing collar, shrunken tie, and metal-tipped shoes shaped like World War I gunboats. All designed, she said, to look so conservative that after the office, in the dives she and Derek go to, she could be taken for a radical.

"What's the diff, half the office will be there," Derek had said gloomily. They seem to Gonchev a couple as neatly trapped as the wildfowl that the mountain people around Elsinore caught and linked to each other with leg gyves. As the evening waxed, Derek would croak slyly behind his hand, as if the devil were listening, "Gotta new place. Want to go?" And she would give that all-American cry which came so lopsidedly from her soft Mediterranean mouth—"Sa-ay. Let's."

In his notebook that night he had written, lately having adopted phonetics: *Bun dox:* place to go if you wish to see the inside of a country jail. *Pee:* to expose yourself. *Wutz thuh dif:* to set up your own boundaries.

There was a comforting fug of leftover food in the room, remains of lobster tails from last night's trays, shared after his appearance at a local college. The motel manager himself had brought the trays—a wide, tremulous man who looked as if he had dressed for the occasion, his large nose in strict line with his flowing tie. He had fussed with the pipkins holding the melted sauce. "Butter. Not oleo." They had complimented him on the lobster tails, unusual on most motel chain's all-too-familiar menus. His own idea, he said. "We're very close to culture here."

His wife, a housekeeper for the college, brought home all the notices. And what language, might he ask, was the mister speaking? "Japanese," Roko said.

"Imagine. And you yourself speak English so well." This town was the crossroads of the nation; he wouldn't want to bring up his boys anywhere else—four of them, one girl. Delicately presenting the check to sign, he slid in his personal guestbook, which Gonchev and Roko each inscribed, under the names of the head actor of a dance troupe from Texarkana and a professor of otolaryngology from Chicago. "And by request," he said, his tie expanding, he would like to ask the mister his opinion. Here the three of them were, practically a United Nations, at his inn. Which was his own, incidentally. Maybe they had noticed the sign, spelled Hollyday's Inn, which was his name—the college had promised to be on his side if any court case was brought by the Holiday Inn chain. "And the lady here might like to know that the School of Social Work has adopted a Viet family, totally."

"What is the question?" Roko had said.

He always asked it of a foreign guest. Didn't they think the States the most original country the world had ever known? And all of them had said yes—so far.

"Tell him yes," Gonchev had said. "Especially his sign."

Outside now the sky is growing light over the morning graces of the kind of small, intermediate city he is getting to know well. Pastoral tricks in the trees, last night's rain glistening on the abandoned railroad track behind the telephone company, early meeting of minds in the coffee shop, over "home-baked" doughnuts bearing on their clear wrap a legend of chemical ingredients as sinisterly appealing as any fairy-tale incantation.

Dawn's confusion is rising in the most orderly fashion, as in any country he has ever been in. The classic repetitions of daily life are occurring as winsomely and banally as anywhere—tugging at the nostalgias, flicking the buried grudges, pulling out the organ stops of horror, biting at a mama's nipples or a girl's. Everybody knows the responses, but as in church, the people who ask aren't always the same as those who get answered. He would bet there was many a divergent moral code to be found for the digging. Only, this country had been founded on mixture, so the din is awful.

Or awesome? There being a distinction, as Roko had explained.

Once he was back in New York, Laura would be pressing him again to begin making application for citizenship. So far he'd put her off, last time saying that until he had been mugged in the subway he wouldn't qualify.

"Let him drag his feet," Derek had said pacifically. "He has to acquire residence anyway."

"But that would take him a long time," Gonchev said.

"Five years."

"No, maybe a lifetime. To get citizenship by birth alone is irresponsible."

Gonchev had only just thought of that but found it true. "Ideally, citizenship should come only on the deathbed." He relented. "Or, since that might be difficult—in stages, according to age. Meanwhile—one has passports." That was more or less what he had done. Technically he had been at times a Russian, a Japanese, and once an Austrian, but in his head he had never been anybody's citizen for the asking.

The most original country in the world, or city, or village—isn't it the one where you find yourself? Or hadn't it better be?

This bed for instance, very comfortable in itself. And for extra, if you put a dollar in a slot at its head—he can see where "25¢" has long since been crossed out—it will jiggle you like a masseur. Or a carnival roundabout. Or a woman.

This country. How its freedoms can lock you in. The whole country is a "hard" offering. Be very careful, Gonchev. Consider the whole poodie-pie.

How good after all that Roko sleeps on so. Now he can awaken her in a way he never has before. At the room's one window a spring day is breaking; the clock says five. A car parked with its nose pointed at the next window is having trouble starting up; Gonchev can see the motorist's face, his eyes bulging abstractedly as the motor whines and dies. Now its driver waits a bit, in order not to flood it. The room light is still on here. Gonchev should get up from his warm, versatile nest and pull down the blind. But he is too comfortable. In a free country there are always these dilemmas.

Carefully, Gonchev inched a hand into the wallet on his bedside table, took out a dollar, and slipped it into the slot.

On tour, at times he is the single attraction, especially in the smaller colleges. In such districts people who had nothing to do with academia, or politics either, might drive over to see what was on show, not who. And a movie man was almost a movie. He is refreshed by these shrewd farm wives who are undertaking the education of "the community," and by their lagging, tanned husbands. Those sit like agriculture itself in the plaid sportsshirts put on for the occasion. The town merchants of seeds and hardware confab in a corner, ombudsmen charged with judging the speaker "from a business point of view." Or there might be the one or two "liberals," malcontents of the region, often in their hale eighties.

Why has the crowd come? Mainly to see each other. What can they get out of someone like him? They soon tell him. "This is the real country you're seeing." And they are proudly showing it to him. After which they might have some further local function, politely hidden from the stranger. After his talk, groups tend to melt away as he approaches them. Why? A host professor once enlightened him. "They're writing you off."

"And so are you, Professor," Gonchev said in Japanese when the phrase had been explained. "No, Roko, leave that out. Just tell him it reminds me of my old committee days. And I'm enjoying it."

But at other times he has to join up with some of his fellow travelers on what Flaherty called "the freedom racket," arguing the term both as a reporter and an Irishman. "Sure and you have to have it, before you can badmouth it. The Jesuit fathers taught me early that just saying that a thing is a paradox doesn't let you off examining it." Flaherty might do a column on just that. "On the deification of anybody on the run from the right wrong governments—only no Irishman, or Arab, need apply. And the crucifixion of any poor slob who dares to say so."

What did he see in Gonchev that made him feel free to say these things to him? Had he heard of Pfize? "Let's have a beef on it, Paul. When you get back. Let me know—hmm—how the wind blows." He went off cocking his cap. He had ferreted out that Gonchev kept an idiom book.

"I don't see this man, Flaherty, as any trustworthy guide," Gonchev wrote, reporting this to Danilo, "on what he calls ideological America. Though I shall keep him on the string. He may be testing the ideology of P.G. But I wouldn't mind meeting up with a Jesuit father." For these letters, which he somehow wants to keep from Roko, he has found a scribe at the Nippon Club—a young Japanese who is, as a matter of fact, a Catholic.

One can't live forever on the nerve-edge of politics, he tells Danilo—not as Gonchev and his kind are expected to do here. For one thing, he hasn't the background. And not only in knowledge. "I don't know the attitudes they expect. For there are correct ones, you may know, even for martyrs. Since I am not one, I don't do very well." Luckily when he goes wrong, not knowing the dogma, they think him naïve, or even sardonic. "Or that I am still suffering the effects of incarceration in that country, if not in jail."

They are making him into a one-dimensional person. "As they do here with all the dissidents."

Men and women of talent, who were now expected to have only one string to their bow—and one subject for their works. All the more so because they are feted for their sufferings. Why should they then recover from their holocausts, partly personal though these might be? For some had left families behind—wives and children—and had done this willingly. He would never have done this on his own—which may be why he is here. But how can they strut so on the podiums, extruding their whole lives across the footlights like virtue itself? Better to be a man without a country—and with no politics.

He has had to see his fellow notables at their own performances to understand them better—Middle Europeans or Russians, most of them, for whom these readings and declaimings are rote, or even apogee. Male or female, they are all Jeanne d'Arcs of the free word. They would burn for that, these proud dissidents, it was explained to him—and more especially so if the words were theirs.

"Wouldn't you burn for the right to do true films as you see it—your films?" one of them said. "Your cities?"

Maybe he would—he isn't sure. Most films here were usually the "truth" of more than one person. Which diluted things, surely, even for those in control. He had tried to cleave as much as possible to the visual—which was truth enough for him. And how could you falsify a city anyway—a place that has everything at one time and is all things to all men?

Yet there was one city, still unseen, for which only a vision still to fall on him would do. Would he burn for it?—to get it right?

He turns to the full table around which his fellows are assembled, in what here is called the Green Room. There is always a backstage room of sorts and one is almost always served a pre-lecture whisky, as now. Usually Gonchev appears at least in duo on the larger circuits, since he is both an oddity as to subject and relatively unknown.

Tonight is a top event, in celebration of exiles everywhere—and of one man, a black still imprisoned, in particular. Gonchev does not know the prison history of any of the five dissidents assembled in that man's honor, all veterans of such proceedings as this, although several are said to suffer from ailments related to their past experiences—asthma, kidney trouble, heart. In his own mind he makes himself assign the causes of injury—foul cells, beatings, the battered emotions of men torn from their rightful places—and marvels that he is here with them, together in this high-candlepower light.

Of the two women, the elder, a poet still resident in her homeland, has circulated internationally for years, presumably with the approval of her government. Now and then in tandem with the true exiles there are special visitors like these, their freedom to move guaranteed by fame. Or somewhere a buried usefulness? If he ever sees Pfize again, he might ask. The other woman, the youngest here, recently released from a prison term served for having joined a protest by musicians barred from performance, is said to have skirted tuberculosis inside. Now they all look as seasonably healthy as any ordinary group of their respective ages.

The oldest, a white-haired Croat in his eighties who never speaks except when addressed, has been in the United States nearly half his lifetime and perhaps shouldn't have been included at all. Probably he is willing to go anywhere without fee. Tonight everyone is appearing gratis, except for the fee one always got, the réclame. That being what keeps some on the circuit? For although it is possible to fade out from such busy-beeing, trusting only to one's work to keep one going, on the circuit one risks being left uninvited if either one's art or one's audience declines. Or, worst of all, if one's very dissidence is no longer to the point.

Tonight almost all are literary personalities—verbalists are naturally the most drawn upon. He notices that the younger woman, dressed in black, isn't drinking; all the men are, including Gonchev. The elder woman carries her own flask and comforts herself like the prima donna she is, in snakeskin leggings and sequin-and-pearl-encrusted boots. She catches him looking at them and smiles, nudging him to look at the young girl. "I wore black once," she said.

On Gonchev's right, his interlocutor still presses him: Wouldn't Gonchev burn to keep the art of film free?

This man, a critic met before in Gonchev's rounds, has his clique in every university café and, he boasts, his "girl Friday" in most of them, and Saturday and Sunday girls too. "One does best with women by the week." Perhaps he asks the same question of his girls, in a form more suited to the sexual arts, such as: Wouldn't they burn to keep their sexual freedom—free to all?

Gonchev catches the others at table looking quizzically at him and his neighbor. That there are echelons of personal honor—not political— among them he has no doubt. As well as stages of American development he isn't sure of. After how many years here did a dissident become merely an exile—to himself or herself, as well as to others? And what if one became a citizen? Some, like the old Croat, who is so rightist that some podiums won't tolerate him, had been "exiles" from the first; for them "dissidence," a modern term entirely, means "the left."

And aside from the political, how far left or right was a dissident on all the other issues of life? Laura maintained that most of the Central European and Russian men were not only womanizers but blatantly antifeminist, whether or not they had wives or companions here. And almost all of them, she had pointed out from her newfound "American" stance, were ethnic chauvinists to an almost naïve degree.

It's true, there are usually no blacks on the circuit he travels. And none in the Green Room tonight, though one is scheduled onstage. The South Africans, for instance, kept to themselves and, except for the most general colloquium, had another set of claques entirely. Meanwhile Gonchev, cashing a check today, had stood on line with an irritable Russian compatriot, a fine poet with a bladder ailment, who had complained aloud that there were too many slow blacks employed by American banks.

Yet how could Gonchev criticize, with no prison epaulettes to his credit, and having arrived here as he had?

He is also the only one with a translator. He sees that Roko is not about to help him on the question just asked. At certain times she no longer prompts him, and not from deference or because of his growing ease. He has an idea she might be building up her own personality, toward what end he can't say.

Meanwhile, his amateur status among these others, and above all his lack of national conviction, give him powers of observation they mightn't have. Or have ceded up. To say nothing of his trade, always so collaborative.

If I were going to burn for the sake of a conviction, Gonchev thinks, wouldn't I want to do it at home? If I had a home. What use to burn here, in this country? One need only talk.

How his arms ache for a camera. I could show it all. I could show you, my talky neighbor, with your fat Ukrainian belly, stuffed like a *lobster Americaine* with what Laura calls goodies, and your curly, not prison-shaved, head. A silent movie is what I would make of you. But I have to answer you. In this land of film glory, the curse laid on me is that I have to speak.

None of the people know Japanese. All of them speak English. Several are Russian, like his fat neighbor. The man is really a butterball.

"You would burn better than me," Gonchev says.

The burst of laughter around the table stuns him—he is so inured to the interval of Roko.

For a moment he doesn't know what he can have done. Then the older woman says slyly, "So he speaks Russian, eh?" Her irises are as gray as her boots. "So you speak Russian, master. In a pre-Revolution accent, I must say."

This time Roko comes to his rescue. "He had five languages once. Russian, English, Japanese, French, Italian." The hobgoblin dialect he and Laura exchanged was always ignored. "But so far, the speaking amnesia has affected all but the Japanese."

The young woman in black leans toward him, murmuring softly two lines from Pushkin that a Russian child would likely know, even one in Kyoto. "You understand?"

He nods.

"Can you answer? In Russian?" Her eyes are blue, and not sly.

His own are wet. He tries but cannot spit out the Russian. "Russian was my other childhood tongue," he says, in the faultless singsong the monks had taught him—and bursts into tears.

"See what you've done, Balabansky," the man with the bad bladder says to the fat one. "But he's a critic, Gonchev. They're always for burning. When he's around, we all watch the soles of our feet." His anglicized Russian is liquid, easy; and Gonchev, who understands but still can't reply, smiles gratefully at him. Roko, who has surely seen that Gonchev understood the man, goes on interpreting anyway, like a nurse with a too rapidly growing child, who can't yet decide what her attitude to this should be.

The two remaining men, a tall, blond Pole and a gypsyish Czech, nudge each other over this handmaiden in her stage costume of black tights, whose clipped onyx hair catches any light. *"Parla Italiano?"* one of them says to her, and when she shakes her head, the other says to him in that language, "Do you suppose she translates for him at night?"

Gonchev, who understands that too, wants to give them the finger, but they aren't looking at him. Nobody is. The signal to go onstage has just been given. But as they all ready themselves to file out, they regard him for a minute, heads cocked, brows furrowed, as one does an animal in a cage. As if he is the prisoner.

A black man, the chief celebrant of the evening, is already on stage. He is here in lieu of brothers still behind bars, and maybe will return there himself; he has no time to waste. He gets the longest round of applause, but that is not why Gonchev envies him. He speaks no language that anybody on the platform, or probably in the audience, can reply to in kind. Yet all can follow him. His skin, sweating platinum drops under the gymnasium's lamps, speaks for him. For the moment, they are all in his film.

The following morning, Gonchev leaves the hotel alone as soon as the shops open. The town, Milwaukee, was described to him as a "German" one, and the draft beer is indeed superior. He is used to towns being classified in some such fashion all over America, although some fought their labels as hard as others courted them. This too he likes. Even if, as in any country, all towns resemble one another more than not, in the States there is always room for argument. Freedom isn't for the Jeanne d'Arcs solely. The holiest dissident can also be an ass like Balabansky. Or something of a bastard like the man with the weak bladder—who after talking tenderly on the long-distance phone to his helpmate and with no sign of drink in him, had had to be ejected from the younger woman's room. Or one could be a strange bundle like Gonchev himself.

Anyway, the Germans made good cameras, neither insanely versatile like the Japanese variety nor depressingly childproof like the American. Just long-wearing trusties that goose-stepped along no matter who was in command. In a shop with, sure enough, a German name, he found a secondhand old box camera, not too heavy to lug about, not too small to be unnoticeable, and with a face that could become a friend. This is all he will ask of it. He isn't planning to use it, only to carry it with him onstage, as women carry purses containing half a dozen tokens of what they are. In the way his own wife had carried her identity. Or as his crew of temporary colleagues did, carrying their books onto the podium although they might not get a chance to read from them.

At his next stop, a small college in the heartland, he does as planned, the camera bobbing with him throughout the day's schedule of classrooms and receptions, all the way to the student's beer joint, routine at the evening's end. The camera is too old a model to have a modern shoulder strap but its box, scabbed with thin black leather, has a molded luggage-style handle that fits the palm obligingly.

He is alone now. Others in the group have dispersed, maybe to larger events he isn't yet privy to, or fitted for. But he likes the small colleges in the country's middle. The undergraduates they produced were often awkward or shy, not stupid, but with a milky goodness, grass-fed and still willing to listen, to chew the cud. Dairy-country kids. Yet such schools also grew avant-gardistes of a rigor he hasn't met even in New York. Gaunt young men, hairy as thistles, whose bristly fathers maybe raised cattle for meat. Doughy girls or long-legged ones, who seemed to have vaulted from Sunday school right over the marriage beds offered in the furniture emporiums onto the bare floors of student housing, where they were these men's consorts. Heiresses of the cornstalk, they had swapped vanity for a yoga blankness of eye, and were sullenly proud of this, in the company of men who approved. They usually hate Gonchev at once. "For ignoring our minds." Meaning that movie directors did?

And for having Roko.

"Tell them I ignore anyone who speaks in chorus," Gonchev says to her this time. "Of any sex."

"We're sixties people," one of the men sneers. "We do that."

Gonchev suspects he is the leader, which puts the onus of sneering on him. Each time he does so he wipes his beard with the back of his hand. Gonchev's eye, still alert to camouflage and other visual evasions, sees that under the matted hair he has an elegant face.

"Sixties?" Gonchev repeats, almost with American intonation. His Japanese lilt is fading.

The polite faculty sociologist who has brought them to the beer joint explains the term. As usual, some people turn to Roko each time for interpretation. Others continue to face Gonchev, hearing Roko as it were through the elbow, as if good manners dictate that she not exist. This professor manages to do both, rotating his bald head so fast that it appears to blur. "He means they've adopted the style of the nineteen sixties. They're not that old."

"*Hai*, the sixties," Gonchev says to Roko. "I was still in Japan." He lowers his voice, talking only to her. Now and then he does this, not because Laura had said to, or Roko invited it, but because with the woman you sleep with this is natural, even if other people notice.

Now he catches a flicker on her face that he's never heeded before. She is too modern to bow, as in the old days in Kyoto one bowed to honor a sentiment, a season, a sacred object. Or person. But that's what she honors him for. And serves him for? Because I have been in Japan.

So does this awed group here. "You were with Kurosawa?"

"With those who have worked with him. I'm not that old either."

They are too solemn to see jokes, where holiness is involved. "We have seen all your pictures," they say, the girls too.

"All?"

They nod ritually. "All." The sneers are merely awkwardness, their style. Or because others here—maybe the good burghers by whom they have been reared—sneer at them.

He blinks, recovering himself. "Ah, I don't mind if you say that in chorus."

Of course they can't have seen all, though he won't tell them so. He listens to them enumerate the half dozen they have seen. He isn't quite sure what they think of these.

"Real raw," they are saying of his Bucharest.

Into whose inoffensively antique scenario he had been able to insert a slide showing that tourist fur store, plumy with white lamb and silver fox jackets, with its two signs: NOT FOR PURCHASE, and CLOSED, and—running the shot onward—one of the armed guards at Ceaușescu's palace door, his bayonet lunging at a tourist who had crossed the square in order to get to the museum next door, instead of going around the periphery.

Sometimes anonymous fans sent him these shots, in mail let through by censors tired of making everything look right. Or now and then some were discovered in boxes of supplies. Oh, he has had his anonymous helpers, well before Pfize.

"Real boss," they are saying, of his London film.

"Why do you carry a camera?" the leader says. "You're a director, not a cameraman."

Bless you. But you may well ask.

"Maybe it's his mantra," a girl says.

He doesn't know what that is.

"Boy," she says, "you really were out of it over there, weren't you."

"Mantra," Gonchev is able to say. It fits very well into Japanese. He reaches over to the camera, on the floor at his side like a dog, and pats it. It already has a devoted face. "So that's what you are. And to think I didn't know." Even Roko smiles, as she translates that.

"How nice he is to go along with them," the sociologist says to her in an undertone, as if the students can't hear. Or perhaps because they can. "The politically serious students had to leave. The Republican candidate is here, you know. For tomorrow's debate." Roko dutifully translates this too.

"They're not interested in politics?" Gonchev asks, going along with this obliquely parental conversation because it amuses him to—not because Laura had warned that he never sufficiently buttered up the faculty.

"They couldn't care less, Mr. Gonchev."

Gonchev makes Roko translate that twice. Such an interesting idiom. Then nods at the beard. "Neither do I."

The faculty man smiles loftily. "Oh, but you have reason. They live in a world of their own."

Gonchev has long since learned to classify how people refer to his situation. Some assume it to be tragic and crave the gory details. Some want to tell him of other dissidents already met, collecting these like movie stars, or stamps. In an opposite corner are the professorial stars, senior, most of them, who resent any outside visitor of note. Such as the historian, occupant of one of those celebrated chairs that so often have a tripartite name attached to them, who had growled, "We've had a spate recently. Of you curators of agony." To whom Gonchev had loyally replied, "Well, where agony exists—why not?"

But the majority of Americans want only to accept him. As Laura says, they are "kind, sweet, dear." In varying shades of what her father feels is essentially a blandness that wants to experience him as a matter of record, in the same way some attend rock concerts, or films. Or at best, hope to touch a world rhythm they fear they are missing.

Derek deems him lucky to be able to earn his living so quickly. "To be a moral view on salary?" Gonchev had replied, he scarcely knew in what language. When the two women had pieced that out, all three of them clucked their tongues at him. "Papa," Derek had said. "We Yankees like to participate."

So this faculty man is merely doing his job. "A world of their own," he repeats. "Don't you, boys and girls?"

Like scolded children, or mutinous ones, they don't answer. One girl is staring balefully at Roko, as if Roko must be held responsible for any sentiments she conveys.

Gonchev leans across the table. "Ask them where that is?"

The professor scratches his bald head. He isn't against them, really. He wants to be with them. More than they want him.

Gonchev reaches for a peanut. So does the beard. The bowl is empty. All down the table, the bowls the barman had put out a few minutes ago are bare.

"You pigs," the professor says with a laugh.

A girl giggles. "We're on scholarship."

"But the college pays for the dinner, sir," a young man sitting offside says, smiling at Gonchev. He is clean-shaven and wears a khaki jacket and trousers, and a collar and tie.

"Wow, you don't need it, Jeanot," a girl sitting next to the beard says. As to be expected of a leader's woman, she is what Laura and Derek's crowd call a looker—if you look close. "You're ROTC."

Roko has trouble with abbreviations, but Gonchev has caught it.

Its meaning is explained to him, in crowed chorus: "Reserve Officers' Training Corps." In return for spending two weeks a year in military camp and promising to serve if need be, this Jeanot is handsomely paid.

"And for wearing the uniform," one grumbles.

Gonchev is delighted. So this must be why the girls are speaking for the men, and so cautiously, one by one; it is nothing sexual. Often he is pressed to report on the sexual sociology here. His usual answer is that he can't, since where he comes from "nobody thinks twice."

But now, in the presence of this young person sitting so hangdog on the sidelines, he feels both exquisitely homesick and at home.

So they too have hangdog watchdogs. Only, like everything here, they keep them, as they would say, "up front."

"Hah. He is your spy."

And Roko does not edit what he said.

It is the first time—as the girls hold their stomachs and even the men howl—that Gonchev feels himself to be an innocent in America.

At dinner later, in an off-campus restaurant pridefully touted to him as "high tech"—an abandoned power station with stained-glass lamps hung from the exposed pipes—Gonchev apologizes to the boy in uniform, who has followed along.

"That's all right," the boy says. "Maybe I am one. Not everything's up front in the free world." He is in the corps because he hadn't qualified for a good-enough scholarship. He'd never have been able to get the education he wants otherwise. He is a film student, born of Haitian émigrés who had clustered in an old Hudson River brick-factory town, Haverstraw, New York. Women like his mother still went out to work domestically in the fancier suburb nearby. As soon as he has his degree—"not that it'll qualify me"—he will plump for the regular army. "And see the world that isn't free. I have an attraction to it." When his teeth flash his face makes the others' seem morose. He will do documentaries, he says. Beginning with the army itself, if they will take him on in the film unit, then privately, when he can. If everything works out, he could retire on army pension while still in his forties and have a stake to go on with. "If I still have the zip."

What adventurousness, Gonchev thinks, appalled, but manages not to say. Having to be translated often seduces him into saying far too much aloud. Sometimes he feels himself being leached of all meditation. At other times he knows better. Being in a foreign country is all meditation in a way, and he has been doing that since he was born. That little demon in his head, his own critical judgment, meanwhile following him everywhere on its motorcycle—his own in-house spy.

Whispering to Gonchev how much this Haitian, poor and Latinate as his origins might be—and of Polynesian physique, with a muscular looseness the uniform can't hold in—already resembles Laura and her friends, those Harvard clones, in the way they propose to conduct life as a business. Youth seems to be cooled early here by that refrigerant—calculation.

In Gonchev's time calculation had belonged to the parents—even in the enforced gypsydom of parents like his. They had expected to funnel their passions through him. Now it was youth that had the foresight, or was expected to. Or if too weak for that, annulled themselves through drugs. Although Roko, whose sister is still in college, says that drugs are falling off there.

He has often been to dinner with her family, who are always gravely pleased that he enjoys their spicy food. They think of him as her employer, although she is paid for by a fund. Roko, like her sister, keeps a share in the tiny quarters their elder brother had managed to get as a music student at Juilliard, although the sister, a graduate student at City College because of the lower fees, is in the quarters illegally. Both the sister and the brother work nights, Sundays, and late afternoons, he as a music teacher in a nursery school and as a church organist, although he is a prodigy on the viola, she as a part-time computer programmer, with a California job in prospect as soon as she gets her degree. The father, a merchant before coming here, is cashier in a Chinese restaurant but is studying to be an acronym—a CPA. The mother stays at home keeping track of this network, a shriveling, peppy little spider on stick-legs, with huge framed spectacles and a fuschia mouth. Both she and her husband are perhaps forty-five.

In the main room there is an impressive black lacquer box, many-layered and with an intricate fish-shaped lock. Since it is never mentioned or touched in his presence, it must be sacred, although he wouldn't hazard whether they keep religion there or money. Every other corner of the small apartment is filled with appliances, all shriek-ingly modern and often competing in singsong, yet the total tone of the household is grave, like their mien at table.

He isn't certain whether the parents know Roko lives with him, or that the brother is gay. Or whether perhaps the father, deep in the Oriental gambling games that take place in the restaurant after hours, protects himself from knowing what the mother, as clever at data as some in-house creatures have to be, would have squeezed from the younger sister and then buried in the family web—with the compliance of all.

What he loves about them is that they are emigrants in a style he knows. His own father, diluted by alcohol rather than gambling, had nonetheless practiced the piano for his scanty engagements. His mother had had a black box, in which no sewing was kept.

As for Roko, his reverence for her family deeply satisfies her. She has been their most expensive sop to the West, and he is the treasure she has brought back home. There she can rest from her labors, for though he and her family exchanged a few formalities when he first met them, ever since then the television and radio are turned on the minute he enters the house, and after dinner, the VCR. Paradoxically, he thinks of that series of tiny rooms as his house of silence. In the midst of noise is where Oriental silence is kept—like a cat.

That neutral quiet is what she gives him. And perhaps he gives her.

As she curls mute on the family sofa, becoming elder daughter, or trots endless small dishes to and from the kitchen, she is released from that ever-pressing Western need for personality, which she might never attain. He does not need to love her. She does not need to love him. That is why he can live with her.

Here in the High Tech, the young people are eating at a gallop, great thick cutlets of red that must only yesterday have been separated from the haunch. "We usually go for veggies," the giggler girl volunteered. "But not today. And not here." The side dishes are a baked potato wrapped in silver, glaring at the palate like the Kohinoor diamond, and cauliflower so abashed that it hides. Gonchev and the Haitian had ordered the grilled bones that came browned. One gnaws at the shreds of meat on the curved ribs and accumulates a great pile of discards, but there is an undeniably good oily taste. "I see you know the food out here," the Haitian says.

"Makes me feel like a lion."

Roko, in the midst of translating this, explodes into laughter she can't explain. Her slim eyes leak merriment. Finally she gasps out to him in English: "A translator cannot always explain."

"I did not ask you to explain," Paul says with dignity, in Japanese. And suddenly he bursts out laughing too.

The giggler girl raises her clasped hands and shakes them at him, giving him the high sign, as they call it here—a gesture descended from what Roman arenas one can only wonder.

"It gets to you," the girl says vaguely, comfortably, and in a minute the whole table has taken up the chant. "It gets to you," they call out happily, rousingly, chucking each other under the chin. There's a sense that all of them know what "it" is but nobody would be stupid enough to say. This was what made for a happy company, a sympathy that trickled in the vein and didn't have to be expressed. He misses that in his very blood. Only when you were very young could you find that kinship at random, as this little crowd could. When they were his age they would look back at themselves and think, Those were the compatriots.

He thinks of a table covered with linen so white that it has turned to yellow under intense sun. Fruit on it, heavy as sculpture. A buzzing fly. There are no flies in this very clean hostelry. He won't bother to remark that. There are enough places in his life now where everything has to be nailed down by talk.

"Dessert?" the waiter said. "Apple or lemon custard *pie.*" He spat the last word, managing to look down on these patrons more than a waiter had to. He is their age, a lithe figure, muscularly compressed, the face above so white that the black cuff of overhanging hair makes the eyes smolder.

The Haitian knows him, and when the waiter leaves to get the pie gives his story. "He's one of the Iranian exchange students left high and dry by their war. A chemist. His family can't send him any more money. They were pre-Khomeini government, and some of them were killed when the mullahs took over. He's had to leave school. If he goes back home, he may be jailed. But our government may be sending him back."

All over, even in this country, these underground stories. Why do they seem to think they don't have them? At Roko's family's place one night there had been a young Vietnamese musician who worked as a waiter too, at the same restaurant her father did. Tall for his race, he had a boxer's physique. It was hard to conceive that a few years back he and his family had been among those skeletal "boat people" shown on the evening news; Roko has a newspaper clip of them. The rest of the family are now working under the sponsorship of a Methodist community in Ohio. Her brother is trying to get his friend a scholarship at Columbia.

Everywhere here this below-stairs ferment. Or sometimes right out in view, like him, Gonchev. Tonight it makes him comfortable to feel so. As part of the centrifuge still at work in this foolish big-eyed country.

"The professor had to leave," the waiter says. "His marriage is in trouble. He paid." Now can he too go home? his clamped jaw says. They have all eaten the pie, even Gonchev. "Order only apple," they had advised. Now they are the only ones in the restaurant. All the other customers have filed out, visibly slowed by food. Maybe to be felled by late-night apoplexies?

In the film he would make of that—a little comic divertimento to be shown only in private or abroad—one by one the lights would go on in the homes of those who had eaten here. The paunched American husbands would be felled on the way to the toilet; leaning over them the wives would shriek with the gawp that knew itself widowed; the complacent doctors would be called. While in one last house a couple would lie in congress, the wife gazing absently at the ceiling, as Gonchev suspects the wives of all too many middle-aged American males do here, her legs wound unaware around a body whose eyes are already glazed.

He pats the camera; how sad it looks! In France, Danilo had written, in a small town where he and a crew were making a television installment, he had taken time out for a walk with his host, whose vineyard was being filmed, and they had passed a whorehouse, outside of which several dogs were tethered. *"Voulez-vous?"* the host had said the following evening, offering him the leashed German shepherd they had had with them the night before. "The dog knows the way."

I couldn't let on, Danilo had written, that his wife had already given me the eye. So I took the animal. At the gate of that house were already two other dogs, one of those nasty white poodles with rheumy muzzles, and a very fine Briard. My, how those aesthetes their masters love their sunset walks.

Danilo had walked back to the house slowly enough for pretense, but fast enough to connect with the wife. The dog wouldn't tattle. The town well might; this was France. But by that time their crew would be gone.

"I may be coming to America sooner than you think," Danilo had continued. As long as the serial he was in lasted, he mustn't leave. But its authors were writing themselves into a trap; either they would have to kill him off, along with the actress who played his mistress, or else the serial would kill itself off; it was being said that the lesbian pair writing it were on the outs. Everything in France was ascribed to sex. He is of the opinion, however, that half the time the French do this so as to be thought men and women of passion, rather than the money-

192

pinchers they are. They knew they had him cornered and were paying him as little as they could.

"Besides," he had added, "under the cheap lights they use I am losing my hair. It's enough to send one back to journalism."

A breath of his light-hearted, never quite shallow spirit came with every letter, that Central European self-mockery common to both of them. Under whose scrutiny, however, the real rats, creeping unexpectedly out of their runs, never went unobserved. Only . . . these Americans are never sure what we are, because of our joking. For depth, they prefer the Russians. Of course everybody respects the Russians for having imagined Raskolnikov.

But come over soon, Danilo. I need a countryman. Oh, Danilo, which of us is in the free world?

Bottom of Danilo's every letter there was the same postscript, like a blot Gonchev needn't read. "No news."

The Iranian waiter was being wished luck. He was hoping to join his folks in Germany; they had heard labor force was needed there.

After he left, Gonchev made a face. "Germany already has too many Turkish laborers. And others, I don't know who, maybe Algerians. But he'll find it rough."

How does Gonchev know?

"I did a recent film on them—migrant workers." He was moved to add, "One of the ones you wouldn't have seen."

"Why not?" a girl asks.

"Official ones."

"You worked for the government that way?" The beard wore a large silver signet ring, clumsily made; he was twisting it.

"He had no choice!" another girl cries, smiling sweetly at Gonchev. She has orange-red hair, the kind that is not a matter of choice.

Gonchev shakes his head. "Wrong," he says. "Tell her, Roko. I did have a choice."

Roko never smiled the easy, middle-ground American smile; her mouth had not been born to it. She had only that masklike ceremonial smile initiated by the jaw. But she had a stare you could see was a smile, if you knew her well.

"You've been going too fast for me, haven't you—for some time," she says to Gonchev in Japanese. So she is on to his increasing English, maybe has been these many weeks. Then she says louder than usual, "He asks me to say that you are wrong. He did have a choice."

The redhead glares at Roko with enmity. People dislike translators here, Roko had once told him. Or even look down on them. If she had known this early enough she wouldn't have become one. "With us it's an honored trade," she had said. By "us" she had meant all Asia, as he has come to know. "Americans don't have languages as we do," he'd said, hoping to soothe. There are so few ways he can; he isn't even sure that sex is one, in the long run. "No," she'd said, with the same gentle ducking of the head that her mother used when contradiction was necessary. "They're afraid a translator may be lying to them." Adding, after a pause, "Especially us."

"He films what you feel inside countries like that," the redhead cries. "Didn't you see the article in the *Voice?*"

"Inside which countries?" the beard says. "Like, what about God's country? Ours."

They stir doubtfully; some nod obediently. They have their politics. And want people to see.

How good it feels, Gonchev thinks. To see all the mime as it comes, without talk. Maybe that's why this job was laid on me. Remember that. For the time may come, Gonchev, when you may merely talk-talk, like the rest.

Roko is translating rapidly now. When she does that, the separate pearly syllables falling like a roulade in music, she is at her most beautiful, though she mightn't like to hear so.

"God's country?" Gonchev says. "Every country is that."

And how easy to make people laugh, in this one.

"He chose to work," the beard says to them all. "His work."

Suddenly he wishes he could show them an early reel or two he'd made in Liguria on that trip with his mother—of a communal christening in the grape season. A precious bunch had been held above each child's head. It was not a lush area for grapes. Each member of the family group around the child had been allowed to pluck one grape from the bunch, one only. The game was to have as many as possible gathered to pluck for each candidate—and to have the smallest bunch. A great cheer rose for the two babes whose bunches were plucked bare. "They are plucking the sins," the priest told Gonchev, "so the child won't have them. Or so they think." The father of one of the successful pair, digging his neighbor with an elbow, had said, "Padre, he will be a priest."

If he had had his way, nothing in those early films of his would have spoken without a folk or earth reason—the voices of land and sea urges, of boats and horses, and of what a crowd says when it is not speaking singly. And when single persons did speak, what each said should never be mundane solely.

What he had wanted to give shape to was that inner fairy tale of vision that comes naturally to a child continuously moving on. To whom sound and even language have to fight to be necessary.

Just as a painting could make Christ swing on the cross, and the stone belly of a Venus sidle with all the fruitions of love—the virtue of each being that it could not really move—a film might at its apogee appear to be holding the world still.

This is why the professionals are amazed that he cannot always say whether a film of his is to be with sound or silent.

"He's asleep," he hears a man say with contempt.

No, heavy with food. And with questions.

"I wanted to work above all," Gonchev says. He looks down at his plate of bare bones, still on the table. "So—I ate their meat."

And so he charms—as he is fated to do anywhere? No strong talent is without its charm. Even the monster talent, although he is not that. Even the ogre, if he is that to them.

"Let's take him to the disco," the giggler says, naïvely revealing that the town must have only one.

"No," the beard says. "We're setting up something at the house."

Roko begs off. She has never done that before. Would they please take her back to the motel?

"But then we won't be able to communicate."

This, from two stolid men who up to now haven't spoken. Hard to tell whether they are glum or shy or merely provincial. There are so many provinces here. But travel has taught Gonchev that the backwater citizen and the elegant sophist can often share points. While the women, of course, bouncing over custom and culture, share all the time, anywhere.

"His English is coming back to him," Roko murmurs, looking straight at him. "Only he can't speak it yet. And I am tired. Yes, I am."

In the back of the huge discolored Volvo, old but still formidable, that belongs to one of the men, she sits on his lap.

"Are you tired of this?" he says in Japanese. Of being his talking doll, who looked so chipper, so New York, in her black, all the more so now that Japanese fashion designers and models had become the rage. He had once bought her a kimono in a museum's shop, but she had said it was a marriage kimono, too beautiful to wear, and had presumably stored it at home, since the next time he was there her mother, ducking deferentially, had mentioned it. After that, Roko had worn kimonos of her own choice on the boat, instead of her college-girl T-shirts and shorts. She is so biddable. Yet taking the kimono as pretext, she had remarked, while chattering as she did when alone with him, that he was as sensitive to women's clothes as Japanese men, and had asked: Was this only because of his profession? Or from his mother, who must have been a lady with taste?

What she wanted was as clear to him as the arch of her neck. She wants him to tell her about his wife.

They have never talked about that. She must know from the newspapers that he left a wife behind, and a son too. Early articles on him had mentioned Vuksica's career as an actress, and films in which she had appeared. Once there had been a call from an actors' agency, taken by Roko, inquiring whether his wife would like to be on their list. Pfize had early explained what an agent was: "An alter ego, who sells yours for money," adding in his chuckling, ghostly way that there was nothing to be feared from being on that kind of list.

A remarkable tact has come from the reporters, Flaherty included, considering how brash they can be about anything to do with his soul. Possibly they think a wife is more private. Souls are, after all, international now, and a man in his position is expected to make his especially available. The rescued were considered to have a duty to the country of rescue. To report first of all, and indeed forever, on conditions in the countries they had left behind. Some who had been on the circuit for fifteen years or more were still being quoted as authorities—and some indeed might have unrevealed means of keeping up.

A dissident's equal duty was to appreciate the new land, far beyond simple compliment. Of course a man just released from a cell—where he might have dined on gruel and lost a nail or two to the pincers, or had his gangrenous toe go unattended but his psychological state monitored—was unlikely to find injustices worthy of his temper in the country that had embraced him, at least not for a while. He, Gonchev, was no such case. Yet he too had quickly found that he shared an obligation.

His duty is to warn Americans of where their own land falls short. Even if his own political stand has been obscure, to have lived as an artist—a man of statement—in a country where statement is controlled has made him a victim, has ennobled him. So that now he too is assumed to be upholding the highest standard of political conduct a man can. As well as being a kind of business consultant on injustices generally—a credential they have in effect slipped into his and his colleagues' breast pockets without their noticing.

A week or two ago he had seen a touchy poet boil off the platform altogether. The poet had read a fine poem. In the question period afterward he was asked not about the poem but about current events, the new tax laws specifically. "What do they think I am? Just a foreigner?" he had growled to the historian who was moderator. "No, you're a hero," this man had replied. "And heroes are answerable for anything."

In the roomy backseat of the old Volvo, Gonchev and Roko are the center couple, between two others, each man with a girl on his knee. He can smell their budding consciences, along with their warm flesh. Freedom can domesticate the flesh. No doubt couples like these watch their parents narrowly. A free government can slide into complications one can't assess as sharply as one can under tyranny. No doubt they watch their government.

It might be hard to be a good young American. Living in open territory, ever trying to remember those who are caged. Across the sea, the sound of some injustice is clean as a shot; the profiles of the heroes rise clear.

Heroes don't have families. Or these are ignorable. Or seem to become so, whether or not abandoned. Most of Gonchev's confreres take some such tack. It may be suspected that some are single as much from a back-home personal choice as from a political or tragic one, but this is not remarked upon. Some of the world-traveling musicians his father's family knew had been like that, exempt from personal devotion or from the character burdens of the ordinary. He and his fellow dissidents are being treated as world-artists, dealing in political morality only—and only in that arena will the moral judgment be made. He too has come a certain careless distance along that route. And perhaps for the others it has been the same.

Gonchev's own world has now stretched beyond the universities. He has small briefings with newly arrived émigrés, is asked to rallies in Lincoln Center, as well as to hostessed dinners, from Chicago to Los Angeles. The politically concerned are always partying. Though he can understand the catharsis, he can't quite believe in it. This huddling together to gain recruits didn't change a situation. One merely recruited oneself for the time being—for an evening or for a world conference. In either place, the process was like talking over bad dreams. Sometimes before you had them.

At most public occasions Roko's presence protected him from the lone encounter—as a multilingual young Dutch woman who was escorting him hinted one night at a Human Rights Congress in Amsterdam. "It prevents you from playing the field," she had said slyly in English, then "Oh, for God's sake, don't ask Roko—I speak a little Japanese." And she had. And in Japanese he had replied: "Oh, what a useful idiom."

What his faithfulness to Vuksica is he can't say, except that it is there. Many of the men and women in his situation—for there are heroines also—do run around, or else have long-term companions, who now and then change. If any have married or settled down, their helpmates do not appear. In their professional life, they need to appear single. Being a hero is indeed a profession—high or low. If aloneness is required, then for him, as possibly for the others, it isn't in itself hard. The cross an exile bears is his meditation, publicized or not. Maybe this is also his faithfulness.

On his knee, Roko is, as always anywhere, a neat butterfly. She shouldn't be scored for her lack of weight. Smart, but in her trade not highly gifted, she would never be of the breed that translated books. She had feelings, but one sensed a posture involved in them, and their sway was controlled, as with a metronome. If he thought he saw all there was of her, this was not to her detriment, but only because he saw so well.

"Roko?" he whispers.

"Hai."

"Are you pregnant?"

"Hah. No." In English—but what is she feeling?

"You would tell me if you were?"

"Hai."

When he leaves her on the motel steps—Does she have the key? Yes, of course, she is always good with keys although she does not say it—he pats her shoulder.

She tilts up at him. "Speak well."

By the time he gets back to the car, he can't remember in which language she said that, but he saw the smile, that of a mother sending off to receive his diploma the son she knows has outgrown her, but of whom she is proud. She hopes I'll be able to do it but she doesn't want to watch.

He gets into the car.

"What took you so long?" the girls in the back seat say. The men, sitting dreamily under the girls' hams, squeeze the girls' waists.

What's he doing here, in this warm potpourri? The girl-flesh on either side of him is merely communal cozy, intending nothing. All he feels are his middle-aged stipulations, more manners than sex. He is maybe being a bit too careful with his thighs.

When they all get out he is amazed, as always, that even students on a pittance have cars here. Besides the Volvo, there's also an early Volks shaped like half a peanut, and a long American wreck painted lavender. In Elsinore he had used a paint blackmarketed from a Mercedes plant in Germany and routed to him by suppliers who were politically acceptable.

Maybe he ought to buy an old car and do it over. Maybe in gold vermeil finish, if his Hollywood agent found him an assignment and he had to go. Laura had said he would have to. He knows she fears his present mode of living could stop if he does or says something too out of line.

He goes up to the car and strokes it. Not a bad job. The boy who must own the car hovers near. Gonchev gives him the high sign; at least he can do that. But he wants to do more. "J-j-j-," he says.

"Jag?" the boy says, smiling. "No, it's not a Jaguar. Pontiac."

Gonchev shakes his head. He has heard the name often, especially in the smaller colleges, and is pleased to have figured it out. "J-ja-lop-ee."

If he's a clown, then by their smiles he's a success. Gonchev motions the boy to write down the car's name. The boy writes down the name. "Jalopy. By General Motors, 1979." Then they take him inside what they call "the house."

Gonchev is familiar with these unisex dormitories. Once or twice he and Roko have been quartered in such a place, when, as Roko said, flushing the orange tint that with her means huff, "not enough respect was being paid." She isn't to be persuaded that not everyone in this vast country knows his distinction or cares, or that by and large he is merely a lucky beneficiary of the great American lecture habit—and on a favored list. Although, as a Czech colleague, a playwright, informed him: "We'll never command the fees they pay their reformed criminals."

Well, tonight Roko's in a nice motel. While he is confronted with what makes a middle-aged man shiver, with longing for the slapdash, ashcan art that youth makes for itself, totally unaware.

On the floor that the republic had provided, their charmed dust gathers, one step short of filth. The white walls are sallowed to ochre by countless impromptu parties, the ceilings spotted from warm beer cans opened with flair. In a corner there's a Mont Blanc of dirty sneakers, offering any inhabitant the right to choose. Chairs and tables have that

naïve invisibility owed to complete subjugation. Yet there are rever-
ences: printed cotton on the beds and rush footstools out of van Gogh.
And everywhere—in the tangle of skis in a corner, the bulbous callosity
that must be a homebuilt stereo, the oars crisscrossed like chopsticks, the
Scrabble board, and the tipsy piles of books shelved on bricks—those
sweaty, infallible signs of youth, counterfeited everywhere by their
elders. Gear.

It makes him brood on Klement. That's always bad. First off, he
always thinks: Klement could live here. He's so good with gear and, after
all, the right age. On second thought, Klement never in the world could
fit in. They would kill him before they understood him. Klement's brand
of snoutiness, nurtured over there in the name of the State, is the one
taboo on which almost all here—even the State itself—seem to agree.

Otherwise, as in any other country known to Gonchev, one can be
most kinds of villain if successful enough at it. Ill-educated murderers are
even sentimentalized as the victims of class negligence—always after
the event. But blood is what Klement would avoid. He is destined to
be—or might already be—that slippery in-between, the state murderer
of ideas.

Yet those rescued like Gonchev—for he has by now acknowledged
to himself that he was more than kidnapped—indeed have an ironclad
debt to rescue those left behind.

Vuksica, however, is another story. Persuasion would be as far as he
could go. That must be why she will not communicate with him.

But his son would have to be called for, like a retarded child, grown
adult. Somewhere in this great American state, which offers as many
ill-advised conformities as any other, maybe Klement could be institu-
tionalized—without bars. According to Pfize, once delicately ques-
tioned, there were many freakish groups here where one could practice
one's intolerances, and moreover enough land to accommodate them.
"The Constitution gives a free run to anybody, short of dynamite," Pfize
had said. "Even to me."

So for Gonchev's own poor monster, borders might be found? Or so
he fantasizes in the vulnerable reaches of the night, where a father of any
humanity cannot leave his son.

Then he would be confronted, as tonight, by these young faces—
"pans," as Roko says. Not all of them peachy anymore, these American
faces, as in the old magazines that in his youth had come his way. All
kinds now, all colors, all shades. And because of that, all the more steely
in one regard?

Once, leaning over Klement's crib when the child was in one of his
red-face tantrums, diagnosed as not from croup but from holding his
breath, Vuksica, up all night with him for a week, had said, "He reminds
me of Göring." And once again she had said it, when they had come
across the child rolling back and forth in his little fists red-and-blue
marbles stolen from one of the games at the cooperative nursery. At first
Gonchev had thought she meant only the actor, known to both of them,
who had played Hitler's Reichsmarschall in a film they had seen at the
Pula festival.

The film had been true to life. Wearing a green dressing-gown the
color of Klement's velveteen rompers, Göring had sifted in and out of
his pockets the colored gems he had loved to collect. In a small sector
of the prison yard at Nuremberg, barred to all except generals, Göring
too had had his tantrums, never displayed in his obliging conduct in the
trial room.

"As long as it's only marbles," Gonchev had said, leaning back from
Klement's crib. Years later, watching the boy's bobbing curls as he
strutted up for his belated graduation certificate at secondary school, and
still later, marking his steamy silences at the sports events he did not
win, Gonchev saw that Vuksica too was being reminded, though by
then nothing was said.

"Ah, Mr. Gonchev, sir. They've left you to wait alone, have they?" The
Haitian boy comes in the door, hard on the sound of a motorcycle
ridden right up to the steps and then let die. "I'll go see what they're
up to. May be a while. Like some tea?" As he goes by he slaps his
uniform. "Had to check in first." There is an obstinacy, a pride, in the
way he calls attention to a uniform he has earned, no matter what the

others think. Were spies pensioned here, like regular army? For they must have them. Did. Gonchev even knows the abbreviation: FBI. To which Pfize had said he did not belong, though there was sometimes mutual accommodation. They call that group "agents" too. Americans have agents for so much.

In Hollywood, Laura's great hope for him, you had to have such a person. "Ah-hah," he had said, "do they too follow you around on a motorcycle?" Nowadays his daughter calls him Paul when she is wroth with him. "No, Paul. They deal in art. For money. Films, books, plays. Other vehicles."

To twit her for her lack of humor was unbecoming in a parent for whom she thought she was doing so much. But he couldn't resist. "Ah, I see. To follow one, they use limousines."

What a follower this ROTC stripling would make. Gonchev can see the two of them going cross-country, maybe at night, through the Grand Canyon, the Yosemite—which they fly him across, these good people, but never give him time or funds to trek. All the way to the redwoods they would go. Which he imagines are like the valonias at home, in their own majestic way. And he would send Laura a card to remind her of what she no longer wants to be reminded of. "Stand under one of these."

Meanwhile, this quietly forceful boy would follow him, at a respectful distance, discreetly vanishing at night, maybe to a CIA motel. The two of them needing no talk, only the covert glance acknowledging the other's presence. Talk—dangerous!

But finally I, Gonchev, would take the plunge. Not the same scenario as with my spy at home. On top of a Rocky, maybe, I have broken an ankle. Limp, limp—I am pitiable. But still in good form . . . Or else— alternate script: He confronts me; after all, this is the States. Our pace is too slow, he says, or too fast; he is getting complaints from headquarters. What can we concoct between us? So that we can go on.

Of course we don't say any of this; he would be wired for sound.

Or maybe I speak? For the sake of a greater goal, I incriminate myself—after all, I am the hero, aren't I? And what is this greater goal? Sincerity.

"Give up this life," I say. "Give up this pension talk. Go for pioneer. For Constitutiondom. For forefather. For face-to-face, man-to-man. For what a man goes for, boy, in God's country. Go straight." And maybe in a whisper, or no, one of those placards the sound crews use—GO FOR LIMOUSINE.

Gonchev bursts out laughing. A girl brings him a cup of tea, lays a finger on her lips, then ducks back into what must be the kitchen; what are they cooking? More than vegetables. A couple of the men now peek out at him. Not the Haitian. Maybe he is outside, watching the only other exit. So, Gonchev.

So. There we will be, the two of us, on the Rocky. Shot of the boy and me, each of us with one foot in space. Shot of the moon—is the moon screen right or screen left? No matter, we are in violet light, color of the gods.

And the young spy is sad, as a good spy must sometimes be. "Old man," he says, "but old man, how are we to follow this goal?" He knows only how to follow. Shot of me—my fist—huge. Close-up of my head, still shaggy, not old. The strong chin, the powerful throat. "Film," the mouth says. "Film." The moon sails in, dead center. No pulleys, nothing worse than a rigged moon. Close-up of the spy. A good face, but as a hero a beginner. And we never see the two of them together again. . . .

Shot of the old man—me. Old now, for real. Majestic, but old. The screen is that yellow you get if you fiddle with the early gelatins. Yellow, for memory. Shot of two motorcycles, riderless, their front wheels pointed up, riding the clouds. One cycle bears an inscription. Pan in toward it closer, closer. But we never get to read it, not this time. Art must progress. . . . Fadeout.

(And what does this film remind you of, Citizen?)

"Noo?" the little frizzed agent Laura had chosen for him had said, pursing her upper lip, on which rode that faint picket fence of vertical wrinkles which the surgeons cannot remove. "Noo—male bonding. Tell him that's what's in. Hot as buried money. Two guys." And she had spurted names like a gilded spigot: Robert, Burt, Keith, Jack.

They were in the lobby of a hotel, the Americana. Inside, it was more like a terminal, with almost every person, male or female, bearing a name card on the lapel. Gonchev knows better than to wear these cards that proclaim one's obscurity; a democratic custom he will never adopt. "It's only to sort you all out," a bright young thing had said to him at a university reception. "Among your equals." Maybe that's the trouble, Gonchev had muttered to Roko. "But just tell her I only do it in hotels."

Laura was worried about the agent, who hadn't invited them up to her room—maybe because it was too cheap?—and hadn't even bought them a drink. And ignored Laura for Roko. "Oh, you're cute," she'd said. "No-oo, not cute. More like that marvelous little Viet who played the chippy in *Diva*. . . . You're not Viet?" Not that it would matter. "Maybe we should do a documentary of you and him." For East–West was also in. So far the agent has had no luck with any proposal. Maybe Gonchev should go for art films? Although that is not her field—she deals only with the major studios.

After she had left, Laura's lover, who had joined them during their coffee-shop interview, said, "Definitely the brush-off." One of Derek's good traits is that he enunciates clearly, although Roko says that this is because he is faking his accent.

Later, Laura telephoned Roko and Gonchev at the boat basin. She had checked at that hotel; nobody by the agent's name was registered. Two days later she phoned again. "You don't think too much of Derek, I know, Papa, but Derek follows through. Right in his own firm, he checked with a VP at Kidder Peabody who knows a VP with Morgan Stanley, on the Coast."

Gonchev is used to these prefabricated syllables of hers, although he is never sure which are people and which are companies. Out on the Coast, it seemed, the woman was known as "the ghost of Annie Laurie."

"Because she looks a little like a famous agent of bygones." Laura said that last in English, in her quoting voice. The woman was an accountant, not a nut. Only she was always trying to break into films. "Not registered?" Gonchev said. "Then she could just as soon have met us at the Ritz."

Laura burst into tears. Over a phone, sobs were worse than when seen, like the dying glottals of a small, human machine.

"Never mind," he said. "Let us get this real person who is named after that song. She sounds excellent. It is a Scottish song." And it is in his library, along with a full file on the great dark-red fortress of Edinburgh, and several slides of the golfing at St. Andrews—he knew the very drawer.

"Annie Laurie is dead," Laura said with a sub-Romanian howl, and hung up.

He rang back, unable to bear it. She had learned a smattering of that tongue at her mother's knee. Vuksica—who in turn had got it from her ex-ex, who had been half that nationality—had spoken it only when affairs were indeed bleak. What he wanted to say was: Laura, poor darling, maybe you are as much of an exile as me. But he couldn't. He was an unnatural father. "I do like Derek," he said. Only he was never in this life christened Derek; that I would swear. He at least managed not to say that, and to invite them to share a Chinese dinner up on Broadway, or carry takeouts to the boat.

He went into the galley to tell Roko. She was sewing one of the remarkable scarves of many colors that were her only adornment when on tour. These days she seemed to him more and more like her mother, who did almost everything in the kitchen, except perhaps pray to the black shrine. What Roko would pray to he couldn't say, but it occurred to him that perhaps the last shreds of Wellesley were dropping off. Or floating down the stream, like the leaves in the picture on the calendar from the Korean grocery store that hung just over her head. The scarf she was sewing on was remarkable. Like a clown suit that had burst in her lap. Or a parachute just about to inflate.

He told her about the agents. "The famous one sold"—he had to pronounce it phonetically—"she sold films that were *bai-gawns.* What are those? Perhaps I could learn to do?"

Roko laid down her needle and the billowing silk and took up a pencil, asking him to repeat Laura's words exactly. A scribble, and she raised her head to look at him, with an expression he'd lately begun to recognize, though not to define. But she pushed the scrap of paper at him with her usual humble arc of neck, as if apologizing for proficiency. BYGONES, she had printed in capitals. "It means 'past days.' When one has been famous."

From her gaze, wide-eyed for her, this must be one more instance among the many she must be collecting—of what he in particular ought to know.

The tea the girl brought is very strong by now; he has another cup. They'd left him the pot; how considerate they are. And how thoughtless, just like himself at their age. He feels an irrational grudge against them for leaving him so long with his memory games. The virtue of a tour is that every moment is prescribed. "As in a . . . a *whirlwing*," Laura had promised. And so it has proved. Almost like work—until it stops.

By touring, he hoped to stay immersed in film, if not in the battle smoke, at least in the shoptalk. American moviemakers did on occasion gather at the various film institutes and museum showings, or in the film departments of certain universities. Roko was a whiz, a spinner, in her element, among those of Gonchev's confreres who had treated him as one of them. Whether or not they really liked his stuff or even knew of it, they were kind—if often with a pitying deference, to his situation rather than to his talent, at which he has learned not to wince.

Viewings of his own films could be the worst, if no one knew them.

"Your stuff is weird in the right way," a manager of a repertory theater had said. "Ever write a play, get in touch." Another theater man, cornering him and Roko on a banquette where they had taken their dinner plates at the party after the preview, had warned: "You're not the first foreign filmist who's made it to the freedom racket. Sure, over here your stuff can do what it wants. Unless you shoot somebody for real, Uncle Sam won't blink an eye. But watch out for the banks."

They'd been in the producer-of-the-evening's triplex, to which a penthouse had just been added. "Let me show you my eyries," their host said. There were three of these, on six levels. "One for living. One for business. And one for show." Their owner's face was solemn. "So I always know where I am in my life."

Gonchev was honestly intrigued. There had been the same luxe—and the same baby pictures—on all levels. "They are like three stages of heaven," he had Roko say, instructing her also to bow. "But in which one of them are we now?"

On the banquette he had protested: "But surely this man doesn't need bankers." His owlish companion had replied, "From the stuff we saw tonight, couldn't you tell? He is the bank."

The last man to make a point of speaking to Gonchev that night had been the most famous there, and to Gonchev the most gifted. Acting under privilege, he entered late. A small man with clever eyes, and hair tufting out of a large-visored polo cap, he looked like a mouse trying not to look famous. When he slipped up to Gonchev, those nearest fell back. The polo cap twitched with mock annoyance at this, but why? After all, he had stated he wanted to speak with Gonchev alone. When he did speak, it was with an air of humorous futility, as if there were no hope that people would not discover that he was a very complicated man.

"Paul. One is so pleased. I am."

Is he implying that there are two of him? Gonchev wonders. If so, he wants people to reassure him that they like both of him. And I do. He has a mouth as sensitive as a puppy's nose.

"Paul Gonchev—I have a confession. But first I want you to know something. In the dark of the Eighth Street moviehouses, Saturday afternoons, when I was sixteen, you were my—incunabula. At the Modern even, when I was twenty. And at Cannes—well—when I was twenty-four." And had won the prize.

A man can sweat modesty, Gonchev thought, but only a few can do so at will. And those teeth, so worn from holding back his self-directed humor. One would swear they weren't capped, yet one knew they must be, perhaps toward that very effect. While the voice that issued from them had the hesitations of a competent knife.

Gonchev had got everything he said. And now understood how the man worked those films of his, one after the other from the same psyche. He was so securely insecure he could risk anything.

In the past months Gonchev had managed to see more American-made pictures than many a professional saw in his lifetime, and he thought he already knew the confession this man was going to make.

"Paul—guess I thought I never would meet you in the flesh. We assumed they had you for life. Or that you wanted it that way. Paul—I stole some stuff of yours. I don't know how I had the nerve."

"Ho, but he does!" Gonchev said to Roko in Japanese. "Because of where I was at the time, he thought he could get away with it. But say nothing."

I did the same once in Japan, Gonchev was thinking. I copied from that obscure Czech not because he was obscure—I was that too—but because the bit I took gave me such delight. Committed by the young, such theft can be a compliment. But this man is not obscure. And not that young.

The man was watching Roko and him closely. Slowly Gonchev let himself nod at him. They held each other's eyes in a boxer's sincere stare.

A cap of that size has its troubles. On a man of that size. It has to look up. For the first time the man addressed Roko. "Does he mean he knows—he knew?"

Gonchev tapped her on the shoulder. "My sequence when the two neighborhoods pass each other. And never quite collide." With the skyscrapers standing in the river and the riverfront dockside shanties flowing in the street. It had been amusing. Actually he had only done it of necessity, because one set of his files was better than the other.

"Paul—tell me in your own words," the man said before Roko could speak. "And chuck the Japanese—excuse me, Roko—is that your name, dear?—but I know he knows English."

"He can't speak it," she said into her neck. But her cheeks had gone almost white. "Haven't you heard?"

"Oh, that. Oh, shit. I thought that was just buzz. For the press." He put a hand on Paul's shoulder, reaching up. He uses his size the way some small priests do, Gonchev thought. "Oh, Paul. And then you've probably had to see all my stuff, including that bit of it. You did see it?

When you'd only just come?" He bent his head over his clasped hands. "Oh, God, Paul. What a trauma, for you."

When he raised his head, the cap hadn't shifted. "I'm so glad I got to tell you—as I was advised. Yes, I was advised." He nodded intimately, as if Gonchev would know what that meant. "But meanwhile, you've been getting the tributes—I know how hard that can be to deal with." There was a glint in his eye—yes, there certainly were two of him. "I was right, those long-ago Saturdays, wasn't I? You're—one of us." He has hallowed his voice.

How marvelous it was to be with an equal. What a relief. Out of the corner of an eye Gonchev saw that daisy fringe of onlookers which had once been his own lot.

"And you," Gonchev answered, letting an eyelid droop—which could be as good as a cap, "you are one of us."

"What did he say?" the man asked.

Roko answered with gusto, "My gentleman says"—for she sometimes used this form—"my gentleman says—so are you."

For a minute the man stood looking down at his white tennis shoes, which were as spotless as if he had flown there, on his own wings. Then, searching in a vest tailored of the same cloth as the cap, he scrawled on a card, pressed it into Gonchev's hand, whispering, "He'll know I sent you"—and vanished. Only to dart back, while waving at a driver now waiting for him, in order to whisper in Roko's ear.

"What did he say?" Gonchev asked, once he was gone.

"He said to tell you that his other hero, after you, is Chateaubriand."

"Oh?" Gonchev knew perfectly well who the French hero was. "A steak?"

Back in their hotel room, this time on Central Park South, courtesy of a management from which Gonchev's sponsor had got the room gratis, Gonchev, by then in his undershorts, fisted his hands to his image in the bathroom mirror. "Stuff. What a marvelous word for it. Stuff!"

Later he said to Roko, "And did you catch a load of his driver? Dressed like a thug. A chic thug. So his master won't be seen going about with a chauffeur. And can wear sneakers."

He was shaving again for the evening. Thanks to the loss of his birth papers, his parents, able to misrepresent his age from time to time for varying reasons, had finally lost count. But whatever his actual age might be, he was still a twice-a-day man. Still chuckling, he had nicked his chin. "What style. But not like Europe. Here one always knows it is style—but do they intend us to? That I am not sure. Did he?"

In bed—for he and Roko didn't have to leave again for an hour or so and, as in the old days, schedule always excited him—he'd said, "In the old Hollywood they used to have a Central Casting; maybe they still do. And if somebody was . . . too true-to-life, the joke would be that he came from there. But I begin to think that everybody we meet here comes from Central Casting. Everybody in the whole country, maybe." He always gave her these small confidences before sex. Since he could not give her his love.

Afterward—for that too was only polite—he said, "You know, I tease too much about this country. That worries me. Teasing means love." Which would be absurd. Loving a country, at this late date, and with his kind of dossier. And what would that do to his stuff?

Her moon-slits shone in the dimness. "You do not tease me."

She saw he was disturbed. Her laugh tinkled. She sprang out of bed, her back to him. What had she said, as the bathroom door closed? Surely she hadn't. "I tease."

Two days later, a Hollywood sheet reported that this director and Gonchev were going to work together on a film, as yet undecided. A rumor that Gonchev denied publicly, to Laura's fury, although there was no use telling her why.

He told Roko. "He's my equal. Equals can sometimes be friends. But they can never work together."

Laura as usual could not be stopped. A quality a father could come to admire, if ever it had the luck to hit the right target. "Roko tells me the Cap slipped you a card."

"Who is the Cap?"

"That's what they call him." She had insisted that Gonchev pursue the matter. "Only a name and address? And his own signature below? That's the way they do now." She had discovered that the best directors no longer waited for the studios but bought up properties themselves, or initiated them. "It could mean everything."

"You do it then, Laura. Pose as my secretary."

If she had, he hadn't heard further about it, so at last, for fear she was hatching something, he asked. After all, she comes from a hatching family. He had waited, though, until he saw her face to face.

Yes, she had even gone to the address, rather than telephone. "As your manager, Papa. Because I am still that, aren't I?"

When she is doleful she is much prettier, softer. And when something has gone wrong. For he is "Papa" again.

"So who was that man sending me to?"

"His psychiatrist."

The beard wakes him. Gonchev apologizes in mime for his doze, praises the tea. The beard is an excellent recipient of dumbshow, prattling along noncommittally in between. "Russian tea—we get it from the co-op. And look here, I'm sorry about the long wait—the equipment broke down. That's why we ate so early. It always does."

Gonchev agrees. He knew all along what must be going on in the other room. Sometimes he waited out the delay in a faculty room, plied with cookies and straw tea. Or in the lustier departments, with after-evening-class dago red. You couldn't trust even the auditoriums. You could merely regret that after a certain interim repairs would be made. The show, all too often the same show, would go on. Only the museum showings were glassy perfect, as impeccable as a trustee's smile.

On tour one expects these mishaps and cheery recoveries; that was what made it a tour. "And I'm getting my college education," he said to Roko. "Like you, a little. On a scholarship."

Often he was seeing again the films he knew, including the ones they thought he couldn't have seen. But also, by persuasion on his part, a lot of what they thought he shouldn't see: the popular taste. And the most interesting, although he kept that opinion to himself. Don't let the barbarian see you know his strength—which he may not know himself—in case you may wish to join up with him.

For he had an idea that in spite of the terrifying excesses here, their screen butcherings of people or emotions, often simultaneously, or their free-for-all vaultings into remote exhaustions of technique, they still didn't see what they had so amazingly done.

What was that leap which only Nijinsky could do? Those decadences that once only the absinthe-sodden French could muster—or that lily-carrying Irish mountebank?

Sixty cameras in commercial quadrille now ground it out every day—and the directors never stooped to calling it art. They can teach a crowd of subway extras to stalk like Giacometti figures—and see itself doing that. They can get a brassiere to pout like an Arp sculpture and slide off into the singing rain, leaving the customers not sure whether they are seeing a breast or a hip. While a clarinet massacres Monteverdi, who never wrote for that instrument, but the child viewer munching Mars bars will remember it forever.

They have gutted the old surrealism to a standstill here. So that any hardhat, lolling in his mall-bought lounger at end of day, can handle those images as easily as he can install a shoji screen in his dinette. The subtly effete, the nastily beautiful, are all the same—and exchangeable with the guy next door. For the Americans were doing a wonderful thing, really, and only what the rest of the world was after—but with God's help, and maybe some from Gonchev, they would do it even better. They were replicating the world as it now is.

His first weeks here he had been devastated. His own film images seemed to him as frozen and static as the earliest travelogues—*Nanook of the North,* say, redone in woodblock, and as dead to movement as any frozen Alaskan fish. Now he saw that his straining against his limits was what had saved him, and had sent his work broadside.

The Americans too were perhaps only parlaying other people's ideas. In films, surely, and maybe in conduct of life. Somewhat like him. But they were not only redoing the past en masse, they were popularizing it. They had this curious tendency to civilize themselves only halfway. To hoard what others called their vulgarity—right in the midst of universal toilets. Given their history, with which Laura's Cooper Union classes regaled her—founding fathers romping with slave girls, or actor-presidents fiddling with "star wars" by astrology—maybe it was their destiny to bring down the bleached towers of the intellectuals and bring up the soiled dreams of the proletariat, to meet.

For no question about it, they had more free-for-all here than in any other place. If they would only give him a camera, and a few shoestring millions, he wouldn't mind abetting them. Maybe he was kidnapped just in time.

The beard has seen his face fall at the mention of the impending older movies. "They putting you through too much of this? I bet they give you the course. Lemme guess. First, the French. All the way back from *Weekend* to Jean Vigo. *L'Atalante?* Uh-huh. And the one where the boys battle with feather pillows? Great, though. Woody himself saw a lot of that. And how many times they show you *Blood of a Poet?*"

Gonchev throws up his hands, groaning, and knocking his forehead. At times, viewing the same old warhorses in the gritty academic half-light, he has bitten his tongue to keep from hissing.

"And *The Andalusian Dog?* I hate that film," the beard says. "Something half-assed about it; I don't know what. Or maybe the way they push it down our throats."

Gonchev shakes his head, trying to say what it was. Danilo had slipped that film to him, as he had most. At first Gonchev had thought, It comes to me too late. Like those nursery rhymes, missed in his childhood, that can never now resonate. Then he had seen the sharper truth. Buñuel had come late to Buñuel.

He tries to say this, but can only emit a noise.

"Ah, that one," the beard says, *"Bê-ête. Bête.* When she croons to the beast-prince. I think that was the first soundtrack that was art." He is bubbling now. "They say Cocteau's shallow. But when those hands on the wall holding torchlights grow forward—Jesus!"

They stand silent, honoring.

The beard smoothes his chin. Gonchev sees that the gesture isn't a jeer but a musing. "Around here it's a case of how honcho you have to be." He sees Gonchev doesn't know the word. "Sam Shepard. Psychology in a ten-gallon hat."

Gonchev slaps his knee.

"One last question. Don't want to throw all my Ph.D. orals at you.

Yeah, I have to do that—and the film thesis. Yeah, I did a film. They say it's too Stan Brakhage." He grins. "I did it on purpose, so they could like recognize something, you know?"

Gonchev agrees vigorously.

"Okay. The question. On a guy around here they say is quaint."

Gonchev purses his mouth. In some circles here, they are saying this about him.

"What's your stand on Jacques Tati?" The eyes narrow, asking.

When talking with a bearded man, Gonchev usually wished he could ask him to doff the beard for a minute, as one takes off sunglasses, so that in the jousts of facial expression they would have an equal handicap. But this man has earned his beard. And there are strands of gray in the brown; he isn't that young.

Gonchev recalled the day Danilo had brought the two Tati films, known to Vuksica but not to him.

"Two," she had said, "two," in exact tremolo between hunger and dream. Reminding him of what an actress she had been, and what she might miss by living in what she had called "daylight country." She never complained, but her remarks could be like the spoor an animal drops openly. More than once she'd said that this country they had consigned themselves to had no real darkness. Odd, in a landscape of trees gnarled overhead like rope, and mountains that at dusk sat like hens on the villages.

In the studio, into which they had crept to show Danilo's contraband, was the dark she craved. They'd never been disturbed there in spite of leaving open a place in the wall through which the screen could be seen. A movable panel about the size of a cat's entry and made by Gonchev himself in that spirit, for the spy.

More than once, the day after a secret showing, Gonchev had felt the man was about to speak to him, but he never had. What a destiny, to be a film critic in solitary. Or a fan?

Gonchev had done the best he could for him. Night after night in his own solitary he'd alternated the two films, until for him one of the two had dropped out of the running. Next day his spy, tailing him, had closed the gap between them, strictly against orders, and zoomed past him with a perceptible nod, two fingers raised.

"Like an icon," Vuksica said when she heard. "You never can be sure what they're saying—icons."

"You didn't see him," Gonchev said. "He feels the same as me."

But this young American sage has maybe seen even more?

"M-m-m," Gonchev says. He would have spat his teeth in order to say that title.

"*Monsieur Hulot's Holiday.*" The words whistle through the fringed lips. "That lope Tati has. Like a stalking grandfather clock. Bust my appendix scar, every time. But in your *Agra*—how did you ever get an elephant to do it? And that howdah, perched out at the very same angle as Tati's neck."

The thrill of having one's art recognized starts in the bladder-anus and suffuses to the collarbone, in a kind of spinal sex. For years now he has never really had it. One doesn't get that from a government. Let the man go on sweet-saying it, like jabs from a syringe.

"You put something in the elephant's quiff?"

Gonchev buries his face in his hands, shoulders shaking.

"We thought maybe some kind of yogi, offstage. Monitoring the beast. But all through the picture? Come on, give." He seems oblivious of the fact that he is talking to a man who can't talk back.

But pure pleasure to Gonchev anyway. The Japanese sprays from him like confetti, while he mimes hammer and nails, whips a cushion from the easy chair where he'd slept, drapes his handkerchief over it, and finally walks on his hands, swaying his buttocks, pad pad.

In a swit of comprehension the beard drops on all fours, opposite him. "You built it," he moans. "You built that elephant! My buddy and I did time with a circus two years ago. We swore you couldn't have."

Gonchev nods. The floor feels cool to his palms. He had had calluses on them for weeks—being Tati inside an elephant.

"But the skin. There were close-ups of that skin. Like you could smell it."

Gonchev nods, swaying.

Old Italian leather, stripped from salon pieces dating from the Risorgimento, and long since confiscated by the state. Dipped first in formaldehyde, then a muddy river, and squeezed by hand.

The close-ups of course had been of real skin.

"But you could never have done the two-man deal inside that thing."

No. It had been a pygmy elephant.

"Or the one-man, either."

The aircraft factory had made the frame. Though for requisitioning a foreign wood, obtainable only by bending ideology, when he might have used home-grown, he had been reprimanded by bureaucrats who didn't know the difference between balsa and oak. Somewhere he had read that the Germans had lost the World War II for lack of ball bearings. In the office of an orthopedist as antique as his appliances he had gleefully found a neck prosthesis chock full of them, on which his howdah could be manipulated. Hidden inside the howdah, purely for his own fantasy, there had been a Hindu mask of Tati.

"Computers! You would have had to."

Strapped to his chest, yes, in order to command the forefeet and the waving appendages—although if given time enough he would have liked to learn whether a human sphincter might be trained sufficiently to move a tail.

"Like puppets actually. Son-of-a-gun!" When the beard, still on all-fours, drops his chin way down, his chin hairs just clear the ground. "Ever seen the Little Theater? The best. Gone now. But the same principle. Do it all from the outside."

Gonchev shakes his head violently. Slowly he stands up. Inside the balsa frame he stretches tall. His hands play a small computer, strapped to his chest and padded to fill out the thorax of the beast. One forefoot and one hind foot are his; the other two he manipulates. His neck alternately retracts and rides forward, while his buttocks delicately protrude, in pachyderm rhythm. He feels in entire agreement with himself; where is dissidence? He lopes.

"Oh look, they're doing Tai Chi," a girl says from the door. "Come on, you guys. It was the projector was busted. It's patched."

The beard is circling Gonchev. "One man? Inside?"

217

Gonchev straightens up, brushing off his hands, retrieving his hand-kerchief—and nods modestly.

"You!"

"*Hai.*"

"You're a genius."

No. A man of limitations. Trained to understand their profound force on a stage set, or in history. In a country, in oneself.

"He did a Hitchcock!" the beard, also on his feet now, says to the crowd in the doorway. "He acted in his own movie. He's an actor too."

No, that's Danilo, my brother-in-law. Always his own hero. He doesn't get self-doubts from playing those. I'm only a director. I send the rabble up the palace steps, and down again. But I stay inside the elephant.

And hope nobody will notice—as they hadn't yet—that pygmy elephants live only in Africa.

Meanwhile he is pleased to be in the company of those who also patch.

A hand falls on his shoulder. Gonchev whirls.

"Jesus, I'm sorry," the beard says, recoiling. "That the way it still is for you guys, even over here? You're so cool, we keep forgetting why you're here. Sorry. But can we kick around one more thing? Tati's *Playtime.* Did the Beatles lean on that or didn't they? You know—in *Yellow Submarine.* Even in *Help!*—that crazy conversation pit?"

There is a wail from the doorway. "Will you come on, Rory? Let him be. We're an hour and a half behind, for God's sake. And what Jeanot's brought—you'll never believe the condition it's in. If we can run it at all."

"Well—it's been great to *talk* with you," the beard says.

The young crowd in the next room shouldn't surprise Gonchev, but always does. Warming a heart chilled by other podiums. Where a whiskey beforehand was needed to brave both the dark exhaust of political protest to come and the distance between the violence of the world, and him and the other spouters in those bright halls.

Here the innocents creep in through the back door to loll on the floor, legs crossed, like yogi, or slouch on folding chairs, lips parted or ready to be cynical. Were there ever any accolades equal to those from the young? Or more to be taken with a grain of salt? For they brought one back to the beginning, even to the crazy idea that one might still be there.

The moderator, one of those blue-chinned glum young men, proves to be humorous. He congratulates their guest on having escaped the student films originally scheduled. "A clone of *Scorpio Rising*, from Rory here. Jeanot's documentary on the West Point military academy—which may have to be cleared by the Defense Department by the time he finishes it. And my own timely little spiel—now that graduation is upon us—*Divorce Among the Unmarried.*" The last quip brings laughter. "Now I'll cede the chair to Jeanot. Who's pulled off such a coup, we may even forgive him for wearing that tie. He's brought us a film no one over here has ever seen before. In fact, here in our little viewing room, for which thank College Housing"—groans—"we may have a world premiere. A film Paul Gonchev was never allowed to show."

They all turn around to look at him. He always seats himself in the last row. He gives them a small, iconic smile.

"Banned," the redhead breathes. "Politically."

According to Pfize, one reason Gonchev was admitted to the States so quickly was the number of his pictures reputedly sent to the scrap heap by his home government. If the latter was Communist, nothing got you past U.S. Customs more quickly. The other reason was that his films had been represented as travelogues, and clean enough to be shown in the schools. Such departures as the sodomy-shaped edifices in his Rio, hadn't been mentioned. Or the smart Roman wedding in Parioli, where the flower girl and boy ring bearer had been making funny with each other, sitting on the far end of the bride's very long train. Which was why neither of those flicks, though so ideologically clean, could be shown in sexually modest China. While at his home base, where such details of Western decadence were very popular, they had drawn crowds.

So it was that he had kept the balance, by seesawing himself a certain leeway. For he had had no films on the scrap heap except those he had put there himself. A museum here, assisting him to make a filmography of his total output, had estimated that less than three quarters were known.

And here is the Haitian lad. He stands tall. Bravo, Jeanot.

"Got this film through channels, yes. CBS—Columbia Broadcasting. Any conscientious objector to that can leave." He grins. "My CO in the Reserve here, he has an old war buddy there, and I went to that guy for a job. Talking film, he tells me they been offered a vintage Gonchev, very early. Almost in the rough. A chance to see the man's technique in the making. I don't know as I go for that. But let the man here say. Anyhow, way it came to CBS, they won't buy. But my CO's friend is hoping to get together a private syndicate." He bows, to Gonchev only, and sits down. Like royalty, not looking behind him.

"A syndicate," the blue-chin says. "That could mean big bucks." He salutes Gonchev. "Maybe we folks could horn in, ha-ha. Okay, fellas. Shoot. And any virgins here, let 'em pray to Jove. That this damn projector holds."

Two girls get up and lower the tattered blinds.

Gonchev knows from Laura what a syndicate is. Suddenly he feels all that tea in his bladder and taps the man next to him.

In the toilet he thinks: I could leave now. I could find the way to the motel. I could hijack that Volvo; I saw the key was left in. Or that boy's motorcycle, a Honda by the look of it.

To the mirror over the toilet he says: No, no, Gonchev. Take the way forward, never the way back.

But these mirrors over toilets, no less—what is it with these Americans? Such an old film ploy of theirs too—a man brushing his self-estimation along with his teeth. But if Gonchev becomes a citizen here, what will he see in all the other glass they offer themselves up to? Those open plate-glass walls at the supermarket, in which they mural themselves in the act of purchase, inviting the world to watch. Or those ninety-story pueblos in which they vie for the sun and then have to cover the glare.

What does he see in the water-closet mirror now? A man whose wife has exported him. Whose son is a bullyboy. Whose lifework isn't even in the official public domain but circulates on black markets that pay him only in praise.

Or does he see the face he's ignored all these years? And never photographed—but never doubted. Sufficient for women, no lodestar to professionals. Pockmarked with European change, the way they like it here. A face with a touch of the brigand, from the habit of command. The way they like it here.

A pan. Of the kind the agent called "the heavy." One that just skirted "bad guy" but made it to "hero." Couldn't he write her a script for one of those?

Or for a man who has a broker daughter. And a podium, of sorts. Maybe not one for the masses, in spite of State Department hopes. Who envies the poets, each of whom is his own podium. Whose whole lives are an open memoir.

Why can't such a face, such a man, make a memoir of itself? For the plate-glass world.

Back in his seat, he shivers with expectancy. Not for the film up on the screen, whose dried-out reel they are still having trouble with— some old film of his he won't mind authenticating, if there's a prospect of proud new work to come. For money in the offing breeds money, Derek is fond of saying.

There is no market for "remake" Gonchev cities, they've told him, and they are right. What they had loved in his "cities" was his fantasy of them—that improbable edge of truth, from a bibliographer who had never seen the books. Fantasies that showed the free world what it was to be free.

So what could he give them now? One of those brown-toned autobiographies, monologued with an over-voice and spiked only with memory, from a man's first hedgerow love affairs to whichever wars, then broadside on, to the power of power, and so declining, back to the green of early Edens forgot. Finale, the wrinkled toecaps of an old man's boots. Or an émigré's.

He will be his own city, somehow. With Laura's help, he will be his own syndicate.

The girl on his other side jumps; he has kicked her. He has remembered with glee why Derek is against syndicates. As in racing, all too often you buy a dark horse.

"Oh, you're right," the girl says. "We're off."

She puts her arm around him.

On the screen the insignia of all his films looms forward, in black-and-white. The premier had been unwilling to allow either the country's name or his own bony surname as sponsor—his predecessor was said to have been shot for advocating more Western involvement. At a Central Committee meeting. By him.

Gonchev had transmitted a suggestion to the premier, careful meanwhile to be away on location at the time. Why not use the initials of the only newspaper in the land, *Zeri i Populi*, these happening to form a word the world delighted in—ZIP. And a word with a sound most appropriate. "Like a shot," he had said.

Next came Gonchev's own logo, the national tree, with his initials artfully intertwined at the trunk. So far no one had noted the Chinese ideograph for the last of the Five Constant Virtues, Sincerity, microscopically inscribed in the veining of a leaf at a time when he'd thought he might need a haven, and travel to that one nation had still been possible.

Next come the interminable credits, actually a complete roster of the Union of Cinematographers, with their statuses indicated in five sizes of print.

The girl's long legs slowly extend next to him, slender and choice. Does the arm now warm at his nape and shoulder mean she is one of those camp followers on his circuit, condoms ready in the purse? Her face is the sweet blur common to females of her age when in movie half-light. Men too can become harlequins there. Even the middle-aged can retreat back to rendezvous.

While he wonders, and the list works itself steadily toward the bottom, she slips a small hard something into his palm. No, not a condom. What he holds is a honeydrop of a brand he himself uses when his voice tires, its bee-decorated wrapper barely visible. The giver, the girl, is of the breed that while it sees and hears, and maybe feels another's flesh, and sneezes now and then from the dust of theaters, must also crunch or suck. So that the sense-trip will be complete. Touched, he squeezes her knee to show that he is popping the lozenge trustingly into his mouth. The projector, as old a one as he has ever encountered, whirs complicitly. Their trip, however grainy the screen, is about to begin.

She is in her snuggery. He is on the long pontoons of light that lead him out to his devotions. His body is his gondola, on that river of picture, the film. From which nobody is barred except a live person. Here one was spared from watching the predicament of living—and millions had rushed to be rescued. He has the same illusions about his audience as any other artist. Buried alive in life, one may enter his palace, and rise like the saved from the tomb—into immortal dark.

"Sir, why do you always sit with your hands on your lap, palms up?" a student had once asked him. Maybe because he was receiving? But he wasn't going to let that loose. "Because I don't watch myself," he'd said sharply, but left them disquieted. A student had come up to him afterward. "We fear for you."

"A film begins as it must end, like a statue turned," one of his Japanese colleagues had said, saying good-bye to him. All present had agreed that a film must unfold like a scroll, and not require literacy. For years after he had left, his brain had itched with their aphorisms. None had been surprised at his choice of country, which they saw merely as a monkish retreat that would set his work on its path. A few have remained his correspondents. One has written: "So—your cities. We marvel. Even at the Tokyo." Whose latest extravagances had been depicted via information not supplied by any of them. "Your highway to the airport looks to have cost as much as it has cost us. And the vase of flowers in the bus driver's galley is quite correct. Although nowadays, in the new Japan, he might have rolled up his sleeves." Their lust for detail had not deserted them. "And we mourn that we cannot see your library. But Gonchev-san, what of *the* city—that one we wait for?"

If, over the years, they'd noted his one major omission, tact had kept them from saying so. But to be certain, he'd written to ask which city was meant. He shouldn't have. The answer came back: a small packet of slides of survivors, blackened and bandaged, but alive. Gonchev's insensitivity had been not to recall that this man's father had for a while been among those. On the back of one photo, presumably of him, had been written: "A detail."

So Gonchev had tried. In reparation. He wouldn't be written to again until he had. He sees now what that omission meant to them. But who could do that city, to whom all fireworks would be an insult?

He had begun the film with bandages—white, pure white, airy, issuing into view like scrolls not yet settled to shaped use—and had meant to end with them. In between he'd arranged his stockpiled horrors: oil fires, battle scenes. Only to be confirmed in what he already knew—that such a city could not be arranged. Any arrangement tidied it. The film had never been sent.

Might this be it, this white continuity now soothing in? Soiled and jaundiced by now, as it should be—for who can do Hiroshima?

But it is not.

What's this mild, dead green sky, amiable as a pin-cushion? Not his London. English air, which he had studied in their Turners and Collinses, was never exactly the right color for the weather of the moment. Channel air was a wrong green, hard to keep in mind. In his London it had been so. Was this the workup maybe? Not with those misty, turreted edifices, like a Venetian wedding cake gone awry. Nor yet his Venice. Nor his Bangkok, a discard, for lack of all that goldleaf necessary for the shrines, for whose sheen he would not substitute.

But these thin-penciled streets of mingy gray—Christ, he's seen those before. And with a jolt now recognizes their ancestry. Someone must have pored over Gonchev's bookplates of Jean Fouquet's *Grande Chronique de France*—the *Entry of King John the Good into the Capital*, especially. And had thought himself capable of imitating that medieval gray, that ineffable blue. As for that penciling—Rise from the dead, engraver Caillot.

Moving his lips, Gonchev can quote the preface of that small bedside edition: ". . . the Paris of which Péguy tenderly sang. City where vice is sold most freely, where prayer is offered most freely."

And here come those accursed curbstones, as thick as the labia of some poor whore. As counterfeited by that whore's son, Stepan.

If Stepan had at least sent this film out as his own. But no. They must have let him do it for the dollar exchange. To keep that profitable industry which my name, Gonchev, has created, that's it. They've sent it out as mine—maybe the first of a long line of counterfeits. By my best student, curse his name. And all his parts.

"Lights!" Gonchev roars. "Lights!" Maybe the language God had used at the Creation. For the lights spring on.

Oh, such a sorry little projector. Must he apologize to it?

"That belongs to the Art Department," someone yells as he slouches toward it, King Kong, King Kong. He understands those animals now, the large leftover ones, and why his head always makes an ark for them.

In a corner stacked with gear he sees what might be the peen of a hammer. It isn't, but it will do. As he raises it, a girl cries out indignantly, "This is a small college!"

No, it's his violence that's too small. And his target. That's what a dissident must feel. He smashes down. Stepan's oeuvre, which had scarcely begun to roll, comes out like a bad egg. Yes, there is the Union stamp: FOR EXPORT.

The hammer is grabbed from him. Too late, he raises his head. The Haitian, defending his borrowed property? No, the girl who had put her arm around him. "Oh, Paul," she says sorrowfully, like to a traitor, and brings the hammer down.

He awakes, not in the Gellert baths this time, but in an American garage, the cars ranged neat as a row of quoits. Three brands he knows—a Ford, a Jeep, and a Merc. And a long, polished hearse. The Haitian boy, and a man in pink pajamas, lean over the deck chair in which he is lying. His mind is clear. He is in fact in a kind of bliss of understanding. He can't be in prison. The man's pajamas, piped in dark blue, are the same as a pair Laura had bought for him. The cushions under him are swollen with quality. Perhaps the college president's? Not likely. Not that college. Not these cars.

The Haitian brings a kind of pierced-steel pepper shaker to his nose. "Breathe in, sir." A breath makes him gag with more understanding. "Sir" bodes well. He shouldn't call the boy "the Haitian" even in his mind. That's what Roko calls "ethnic."

"Now, just hold it to his nostrils," the other man says. "Ten seconds. Then he'll sit up." He checks a watch dial deeply imbedded in a fleshy wrist; he must wear it to bed. "Right," he says then. Gonchev has sat up. "There you are, Jeanot. Antifreeze, of a sort. Put it back on the shelf up there. Won't get that out of the procedure on concussions. Works though, most times. What hit him?"

"Piece of a fellow's hang-gliding gear. And a girl."

"How come?"

"The equipment's no loss. They need new. But he was holding the film print high over his head. And the hammer. Guys rushed him. They never meant to hurt him." The Haitian—Jeanot—starts to laugh. "Excuse me, sir. He stopped them cold."

"With the hammer?"

"He spoke."

"So? Isn't that what these fellas do at those sessions?"

"In English. He's the one who couldn't speak, except in Japanese. A case."

"Sonofagun. What'd he say?"

" 'I pay for what I break.' "

"Spoken like a good American."

They both laugh.

"But then Rory—you remember Rory?"

"Drove for me once. 'Bout ten years ago."

"Everybody has. Best-paying job in town. When there's work."

"Don't joke," the man in pajamas says. "I take care of all my boys. But no jokes. It's an honorable profession like any other. Like my old man before me."

"Sorry, sir. And everybody knows you've brought the Corps back to—where it was."

"With the help of you boys. But Rory was never in the Corps."

"Big guru on campus now. Still going for his Ph.D. in film. They let him teach one course. Anyway, Rory jumped this guy too, yelling he might be a hijacker, and grabbed for the film."

"Is he? A hijacker?"

"No way. A real chief, in his line. For me to meet him, well, to a former army man like you—like General MacArthur coming back. But he says the film is not by him. Said it clear as a bell, before he got conked. 'This film is a faker.' Before he went berserk."

"You put any money down on it?"

"Nobody did yet. But no harm checking. When we heard a film by Paul Gonchev might be on tap."

"Russian?"

"The good kind. They bounced him. And he grew up in Japan."

"Those Japanese. I just bought one of their computers. My business here doesn't justify. But I couldn't resist. . . . Look, I think your guy is coming round."

"I just want to get him back to his motel."

"You amateurs," the man says, chuckling. "Well, okay." He bends to lift one of Gonchev's eyelids, then feels his head. "Hey, feel this. And this here. I was in a medical unit, you know. This man's had a concussion before. Hard head." He checks the other eye. "He'll be okay. But you want to take him to emergency?"

"Saturday night? Half the interns at the disco? He'd be on the bench 'til dawn."

"Anybody at his motel?"

"Just his girl. Or, I dunno. She maybe—"

He's made a movement. Gonchev can't turn his head to see. But his mind is clear. Those pajamas are exactly like his. The ones back at the motel.

The man in them sighs. "Look, we better walk him. And hot coffee. I'd take him upstairs to the house, but you know my wife. She likes to keep the business separate. But there's a coffee machine in the . . . you know. The ell. Want to go fix some?"

There is a pause.

"Any bodies there?" the boy says.

"One. But all done."

Another pause.

"You'll never make an officer," the man says.

"Oh yes, sir. But there I'd be the one killing them. After a struggle. The body in your refrigerator might be somebody I know."

"No one. I guarantee it. We scooped her up with a spoon on the interstate. Accident. And she's packed. . . . Okay—I make the coffee. You get him started walking. Slap him if necessary." He backs out a door. To one side of it two hats are hung on wall hooks—a fine black fedora and a visored military cap. Neither looks as if it belongs to him. He has the roundish face and lumpy, slightly gone-to-seed body of the American male who typically wore what Laura called a porkpie, a kind Gonchev must not buy. Lower middle, she'd said. Middle what? Class. Oh, Papa, you don't fool me. You're the real snob. That's what Mama loved you for.

"He's all right, my CO in our ROTC unit, don't you worry," Jeanot says when the door has closed on the other man, meanwhile hoisting Gonchev to his feet, which isn't easy; his ankles are jelly. "He just never got over his war. And having to come back to the family business. . . . There you go. Can you make it?"

Gonchev blinks. He isn't going to let himself be slapped. They walk back and forth. Now and then they pass a table on which lies the snarled roll of film, a kind not used here anymore. Each time he eyes it, his knees are stronger. It wasn't a bad knock, only another one. He doesn't feel too sleepy; he feels awakened. This isn't the Rockies, but he and this kid are getting to a mountain top.

As they pass the cars for the twentieth time, Jeanot gestures to them. "That's his family." He points to the Volks. "His baby girl. She's thirty, and home from her second ex. And that's the wife." The Mercedes. "And the Ford? That's him. He's really a lonely man."

Well, of course he would be. With that ell to handle. Where he is taking such a long time to make coffee. And a hearse in the family too.

Television shows here, the eerie ones, often made use of such places, with ghostly sound effects and blue-black interiors—whereas most of the real undertakers were probably like this, porticoed old houses with storage space to burn, and located just barely on the safe edge of the rundown side of town. Or within "parlor" distance of a church.

In Harbin, Gonchev's family had lived next door to a man of just the same function. An ancient, rumored to be old enough to have once worn a pigtail, and to have been a part-time executioner, as well. But what else can men of such professions be except part-time? Gonchev's old neighbor had inherited his business also, and he too had had a second vocation, in his case as a scribe. It was said that his brush and pen knew as many characters as he had known corpses.

It was from him that Gonchev, in Harbin again on a movie errand, had got his ideograph. Which you had to be given; you couldn't choose. "For who would choose Sincerity?" the host had said, peering up through the tiny, flat-lensed, iron-rimmed spectacles that had been his own father's. "Or any one Virtue," Gonchev had added, priding himself that he still knew how to talk to the Chinese. "I've never been to the cinema," had been the scribe's reply.

"You are thinking," the young man walking Gonchev says (for a person who walks one is no longer a boy). Gonchev nods. Yes, I'm thinking what I will say when that coffee comes through the door. For I will say something.

Just then the pajamaed man enters, carrying a pot and three mugs, no, four. Maybe one for the corpse? "Cold in there." He is wearing a porkpie hat.

The coffee is black and strong, the best that Gonchev has had since he came over. Still standing, he smacks his lips.

"Dragon's blood," the younger man says, grinning.

"His mother gets it for me from Haiti," the man says to Gonchev, sitting down on the deck chair Gonchev had vacated, hat knocked back on his head. "Have my coffee, I'm up to anything." He nods toward the ell. "Had to give her a little touch." He sighs, as a workman does at a task completed. His hands are soft and white.

From rubber gloves, no doubt. Gonchev feels light and easy, repaired. It wouldn't be that hard to speak. Do Americans realize how much farce flits through their normal daily lives? Or is it so only to the eye of the exile, requiring him to think thoughts more profound than he is used to, as antidote? A damn nuisance, a burden. Until he stops doing this he won't really be in America. A second blow to the head should have helped.

Does he actually want to be here? Even in this ghoulish, faintly ridiculous garage? Yes, he does. The man in pajamas is now putting the fourth cup on the cement floor back of the open overhead door.

"Milk for the cat. Comes in from his amours when he damn pleases," the man grunts. Rising from his squat, he massages the roll around his belly. "Wife wants him altered, but I won't allow." Glancing at Gonchev, he grunts again. "Hah. Lemme see the eyes again." He peers in, blinking. "Good. Now stretch out your arms." Gonchev does so. They quiver, but minimally. "Good enough. Raise your right knee." He hits the reflex with the side of his hand. The leg kicks. "Right!" he says, and extends the hand to Gonchev. "Glad to meet you."

The Haitian is beaming. "Director Paul Gonchev, Captain ——." The name goes by too fast for Gonchev to get it. "My commanding officer."

Gonchev lets his hand be gripped. It is still too Japanese. Too limply European, even. A gesture is owed, a friendlier one. He extends a finger and pokes the captain's pajamaed midriff, then his own. "Brooks," he says, enunciating carefully. "B'rooks B'rothers. I have the same."

"Sonofagun," the man says. "Hands across the sea, huh? You get their catalogue?"

Gonchev shakes his head. Whatever a catalogue was, he didn't.

"We use their pajamas a lot in this business," the captain says, flicking his pink sleeve. "For the unidentified especially. You'd be surprised how many families won't give up a good suit of clothes. Top people." He muses. "So you're a director. You too. But not the same as me, huh?" He articulates the English, as people do here when talking to foreigners.

His junior officer looks embarrassed. Yes, that's what this Jeanot is—an officer in the making. And on the lookout for the documents?

Gonchev takes a last sip of coffee, cleansing his teeth with a tongue still fuzzy. So he is a snob, is he? Interesting to see how Laura and Derek would act, if they were here. Ask the cost of everything? All countries are multiple, he thinks excitedly. Even the one I just came from. But this one is more multiple than most. And I am just at the beginning of this one. Only, Gonchev, please. Spoil it all if you're not careful. Stop being profound.

Taking a deep breath, he points to the film on the table, meanwhile shrugging disarmingly. Jokes would be chancy in this place. "Stinks."

The captain does give him the eye, then bursts into loud laughter. "Sonofagun. So what're you going to do with it?"

Gonchev bangs his fists together, wrenches them apart. Mime is often so much more satisfactory than speech. He expects to miss it.

"Can you tear up film?" the captain says.

"Dump it, maybe." Jeanot catches Gonchev's baleful stare. "Exposing it again first of course, sir."

"Oh," Gonchev mimes. "Maybe. But I'm not sure." And not sure you would destroy it.

"And who holds the bag?" the captain says.

"The source, sir," Jeanot says. "Trying to palm it off; what can they do? Not that they wouldn't have another print. Everybody does."

You don't know Elsinore, my fine boy. Ten forms to fill out for every inch of film. And when you've done that, a mustached little old lady doling it out. But let them have fifteen prints, fifty, I want to get my hands on this one.

"Who made it, by the way?" Jeanot asks.

"Former—student. My—best." Pronounce his name, Gonchev. And in English. It'll do you good. "By name—Stepan . . . Sefaru."

"Why would a guy forge a film?" the captain asks. "Why not just do your own?"

The younger man leans forward. Even at this hour all of him glistens, teeth, eyes, hair. "He wasn't selling it as his own, sir." He turns to Gonchev. "There was a rumor, sir"—how elegantly he manages his "sirs"—"that the one city you always, you never . . ."

For people to mark what you don't do . . . yes, that must be fame.

"He had—ambition, our Stepan." But for what? Not just for Elsinore. They had all begun to despise it, Gonchev, and you knew it. They wanted the real thing.

From across one quarter of the planet—be accurate, Gonchev, one sixth—the answer floats to him. "He wanted to sleep with my wife."

At that the man in pajamas rises, prowls uneasily, and finally speaks. "Why don't I get rid of that thing for you? In the ell."

The Lord has sent me here, Gonchev marvels. And, of course, Vuksica. "I accept."

On their way in, the younger man, this budding documentarian, half proposes to join them, but Gonchev turns him back. "Brave of you, but no need," he says haltingly in the best English that has yet come to him. "Some people . . . admire the dead. For having gone through death." That is his feeling, just this minute gouged out. "Some are repelled."

"I admire everything you do, sir. And that is the truth."

"Come along then," Gonchev replies.

The captain leads them in, a little pridefully. The long room, ready with glassed-in cubicles, is as neat as a good housewife's refrigerator, and as cold. Only one recess, up front, is occupied, by a body wound with broad white wrappings. The head and neck are still unbound. A cloth lightly covers them. "No coffin yet," the CO explains. "Still hunting her relatives. In case they can pay more than the state fee. Put her in the standard job, we might offend."

Above the rows of shelves on the wall opposite Gonchev is the man's license to operate, in good diploma script. On one shelf, among flacons and bottles, Gonchev sees the pierced-metal object that had been held to his nose. There is a fierce prophylactic odor to the room. The air conditioner whirs softly.

"Over here." The CO leads them to a wall of sinks and vats and lifts the lid of one. He has the reel of film in his other hand. On second thought, he offers it to Jeanot, whose eyes are half-closed.

Gonchev quickly grasps the reel, holds it for a moment. Like a priest, he thinks. Or a choirboy. What communion am I making? There is a vibration in what he holds, something he ought to know; had better not know. He tosses the thing into the vat. The lid drops.

Jeanot groans, bent like a mourner. "What was the subject?"

Next to the door, the coffee machine starts up softly, the CO watching it.

A lie can be so symmetrical that it is art.

"Hiroshima," Gonchev says.

7

Ethnics

Is IT BECAUSE Americans don't know the way of the world that the story of Paul Gonchev may give them a shiver or two? As well as a devilish wish to be amused? Or is it because they do know the world's ways and never cease to enjoy those?

What's a movie director like him doing knocking about history as if he belonged there as much as any obscure Greek general in the old mythology, and with as forgettable a name? In the nineteenth century, too, one found these troubled observers creeping into one country armed with the moral stance of another, their carpetbags slung over their shoulders, as if these sometimes dirty, even blood-stained, sacks contained only virtue. As for the eighteenth, which was when they here had the wit to found their country, while Gonchev's crowd were still serfs—what a rip and roar! Marquises holding their noses at us savages, while a hand stole out of their silk breeches and signed away our lands. Or English ladies, holding up their petticoats against the American savannahs and wetting their ankles in rivers the size of which their minds could never ford.

As for the twentieth century, whose villains the Americans are certainly going to be, wouldn't you think that they and we all might want to free ourselves of its grim capers, now that we are leaving it?

Gonchev knows better. History always scares. Just enough to offer some pinch of encouragement. Best anybody can do is get to know it intimately. Some corner of it.

So let them regard Paul Gonchev, in the town of Pipestone, Minnesota, leaning over one of the Indian ditches that are the pride and tourist attraction of the region, while a lovely young woman weeps her heart out at his side.

The birth certificate of this man may once have read *Pavel Goncharoff*, or *iev*, although he has never seen it, and by now the exact syllables must be lost even to any Central Intelligence. The girl may look to be in a dead-black mourning suitable to her storm of tears but is merely dressed in the New York City convention that goes with her age, occupation, and milieu. So cheer up; she's no widow yet of anybody. Although back at the prim ranchhouse-style "museum" that monitors this sacred place, the two women who preside over a sales booth stocking feathered earrings, printed guides, and larger items of bead, leather, and even fur, had stared at her. A tribal pair themselves, no doubt, but of some smallish ochre-skinned variety, Indians of the Midwest rather than the hawk-featured East, wearing sweater sets, and with permed hair. Who can blame them if this elegant creature, light-yellow-skinned and black-haired too, is like some affront they can't define?

A tourist did it for them. "Oh, look at the lovely ethnic," he whispered. Nobody gave a second look to her companion. And she wasn't weeping then.

The ditch the pair are staring into has been scraped clean of all myth. People around here are tidiers. Yet the field has a sparse aura still. From these small, ledged recesses the red stone of the region was mined, and the ritual too. And the thousands upon thousands of clay pipes. You may prefer the town of Pipestone itself, part of whose main street is still built of that local stone. The red fronts, sanded by wind, look like weathered cheeks.

"There's nothing here," Gonchev says, and knows on the instant that he is wrong. His camera, though slung laxly on his shoulder and impotent without film, says otherwise, speaking to his eye. In the grain of the buffed dirt might its lens detect cross-hatchings from ancient moccasins? In the empty coliseums of these small narrow diggings, is there even now a coarse black hair, caught in a cleft that has kept it safe from two centuries of wind? A camera is memory-of-place made visible; it can film where people have been. A good camera would see that this ground isn't just ground. Lives were made here, and undone. Clay into pipebowl and stem, each a small white hearth of a life, with a thin span of years attached. Pipes by the thousands, sharded back into clay. His camera would never need the drumbeat of words. Afterward, one could add music, but to him that convention means little—the sound only a kind of web the film exudes, binding the buttocks to the velours of theater seats. He knows nothing about the Plains Indians—and everything. Their lives had been smoke.

Roko is walking blindly but surely ahead of him. Her tears are her lens. He had seen this happen with his mother. Whether or not she had liked the city or home they were deserting, she always wept on leaving, her wet face an encouragement carrying her forward, a small Russian émigré lady, her face held high.

Roko wears boots by the same high-tech Japanese designer whose wily black bodysuits she favors. The suit is as slick as a surfer's; if the air were water she could swim. But the boots, black also, are intentionally clumsy, though with a machined sparkle circling their gloomy pointed soles, and a wag of leather behind. What are those boots leaving? He follows them.

As with many excavations, the paths between the ditches lead back to the base one started from. In the distance he and she can see the small building, scarcely an outpost, that houses the store. At the very end of the circuit he and Roko stop dead. She has let the tears fall without blotting them. He touches the wet salty face. "What are you crying for?"

She doesn't answer. Has he said it in Russian?

He says it again for sure, in Japanese.

Still she doesn't answer.

He knows what she wants. We each want what we fear, don't we? he says to her silently, cupping her face. It'll come to you like pipe smoke.

I can't bawl, he thinks. But from now on I'll be knowing what language I am speaking. That too will be a leaving. She knows.

She wants him to say it in English! Who are you crying for? So that she may answer.

For us, will she say? For all translation done?

Better to walk on.

Then what? The hotel in Pipestone, an old hostelry built for pioneers, had been renovated into "period suites." The lady desk clerk last night conducted him down the empty corridors, asking him to choose, and when he shook his head at decades whose names he had never heard of, allotted him "The Victorian," according to a brass plaque on its door.

Inside, two high-backed wooden beds had confronted him, both double. Here, too, did one have to choose? And were these huge installations meant for orgy or for family—which was Victorian? He knows the answer for any era: for both. But all the long night the flowered paper was too lively on the walls, and he dreamed what one does when one is the solitary guest in a hotel and the reservation has been for two. In the morning he had taken a cab to the first motel he came upon, and from there had traced her here.

Let's go back, he could say. Back to the hotel. Where we'll work this out. You choose the bed.

She's digging the toe of her boot into the path, but the ground won't give up a crumb. The spirits of those once here may be proud of that. But she isn't going to let these ledges resist her. Dropping to her knees, she scrabbles at the ditch side with a long almond nail. A clay shard falls.

"Watch out," Gonchev says, with a guilty glance toward the mission house, which is what the museum shed looks like to him. "In Harbin once, an Englishwoman who picked up a splinter of blue china on the street found a guard at her hotel when she returned, and the property of the people was demanded back. Everything must belong to the reservation here. Even a pebble."

But she tosses her head and, standing up, slides the shard carefully into the bodysuit's one pocket, a mere slit at the hip. Many people would forget such an acquisition later, but not Roko, schooled as she has been by Asia, in the retention of detail. Though she has never treated him like a detail.

Far from it. Sometimes, when she turns toward him from whatever else she may be doing, or from another conversation, he is reminded of the way orchestra players tip their faces to the conductor when about to shift to a major key.

Her face is still wet.

"Have a handkerchief."

"No, the wind is strong." She turns to the wind as to a brother who would defend her.

Her face has dried by the time they stop again at the museum shed. There she buys six pairs of the feathered earrings, to be wrapped as gifts. One of the women starts to insert an earring also in Roko's ear, but she demurs. "I'm not Indian." The woman nods solemnly. She was only trying to make an extra sale.

Roko spins on a boot and takes in the whole set-up. Tan walls—the color of state money? Cardboard histories, on placemats. Going cross-country, Gonchev has been in a lot of such local outlets, shown the foreigner as a matter of course.

"No wampum for sale?" Roko says, paying. The woman laughs a little, as at a lame joke.

Outside, she tells him what wampum was. "Bead money. Folk art, now. Very valuable."

She had hired a car to get here. They sit in it.

"Who are the earrings for? Your mother and sister? And who else?" Why exactly six sets of them?

A Western smile, though they are still speaking Japanese. "My house sisters. In my old dorm. I have a college reunion coming up."

"Oh. But why not—"

She is quick. "Something Korean? The stuff you can get in all the souvenir shops? People never had that at home."

"Your mother's black box. I always wonder what's in it."

"What do you think?"

"Money? Prayers?"

Roko sighs. "The box. Is the box. Is itself."

No matter what tongue he and she are speaking, this is the language of farewell.

"Itself?" he says. "Nothing more?"

She hitches in the seat, impatiently. "For us that's enough."

But what is not enough? "Roko, why do you cry? Please."

"I was weeping. Not crying. There is a difference." Her voice shakes. Not her pedant voice.

What wonderful women I have had, he thinks, shaken too. Can a man be forgiven, or understood, for wishing that this girl and his wife could meet? Not over him. Or not precisely so. Only for both to understand how this moment has come about.

"So, you were weeping, then. For what?"

Her small underlip curves down. The nostrils flare. "For ethnics." Her head bows.

Not geisha anymore, he thinks. Not tea ceremony. But ceremonial still. They still hide their hurt in ritual. Oh yes, there is something in that box. If only Korean air.

He touches the ear that wouldn't wear Indian feathers.

"And because I am going to marry one," Roko said.

Later he would be grateful that he hadn't twitched. A man in his plight might be forgiven for imagining—for just a second—that she had somehow meant him.

But it is the young man who plays the cello. All has been arranged, she says. He hears the details distantly, like over a poor phone connection. He, Paul, would be expected to attend the ceremony. "Otherwise my parents will be ashamed."

"So they know about us?" His voice is hoarse.

Again she bows. "How else?"

Then she sits up in her seat. "And now I will drive you home. And me. And return the car."

And not go on to Los Angeles? Are those her questions, or her ultimatum? He isn't sure.

Her hand lies on her black lap, a glass hand. Not a hand to kiss. Not one to remind him of European manners. That had been its calm for him. But is it waiting?

If he asks her to do him the honor of one last night with him, will the Western part of her smile with scorn? If he asks her to give him the pleasure, would that insult?

Crudest of all, how can he tell her that if a man has been capable of stopping his life for a woman, of damming it up into an oasis for two—this can only happen once?

Plain English will say it.

"Come back with me. To the hotel."

She chooses the other bed, although the two walnut headboards are exactly the same. "You slept in the window one, yes?" As he always did when a room had two singles. "Then I'll take the one by the door."

Here in the Victorian era, where both beds are double, they could use only one. Instead, now and then through the night, they make use of both.

At the outset, standing in the cleft between both beds, she says: "Make love to me in English."

They have never been much for love-talk. The days have been so spiced with interpretation, so squeezed dry of language by nightfall.

Now he does what he can, whispering such confidences as he can muster, even editing orgasm's noise. She has been his body-servant; he can do no less for her. He can do no more.

During the night she gives him two shocks.

He awakes by the window. The bed by the door is stained blood-red, down to the sheets. She has cut her wrists and lies there white and drained, in her own blood?

Then he sees that she had turned on the bedside lamp, a huge veined tulip protruding from its maroon stained-glass shade, and had fallen asleep under it. The wrists are unmarked. Still, he gathers her up and puts her in his own bed. "Word angel," he had whispered to her earlier, meaning that this was what she had been to him. One of the grateful synonyms one finds when one cannot cede simply love. Why couldn't he see her as a real girl?

She had one flaw any of those might have. End of day, she would sometimes groan or blurt in her sleep. Sometimes these were intelligible fragments of the straining, sweated hours they had spent together in projecting Paul Gonchev on the world. At other times he seemed to hear repetitions of himself, but sea-changed into her version of him.

He had never told her of this, out of a rueful sense that he must continue listening. She would never willfully misrepresent. But languages had corners, edges, and depths, the way pictures did. As his English improved, he had caught intonations, lilting ones, and even odd phrases that had made him worry over how one person might emerge from another's throat too emphatically improved.

Of course that happened every day here, in politics, and elsewhere. At times the whole country seemed to him a grandstand, rah-rah-ing almost everybody who belonged to it. Compared with the acid French or English newspapers he had read in his youth, the press here was benevolent, if with a certain gaga tumescence. "Upbeat," it was called, and as he recognized the attitude he began to think that it did more harm to the truth than a direct lie.

"You sometimes make me sound as if I am running for president," he joked to Roko once.

"Americans like shiny people," she said.

But from then on, for any lengthy interview, she provided him with a transcription in Japanese afterward. When he complained that there still did appear to be some gloss he hadn't contracted for, much less said, she replied: "An interpreter only does for a person what you did for your cities." So warned, he had listened harder. What kind of hero was she setting him up to be?

Recently he has heard nothing of her sleep-talk, or only murmurs. Here and there, in towns where it was clearly expected, they had had separate rooms. After which they rejoined each other refreshed, as from some hibernation, and slept almost lover-deep.

Tonight, he wakes for a second time to a word caught in the sleeper's throat. Thrice repeated, and thrice again. She lies next to him, her face tucked against her collarbone. He slinks down, his ear nearly on her mouth. She is breathing evenly; maybe the word won't come again. Then it comes. Not a groan, but not upbeat either. A translator's tone, tentative.

"Vuk-si-ca."

8

Vuksica at Home

FOR WEEKS AFTER GONCHEV was abducted, Vuksica would still feel herself to be that woman in the window, sitting by a telephone over which she has just alerted an ambush, watching Gonchev lean into the wind as he circled the house, and unable to wave him off. Thinking: He can trust that motorcycle more than he can me; it's known him longer. She's always been jealous of it. Shortly it will know what happens to him, as she cannot. There's a possibility that she will never know. Yet when first planning what she now has done she'd discounted that. All her life with men she has got what she needed to know from them. And when Gonchev is free, she will hear from him. One day she will tell him why she'd been able to do what she has just done. "I trusted you. I absolutely trusted you. To stay alive."

In her young days as an actress she'd attended a class where they dissected the larger emotions. Now she could have told them that guilt comes on you as a kind of residual silence, washing over you from each of those with whom you have to maintain a front, and invading you at the least slippage of your mask.

After a while she left the window and went as usual to check first the covered tub in the pantry where the bread dough was rising, then the vat in the drying room where the linen was soaking; then she went outside to test the autumn wind with a wetted finger to see whether the linen could be hung outdoors for one last time. Some distance from the washlines there was an outdoor oven where on fine warm days the cook would bake the last scraps of the dough into a flat pie sprinkled with salt and topped with bay leaves plucked from a bush nearby. The oven had been built under Gonchev's direction, along with a small carved stone table outside the kitchen door, where he and Vuksica would sit with glasses of their own rough red wine, watching the cook shovel in the pie dough with her long-handled scoop.

Vuksica plucked a leaf from the bay; after a certain age it should not be used. Eyes half-closed, she smelled the leaf. The bay bush confronted her, awareness on every twig. It must know that Gonchev is gone.

She went inside and told the cook: "Master hopes to be home early. We'll have a pie. But see first what you think of the bay." The cook nodded—if the bay was too bitter, she would use the tomato-in-oil, as she need not say. "And tell 'Risa to hang the wash out one last time."

She and the cook smiled at one another. All the household took glee in outwitting the weather. In this alternately harsh and tender country all the populace did. In snow her scheme for Gonchev would not have been possible. But her housewifery, doubly scrutinized because she was a foreigner, had long since been approved. Now and then, for the sake of the servants' national pride, she committed an error, maybe some sewing that had to be rectified, or a local recipe, attempted in laughter, that turned out to be unchewable. But when she'd first painted the garden wall they had all stood about, marveling. Careful not to appear to be setting a bourgeois fashion, she had let it fade.

Could she flatter herself that by then they'd forgotten she was an actress? Previously, it hadn't seemed that they were especially watching her. Shortly, they would be able to report that they were.

This happened sooner than expected. The dried linen had just been taken in. She sat at the stone table with her wineglass and Gonchev's waiting one. "Sun's going down, Cook. Better put in the pie." They had been able to use the bay. She was watching the long scoop slide the

242

dough in on top of the hot ashes when the arrival of Gonchev's committee was announced. "All of them?"

"All."

Everything is known here. Vuksica herself knows every phrase of Gonchev's relationship with the eight men on her doorstep, as well as what each man craves professionally and has or has not achieved. So does the housemaid.

It's now her business to be innocent but in command. They don't expect her to be as simple as they think their wives are; she is known not to be. But in the end she must be as naïve as they think all women are. She remembers, a little uncertainly, how a professional would handle this. You substantiate what people are already schooled to believe.

The committee has come to tell her of "the accident." They are all in dusty black, but then they always were. Still, their coming unannounced and in force is not usual. She lets herself appear tremulous, the more so when she sees the woman they have brought with them, the senior member's wife, a whiskered old biddy given to such services, whose presence outside a mineshaft or a quarry swimming hole always signals woe.

What they let Vuksica know is surprisingly in order with what might be the facts. Gonchev, who had put up a fight, had been knocked unconscious, then spirited offshore.

She doesn't faint; they wouldn't expect that of her. "Ah—he put up a fight," she says, proud. "With whom?" She even lets them see that she's surveying their faces for bruises—at which they shift their feet, and the old man quavers, "No." She doesn't ask who informed on the "accident" in such detail, only hoping that the spy has survived.

They ask to see the invitations from abroad that are always coming, and Gonchev's responses, all censored in any case. She takes them into his study—not the lair of a man who had planned flight. When she sees the strewn desk, the murky glass paperweight on which he had a habit of resting his hand, she knows that he is truly gone.

243

At the house door, when they are leaving, the old man grumbles, "If we'd rescued your fine fellow, I'd have put him in prison anyway, for bringing us all this Western attention," and she almost does faint with relief. The die-hard old partisan, a hero whose senility has to be tolerated, often drops clues to the general opinion. Other than telling her that her children—both away from home, and this too calculated by her— would be alerted, the rest offer no plans for her future life, the truth being obvious, that they aren't up to it.

"No," she says finally, to a query that seems to come from the whole lingering group rather than from a single mouth; Gonchev for the last year or so hadn't spoken of any wish for a visit out. She rather thinks he has given up such ideas, now that television might be tried. Their faces go blank, too suddenly. Hers is all streaked with wet and softly open; they have never seen her like that and never will again. "He was too fascinated with that idea to want to leave—you know him."

No, she has no idea who could have initiated the "accident."

Then, inspired, she hunches her shoulders, clasping her elbows. There exists a picture of Duse like that, only with a shawl, and even one of Vuksica herself in a sketch à la Käthe Kollwitz in a Belgrade café. "But where is Stepan Sefaru? Why's he not here with you?" And saw happily that the suspicion had already occurred.

Now she waits. Everything goes slowly, a condition the country prides itself on, claiming that its antique ways extract twice as much from life. "A slow train lets you see the scenery," one modest beer poster proclaimed. "Too much electricity and it's all over," underlined a cartoon of a man at one end in an electric chair and at the other a family overwhelmed by electric appliances not procurable here. But no wag ever whispered of how hard it is to wait in scenery calculated to stay half a century behind the actual one.

Meanwhile, a secret balloon labeled "Outside" might well grow in a child's chest. Had grown, in Laura's. To Klement, the protectionism here is balm. Glory can be squeezed from it. He is more native than those whose progenitors had crouched in the country's caves.

At the moment Laura is in the capital, working at one of those post-school apprentice jobs open to the sons and daughters of people of influence. Her lawyer employer, in whose house she is quartered, a brother-in-law not of the premier himself but of the premier's aide, is a deft politician, of whom it was said that when he greeted you with the double kiss on the cheeks he also patted the cheeks of your behind, but only to leave his calling card pasted there.

"They keep me under a veil, darling parents," Laura had written. "Your daughter is safe. Off the streets after six. After dinner we have what you might call non-prayers. You and my father were always such relaxed unbelievers. Why didn't you tell me that when atheism is the official religion of a country, it is worshipped like a god?" Anyway, she wrote, the lawyer's daughter, her own age, was fat from kneeling to too much family regimen. "And has warts, from never seeing any young men." Any single man admitted to the family circle was over fifty, and her host's daughter was currently smitten with one of those.

Laura's lively spirit rose from her letter as always, like the bouquet of a fresh young wine. Let it not sour into sarcasm, her mother had thought. But Gonchev, when shown the letter, had merely grunted. Like many another father, he had no humor where his guardianship of his daughter was concerned. "That's not the way to keep a girl like Laura safe," Vuksica had said. Like mother like daughter, Vuksica thinks now. Whatever Laura ultimately does, she will use her father's disappearance as excuse to leave the capital. But she will do all discreetly. And will find the funds. Her fingers always found money, and legally too.

As for Klement, as might be expected, he is now aide and virtual heir to an aging commandant of the security police—and by carefully entering only second-class competitions now wins every decathlon in which he participates. She will not yet let herself imagine what Klement may do.

She finds herself already profoundly beset by the sheer physic of being single. Any observing woman could predict the politics of widowhood, absentee or not. One was immediately removed from the sedate goings-on in any rooms given over to double occupancy or coupledom. But what she is feeling is more emetic, and entirely personal.

She is now free of the burden of being possessed, and of being possessed by love. The two burdens are not the same. But in the absence of the beloved the two blur into one heady freedom. She is no longer formally possessed, either to observers or from within. Her own action has separated her from living, as she had lived, under that double concern. What she has done has freed her—if only for a respite—from the yoke of love. Gonchev, if alive, as she feels he is, is now equally on his own. To live in tandem is a strain even to the loving, especially if personalities are strong.

What had saved her—or kept her as "safe" as some Laura preserved by marriage—had been the extraordinary backdrop of this country: lushly stage-green, lit by a forbidden horizon, and as complicated as any opera set, in front of which she has acted out her life. Women make their own Elsinores. And are trapped by them.

Be honest—and, alone now, she can be—she had wanted more than merely to rescue Gonchev. Although that had been her motive as first conceived, with time this had diffused, as motives too long held can do. Gradually, had she come to crave a vacation from love? And not only from Gonchev. From Danilo, most of all?

It isn't love she feels for Danilo so much as the intricate drama of twinship. He has many habits and vanities she dislikes but can tolerate. And the truths he knows about her are terrible only in quantity. Two lives under one speculum; that's a twin's normal lot. In the future, maybe very soon, she may miss that.

But for once she is glad not to have to answer to their double memory of one another. Glad not to be so committed to it that anything she does would be seen in the light of all he so minutely knows about her. What she's done may be unprecedented—to ambush, even for his own sake, a lover-husband, already missed. But as she stands of a Friday morning in the shallow dew of her squared-off garden, she is supported by that unconsulted act.

Friday is unofficial fish day, even in this half-Muslim country. Friday is family day, in this place that can only salaam in secret to any Allah. Friday was always Danilo's day, and he often came bearing fish, well wrapped, of a kind one didn't get here—making the Gonchevs gasp once again at how near the "outside" was. Anywhere Danilo went, even to family, he was in himself something of what others didn't have. To his lady friends especially. And to his sister. More and more he had come to signify what she didn't have in her elected life. So she is single in that way now too.

For of course Danilo is a suspect. She herself could have written the charge. Smart actor, privileged visitor, what couldn't he have arranged for his brother-in-law under a false cover of violence? In her own heart of hearts, could she have thought of that too? No, that's "too Stanis-lavsky method," as her pals used to say. Still, that old theater phrase for emotions too thoroughly dissected comes to mind. Over the years she has taken advantage of what theater she can. So this being Friday, and the hazy, good drying weather still lingering, she sits outside with her glass of wine.

Over the week, gossip has filtered. Sometimes from the staff, who whether faithful or not have a vested interest in the drama they work for. From the head gardener—saying with his face stiffly averted, "Now that the guards at the airport have been changed, mistress, I can't get the bulbs the big one used to bring us from his mother's province"—she learned that. From the mute who came to deliver eggs and was always fed a tea break by the cook—he was late, his note said, because he always set his clock by the motorcycle man, who was now in hospital, although doing well. And from her five women friends, whom she can trust at varying levels that still amuse her—the rest.

Gonchev is believed by some to have been hijacked, very probably by Americans. This is a policy relief for everybody. No one credits that it could have been managed without local collaborators, but those could have been "the Italians," now blamed for the ever-increasing contraband. Or Gonchev had been "captured" because his wares were too good for the exchange here, and the capturer's economy was now in dire need of him. Or the Americans are jealous of his expertise, recognized so early here, and plan to torture him into revealing all. Or, or—the stories grew wilder, always on the same theme. It was sensible, and unproveable, to blame that worldwide bogeyman for everything.

Meanwhile, there are rumors that the spy, or the "guide," as he is referred to, has been exonerated, though not because he had been pulped to a purple mess, nor because he had begun to recover, though his stamina is admired, but because he knows the terrain at Elsinore better than anyone else. For Gonchev had kept his domain like a picture puzzle, assemblable, even by the cinema staff, only in parts.

Gonchev of course is the prime suspect. But it would needlessly divide the country to say so. When you have borders such as these, you must believe you are a sufficiency. An artist who stays is therefore an emblem, a crown.

Though some are hinting, since everybody knows that some liberalising is on the way—foreigners no longer being doused in disinfectant at the border; the penalty for beards lightened though not lifted—that Gonchev, whose devotion to his fief of cities is a byword, would have left only because he had been bought by the promise of a bigger one.

Or else—he has been sold. Exchanged. By the government itself. For arms. Which verdict, since it is the one most people believe, can only be mimed.

And what are they saying of Vuksica herself? A victim, sadly left behind? An adulteress, seduced by the muscular sexuality that so often attached to the smuggler's trade? A too loyal Yugoslav (for now and then some of that nationality surface offshore)? Or a sister coerced by her charming brother, who in spite of his poor status at home could be a countercounterspy?

Except for "victim," a classification she'll reject in any case ever held against her, she can't voice a preference.

And here is Lola Trim, circling the house to find her.

"They don't know what to do with you," Mrs. Trim says without preamble. Her voice is soft, as the voice of the wife of a man said to have murdered his predecessor might have to be. It is sometimes rumored that she did the job herself. She has brought Vuksica a bouquet, maybe on instruction and therefore not a dangerously sympathetic act, although, not to cause comment, the flowers are neither pretty nor fresh. She is ruthless and could just as soon cut off your head—no, have it done—if she is not on your side. If she is on your side, then she is just the sort of friend to have.

"Ah—?" is all Vuksica lets herself say. In a socialist nation, a person they do not know what to do with is not safe. Your friends must make adjustments accordingly. From no longer being reachable on the phone, to letting out ruinous gossip, to the worst of all—no longer exchanging contraband, including books. "And what of our other four friends?"

Mrs. Trim hasn't sat down at the stone table. She too has her spy, a beetle-faced woman in a tiny car, who functions as the arrière-garde to Mrs. Trim's old state limousine. "Oh, don't worry. They'll rally, no matter what. After all, you have all those pills underneath that bed of yours." While laying down the bouquet, she has scraped up a packet with her glove. People think her ever-present gloves sinister, imagining a concealed stiletto, or a skin with no fingerprints. Actually her hands flake from a mild psoriasis and the packet she's lifted contains not only a supply of birth-control pills far fresher than her flowers but an ointment labeled "Betamethasone (Valisone .01%)," procurable only in the United States. All of which system she initiated, but has routed through Vuksica, whose servants are inured to Gonchev's having as many curious substances around the house as an alchemist.

They smile at each other.

"No more cigars for Trim." Vuksica makes this half a question.

The Etruscan brows rise. The only thing Vuksica finds sinister about her closest friend is that Lola's eyes seem ever farther apart. "I suppose—not."

Which in this country means never. So Danilo will not come here again. The "never agains" in her horoscope are rising too. "And the children?"

"They will come."

"Ah."

Mrs. Trim bows and makes off. Thanks to Danilo's Nikes, or exact copies thereof, she no longer trundles.

Vuksica sits on, sipping her wine. By the sundial at her elbow—once at her and Gonchev's elbows—she has another half hour to be calmly on display. She has done this every evening, keeping their usual hour here. The sundial, designed by Gonchev, is not a usual one. Its dial, though on a pedestal, is set in the torso of a recumbent woman, otherwise armless, headless, and tastefully legless. "A woman's stomach is sacred," he always said, to any comment. "The nineteenth century went in for Venus de Milos with clocks. To wind their navels was a joke. But the sun is no insult."

A long speech, for him. He had talked more, years ago. And if things went well, would again.

It is not a good day for drying after all. She and the maid haven't outwitted the weather this time. The wash hangs chilly and stringy over the sundial, a man's pajama bottom brushing the torso. What's all this wash for, that she's left with? A man's sweatshirt, then another, both shouldered by the years into the outlines of work. A favorite pair of those boxer shorts that don't pull at the crotch. Had she at least sent Gonchev off wearing some such consolation? She can't recall.

She is learning how evening attacks those whose life up to then had been dual and bed-charmed. In the house behind her the big bed stretches like a platform on which one never had to speak. Under it, like the bumpkin lover in a farce, is the plastic-wrapped bundle of pills. She now avoids the daytime sight of the bed and its nighttime embrace. Desire itself may attack her later on. She refuses to imagine the man she might feel that for. Having been possessed—in all the other ways as well—is what she misses most.

Her hour for receiving is almost over. The cook will soon emerge to take from the oven the uneaten pie. In the near distance is the playhouse Gonchev built for the children, behind it a quiet truck garden in which the last of the squash is still yellow. Over there, four-year-old Laura, eating sorrel, a crown of daisies on her head, says again, "I'm a queen, a queen does not die." Gonchev, chucking her in the belly, answers, "How about the kings?"

Beyond the garden is her own landscaped pasture. There Klement at about the same age, bumping into one of the conifers that rimmed it, had said, "Sorry, sir." His manners have always been the best of him. Farther on still are the tobacco huts, that steadiest of crops. The autumn star burns low. What a salon she has had here. Will no one come to tell her what's to be done with her?

Yes, here comes someone. That student, who is now a man. A good artist, Gonchev had said, but no artisan. Yet a man to fear, as the man's colleagues do. Why? An ascetic, Gonchev had told her, who will steal me blind. Yet you don't fear him. Why? She had known the answer but relished confirming it. Because I don't need to steal, Gonchev had sighed. Or not yet. Anyway, I can afford to feel sorry for him. Why? she had asked. The women all pine for those haggard good looks of his. Oh, he could play either Jesus or Judas, yes. The men call him Jesus Iscariot. Gonchev had meanwhile got hold of her nape in a way habitual to him, as if she were his cat. But he's said to be hopelessly in love with an older woman. Who has never rejected him. Because he has never asked.

Laughter between two in bed can be cruel. But no one hears.

And here he is, with his gaunt cheeks and butcher's glare.

"Yes, sit down, Stepan Sefaru."

The cook comes to remove the pie.

"Serve it," Vuksica says. "And bring more wine."

"No, this will be enough." He stares into the glass she has given him, then drains it.

"The bay is a little bitter," she says, eating.

"Not bitter enough." He stares at her mouth.

She can understand the women. His hands look talented, long at the joints, a capacious palm. A man doesn't have to be an artisan as well.

The wind is coming up. She can hear the first harmonics of autumn in the trees. "I shall have to go in." But only I. "The children are coming." Her first lie? But hope is not a lie.

"I saw Laura with you in your private garden, once." He points. "She's your daughter. Though she doesn't look like you." He stares at her eyes. Not into them. What does he know of her privacy? "But is Klement your son?"

The cook, pussyfooting in on pretext of clearing the table, takes warning at the sight of them, drawn up for battle, and sneaks away.

"I mean—you were married before—perhaps a stepson? Or adopted, some say."

"He's ours." She swallows, saying it.

He stands up.

She stands too, to meet whatever it is. "He hasn't—?" No, Klement would never. He had always sneered at Gonchev's tales of ritual suicide in Japan.

251

"Klement has advised the council to burn Elsinore."

She can't reply. She is with Gonchev wherever he may be, running aghast at his side.

"Your son is very angry. He feels that Gonchev's—departure—has cast a cloud on him."

Departure. So that's what they're now calling it. How does that bode?

"He has been angry all his life" bursts from her. She bites her thumb. And so have we been, I guess. At him.

"They want me to do the job."

She has to look up, open-mouthed. That canny crowd. What a snare this man is in. They're testing him. "And will you? Burn. Elsinore." She has given the words their full weight.

"I'd rather inherit it." His teeth are not pretty.

Why not? does Gonchev say, running at her side? Let them burn it. Without me it's a bundle of sticks.

But can she be sure? That he is still at her side?

"Will he be coming back—Gonchev? If he's alive?" He is staring at her neck. What can he see there?

"If—he is alive? Do you know otherwise?"

"No, I know nothing. Though no one believes me."

"Nobody gets back inside here. Who has ever been out." She hadn't had time to think of that, but it's true. "And if he could—for what?"

He stares at all of her. "For you."

She'd honestly never considered that. What she has been mulling has only begun to bloom.

"The committee will return. To ask your advice."

So she too is in the snare.

"They respect you. So—so do I."

That's been hard for him to say. When one would rather say "love."

He spreads his hands on the sundial, smoothing it. "You never had the quintuplets. For that five-breasted bed."

She can feel him looking down at her. He wants her at least to recall that old exchange when he was a student. She doesn't look up. Or answer. The hair at the crown of her head is mixed with white. For the first time since it began to whiten she has forgotten to gild it. Let him note.

"Burn it then," she says. "For him."

The hand on the sundial smoothes the face of the dial, then the stone torso beneath, then falls to his side.

"You don't change."

He is gone.

She goes into the kitchen to see the cook.

"Autumn has begun. No more pies."

That night, she is lying in the bed unable not to keep to her side of the mattress, when an expected tap comes at the window. The window is actually a French door of curtained glass, but she does not move to open up. Whoever is out there, if the right person, will circle the house three times, as agreed, to check on any interferences—although none has so far occurred. The cook and the maid sleep in their separate cottage. At times they may be visited also, though their callers would be different. The head gardener, who has only day help, goes home to his family at night so is spared the embarrassment of ever catching his employers out.

The art of smuggling here, either of contraband or of sex, is akin to practicing the piano. One makes arrangements with the neighbors in order to spare them any "inconvenience." A late party maybe Thursday, you say; pardon if there is noise. On occasion they may give you the same warning. That way, you protect each other from stumbling on anything that will incriminate. There is rarely any noise.

Yet occasionally the authorities must raid, in order to save face, and for sins publicly discovered the penalties are as terrible as any purist might hope. Therefore, you circle a house three times, blade ready— never a gun—meanwhile marshaling your one or two ragged aides-de-camp, like von Moltke his troops, and wearing a homemade headguard against the lasso. Once, when she was first here and was walking innocently early to see a local oasthouse of ancient repute, she had blundered into an old ruffian wearing such a guard. He was tiddly. "It's a birdcage he's bringing to market," the men drying the hops had said, white with fear, and pulling the old guy in.

It's like a farce I'm in the middle of, she thinks; if the exits and entrances go like clockwork, all will end well. And the safest hiding place is still under the bed. Yet she is unnerved. As for Elsinore, without Gonchev it won't be Elsinore. In that matter he would say she's doing right. And in time, maybe, even that she has done right by him. But without Gonchev somewhere in the offing and aware of what may happen now, is she Vuksica?

Explaining the birdcage to her, he'd laughed. "This is still Europe, this country. Yet almost Asia. Children here are born with black-market dirt under their fingernails." She might continue to procure her chocolate and even other scarcities—known in the parlance here as "doorstep" goods, often counterfeited. A bar of chocolate, say, crudely packaged as Cadbury's but more likely from Italy, or even Holland, and actually good Dutch stuff. What one must never do is allude to these benefits, even in the act of making use of them, even in the presence of the closest friends. Never notice the white sugar on the table; merely sprinkle and move it on down. "The discoverer here is punished as severely as the offender, Vuksica. That's why it all works out." And although Gonchev vastly admired the handicraft, he remained wary of collecting certain underground objects, like that "birdcage," or the hammered silver chastity belt, even for study in his own workshops. "If I'm hung, it'll be no consolation to know that the rope is handmade. Or how."

Officially, he'd known nothing about her female cartel, although he was obviously amused. Just so she had very slightly mocked the interest in the pirated television set that had led him to a night with Mrs. Trim. Their marital tone had always been light.

"Are you bored with being able to trust me?" he'd said that time.

"Not at all."

He knew her own past was more rakish for a woman than his for a man. Gonchev, like the many men who were not Danilo, had merely taken whoever was attractively at hand from time to time, without emotional doom. And once doomed to her, had rested there. Perhaps the drama of being beleaguered here with him had helped keep her faithful—along with the lack of candidates?

Anyway, faithful she has been. Yet now she scrutinizes what she has done, in a mode maybe only women and Jesuits bother with. Has she sent him off for his own good, but also a little bit for hers? If she had been growing restless, was it only because he had fallen below what she dreamed for him? Or has she grown used not only to a little dirt under the fingernail but to the smuggler's practice of keeping back a little of the booty for himself?

It is otherwise with Lola Trim. Sexually she seems Muslim to the core. She had come to marriage, as the saying had it, "a virgin two times over." Which by convention made it easier to live with a brute. She did not expect to live with her husband's psyche. In a limited way, that kind of companionship was to be for women. Who might smuggle for each other in amity—but most because outwitting the men was women's lifelong work. What Lola had learned with vigor from her so-called Premier—actually a provincial governor only—was the style in which power bred on itself. Which is why she collaborates with him—and why the women of her circle think warily of her as Mrs. Trim.

Vuksica has called her Lola from the first, a show of power that has earned her a weighty gift—the woman's confidence. Which Vuksica can honor, if not return.

Gonchev has been her own sole confidant. Yet, loyal to her friend, Vuksica never revealed to him that Mrs. Trim—who in spite of her statuesque good looks is a figure of fun to him, and to Danilo, especially—has developed a very vulnerable Achilles heel in one of those big feet. Danilo had once commented that in a well-known piece of Etruscan statuary that much resembled Lola, the female bust had been formed not by casting but by riveting pieces of bronze together. How surprised he would be to hear that there exists a man over whom Trim's faithfulness, though so far steadfast, is being sorely tried. As Vuksica's own is now threatened. And by the same man.

Very different for herself though, a woman whose man has been her confidant, in spite of the remembered motherly advice given her on the eve of her first marriage: "Vuksica," her mother had said. "A smart woman always conceals something from a man. If only in compensation for our being rated such a chatty sex. As most of us are. Men by and large don't talk so much. So concealing isn't the same for them. But when they do bother to, mark my words, darling. Except for a few scoundrels, they're not nearly as good at it as we are."

After Vuksica's successive marriages, and her open style of living in between, her mother had fallen mum, and remained so until her death, at which nothing further of her own simple life had been revealed. "I have to act so much elsewhere," Vuksica had pleaded to her. "I can't be an actress in my life too."

Now that has been reversed. It is her life she must act. With her only confidant—in the early years so profoundly that—receded little by little into his work-at-hand, then in her eyes increasingly compromised—and now gone. Yet to live in an alien, difficult country with the person of your choice can be profoundly uniting. Perhaps that was why she had chosen to. And even at the end Gonchev could be winsomely close. He had no barriers against women in matters of the mind. Speaking as equals, he and she had been pushed even closer. Even not to speak—for instance, about their disturbing estimate of Klement—had been a bond.

Is that how she would explain her years here to her mystified friends in Belgrade? An eyrie, a nest with our nestlings, within the oh-so-accommodating wild? And hear their verdict this bosky evening? "Pushed to adultery, she says, only by politics? La la."

But if she goes by the books slipped to her by Danilo, they in Belgrade have also been subtlely eroticized. The men especially. Making their dream nests in the heart of the socialist dishonesty, with some naïve little cunt they can beat for it. Even Danilo, with whom affairs are habitual, now has more of them. Little affairs. Where one can still dominate.

While the women act accordingly. Slam down the equivocal newspaper, whose evasions your civil-servant- or artist-husband has at breakfast detailed. Slap or embrace the worrisome rebel child. You love them both. You love everybody who is suffering the cramped, brave, bitter, not quite murderous life of Central Europe. So—seek out some tiny shop where your vanity can be appeased; waltz off to the café, that haunt of all the mercilessly politicized. Seek the temporary heart in another pair of eyes; celebrate that in a circle of other eyes on the hunt for the same. Silly not to enjoy your only open secret, that cunt. Silly not to enjoy being one.

Else end up like Rémy, a gabbling demi-intellectual, one of those women who, whether they work for or against the party, are like the cream in that long-term milk now made to last a month or more—never able to rise to the top.

Yet you, Vuksica—backslid movie star, veteran wife, apprentice hijacker—do you now know any better what to do with yourself?

And why hasn't the man rapped again? Has a trap been set for him? Throughout all his and Vuksica's arrangements concerning Gonchev, Lola Trim has been so proud of their intermediary's cunning—"Not all muscle only, that huge man"—and of his wealth—"Runs their operation like a factory, his partner, my brother, tells me. And as rich as his own grandfather. Legal or not, people always get rich in the shipping line."

Poor, dazzled Lola. Who has no idea of how far below-the-salt, or sideways, an accomplished bandit's interest can range. Or does she? That too is possible.

There's his second signal. Not the usual knock, or tap. A sibilant rubbing of the glass. All his languages sound like code. Even his native Greek, which she doesn't speak, but Lola does. Their three-way conferences had been like something out of Molière: he speaking to Lola in Greek and to her in showy Sicilian or sailor's Serbo-Croat, saying, "In Piraeus one hears everything"; she answering as she pleased.

To Lola he'd given a snapshot of his grandfather and himself, the shipowner's boy, at thirteen, his lip already bee-stung with know-how. The grandfather was even bigger than the grandson is now and, according to his story, was a man who would regularly knock the boy down for calling him Pasha, so insinuating there was Turk in him. There'd been too much legality at home, the grown man had told Lola—five lawyers in the family. "Sea lawyers. Even so, I had to do something else." But he still uses the family's ships. He told Lola that this was the one coast he and her brother had up to now held off smuggling from. "But I had heard of you, Lola Trim. In our trade, your brother is a mere businessman. But you—you're an adventurer." Or so Lola reports. "He would like to be a pirate," she sighs. "But there is now the radar."

To Vuksica he has said when alone with her, "Soon I must marry a young girl and start a family." Although only women in their prime interest him, even now at forty-three. "And I will stay home." This she hasn't told Mrs. Trim. Nor that, although he would do what Vuksica asked respecting Gonchev, he had informed her that she could not pay him in any useful currency. This has turned out to be true. Neither of her family treasures—a reliquary set with malachite and an eighteenth-century vestment, brocaded in pure gold—are marketable in his sense, since he deals in munitions only. "Small arms mostly, my dear"—in case she had any of those? Of course she hadn't. But he has his price.

What the premier may be buying from him from time to time, via Lola, she isn't likely to know.

He steps inside the curtained glass door on cat feet, the way boatmen hop from barge to barge. Hair enough for two mops, but in curls strict enough for a prima donna's wig. Sweatshirt worn as if it bore an admiral's buttons. A lout's slouch.

As an actress she had early become too used to handsome men—or to men who too consistently acted the lead—ever to fall for those qualities solely. But he brings his own presence. He is a man without a century. Who wears the most modern of guns, strapped to a leg.

But normally he doesn't have a black eye. Maybe two.

"He insulted my mother," he says, striding in. "Had to beat him up. And maybe a little bit because you are his. But we got him off safe."

She sits immobile. How can she have any other thoughts? Safe.

He's squinting at her. "Barricaded yourself with books, have you? It wouldn't help. But I don't rape." He laughs as silently as his gun is said to shoot.

"I do that when I'm nervous."

"You never look it."

"No."

"Ah, my God—brandy." He pours, swigs, sits.

"And fruit." And meats and cakes she's sneaked from the larder like an adolescent on the run. She has set herself up half like a tart, the nightgown too. And half not.

"The other night you wanted me," he says, drinking.

In a moment alone together in Lola's house, Lola on the phone, they had kissed passionately. To seal their bargain, he'd said. And to be frank about the price.

"I did. But there's something wrong with me."

He's straddling a chair backwards, leaning the cleft of his chin on its carved back. There's theater in him, all right, even if no present-day actor would dare that drawing-room pose once so favored by juvenile second leads. The rough-cut face is what the studio used to call pure movie-movie. There's no stagecraft in him, though. She's never before met a man she wanted to teach that to. It had been a matter for pride that she could teach Gonchev nothing there.

He scans the nightdress, which is sheer. "You're not in your blood?"

What a phrase. Natural. With him, everything would be. As with her; she's no prude. As with her and Gonchev. That's where her body sticks. Stubbornly. She can't push it on. Though her lips swell, expecting this man, here in his presence her hand won't glide. "No."

"I wouldn't mind." He sits on the bed. Its size doesn't surprise him; he's no Sefaru. One by one he slides the books off the bed onto the rug, not looking at the titles but handling each like a piece of machinery he doesn't know the uses of but must respect. Remembering how Gonchev rids her of her books—slam-bang—her breath catches. When the last book submits, he says, "There. Now all your friends are gone," and sits. When she makes no move, he wraps his warm fingers around her cold, naked foot.

It hadn't occurred to her that the brute might be tender. She's been trying to make him into a brute. She is about to cry. For Gonchev. For herself. Up to now, she hasn't.

She hasn't really wept since the children were born—afterward, when each baby was placed in her arms. Yet she used to command tears at will in the studio, cheeks shining obediently; that was how she had got her first acting job. A girl desperate to earn at her chosen trade, in those postwar years that were coda to agonies and putsches she and her crowd knew only by hearsay, but when everybody was poor, and chilblained, and gay. And that day—by thinking of her roommate, who had been soaking her white frozen hands in ice water to make the red come back, while assuring her, "A snort of slivovitz and I'll be fine," although there was only tea in the cupboard—she had easily made herself cry. Brimming over on the breast of an unknown actor, she'd sobbed out in professional tears her private woe. Saying when complimented later, "Oh, it's nothing—a muscle. Like wiggling one's ears."

Nothing but a wiggle, this would be. With a man who's only an actor in your life. But while Gonchev rides, rides, in your mind's eye. You made too difficult a bargain, that's all. And maybe too devious a one. Desire rides its own way, hunched on its unicycle.

She hunches forward herself, grasping her ankles. He's let go of her foot—good. If at this moment he and she touch, they risk being friends. "Nothing's wrong. Except—twenty years of nonadultery."

He laughs. "It can be cured."

In the head, yes. The will is adroit. But this is in the flesh. With all her old affairs before Gonchev rattling harmlessly in her past, she can scarcely believe this of herself. Flesh faithfulness—who would have thought it? Maybe the result of the Muslim atmosphere here? No, there's a unity in her body—of this body cleaving to one other body—that she wishes not to dislodge.

Although the man's shoulder is bent to her confidentially, his head turns on its axis, listening. The French door is slightly wavering. Thanks to the covered walkway just beyond, any draft will do that, even a dog passing.

Suddenly he's there behind the door to one side, gun drawn. A footpad! Like the ones in that *Beggar's Opera* production she was in once—in English, for an opera festival. It didn't go well.

"My bodyguard," he says loudly, and shuts the door. Back at the bedside, he whispers, "Our go-between. Mrs. Trim. Can one see through the curtain from out there?"

"A little. The netting comes from the state store. Everybody uses it. Not to use it would be thought odd."

"Hah. Thank God I'm Greek." He's slipped the gun away and is palming a roll of money out of a pocket.

"I should think that gun would come even faster from the hip," she finds herself saying. A prop is a prop. Then with an inkling of rage to come, "What's that money for?"

His back is turned to the door. "You're to be seen giving it to me, when I leave," he whispers, palming the thick roll to her. "We had a bargain, remember? And I shall leave. It's not the right time."

He stands tall beside the bed. "If your husband were around, you could deceive him. It's because he's not—and why—that you can't."

She won't hang her head for any man. But he's right—in part.

"You're an honorable woman. I saw that at once. Otherwise I wouldn't play such a trick on another man. Who can trust a wife, an ordinary one? I could see you were not that. But now—here we are." His teeth are white, the smile lifting at one end. "Even with widows, honor can't last forever. And you are not a widow. He's alive." He rubs his bruised eye, the darker one. For the curtain's benefit, he's explaining the bruise and extending the hand for her to clasp.

"Alive. And in Paris." She can say it aloud now for Gonchev, for his dream, hoarded for so long. Once he's in his city, how can he blame her? Making his pilgrimage to the Salle Pleyel, he'll know why he is there. Sliding his boots over curbstones as thin as French lips. Free.

"Ah . . . Paris?" The man is shaking his head. "Ah, no, we couldn't arrange that."

She sweeps her feet to the floor and gathers up the robe. "What do you mean you couldn't arrange? That was the bargain."

"I warned you. We deal with whom we can deal."

True. But she'd cast that aside.

"With things in this country beginning to loosen up, it's all the harder for people like me. When everything was tight I could do as I pleased. Never had to bother with your politics; it was all the same. But once a country starts opening up, everybody has his opinion. On what a respectable black market should be. And the most profitable one. Right now all Europe is off-limits for your diehards here; they've taken a hate to it, like they did to China, once. Ten, fifteen years ago, you saw the damnedest people here, coolie hats right in the capital. Then no more. Now it's Europe they won't have. When a country's walked blind for so long, it gets big ideas."

He's all brigand now, and businessman. "And here comes this accommodating new customer. Money no object. And all the paperwork—I like things legal, you know—done. Clean as clean." He laughs. "They're big on that, you know. Your man'll have had a change of shirt in no time." He's eyeing her robe. "Local work, eh? Eh, well . . . Anyway, they're tickled to be the ones getting him out—the big gun especially. They fancy themselves that way, you know. He said that for your man it would be as good as coming home."

"You've sent him to Japan?" she said, dreary. Tap tap, Tokyo. "But he came from there. To here. And it's so far." And what point to it? While Paris . . . And with Danilo there as well . . . And maybe Laura next, and then I. First things first, like in that conserve that one layers with different fruits, week by seasonal week. Adding a measure of rum. Or a dram of love.

"Japan? You flatter us. We work Italy's boot, the Dalmatian coast. Not the Turks; they cut out your tongue. Or worse. At a pinch, North Africa, but only from there. No export." He lowered his voice to a whisper. "We got him to Opatija. I know a former countess there, runs a pension right on the sea. The customer did the rest."

"The rest?"

He lolls, staring at the vacated bed. "Such a boat they had. Like a swan with a golden beak. Preening like a rich man's toy. You would never suspect it. My grandfather was in their country once. He would be pleased."

"I was the one to please." Her knife voice, the children call it, saying it could cut cheese while still a yard away, and penetrate even Klement's thick backbone. "Where have you put him?"

"Where else? Your kind of package—they eat him up. America, the U.S.—where else?"

Of a sudden, Europe grips her in a great tumbling of images she hadn't known were so dear to her. Arcades at Bern, under each archway a monk centered like a fist, holding out orthodoxy to the visiting Serbian child. Versailles upside down, its spires pointed hellward, as if fleeing from the Renaissance. While embedded in its very rotunda, among the stone persons who seem to be holding the human race in their carved hands, is that nearby honeymoon restaurant, floating like a rose blown above a crowd, where she had eaten a lark.

Or the black-and-white floor of the basilica at Siena, where a troupe of actors, derelict after a failed play at a festival at the university—and all young, of course, so without contract or funding—had mimed and begged among the sarcophagi. Until—presto!—they were whisked home by the mayor of the town. To a soiree where what must have been the biggest Bösendorfer on the continent was being played by a fly-away Italian the size of a bat, while women in nose veils and men in silk vests ate from sideboards jeweled with the fishy ivory and crisp succulents of civilization—and the young actors too were fed.

Who'd have thought the old memory had so much blood in it—or that she still had access to the actor's habit of caching thought in any dear old nosebag. Friend Shakespeare's being the best. It occurs to her that her vaunted calm has come about at the cost of her not working. She's been the other side of Gonchev's picture, of the movie that any life is, and this wasn't seeable until he had gone.

Had Gonchev already known about this sleep of dependence that she has fostered in herself? A kind of Muslim sleep that a woman gets into, stretching herself only to the length of a washline, to the breadth of a pie. Or to the depth of a man's probe. A sleep that can go on anywhere in the world. And had he gone on willy-nilly by himself, forgetting how she was before?

It occurs to her with a little rat squeak of the heart that she too is Europe. She is the part of Gonchev the United States won't see.

The man is leaning over her books. "I'll take one. For a souvenir. Once a job's done, it's nice to read, on a boat. Which book shall I take?"

Too dumbfounded not to reply, she stutters, "They're all in English. We women have a reading group." And when he waits, unimpressed, "There, take that one; he was Greek. A poet."

"In English, eh. I went to the naval college. I speak English too. Not just that Yugo-Italian/Deutscherei they call sailor's Swiss." He picks up the book. "Oh, him. Everybody in Athens knows that name. A man lover, he was. No, we are supposed to be proud of him, but I am not that kind of patriot. No, give me a kiss instead."

"You forget our audience."

"Good for her to be jealous. Good for you."

"How so?"

"Maybe she'll help you. Again." That last word is almost inaudible. *To stay out of sight,* his lips say without moving. *Or even—to leave?* He has turned to scan the bed. "In that bed, I could speak Hindu. All the dialects." He faces her again. "What's to become of you?"

"The committee is to return. They haven't yet. My daughter has been allowed to phone. When she is finished her finance course—world markets, for the love of God—they will let her come home. My brother—he was to be here that same Friday. He wasn't. Later I got a telegram. They let me get it, you understand."

"What did it say?"

"It said: 'I have been stopped.' "

"Did they let you answer?"

"I sent one. I don't know."

"Ah."

There is a tinkle from behind the door.

"Falala," he mutters. "Even her bracelets shine red in the dark. Like her eyes." Suddenly he shouts, "Just finishing. The bargaining."

"You'll raise the house."

"Better so. Keep people hearing you, my dear. And that you have friends. . . . Have you heard from that son of yours?"

"Not—not directly."

"Ah."

She won't stoop to ask him about Elsinore. That belongs to Gonchev, still. Maybe it's all that now does?

The man she's dealt with only as Demetrios is bent over a small bedside table, apparently musing. "Ships are finished in this business. I'll be expanding by air. With such fine customers, why not? I'll leave you my card."

Standing in the middle of the room, he bellows, "Give me my money then, madame."

She passes him the bankroll.

He bows low. A hand rakes between her legs, along with his whisper. "That's where my money is. I'll be back."

Outside the door he says clearly, "Ah, there you are, Lola. How good a friend you are to her. You know me. But she's safe. She drives a hard bargain, that friend of yours. She has a tight crotch." He says that last in the local slang; he's informing the house.

As the two move off, she can't help smiling at the impudence of him, maneuvering his roster of women as if they are boats. A former countess, no less. No doubt a woman in her prime. No doubt if he switches to air he will still attend to that detail. If necessary she would trust him again. He is a marvel at his trade.

She sits as she is for some while. When next a draft of air comes through the door ajar, it is indeed from a passing dog.

When she moves the small table in order to climb into bed, the napkin slides from the platter of fruit. Something else is nestled there. She picks it up with great care. In bed, in the worn double hollow now too big for her, she places it next to her—a prop most theater people know how to use. He has left her the gun.

"Mamma."

Laura falls into her arms. She's wearing the pixie headband with waggling antennae that all the girls made for themselves last year, until it was officially frowned upon (How do they pick up these underground fads?), plus what looks like French dungarees (Where did she get those?). The headband is too childish for her now; she is filling out. Though barely of age, she could pass for a young woman well into her twenties. And she will pass, Vuksica thinks; she's like me. At fourteen, in Novi Sad, I played in *Mayerling*; there was scandal, but my name was made. And I had filled out. Laura will be an actress too—but at what?

In the midst of their embrace Laura murmurs, "Mamma, bravo." The antennae tickle Vuksica's nose. All is well.

Later they are in the playhouse, wedged in the small chairs, looking out on the fields through the open door. "America," Laura says. "I always knew you would finally do something. That you would be the one."

"How did you know?"

"Parents are like trees, to a child. They talk, even though they say nothing."

The horizon is calm, immovable. So is the blessing of a child.

"And imagine, Mamma, I know somebody from over there." Or rather, a girl who is a frequenter of the lawyer's house where Laura has been staying knows him. This girl's own cousin. "A former playboy, still very rich, the money safe in Canada. But in America he is no longer a playboy but a student. At a Wharton School of Finance." The syllables roll off Laura's tongue like pebbles tossed out the child-scale door, onto that miniature green that was once a child's world.

The girl's family are escapees from Iran, distant relatives of the former Shah. "They were living in Paris, but one of their relatives was shot." Even the girl's school in Switzerland was no longer safe. So they had come here. "She's in my finance class, learning how to manage their money." The girl could paint her fingernails with bullion, though of course she never would; she's a plain thing. But not ignorable. "She says what they teach us in class is pitiable. Theory from the great economist Lukacs, beautiful—but nothing about what she calls 'stocks-and-bonds.' She wants to 'deal' in those." Laura giggles. "She says the banking talk in the mess hall at that Swiss school, even the crumbs that fell, you could feed more than the birds with them."

"How old is this girl?"

"Twenty-four—she says. They are keeping her in school, she says, to pretend she's still in her teens so that maybe some good Iranian catch will still marry her. She lost precious time during the Iraqi war." But Laura and the lawyer's daughter think the girl visitor is even older. "In the bath, you can tell. And she knows too much history."

"Too much? We taught it to you."

"I know, Mamma." Laura is impatient. "But on her own. And like she lived it."

"The way we learned it. Nobody escapes."

"Ah, Mamma, I know." A slightly greasy hand pats Vuksica's wrist. The tiny table is heavy with the cook's welcoming food. "They like to stuff themselves with my goodies," the cook said, her pig eyes intent. "Will it be both of them, mistress?" "Have we heard from the young master?" the old gardener said more bluntly. And at Vuksica's head-shake, "I am tuning up the old car. In case we have need of it."

Through the doorway the background hills are as ordered as any in a cinquecento frame.

Laura waves a pastry at them. "Beautiful. But no 'deals.' "

Vuksica smiles.

"Eh, Mamma. Or have you—a deal?"

"You are at the age when, if I told you anything, you would say, 'I know.' "

"Hah. So you do have one." Laura wipes her hands with the lace-encrusted napkin the cook had put out. Worthy of a folk museum. Maybe it soon would be in one, Vuksica thinks. I am not going to open a pension.

"But you are wise not to tell me," her daughter says. "Like about what was going to happen to Papa." Laura's face screws in that sadly truthful estimate of her own nature which few can resist. "I let things out."

She is going to. Clasped to her mother (Who is holding who now? Vuksica thinks), she gasps out, "The Pahlavis are leaving." That Iranian girl—her father thinks the protection they came here for isn't worth much anymore. The boundaries will be breaking down. At the same time he would like to be in on the ground floor in a country that will so soon be opening up. One of the last such countries left. So he is buying up real estate here through a dummy owner. "But the family itself is moving out."

Vuksica stares at her own real estate. It has merely been lent to the Gonchevs by the government. Else what duennaship mightn't she be feeling toward all this green? Land grips you either because you have never had it, or because you possess it. Thank God she's never even given this loved place a name. As it is, what else must she guard? "Your father used to say, Laura, that some refugees fall on their feet any-where—and that the Gonchevs were like that. But that some who were on the run—they ran so hard that they somersaulted into wealth. And the Gonchevs were not like that."

Laura is very quiet, for her. This girl who thinks that anything that is not 'a deal' is merely beautiful—why isn't she saying, "Mamma, I know"?

"And where are these friends of yours going?"

"They are not my friends, Mamma. Like they are . . . business acquaintances. That's all we talk about. They're going to Rome first—but then to an island, they don't say where." She giggles. "They don't want to let anybody else in on it. That is what you do."

"And why are you telling me this mishmash?"

Three guinea hens strut past the little door. They are not allowed in these gardens. Normally they are made to roost in a grove of trees outside a small barn. Who has neglected them?

"Because the capital is weird, Mamma. Nobody knows the rules anymore. Nothing has officially changed. The prison doors still open—and close. Yet you will see a man walking down the street with the forbidden hair on his face—a mustache, maybe even a small beard. Three men, even. Four. The next day two of them say when you meet them, 'That wasn't me.' " Some of the churches have held masses—but only in the dark. "But the priests are going around saying, 'Soon with candles.' " One heard that the government itself wants to ease boundaries. "But isn't sure how to do it. Which makes people even more scared." Laura is scraping at one pointed fingernail with another, both nails lacquered a daring deep pink. Women have been flogged for less here.

"Nobody in our time has seen that kind of change, this part of Europe. It's all gone the other way." Vuksica has surprised herself. "But who are we to apologize for governments?" She grasps Laura's picking finger. "Haven't you the liquid that gets that polish off?"

"I forgot it. In the city we are showing fingernails again."

"I'll look in my old kit. Maybe a bottle there." What had it been called? Remover. She recalls its sharp acetone scent. The cook will report Laura for vanity, in order to earn credit for herself at her union circle. Vuksica sometimes buffs her own nails with a once-rosy powder pressed into a faded cake she had brought with her from Belgrade. Little shine comes of that, but memory assaults. When a housemaid helping to turn out the drawers inquired once what the powder was, she had answered,

"For silver. But it's no good anymore." And she had been careful not to acquire too much silver. She leans out the tiny doorway. Those three silly speckled birds look so daring, pecking in the stubbled cornrows. "Look at the revolutionaries," Vuksica says.

"Turn around, Mamma."

For a minute she is afraid to. Wary these days of any command from behind. And heartsick that she cannot control this, even with Laura. It comes from having betrayed someone. From then on you suspect everyone.

Laura is holding out a long, slender document.

"An airline ticket!" She fingers it. She hasn't seen one since—when? Since just before that last border-hop to here. A journey tossed behind her as casually as a day trip.

"Passage from Rome airport, Mamma. To London. Good for sixty days. If one can get to Rome. It came from the Pahlavis."

"Is it a trap?"

"No, no. They played like it was an extra ticket, for a servant who was refused permission to go. But that's nonsense. They wouldn't involve themselves that way for a servant. And I doubt they're going anywhere near London themselves. No, they picked it up somehow, in a deal. It's because I coached the girl. But one would have to get oneself to Rome."

"Then—go." She takes Laura's face between her palms. "Go quickly, Mouse." Using the old pet name, she strokes her. "Mouse. Mouse."

"No, Mamma. You."

It takes the young no time at all to dispose of excuses. "No, Mamma, of course you wouldn't be leaving me behind. I would be going. But another way."

"What way?"

"From the capital."

It seems that the pilot who had been bringing Danilo in all these years comes there now, bringing certain people in. He comes to the lawyer's house as well. The lawyer thinks he is courting the warty daughter, and he allows this in order to egg on her older suitor, who is lagging. "Mikhail is nice, Mamma." The pilot. He'll get Laura to Belgrade if she'll stop off with him there for a while; he doesn't expect more. Though if she were willing, he would give her a marriage ring. But she will go on, to Rome. "I've known him ever so long. Maybe too long."

"How can that be?"

"Ever since you and Papa started letting us go with you to the airport, whenever Danilo came. For practice, Papa said. To get to know the layout. In case we ever."

Vuksica recalls what year that was. The same year Gonchev started his rides. "But you were only fourteen."

"Yes, Mamma." Laura gives her a look. "We used to sneak into the guards' bathhouse." She sighs robustly. "It was like Romeo and Juliet. Only we think the guards peeped."

"The guards never . . . bothered you?"

"Oh no. Mikhail brought them cigarettes. And other things."

"You couldn't have known what you were doing, you crazy."

"Oh yes, Mamma. I sneaked the pills from under your bed."

Laura waits, a little mischievous, but plaintive too.

"Stop calling me Mamma," Vuksica says.

In a while, after they have wrung hands and kissed again, she says: "Let's get out of this toy house." Although the toys have long since been cleared away, she feels like a lumbering giantess, who has been deceived by elves.

They walk across the fields, away from the main house.

"So it's agreed—you'll leave," Laura says.

"I? How?"

Laura plants her hands on her hips. Although her figure isn't at all formidable, she manages to be. "You know—and I know. How could I have told you about Mikhail otherwise." She points toward the coast. "The way you got Gonchev off." Quickly she drops her hands. "I shouldn't have pointed. Cook's watching. She does it from the store-closet window."

"You seem to know everything."

"A lot."

They walk on.

"So you're calling your father Gonchev now," Vuksica says, after a pause.

"He was always that. To all of us."

"Not to me."

"To you most of all. He was the tree under which we all stood. Otherwise, why would you do what you did. And the way you had to do it."

"Who said how I did it?"

"Four of the women." Three loving notes that braved the censor to tell Laura, in different versions. And one oh-so-friendly phone call. " 'I'm taking my life in my hands to tell you this,' that one said. I said, 'Hang on to it, that life of yours.' All of them said I was to come home to be by my mother's side. None of them quite said what happened. But between them, I puzzled it out."

It's beneath her to ask precisely what Laura has guessed. Beneath both of them.

"Nothing from my—fifth friend?"

"Lola Trim?" Laura grins. "No. So I decided she must be the one in on it. And that maybe she was crazy about Gonchev. Um, Father."

Vuksica gives her a long look. "Maybe."

They are approaching the house again. Now that the leaves are down, the details of Gonchev's landscaping emerge, rectilinear, clear. Marking the small estate for human notice, then folding the outer fields back into the hills. "A farm ebbing gradually into the wild," he'd said. "Life can't be like that anymore. Or mine can't. But the architect can pretend."

Over there is the small outbuilding where he viewed the films received under special ukase at the studio, and somewhere at its base is the flap he had carved for the secret viewer, their follower. The sumac bushes flourish, models for the painter Rousseau, he said, as well as home for quail—and not really poisonous, he had told the children, except to those unaware that the bushes were part of an industry as well. And over there is the odd, loaf-shaped natural rise that Danilo had dubbed "Paul's podium," having ferreted out that when brooding there one faced toward Elsinore, even if from thousands of versts away. "Only toward the library," Gonchev had replied, always literal on construction points. "The sets all start farther east."

Everywhere here, the husbandry of Gonchev's eye. He carries his trade with him, leaves traces of it behind. Has he at all disturbed the architecture of his life?

And over beyond, only a motorcycle ride or a car trip away, the coast.

"For your information, Laura, I managed without having to make good—my end of the bargain." How pompous that sounds. She's sorry at once that she said it. So much of what one says to one's children is the kind one is sorry for.

"Indeed," Laura says. Doesn't she approve? She widens her eyes. "I understand the bargainer is—quite presentable."

On impulse they both make for the podium, which is broad enough for both of them to stand there, their backs to the house. "Cook's probably still watching us," Vuksica says. "She does it without turning on the light."

Laura nods. "Klement and I once put a mousetrap on the sill where cook leans."

So they've at last mentioned him. "And . . . ?"

"He went next day to check whether it had been snapped. Not turning the light on. And caught his finger in it."

Neither of them laughs.

"Cook lets me know she watches, these days. In order to keep me comfortable. The servants feel it's worrisome to be in limbo here." She won't say she agrees with them. "So far, I haven't been awarded a spy."

"Why should they bother? When there's one in the family?"

"Laura. You haven't the right to say that."

"Why else do you suppose I came running? And why hasn't he? Your own son. You've never faced what Klement is."

"Haven't I," Vuksica says.

For once Laura is taken aback. "Ah? You and Papa never said."

"No."

"Papa too feels that way about him?"

"We never spoke of it."

272

"Ahrrrrrr," Laura says. "You're in the soup for that, now." She sneaks her hand into her mother's, holding on tight. The cook can't interpret that. "Here's the stock sheet." She has trouble going on.

Vuksica laughs. "Ah, Mouse."

"Stocks and bonds tell you about people. Sometimes too much." Laura's eyelids redden. "So listen."

"I'm listening."

"You are now a blot on Klement's career. So am I. A lesser one. But still, a blot. Yet the family is all-important here; he can't just murder us. Maybe he's not even capable of it. But here the government is the biggest family of all. He has to signify very soon where he's putting his money. Or his heart." The tears are running down her cheeks. He and she were culprits together once, siblings close enough in age. But she's speaking quite measuredly. "He has to walk a chalkline now, my brother does." She swallows. "And he's not capable of it."

Vuksica gives her a handkerchief.

"That pouch of yours," her daughter says, staring at the sacklike purse always hanging from Vuksica's wrist. "Part of my life. But it better have some smart magic in it now."

Vuksica stares down at the pouch, always full, with anything from keys and kerchiefs and lists to carrots just pulled, stashed in an oilskin-lined recess for just such a chance. Part of their lives. A small extra lump is not noticeable.

"He's on maneuvers now, Mamma. With that Youth Corps of his. Not his idea. Just his good luck. Kept him from raring off—for what I won't take time to say."

"You don't have to. He wanted to burn Elsinore."

"To show his allegiance, yes. His idea of it."

"Will he?"

"Too valuable. They'll make a museum of it, my friend hears. If the sensible ones have their way."

"Ah. Sefaru."

"No, he's decamped. With half his crew."

"Over the border?" Her tone has in it all that the years have done to her. She can hear that herself, even while Laura looks her down.

"Yes, Mother. The price isn't—what it was."

"Oh?" Vuksica, shading her eyes, can see the far web-line of the larger mountains behind these foothills. "It'll be strange, living here, then. Not knowing the rules. And they mayn't tell me. That could be my punishment, for a while." She leans forward. "I can imagine worse." Though borders made of ravines and passes are not the same as a coast.

Her daughter is shaking her. Shouting, almost. "Then imagine it. Your son, Klement, will be going to interne us. Not here. In the capital. He'll invite you there. To share his residence. To show your sympathies. To be his bright mother-star. And he'll mean it. I know my brother. He's stupid enough. To think you will."

"And then?" She stands so straight that the backs of her knees ache. "If I won't?"

"There are places. Just outside the capital, some of them. Where with all due respect a man of influence can keep a family member who is a danger to the state. Can protect them from themselves. Nursing homes—that are a wee bit like prisons. Or for the obstinate, prisons. That are not too much like nursing homes."

"How can you know all this?"

"Warty-face. We have a deal. She tells me all her father's market talk with the old lover. And once, when we were out for our exercise, she showed me one of those buildings. The nursing unit. Jokers call it the Granary. The other one I didn't see. It's called the Millwheel."

"I can't believe—"

"You and Papa. You've been living in a movie dream."

"Maybe. Yes, maybe it would be that to you."

"Maybe that's why Klement and I are the way we are." Her daughter is regarding her sullenly.

"You are not like him."

"You don't know the deal I made. With Warty."

"What deal?"

"I promised her Mikhail."

"Hoo. Dear Jesus." She half wants to laugh. But she is like her women friends, where men are concerned—she is greedy to know, even about her own daughter. "And will he?"

274

"I promised him Belgrade."

Vuksica tousles her daughter's hair. Laura isn't quite a woman yet after all. What woman is, all her life long? But a mother has to be. "You're not so bad. You just let things out."

Arms around each other's waists, they watch the sun disappear behind that web-line of mountains. She feels as if this afternoon she has tasted all the sludge of the capital—what it does with its money, its bodies, its walks, and its dinners, its marriages—and its armies. All at once, all the façades. Even that backwater is a capital of all that there is or is to come, anywhere in the world. Is she living a tragedy or a farce? Or to be living to the full, did you have to be down so deep that you never knew which?

Danilo would tell her. She sees him as she has seen him dozens of times, shaving her face in his mirror.

Vuk-si-cah, he'll say, as no other tongue says it. After a certain age, dear sister . . .

"Laura?"

"Yes?"

"After we are a certain age, maybe any country is a movie dream."

Laura can't see him, of course. And what does he know about what Gonchev came here for? Or why she herself, almost to term with Laura, but not caring a fig for that, agreed to come here. For the theater she had to have.

"Come on down." On the grassy flats below, Laura is holding out her arms. "Climb down carefully, there's a nasty pitch there. And Mamma . . . Vuksica . . ." There's a sob in it. "Promise to do what I ask."

She starts down, only turning for a last look in the direction the podium points. "All the same, I wish he hadn't called it Elsinore."

As they near the house the cook comes out on the side steps, waving her arms.

"A phone call. She never gets used to them."

"Klement," Laura says.

From inside the house, the outer light is now extraordinary. The trees hold autumn fast by its frog-green glare. The fields are as jittery as van Gogh's.

On the phone, it's Lola. Klement will arrive this time tomorrow evening. "And we thought—all five of us—you might wish us to be with you."

So she is warned. But she refuses them.

Next morning, Laura goes. Neither of them has slept. "Use that ticket," her mother says. "Go for your reasons. I stay here for mine." At Laura's agonized face she adds, "But I promise you. Wherever you land, I'll someday come. I promise you."

The face lights up, a girl's. "We will be refugees. I'm glad."

As Laura bends to pick up the flight bag that holds all she can salvage from here, her mother whispers: "I have to stay, don't you see? I have to give Gonchev time."

When she had torn herself from Laura's abandoned room and closed the door on that girlhood, she went down the corridor to Klement's den and unlatched the door. At age eight he had demanded locks, with a military fervor that had at first amused. His keys are now kept above the door, for decency's sake, and for the cleaning. By some mumbo-jumbo of placement he knows when they have been used in his absence, and reports on that even now. New maids always say, "He keeps his room so smart, I'm scarcely needed; how lucky you are in such a boy." Then they see the separate showerbath—built for him in his teens in order to get him out of the family bathroom—its walls yellowed by the steam of his hour-long showers, the floor rotted from towels flung there, sopping, and left. "He leaves his dirt inside there, whatever it is, and the inch of rebellion he can allow himself," Gonchev said. "We are wise to help him confine it." Now and then the shower floor is replaced. The ever-drying towels, always a dozen or so thick Turkish ones on a separate line in the yard, are part of the horizon of their lives.

In company, after people have batted cheeks with Klement in greeting or clasped hands in farewell, he can be observed to be restless and will shortly absent himself; any later bathroom user will find the soap swimming in its dish and the telltale towel. Catching him at a more public ablution—at that picnic, say, when a bravura twirling of his bike brought him down in mud, and a basin was brought—if one is privy to the distorted flourish with which he ends his scrub, one understands better why. All cleansing tools must be dropped, leaving him pinkly himself, for the moment freed of contact even with those.

Yet her son has his sweetness, or tries. Once or twice a calendar year, the dates being dependent on his completion of some athletic trial or organization event, he opens his room to the family, a favored crony or two, and his own current girl, for what he calls his show. All the new trophies are trotted out and the new photos aligned. Sweetmeats and wine, lavishly bought with his own savings and decorated to the hilt with paper flags and the slogans of the moment, are served them all, with that intensity of purpose which, for him, must be love. Even if afterward he counts the leftovers.

She hasn't seen the room since the last of his shows, a year ago or more, before he went on active duty. It no longer shocks her with its conformity. Klement is a scholar of the ordinary, only more tied to it than most of us. In the closet are all his uniforms from childhood on, kept there after he had a temper tantrum when the first one was got rid of. Some parents cherish the height marks penciled on a wall; what's the difference? Here's the glassed-in cabinet where the dated photos of Klement's successive girls stare in chorus. Each one she had met seemed to her to have been curvetted here by the practiced flick of a whip at their heels. There is one girl she hasn't met.

Picking up the photo of that girl with Klement on a ski trip, she dislodges another of him and a former girl, in hiking boots. Both snapshots slip to the floor, face down. Inked on the back of the hiking picture are markings, groups of four verticals crossed off with a fifth line—the traditional counting-off in fives. On the back of the ski picture of the girl she hasn't met—a tall girl, quite as handsome as the others— the penciled marks are zeros, three. Should she blush—a mother—at the scoring her son obviously keeps—or laugh? I'll decide, she thinks, when I meet that last girl.

Yet the room asks for some response. Does it depress her with its imitation? Anger her with its ideology? Scare her with its ego? What? Summon all your knowledge of him.

He is not bright politically. Instead, he is brutally devoted to the facts.

And can be trusted never to originate. Meanwhile, Roman-curled with youth, he has the head and bull neck that have marked certain leaders of men. She has often heard how difficult it is for parents to descry their own qualities in their children. According to Danilo, when Klement is satisfied, he moves with some of her own heavy ambience. When he is thwarted or threatened, he lowers fretfully for the charge, in a childish version of what to her is Gonchev's poetic restlessness. Reared by parents who each had a sense of personal direction, he can imitate their posture, if not their performance. Will that be enough?

She turns slowly, an improvisatrice, receiving data from a supporting actor on a set they both occupy. What's meant to shine here shines, those steel javelins most of all. And the silver prize-flagons. All his "firsts" are prominent, including a brown stone mug she recognizes, token of his first beer. Conversely, whatever might stink a little—the boots lined up in category, the sweatshirts grayed with use—is placed well back. There are no books here. Nor anything visual on the walls, unless one counts the slogans, in their repetitions grossly—accountable? Careful; don't pun; Klement has never caught on to puns. Over his head they fly. Or under his skin.

Count the mirrors. There are those. Two of them full-length.

Otherwise, no clouds, tints, shadows, illusions, all those in-betweens of vision, those velvets and atmospheres of the eye. And of its depths. Perhaps Sefaru was right in a way. This man is not his father's son.

There's even a flicking sensation at her heel. Is she being asked to move on?

The room tells her that Laura's warning may be real.

Moving in the wind outside the window, an old metal mirror, bracketed to the frame and pointed down the hill—a trophy found in the Tirana bazaar, said to be from a Western truck and given to a ten-year-old by a still-doting father—shows her that the owner of this room is now arriving.

She stares down the hillside. Painters in their old age often painted from behind windowpanes, Gonchev once said, pointing to a copy of Pissarro's *La Place du Théâtre Français* in his study, painted from above, in which the carts and horses stood in peculiar stasis, and one could see that the pavements of Paris were pink. "Is Pissarro your favorite painter?" Laura had asked. "The good ones are all my favorites," he'd answered. "They belong to us all. They belong to you." Reproductions were all over the house—Gonchev had brought a few personal possessions with him at the outset, although some, including a Cranach nude, had had to be left at the border. "Does Matisse belong to me?" Laura had said in awe. Gonchev had chucked her under the chin. "You belong to Matisse. You women especially."

To whom does Klement belong? She looks down at him as he draws up to the house, not on the motorbike acquired when he was sixteen and for years curried like a horse, but in an open touring car, with a driver at his side. The car is ancient enough to have driven Mussolini. Maybe it once did, drifting down afterward through the subterranean exchange marts of the Balkans.

Fifty years back, this is the way a leader exposed himself to the populace. At the moment there's only the cook twisting a knot of her apron, a head gardener with pockets that clank, and one of the tobacco crew, stinking so from his own chaw and spit that from habitual rebuff he gawps from several yards back. Now Klement is bowing, left, right, to these denizens of his childhood. Their faces judge him. In the theater it's bad luck to watch a botched performance from the wings; even the stagehands leave. She can't.

The driver sits like a dummy. She can see only the cap.

"Oh my, my."

'Risa, the maid, has seized the opportunity to sneak into the off-limits room and is peering over her shoulder. "Master Klement has gilded his hair."

So he has. A pompadour brighter than hair could ever be juts over his khaki collar like the biggest of brass buttons. Wind is jiggling the plane trees that line the driveway. If she raises the pane she'll hear a drone like invisible insects by the thousand rustling their legs. This the bora, the dread seasonal wind. As Klement gets out of the vehicle his muffler flaps across his face, but he's not a brigand; he'll resist any loosening of the law. Laws are his prop.

"Help me raise the window, 'Risa."

"But, mistress, this room we never . . ." 'Risa is shocked.

"Help me, I say."

The wind comes in, smelling of the sea. This region doesn't get the bora's full force, but during its season small craft cannot land along the coast. The wind is advising her. She must act on her own.

Down below, Klement looks up, the scarf whipping free. The house is a mere story-and-a-half high. As he marks the window she's leaning from, she can see the red rise in his neck like wine in a bottle. With an effort he salutes. She closes the window, still watching him. Only of police rank, he rates no gun but has a convenient little nightstick, with which he's marshaling the cook and the gardener into the house. Even the workman, hanging back and gesturing to his encrusted shoes, is tapped in.

When Klement and the others have gone in, the driver climbs stiffly out of the car, favoring one leg. An older man, then, as drivers often are here, because of their old-car lore. Or else a disabled veteran of some internecine war or feud.

As the man attempts the first of the three steps, she recognizes the stooped question-mark frame. "Our punctuation mark," Gonchev used to say of him. "But is he telling us where to stop—or to start?"

The man's seen her. The face lifts farther. That's hard for a face used to craning sideways, but the long neck stretches up, up. He lifts his cap. He has never before done so. They exchange the glance that people give each other in the extremities of trust.

Behind her she hears the squeals of the cook and the gardener's grunts as they are shunted up the stairs—and the door bursts in.

"My room!"

Klement sees the dropped photos at once. In a fortress, any crumb of change is visible. He half drops to his knees, then remembers who he is now and covers them with a foot, but can't resist. He crouches and rises in a flash—those knees, muscled and oiled by the bike, are the best of him, along with the biceps which have won him his only earned merit.

Holding the scooped-up photos, squinting at her meanwhile—so she's seen the markings that tally his luck with girls, has she?—he opens the cabinet, thrusts the photos in, regards them, and with a hand quivering with compulsion edges them to the exact position they were in before. Then, spreading those arms tenderized by the javelin—huge arms that his military-cut jacket, smartly indented at the waist, fits precisely—he stands back, saying—"Memme."

"Klement?" He's never said "Mother" or "Mamma" in anything but Serbo-Croat or English. *Memme*, or *memmo*, is the local word for "mother," or "the mother"; she isn't sure which is the form for direct address. Or the form for sentiment. Nor maybe is he.

"So—I am here."

"So you are."

They do not embrace. At about fourteen, grown tall and burly, he shrank from that, which Gonchev said was normal. "When he's man enough to resume that, he will." By then she and Gonchev had long since stopped being physically demonstrative in front of the children, although their after-lunch naps couldn't be concealed. But perhaps the damage had already been done—if it was damage? Laura, going off to be Juliet, at Juliet's age? Girls matured early physically here, but often late emotionally. As for Klement—"All Klement's pals' parents are Muslim," Gonchev had said. "If any of their mothers have a belly like that Cranach we had to leave at the border, Papa doesn't mention it—and maybe goes elsewhere, except to propagate. Our loving ways—Christian ways, such as they are—embarrass him. On all scores."

"You Gonchevs seemed to manage fine in any country," she'd said. Pictures in Gonchev's study show him arm in arm with his parents at several ages. As he grows taller, and they shorter, his arms encircle them.

"Ah, we were refugees," Gonchev had replied. "That was our strength."

Klement is prowling his room, aligning a ski pole, fussing with the tongue of a boot. Can he hear Gonchev's voice in her head?

Here comes cook, beamingly carrying a load of white cake-boxes. "From the capital," she says. "I can't wait to see." And there's the gardener, bearing a whole case of those little splits of Austrian champagne, not seen since—when? Since Vienna, where she and Gonchev had a final splurge, talked about ever since, before they came here.

"We have those in the capital now," Klement says.

"Ah, yes, I can see," she says. "Everything here is from the capital."
And Klement is having his show.

"But where's your driver? After such a long ride, won't you ask him in?" She must keep the maternal chiding from her voice.

"In Papa's study. Packing the big map. And—other things."

"To go where?" And when he doesn't answer, "Ah, yes. They're not going to burn it down, then." She is careful to say "They."

"We'll drive him to the airport with the stuff. They have a plane ready for him. You and I will drive on."

"On?"

The cook has been bringing out the cakes with "ohs" and "ahs," setting them on two folding tables, made in part by Klement, and finished off in Gonchev's shop, for youth meetings that never materialized. Cook knows the routine for the shows that have taken their place. The cakes are grandly tiered—a white, a mocha, and a pink. "From the bakery in the old quarter," 'Risa breathes, and then squeals. The last box holds a domed blue velvet jewel box.

Klement takes it from her. "Not for you, 'Risa," he says, mocking. "Nothing for persons who unlock my room."

"That was me," Vuksica says. "Your father's study has never been locked. But you are wise. There are vandals about."

"He's gone, isn't he." Klement's voice has no color. But then it never had much. He is opening the box. "And I've brought you a medal."

Medals are struck here for every occasion. "They do it in place of parades," Gonchev used to say. "For which the terrain is largely unsuitable. And the military display unobtainable. And for memorials," he'd added, when the children were out of hearing. "After a political killing." The workmanship of these pieces was often very fine. But Gonchev had never accepted one.

"From the bazaar?" Where secondhand medals abound. Klement and his chums used to collect the lesser ones.

"From the state. I persuaded them."

He would think in that style. Communards of the old school, like that elder partisan and his whiskered wife, hung enlarged metal replicas of such medals at the front doors of their houses, as one might a flag.

'Risa whispers to the cook, "Will it be gold?" Many medals were not.

A pill Vuksica will have to swallow in any case. "That's thoughtful of you, Klement."

"Wasn't easy, I tell you." He's always suspicious of praise. "I had to sweat for it. The stories they brought up. Is it true our name was Gonchariev once?"

"Your great-grandfather belonged to a household of that name. But rest easy. He was a serf."

"But a freed one."

"Ah, don't worry about that. At that time, in that country, they all were. Anyway, you've done your bit for your mother. So that she can go on living here."

At the doorsill the old workman is shuffling his feet. "Come in, come in, don't fuss about the carpet, 'Risa'll clean up," she says. She motions to the head gardener, whispering, "Break out the wine." Why is she whispering? Because she knows the gardener to be her ally?

But it's her son who's at her side. And what's he saying?

"No, Mother. So that you can live with me."

Cook is cutting the cake as silently as if it must be done that way by law.

"But you don't live in any one place, Klement. Or only in the barracks."

"A house is available. In the old quarter. It was used in a film once. You admired it. The big gray one. That extends underground."

"The old waterworks?" She'd admired it as one does the improbable. Tomblike, uselessly turreted, it had the ill-starred air of a project whose architecture was too handsome for a back street. "House of the Cat Queen, whose ranks have deserted her," Gonchev had said of it—had Klement heard? "But, Klement, nobody's ever lived there."

"Laura will keep you company. And I'll visit. When I can."

"But it has no windows on the ground floor."

"You'll live at the top."

The cake knife has stopped. The tobacco worker's boots also. And the clink of opener against bottle, in the gardener's fist.

"I had such a clear path," Klement says. "Now—I have to cut my losses."

"Then what's the medal for?"

"I may never be Premier now," he says. "But I'll be a Premier's right hand—you'll see. I was brought up here. And I speak the English they'll be needing. You've educated me. In what they'll need."

His English is not that good. He never liked the family's use of it.

He comes closer now than they have been in years. His breath stirs her hair. "A Premier's right hand. You'll be the mother of that. And you'll wear the medal. To show that you agree."

And atone for the stain on him? Gonchev, if he had been here, would have laughed and thwacked him on the shoulder. And been knocked down for it? He hadn't seen Klement's clumsiness grow into power. Already so much Gonchev hasn't seen—does she envy him?

"And what if I don't agree?"

"Oh, mistress . . ." The workman speaks through a blob of cake. "From what's doing in the barn, you'd better. And take what you can with you."

The driver enters, carrying a long cloth-wrapped cylinder higher than he is, which he stacks in a corner. "Beautiful maps. I found four altogether. Along with all the blueprints . . . and what's doing in the barn?"

Nothing can undo the sidle of the driver's head, fixed by hundreds of hours leaning from his motorcycle, peering in at meetings, casting eyes modestly aside. But now, in authority, the face is more frontal. When he sees Vuksica, shuddered now into a corner, he bows.

She nods. What a long relationship they've had. He's an actor too. And, like her, one step removed from the general history. She's never before spoken to him. "So—you follow my son now. You're his."

He doesn't quite answer. Habit holds him. But the head cocks. The face has a wry smile.

"He thinks I'm his" bursts from Klement. "Young Gonchev, at the end of a puppy string. Guarding his museum for him."

"You're being sent to Elsinore? You?"

"Because I am my father's son, they say. They call it my duty, but it's my punishment. To obey all the staff there. And him here." He clicks his heels together, and a fold at the back of his stiff jacket brushes the tier of a cake. "But my boys don't ride the borders to learn to be ratcatchers. We'll be back."

There's a crash of small bottles. The gardener is standing up. "Two of them were here yesterday. There's cans of oil under the hay. Under the cellar steps here, even. When I and my men go off for the night and you've been taken away, mistress, they're coming back. To burn the place." His voice shakes with anger. "And they've left the horses in the barn."

Klement has a gun in his hand. So it's true.

"And cook and me," 'Risa wails. "What about us?"

The gun wavers, settles on the gardener, lifts again. Comes to rest pointed at the spy—if that is still the man's rank. The gun circles them, Vuksica too. Can't decide. Maybe shoot them all? They can see the progress of the gun's thoughts, of how an assassin is made.

Clutching her purse, she yearns to harness Klement again, as she had had to do in order to safeguard the lumpy, blundering child of two.

"Oh, Master Klement," cook says from behind him, "mocha, all over your lovely coat."

In the moment he looks down, Vuksica shoots.

There's no noise. As in a pantomime, the right arm seems to shatter, the gun drops, he sways.

In a vise of horror, she holds off from shooting him in the leg.

Cook forestalls her. "You'd have left us to burn." Her plump hand smears mashed pink-and-white icing from Klement's collar to his crotch and across his insignia. "Now, go to wash."

The gardener pulls her off, meanwhile snarling to 'Risa: "Bring linen." He is first-aid man for the farm. "There's not much blood," he says, squatting, making a quick tourniquet of his woven cotton belt. Klement, lying spattered on the floor like a boy in mud, doesn't resist.

"You shot well," the gardener says to her. "As a mother must."

She can't yet look at the wound. But when the arm is wrapped she kneels to him. She sees him in his crib.

"Doctor or hospital?" the gardener says behind her.

"Doctor, first." The hospital is forty miles away. But the doctor isn't much. She looks around for the driver. Gone.

"Gone to see to the barn, ma'am."

"Can you make our car do it?"

"Been on the ready," he says proudly, "ever since the master went. We'll have a cart trail us just in case. But I don't fancy using one. Carts make a wound bleed."

It's said a wild pig cries when stuck, out of humiliation. Under Klement's gilded forelock the eyes stare back at her, swimming in their own brine. She speaks to them from behind her knuckled fist. "We didn't do enough for you."

They carry him out, he struggling to walk but beginning to bleed again. Her gun is safe in her pouch.

In the car to the airport, hours later, she thinks of how Gonchev and Danilo used to envision their leaving this place—either with the children, or the children alone, or Danilo with them, or all of them, even gathering in the spy. And of how none of them have left in any of those ways. She thinks of how they'd considered the likelihood of getting a gun, and of how it has been got. Her belongings are packed as she might have packed them. The spy is driving. Returning from the barns, he hadn't been able to use the new-style talker strapped to his chest after all, in order to check with his superiors. It had been "shipped," probably as contraband, without batteries. She had led him to the telephone, all without speaking.

Men are coming to guard the place, the gardener reports. After which, gossip says, it will revert to the state. The car held up until they got to the hospital, but he has had to return by the cart. Klement will be kept in protective custody for some months, whatever his injury. Telling her this, the gardener avoids looking at her. When members of the Youth Corps failed at what was valor to them, they often killed themselves in the old style, which dishonored the state.

"And the arm?" she'd said.

The hospital will phone.

"Madam . . ." The gardener had always been respectful. But the change of address from "mistress" was significant. A tall grizzled man, important in the village, he always reminded her of the host in the inn scene in a Vienna production of *Rosenkavalier*. In which, though already known in her own country, she'd worked as a nonsinging ensemble player, in order to observe a great diva.

"Take heart," the gardener said. The village was agog, but not as she might think. It was felt that she had shown *trim*. "Like one of us."

This is still the back country of the blood feud. In the old days, men were killed off privately as commonly as in military service. Women went to pick up their dead as they once did in medieval war. Indemnity was paid by the killers. The slate was wiped clean.

And these are still the old days here, like the bottom floor of the house Klement intended for her. Maybe they'll respect her, for what she's done. Not striking a medal. But in the end she will pay up. As both she and the gardener know.

"You did it for us," he said. "And for the horses."

He had kissed her hand. And had relieved her of her gun.

The gaunt workman had decamped pronto, taking with him his rightful split of champagne, to flaunt his story at the local bar, where Gonchev used to go, he said, to sit inside the peasant mind for a while, an outsider, but the cockles warmed.

She hasn't been in a bar of any kind during all the years here—she for whom bars and cafés had been a routine expansion of one's hours, and of her personal life. For women, such places do not exist. For the women here, perhaps she herself doesn't now exist. Cook and 'Risa, after helping her pack in frightened quiet, had accepted the keepsakes she offered and disappeared with their own bundles. Nothing has been heard from Lola or the others. She has exceeded their boundaries.

Later, booted and furred for the mountains, she stood in her own driveway and watched the draft horses being led away. The brown-and-white house sat sturdily in its ruff of green, on its south wall a fading fresco of flowers. Fading might proceed quite comfortably when a house was occupied, but was like dry rot on a deserted one. Granaries and gardens cannot be safely locked up against the seasons, or time. The house would wait under guard for some functionary either willing or commanded to deal with its unorthodox fancies—and from now on, with its legend. It will not wait for her.

At the airport the new guards are the same types. Thick jokers, bored with their own brawn, and negligent, they let her pass without noticing her. But Gonchev, Danilo, Laura, and Klement are all there also waiting for her.

Ghosts have their own baggage. She can see right through them, to the land she and they have loved in spite of all. Its trees, its work dirt under the nails, its people, reflect in their ghost eyes as on the air her own lips taste. They are holding in wait what cannot be lost. Are they waving to her? Or is she waving to them?

The plane is bucking the air currents over the mountain range that cups Elsinore. Down in the plains the *bora* is sandy with North Africa, tropically fierce even in a blow. Up here the winds are cold with the genius of the hills. Above those even higher peaks ahead must be that freezing temperature which foreshadows vacuum. Winter skies here are as hard as opals. On their Alaskan stretches the eye expects to see white bear. Why is she thinking of the American continent, when the Himalayas are so near?

She has always held the name of Gonchev's plateau against it. A Hamlet dream, tied to a Hollywood kite. Now she sees how right he may have been. A man like Gonchev will have his final emigration in his bones.

In which of his cities will they quarter her? She won't find that eerie. A stage set doesn't come alive until it is used; until then, it's a rubbishy attic, or a deserted bal masqué. Besides, as she once teased him, all Gonchev's cities smell alike, and all their seasons. They smell of new varnish, of the old doll-stuffing that costumes and rented sofas always seem to be made of, and of hot lighting trained on this year's emotion and last year's dust. Now and then one gets a whiff of lurking animal, remembered from a back production, or from as real a cat as the night watchman can find. Always there's the sweat of actors, dead or alive. If anything can heal her, the smell of theater may. Persuading her she's merely shot a boy cast as her son?

At the moment she's more of a mother to Klement than she has been since he was the small boy who she already knew would never grow into the endearing gosling that so many of his playmates were coming to be. Even when tiny he'd had that beetle brow, that gingery brush hair with no cowlick for a palm to ruffle, and fat fingers that stuck out like prods from his ever-acquisitive fists. It had been her duty not to let him know he was unlovable. Animals cast out the misfits of a litter. Humans try to love, and fail.

The news from the hospital was that if the local doctor had set the arm properly, Klement would regain use of it. His political fortunes are less likely to recover. But the country is opening up, and is money-hungry. And maybe status-hopeful, in the prevalent way? If she thinks of this country as Lola and "the Premier" personified, she can hazard better what it will do with Klement. Under their new ethic—or the old blood-feud and smuggler tactics refurbished—a use may well be found for him.

Gonchev's voice, consulted, says, "You shot him because he was dangerous, not because he lacks charm."

But the womb has its guilts. She wonders how such a mosquito of a plane as this one can stay aloft, carrying a woman with such a heavy stone in her breast.

Her companion, who can no longer be called a spy only, is in the jump seat next to the pilot, near enough to touch. The rest of the tiny plane is filled with the baggage rifled from the house. All the contents of Gonchev's study must be here, though he has preceded them. She now has no guilt there, only the hope that his voice will stay with her.

Whenever the man up ahead speaks, to her or to anyone, he does so with difficulty; silence has been so long his habit. When he came back from the barn she had said: "I don't know your name. We never have." Direct address made him blink and summon himself. "I am a Tosk."

From history lessons gone over with Laura she knows that the Tosks were one of two early tribes, the other being the more Greek-sounding Vlachs. Turk, Slav, Greek—it's all the Balkans, her ledge of Europe. Which leans more than a little toward an East beyond Europe. And on summer days tilts toward Africa. But can never finish its own wars. Yet once, in such a summer, had started a flame-throwing that more than the horses had not escaped.

After which this country had holed itself in on a scale that even she, a Slav inured to living in between, could scarcely believe.

"It's a badger of a country," Gonchev says over her shoulder. "Holing itself in." Under these very peaks the plane is threading—"Which rise," Laura's little school-voice is chanting, "to a height of eight thousand feet."

"I admire it, though—this little country," she'd said to Gonchev.

"That's because it appeals to the badger in you," he'd said. "And in me."

She hugs her breast. What's she doing, sinking into this abyss of history, geography, while the plane rises in its tussle with the mountains and slips down in its race with the night? She knows. She's traveling. We all are. Laura, my dear. Gonchev, my life. Danilo, my family. Even you, Klement, my stone—over a boundary you thought never to cross.

What she craves is a book. On top of her stacked luggage is a nylon see-through shopping bag, contributed by her brother, with a caustic "Find them in Tibet probably, but not here." It holds her real purse, a pair of pajamas—no more nightgowns from now on—her mother's cookbook from Novi Sad, and at the bottom, pushed there by 'Risa, who had stolen a look beforehand, the blue velvet box.

The medal stares up at her, unblinking, naïve: a woman in a headshawl clasping a baby to her with her right hand. The face is almost noble. The babe is crude, in profile like a heavy-chinned man. But then these holy babes are often grotesque. The nurturing hand is as large as the woman's face. The bright metal must not be gold; its reverse has worn to a brassier color. The inscription, encircled in a wreath just inside the rim, is in clear relief:

WE

SUPPORT

THE BRAVE

SHIELD

THE DESTITUTE

SAVE

THE WOUNDED

———

A.D. 1917

Turning it over again, she can just read the worn letters that span the woman from shoulder to shawl-tip: NEW ENGLAND ITALIAN WAR RELIEF FUND. The medal too has trickled down, from the years when this grim, never-quite-ravaged terrain was an Italian protectorate.

Perhaps she'll wear it. She has had nothing to do with the mandate on its back. But the sculpted face is appropriate.

Holding it tight against the wild dipping of the plane, now alternately gunning itself upward and veering from looming crags just in time, she taps the shoulder of the man in front of her.

He thinks she's alarmed, and shivers a hand reassuringly.

"No, I just want to know—where I'll be quartered."

The pilot speaks without turning his head. "With luck, in a good soft bed."

He has spoken through clenched teeth. After a moment he adds more softly, "They've a staff building. Very nice. Which we'll deserve."

She wills her own tone to be soft, relaxed. "I meant—which city?"

"I could not say," the spy says. He swivels in his seat, the lurching shadow in the plane dappling his face, on it the first expression she's ever seen there, though she can't name it. "When there, he lived in all of them."

She focuses on the two napes in front of her, meanwhile walking with Gonchev in his domain. Those space-and-object mongers, the modernists she had known in Belgrade, even now would be pacing their studios, flying up and out courtesy of an aluminum wing or a twisted iron ladder, as if toward a philosophy.

Gonchev she sees in more domestic poses. Having a sandwich, on a park bench whose curve and placement were already engrained in his eye. Curling up to sleep, in a crypt he had built and knows as well as a mother's womb. Or on a lonely evening in that same mock cathedral, lying down with a sexy smile on the long stone tomb and slender body of a faked nun. Living the mythology that kept life real.

What if she's been wrong, wrong to drag him from it because of her own political shame? Those churches that soared on temporary buttresses—he may have worshiped there. Who should know better than she that a drawbridge built for a two-week's run, across a stream sparkling with tinsel, can support a dialogue so true that it hurts? But does not kill.

What if people like her and her crowd, doomed since birth to hop between one political ditch and another, have forgotten the depths of reality that exist far below any of those?

"It has snowed," the pilot says. "Can't see the landing strip." He swears. Curses in the language here are as solid as nutmeats.

Nothing is all illusion. Nothing. I used to know that.

"Where do you suppose he really went," she says, "on his rides?"

"Ah, those." The shoulder in front of her curves almost like a hump. "I wore out two machines."

"Remember the cat-flap he built for you? So you could view the Tati flicks?"

He almost smiles. "My daughter who keeps house for me—she thought I'd found a woman. Kept urging me to bring her home."

"You were his friend. His only one."

"He spoke to me. More than once."

"I know. I was afraid for you."

"Not for him?"

"Gonchev? I'm never afraid for him. I don't know why."

"Ah. My wife—blessed be the dead—was the same. It's a gift."

The plane takes a steep drop. In the downward swoon she gasps out, "In his Madrid, maybe. It would seem warmer."

The plane rights itself. The spy and she bow their heads and breathe again, as people do.

"Or Tokyo. That tiny restaurant he made? With the two-mat rooms for a family, in the rear? The plastic foods for it were in his study for weeks. The children kept begging to take some to school, to fool their friends. I still have a fried egg." She glances at the baggage. "Or had."

"There was a picture of Director Gonchev in the studio. Leaning on that counter."

"Yes, he lived there too," she says. "And I've banished him."

"Ah," the man says. "So it was you."

The pilot says, "We have landing lights."

The plane is descending to that great bowl of flatland, sunk in gently flowing rises and romantic fissures of the earth's crust, which Gonchev had found here. Leaning over the maps now heaped in the plane he had chanted: "Caucasus, Trans-Caucasus—and a fifty-minute hop to the Alps. All mountain ranges are related. We only make the postage stamps." He'd like to make a Tiflis, he'd said, while blocking out the cities, and smiling like that sharpy boy who'd first discovered in Harbin what the world was. "Some of my father's folk went to school there. And Stalin. But it doesn't rate."

The landing strip is now visible in the snow, a long narrow gash as smooth as civilization is supposed to be. She feels that last bubble of flight in the body before a plane hits, then the syrupy taxiing. Far down the runway as they come to a stop is one other plane, larger and familiar, belonging to the nationally run line that twice a week flew a domestic plane over her house.

They walk toward it in the near dark. A faint searchlight swings up and over them, receding again behind a small building from which it came. A halloo, scarcely amplified, tells them to wait where they are.

"I won't have any airport Babel," Gonchev says. "I want to hear carpenters' hammers, cranes grinding, all the rattle of the metropolis— even that demented violinist who drives the neighbors cuckoo. And his scream, as they smash his door in."

"Ah, thank you, Gonchev," she says, "your voice is clearer here. I was right to come."

There is no sign saying ELSINORE. He had taken such delight in naming the place both for Shakespeare and for a small California resort town— "One hot mineral spa and a state park"—in which a few Romanian and Jewish rascals had first planted a claptrap studio. But he'd never allowed the name to be put on any sign.

"The place knows itself," he said to the authorities, who had half-pressed for that. "The way your country does." Afterward he reported to her gleefully: "You know that toady murmur all Marxists have to make in public? 'He is a true patriot,' they said." Still later he confided to her: "A country that's been passed from Byzantium to the Ostrogoths, from the Ottomans to the Neapolitans, and now to these people—does it really exist? My name for it says that."

But, Gonchev, that was when you were first here.

The air is fresh on her cheek. The two men have pulled out a footlocker for her to sit on and are sitting on suitcases, in quiet silhouette. Can they hear him?

A few years later, by which time the house was built, the children were grown into personality, and she had friends he could twit her about, Gonchev was sent anonymously a jerky print of some reels actually made at the California place—a comedy, American dialect. "Moom pitchers," he said, excited, spinning on the narrow heels of boots patched so often that she had teased, "Your boots—they don't exist."

He had taught the children the phrase, telling them that this was how Americans refer to film. "You'll have an international education," he said, tweaking Klement's ear. "Say 'moom pitchers.' Say it, my boy."

Later the phrase would depress him. "In Chicago, would that be the way people there talk of my film?" he said, coming late to the dinner table. By then he was often late. The rides had begun, although only in the daytime. "But, Papa," Laura said, "your films don't talk." Gonchev had snapped, "So they don't."

Danilo, there for the weekend, said: "Isolation depresses any artist." He was always saying what shouldn't be said. "Artisan is what I am," Gonchev had growled, but Danilo had only shrugged and replied, "Isolation makes them pompous as well." Gonchev had given them all that smile whose charm she can feel in the pit of her stomach, almost seeing it, a small nimbus on the mountain dark: "You always have the last word, Brother-in-law." And Danilo had sighed, "That's what actors have."

Her eyes smart now, with that truth. She recalls admitting to Danilo later that his antics helped. "You have no humor," he answered. "I'm the humorous twin. But don't worry. I'll survive because I have it. You—because you don't."

Gonchev entered in time to hear that. "I sometimes thank God," he said, "that I am not a twin." Her brother said, "So do we."

The scene plays itself out like a genre picture, long gone.

In its place are the cities. She looks forward to them. In each there will be a voice.

When instructions come to walk forward she stumbles on the flinty path, but her body is electric with vision. She has dealt with her life.

The spy limps behind her, guiding with a flashlight. The pilot strides ahead, his flight bag brushing her. As they approach the other plane on the strip, it is swiveling. When planes position themselves they look like birds of prey. She'd forgotten this—and that airports are more amiable when there are crowds. The shadows here are Prussian blue.

The plane has stopped moving. Two men in the gray-and-black uniform that guards wear in the capital step from behind its wings. Above them the plane lights up, shining on their silver braid. They look to be the overlarge, slightly doltish men recruited for such posts. Tonight they're without their token bayonets. On air duty those would be cumbersome.

The man who has been spy, follower, driver, audience, is separated from her, though not roughly; he is even allowed to kiss her hand. "Get along with you," they say to him then, "you're needed here." She thinks of all the incarnations of his service to the Gonchevs, but cannot find words in time.

The pilot vanishes to his soft bed.

Orders are to return her to the capital.

They know now, what to do with her.

PART
II

9

The Real Land

"CALIFORNIA'S THE REAL LAND of the free among you Americans, isn't it?" Gonchev says to his hosts, on their patio. "Any Californian I met my first days here was happy to help me make that discovery. Though you no longer feel much need to tout it, I gather. You seem to have your own civilization out here now." He's so happy to be speaking Russian, and in this antique style, his eyes moisten with Russian tears. That he should feel the long-buried need to cry, after a full meal washed down with an excellent, suitably scarce local wine and eaten in front of as broad a stretch of the Pacific as an eye could accept, was what made the tears Russian, of course.

His host, Malkoff, a physicist, once Malikovsky, wears spectacles, thick ones, but his voice is moist. "We Russians. Freedom makes us cry. We know how to bring the tragic sense of life to the table, and talk it down."

Behind Malikovsky-Malkoff is a life at first glance exactly the reverse of Gonchev's, underneath which lay sympathies that much more intense. His father had been an émigré basso who had died of apoplexy onstage in Pittsburgh, leaving behind his French consort and their son, who had grown up to be Malkoff, a bilingual prodigy from Carnegie Tech, for many years now persona grata at Moscow scientific conferences. At one of these, perhaps, would he have acquired his wife, Daria, bringing her to the States during one of the briefly warm periods of the cold war?

At least she appears to be his wife, although maybe the family tradition of consort carries on. From an early picture of her presumably taken at the time of her arrival—on Malkoff's arm, a round dark girl with plump cheeks, Gonchev, invited here during her absence, had expected a matronly development. What he has just met, before lunch, is an angular woman in high-heeled red shoes not suited to the territory, sporting a long bag of frizzed hair that must endear her to the rock musicians whose favorite video-aide Malkoff had told him she is—and wearing the sullen silence that so often enfolds the female photographer.

Although she had apparently been out all night or longer, and Malkoff clearly doesn't yet know where, she had made no move to tell him, and this seemed to suit them both. He and she plainly have a rapport. Considering where they are, in the most expensive of gardens-by-the-sea and in a villa to suit, yet childless and seemingly without other family, it may be merely that they have settled for the physical life. Either separately or together.

Malkoff, a prize-winning physicist, is surely paid a top salary by the great state university system here, but the "real" money, he'd informed Gonchev, comes from "a couple of silly patents," commercialized when he was too young to know better, that he should have given to the world without fee. By now, however, he is "almost of the opinion" that he can administer such funds as may accumulate quite as well as the world might have done. At his and Daria's death the royalties, if they persist, are to go to a foundation already established.

Since Malkoff looks about fifty and she a few years less, this is maybe why they contemplate that eventuality with such calm. Or is it that in a country which so medicates against death—to the point, Gonchev has noted, of being almost disinclined to acknowledge it—the rich, more accustomed to meeting early with their lawyers on such disposals, seem more matter-of-fact?

Daria hadn't seemed to mind finding Gonchev ensconced in her house for the weekend, before beginning the university duties Malkoff had found for him. Of course there is staff—two Mexican women, maybe mother and daughter, the younger one flitting noiselessly about the house turning down beds for siesta, the older one serving the meals, and no doubt cooking them. And, hanging about the kitchen when Malkoff and he passed it from the terrace, an anomalous boy peered at them. "Some relative," Malkoff said, sighing with master-race satisfaction. "We never know who."

"Like in the Orient," Gonchev said. Where even his parents, whose strained budget could stretch to the few pennies for a servant, had had to tolerate a kitchen flow of the servant's kin. "Part of what we used to call 'squeeze.' "

"Oh, we're very like the Orient, here." Malkoff stopped at the foot of the stairs for this analysis. "And very like Europe. The vineyards, you see. Not to speak of the bidets." He opened and closed a door just behind them, yielding Gonchev a brief flash of a gilded bathroom. "New York, I hear bidets are still against regulation, some buildings. Have to bribe the plumber to install." At the top of the stairs, which he mounted with an ease he couldn't help pointing out came from a twice-daily swim, plus manning his own boat on Catalina—"an island pristine, we'll take you there"—he popped his glasses by waggling his thick eyebrows, something Gonchev had often seen done by ham actors but never by an ordinary person. "And we're very like *us*. Come downstairs whenever you please."

Now the three of them are finishing the remnants of a meal indeed fraught with the international: tortillas, polenta, huge gray crabs lying stunned on the platters or wrecked on the plate, pastry more forthright than French but still tasty, fruit either pompously large like those strawberries with inch-high haunches, or else like those tiny yellow ovals— loquats?—knowingly small, and too much like certain faces—a face.

Malkoff can't wait to tell Daria how they had met. "On the train I made the conference book me from Chicago. About time I saw my own country—not just from the sky. And man, did we. Every whistle-stop. So, at one of those, not too far along, I see this gentleman, being left off at the platform by the most beautiful Asian snake-hips you ever. In a huge white fur parka. For a minute I think you and the band have followed me up."

Malkoff pauses, to wave them all a second espresso. The boy from the kitchen serves them deftly, his eyes meekly lowered but darting. "Hmmm, Jesus," Malkoff mutters once the boy has gone through the kitchen's swinging door, "now am I supposed to hire him too? I bet."

He resumes. "Daria did that once, when I came back from a roundtable in Honolulu. Met me with the band. When she first had it." He gives her a grin. "Not since." Daria does not respond. "Anyway, then the girl drove off. On her motorcycle, no less."

"We borrowed it," Gonchev says. "I was going to miss the train connection. And the cab agency in that Minnesota town wouldn't rent us a car except locally. So we made a phone call to a young officer we knew." Bring a friend if you like, Gonchev had said to the Haitian, the room's paid up for two nights—but whether he had, Gonchev didn't know. Borrowing the cycle had been Roko's suggestion. She would bring it back to its owner and take the plane home. For good.

"Until then I didn't know she could ride. Or she me," he tells the Malkoffs, squinting over the memory. Going to the train, he had taken over the cycle. For a fast ride that had said good-bye to all his wild ones.

"Sounds like a close relationship," Daria says.

Wham. He doesn't ever answer this baby hostility the women seem to trump up here. Like in those balloons in the old comic strips. Biff! Passion against a man—not men—he knows and respects. As well as, God knows, passion's acts.

"She drove off like a shooting star anyway," Malkoff says, oblivious.

Malkoff's not insensitive, Gonchev thinks. Merely used to the biff. "Her brother was a messenger all one summer, it seems. For the telegrams."

"You know all the proletariat, hmm?" Daria says.

Gonchev realizes he is hearing her speak for the first time. What's her resentment? Every corner of the room is sparked with flowers. The chairs are those huge, flowered discs, on whose pillows one can grill like a fowl in the sun, or soak up food and shade. Should he give her and her room full of chain-store life a mean stare and reply, "All of you"?

The walls are lined with her photographs. He doesn't mind rock music, the sound of it. What he minds is its linkage with film. Armies of teddy bears crying for the bottle, to a tomtom background of orchestras that have never learned the full scale. Visually, "rock" seems to him like a *commedia dell'arte* for children who can't dream, or maybe even hear, yet have caught wind of such practices. Graveside harlequins, clutching the mike as if it's an extra skull. Girls as thin as soda straws, and as scantily attached to life by what flows through them, whispering their egos through their hair. Rock's pathos was that it could transfix you only for the moment. Its power was that it could bury you in its routines.

Daria's photos, one to a panel, on walls covered with the grasscloth used by galleries, had caught all of those. She had also caught rock's lack of change. Here is the familiar yap of the stretched mouth. There the thicket of the token wig, filling the screen like a landscape—a private grove. Yonder, the vacant nod of the drummer, above his battery. On the farthest panel two final shots: an iridescent thigh, convulsed, and the dead-set statement of a leather boot.

"You don't like rock?" she says, ready for that.

From his long fraternity with cameramen he knows that one must never look to them for interpretation of what they saw. They were like the camera itself, merely present, or maybe one or two button-pushes above that, and if "good," with the earnest habit of being the right eye in the right place. Or else they were visual geniuses from birth, getting what they got through the fingertips and the back of the head, and like any sensible creator, scorning or fearing to scrutinize how.

But this woman, being Russian, must have come late to the rock phenomenon. Matter of fact, Malkoff had said, it was when she had failed orals in bacteriology that he had bought her the band.

"I mind—that I don't mind it enough," he says.

She makes a mouse movement, like a child told what it already knows. "You telling me the story of my life?" she says, and kicks one red shoe across the room.

Gonchev has heard Laura's friends say this, one of the catchphrases they spin like quoits across their lazy patterns of Sunday afternoon drink. "You can say that again," they might respond. Yet the clichés of one language are another's marvel. How they diagnose themselves here, and so openly! And with such pith.

He ponders how to compliment her, as one does when one considers a woman to be without charm. For it was no wonder she'd chosen such a band as her hobby. So many of whose creatures were likely born charmless too, and were working themselves up into anti-beauty instead. Yet even her pictures were not ugly enough. Nor she.

" 'The story of your life,' " he says. "How Russian you still are."

She gives her husband a look across the table. "No, that's him. Second generation." Her American accent is perfect, even a little dull. "They're like converts. When they really get the bug."

"Don't you want to hear how I corraled this marvelous guy into coming home to us, and for the college?" Malkoff interrupts.

"And if their father dies onstage," she says to Gonchev, ignoring Malkoff. Then she rests her chin ostentatiously on her palms. "Go on. Tell." But at the same time she rings for the maid to clear the table.

It is the older woman who answers this time. Looking at everybody and nobody, like underlings everywhere. If you could catch that look on screen and in large numbers, Gonchev thinks, you wouldn't need theses on revolution.

"Maybe the guest should tell how we met," he says, hoping to pacify. He doesn't quite know how these two are using him but knows he is being used. With the dreadful American openness. Pursuing which they can maybe sleepwalk through their lives more easily? And quarrel domestically, with an audience. And never come to grips.

Maybe this openness is the last of the pioneer energy? Maybe he should try for it too.

"We—were on a train," Gonchev says.

Malkoff gives a great laugh, reaching down the table to pat Gonchev's arm. "Good try, Paul baby. But let me." He interrupts himself to say thank you to the maid and add a request in Spanish. She brings cigars. Daria takes one too.

"So we were on the train, yes." The cigar smoke curls from the three of them like proper drama. "I see a fella shivering in his turtleneck. He looks real down. And a foreigner. Shivering, jacket like a dirty eraser. But a good wristwatch. And there's snow. And here I am, in my winter underwear from Bean's. So—how do I begin? 'Lovely girl,' I say. But this schmuck doesn't answer. So I'm intruding. But what the hell, we're going to be on the train for two and a half days. So I say, 'They say we'll see bald eagles on the way, if we're lucky.' And he says, 'Excuse me—would you repeat?' And when I do, he has a laughing fit. 'Your national bird,' he says, 'it is bald?' "

He and Gonchev laugh together now, with the cheerfulness of thick-cropped men.

"And it's then I realize we're speaking Russian. Something in his looks must have made me. And one thing leads to another; we spend most of the time in the observation car. I find out he's on his way to Berkeley as a visiting Regents Professor; he's their movie king for the semester. So I say, 'Berkeley? No you don't. A visitor, Regents Professor rank, any college in the system gets its dibs on your time. I'm going to see that you come to us first.' And it's a bargain. No skin off his ass, he says. If I will speak English to him all the way."

" 'No skin'—did I say that?"

"You're able to now," Malkoff says, pouring more wine.

Gonchev is beginning to feel pummeled again by American life, by the scheme it has devised for him. But he is riding with the punches, as Laura advised. And escaping? What can a man in his case further escape? He hasn't yet called Laura to let her know where he is.

Maybe they will give him a movie out here.

"And you help me keep up my Russian," Malkoff says. "She would rather I didn't."

The "she" kicks off her other shoe, which lands expertly beside the first. She must do this regularly. "See any eagles?"

"Two. They're on the table there."

This Gonchev can applaud. In the country he had left, such a statement would still have meant that you had literally shot them. Here almost everybody understands that what you see you can now own. In the observation car there had been a great exchange of camera slides. At the time he left Japan it had already begun to be that way—a land that honored the visual as a nimbus to a second life, and accepted any currency that obtained this for you, whether it was technology or a Shinto shrine. In much the same way, he had long ago agreed to give a bitterly enclosed country its voyages.

In the observation car the conductor had pridefully brought out his own slides. "I got the Louvre," he said. And he had. "Just a minute," somebody had said, "look at that window." On the railroad siding whizzing by, deep in snow, the long, swaying weeds were imprinting a border pattern between pane and snow that to him, Gonchev, would be Montana forever. "Get it," somebody said. And several of them had.

What could he bring to this country—give to it—that it didn't already have?

"I got your parka girl too," Malkoff says.

Daria, who hadn't stirred for the eagles, now rises from her chair in one hip-push and brings two snapshots to the table, stooping to pick up her shoes on the way. Both shots are of Roko—nobody with any sense takes just one shot of anything. Maybe Malkoff had already discarded others. Surely the eagles would be at best a blur—if of a kind that you could keep forever. As an endangered species, Malkoff had said.

Here is Roko. Seated on the motorcycle and ready to go, her body leans forward, the tip of one hip-high satanic boot grazing the ground— all of that black-clad torso in tune with the surfer-and-marathon-runner energy of her time. Above the forward-tensed shoulders her head faces the camera, toward where he himself is standing in the limbo of farewell. Framed in the white "native" ruff he had returned to the museum to buy her, her face stares after him as he must always have refused to see it, the slant eyes earnest with the calculation postcollege life is teaching her, the parted mouth still pedantic with hope.

Daria leans over the picture he holds. "Unisex?" Not waiting for an answer she jerks her left thumb over her shoulder at her husband and leaves the room, carrying her shoes.

"What does she mean?" Gonchev growls, and when it hits him, hauls himself out of his too-deep chair to hurl after her, "No!"

Then he is embarrassed. This is no way to act to one's host, to yell so at the wife. Yet maybe it is? Is Malkoff—gratified?

306

"She gets confused by all that music," Malkoff says. "And that crowd."

"Hah. Music can confuse film too. You have to keep it down. Like a dog."

"Oh?" Malkoff isn't really interested in film, as Gonchev has found. He takes snapshots merely to do what everybody does, like driving a car. But he sits up suddenly. "You don't mean—you want to do silents?"

"I have thought of it." Like cartoons, only with people, with maybe now and again a rattling little *pick-pock,* or a hornpipe. Or like in a land documentary, only the great rippling harp cadenza of the sea. He smiles at his host, almost happy. "Or maybe only conversation." Although in what they called cinema verité here, they were inclined not to let you hear more than a blurred slur. Like the eagle, he thought, excited. *Endangered conversation.* I could do that.

"Oh, good God, Paul, no. I told you. It's not the medium that matters here. No matter what they tell you. This country began itself as a mishmash, and that's what we'll give the world. Single-minded, you don't get far here."

Malkoff himself is involved with some scientists down at the Salk Center in La Jolla, who are studying cancer microbiologically. Sure, he himself is an atomic scientist with astrophysicist leanings. Didn't that have to do with the stars? Gonchev had asked. What had that to do with cancer?

"This is a mixed-media country, Gonchev. That's how it began, yes. And that's what it's already giving the world. Man is a mishmash. And so are his diseases." Malkoff doesn't seem sad about it. He stamps out his cigar. "There are stars in the flesh too, guy. Depend upon it."

He looks very single-minded as he says that, Gonchev thinks. And that is the way I would show him, on film.

"So now—we swim," his host says. He leaves the room abruptly, giving Gonchev a push on his way. "You'll find a suit in your room."

He can't find one. Somehow that makes him feel utterly forlorn. The way you feel when you discover yourself to be on a crowded bus with nothing on, a dream he used to have in Harbin. He had got rid of that in Japan, where life was so directional. Yet here he is again—on a very crowded bus, the way things were going. Maybe that was why his host kept giving him directions. Meanwhile telling him to please himself. He would like to lie down and consider. What if he did that, and just didn't appear?

Just then the boy he'd seen in the kitchen brings him a pair of bathing trunks, nodding and bowing, and leaving behind a strong smell of cologne. Everybody in the house does, even the cook. Maybe the servants steal it—there's a large bottle of the stuff on the dressing table. He lifts the bottle's huge, winged stopper. Yes, the same scent. Maybe it's intended that they steal some. Should he? Near the cologne there is a phone. He had better phone Laura.

"Oh, Daddy. Papa. Father."

"Yes, your mishmash," he says.

"Oh, Paul."

His spirits rise. She worries, poor dear. About him.

But no.

"There's been a crash."

"In Derek's car?" He had never trusted that Corvette, streamlined like for the races at Le Mans, but with lambskin seatcovers and a stereo. Plus a sign saying THIS CAR HAS NO STEREO.

"No. In the market."

"But you all said it was going to happen."

Laura and Derek's last cocktail party, before he went West. All those pink-cheeked girl vice-presidents, with their long, shapely nails on hands that had never scrubbed or cooked, and their squarish or skinny but always sharp-eyed young men, bringing the girls the white wine, and helping them choose which restaurant to invest in for dinner. They had all said it would happen. Smiling high.

"But now it's happened," Laura says.

And Derek had lost his job. No, not she. The lower-paid women were being kept on at her place, if they would take a cut in pay. "I will, of course. You can go a long way without pain on forty-five. And the price of things will come down."

She'd never told him what she is earning, saying he had no conception of money. Which was true. Sixteen years in a country that had run itself like an all-but-self-sufficient homestead farm would have done that for him, except that his habit of working for the sake of the work alone already had. But this was America, as they kept saying. He is learning money's value, surely.

"Forty-five dollars per week. I cannot believe. They are exploiting you. As a foreigner. And a woman. When they pay even me—my God." Seven hundred, was it?—just to speak. And once, a thousand. What the university was to pay him for his ten weeks he doesn't know. She takes care of these arrangements.

"Oh, Paul. No wonder I have to know about money. No, forty-five thousand. Per year."

"Oh. And what do I make?"

A pause. "Not nearly so much. But then you are not working by the year."

"It feels like it," he says. "Or like I am going to. Out here."

So finally she does ask where he is. The last few days his itinerary has slipped her mind.

She gives a squawk when she hears his change of plan, from Northern to Southern California. "Papa. You are in the promised land."

"No. Laguna Beach."

She laughs at his joke. So she is really all right. He is surprised at how much love there is in his chest. "And, Laura, if it helps—we are going to dinner tonight at a millionaire's. Or maybe a billionaire's."

"Both could be in trouble." But she giggles. "I wasn't in the market myself. Not recently."

"Where were you?" At least he knows from Derek how to handle that lingo.

But maybe he isn't convincing. He hears her sigh. "In a drugstore. And a launderette. Not stocks. Property. Basics."

"With Derek?"

"No." She is suddenly stiffish. "He and I may split."

"Why?"

"Because—he wants to stay."

She is like her mother in that.

He doesn't have to say so.

"No news," she says. "But soon maybe—news of news."

"I will come home at once. Tomorrow."

"No," she wails. "You. You'll spoil everything. You have to stay where you are. Wherever you are. So that they can see where you are."

"They? Who?"

She won't say. "Where are you, exactly? Who you are with?"

He wants to correct that sentence but doesn't. Being with Malkoff has infinitely improved his English; he can talk almost like a professor now. But he doesn't much want her to notice—and maybe ask about Roko.

So he describes the household here in some detail. Also how his hosts boss him, yet seem to use him as intermediary. Because maybe they were bored? With their beautiful situation. "Their property is beautifully situated." A direct quote, from Malkoff, on the train.

"Oh, Papa, of course. Then it's all right. You are in what is called 'the weekend.'" She and Derek have been to two, one in Westhampton, Long Island, one in Vermont. She chatters on. In one place she and Derek had to help cook, in the other they hadn't. But in each place they had been invited in order to admire. And to be audience. "Derek said they always say they will leave you time to be on your own, but they never do. We went to three other people's houses, for them to meet us." And always lots of extra people to dinner. "But even the children knew we weren't any of us real friends." She sighs. "Maybe the hosts just don't want to be alone, really." So whatever his hosts promised—an introduction, say, or a party to come—he was not to believe them. "It is just the weekend. But Monday will begin the week."

She is full of sighs, that girl. So for Derek and her it hasn't been only the crash.

Then she is quiet. He is suddenly sure she knows all about him and Roko.

"We are speaking the beautiful English," his daughter says. "You are."

"So she is home?" he says.

"Two days ago." And Roko had gone to the boat and taken away all her clothes.

His turn to sigh.

"Don't you do that, you," his daughter says sharply.

All women are together. "So I'll go back now to these odd people," he says haughtily.

"Not so odd. I told you. Par for the course. What's *she* like? The wife."

"Maybe not a wife. And not even foreign anymore. Like your American girlfriends, she reminds me." The same air the smarter ones have. Confident though you are, Laura, you have it too. Though this he wouldn't say. Maybe he didn't have to.

"Like what?" his daughter said.

"Like . . ." He thinks of Daria's shoes. "Like they are—unsuited to the territory."

Phones are tricky. But he has a feeling he has touched her. Or reminded her.

"To worry so," he says. "That they don't mind their comfortable life." Daria more, because out here women are more restless to begin with. And more comfortable? But Malkoff has it too.

"That's the golf game, yes," his daughter says. "In the States."

He thinks this over a minute. "You are getting more and more American."

"You are liking it better in Europe?" his daughter says. "Where somebody else could do that for you? Mind that you don't mind your life? Worry about how comfortable you are? Like Mama did for you? For all of us?"

One no-good child, he thinks. And one scourge. Is that par for the course? Anywhere? "Why do I have to stay here then?" he whispers. Surely she has heard something, from somebody.

"You have to stay on view," she whispers back. "So nobody questions."

So she has heard then. He recognizes these whispers that gather around Pfize.

"So, I can swim now," he says to the dead phone. He certainly wouldn't sleep.

"Glad to hear it," his host says, entering. "We were wondering."

"An expensive phone call," Gonchev says. "I'll pay for it."

"No, our pleasure. Come along."

Although Malkoff had entered without knocking, he waits outside while Gonchev strips. Gonchev reminds himself that the lines between rudeness and delicacy are everywhere different. The purple trunks fit him about right.

"Yes, we keep a supply of suits," Malkoff says, scanning him. "And Daria is a good judge of bodies." He catches Gonchev's non-expression. "She does costumes for the band."

"So now to your pool," Gonchev says, exhilaration swelling him— because of Pfize? It was the amateur spies here whose action made news. Meanwhile, no harm in letting Malkoff know that he is acquainted with such luxuries as pools.

"No, we have white water."

"White? You mean—milk?"

"Ocean frontage. What they call it."

A pity. For a second he'd imagined oblong lagoons fringed with natural quartzes, in the ice-cream colors that palette the average vision here. People of all ages would immerse themselves for beauty's sake in those tepid, lactic Jacuzzis, only to rise like children, bearing the milky mustaches of health.

But he and Malkoff emerge from the front of the house to a reality so exaggerate that imagination fails, not up to even the normalities here. From the deep inner core of the room where they had dined and lolled, he had indeed seen water, but so framed and hoarded that he had scarcely noted whether its solitaire blue was liquid or glass. Now he can only compliment this valiant shoreline, which has got itself together again in spite of the array of houses that swooped and dove on it from all directions, dividing the spoil like a pack of gulls.

On either side of him and above him, the house extensions flutter, curve, angle, and spiral, intent on one-upping each other's view. Nearest him, on the house next door, a long toucan's bill of a window is answered by a kind of pelican's pouch of a second story jutting from the house on its farther side. Only to be outdone by a periscope extrusion, triumphant with striped umbrellas, on the house beyond. The lower stories of these houses have also deserted the square. They sidle or shoot forward, forming angles so acute that one must have to warn any small fry playing tag—anywhere there is ground to play. No doubt these add-ons are all legal. The architects must be like what Derek maintains all Wall Street lawyers are—enemies on top, all friends together underneath.

Or vice versa?

Gonchev deplores this inner habit of vice-versa-ing, which had come upon him as a young man in response to early confusions. Such a course made for an easy but shallow response to life's paradoxes. One is left, in effect, without conclusions. Although in his present situation perhaps that is best.

I must remember, Gonchev tells himself, that just because I have been thrust upon this huge and no doubt important sector of the globe doesn't mean that I owe it an intelligent response. I have my own life to lead. Even if at the moment it's only in what they call a cabana.

The Malkoff's cabana flutters in the center of their strip of beach like a medieval tournament tent, its multicolored vertical canvas flaps hanging from a peaked metal frame, which, however, bears no crown.

They stop to have a drink there. A radio and a pair of binoculars stand on the bar, with the air of being in a still-life painting that man-made objects tend to have at seaside.

"How's your swimming?" Malkoff ignores the charivari line of houses behind them. His own house, on a double-width plot, had settled for its one long chute and a fantail above. Encircling it, and all along the beach, foliage of which only the tips can be seen screens and cavorts.

"I swam in the Adriatic."

"Good."

"But is that a shark?" At some meters out, a dark fin rides the creaming green. In Yugoslavia, where Gonchev had been with Vuksica, the hotels hadn't always posted shark warnings, not wishing to scare off the tourist trade. The local joke was: choose one of the plump German fräuleins and her man, and let them be the first to plunge in—as was usually their intent anyway.

"No, that's our rock. Big, but smooth."

Daria comes out on the sand, her pubis in a star-patterned indigo triangle. On top, a slanted bow of streaky gamboge and magenta touts two tiny poached eggs, her breasts. She and Gonchev give each other

the covert glances people exchange when first uncovered to one another. California clothes do call to mind comic books. He likes their lurid
assault. If insulted, those nipples of hers might squawk. Her legs are wan,
though. Not to be burned is surely a social stigma here. Her boyish
pallor increases her air of sullenness. Was she after distinction at any
cost? If so, she has made the wrong choice. Maybe is always doing that.
As she walks past the two of them, her tiny toes crimping, she looks like
a lady accountant, out for a glorious afternoon but unable to keep from
totting it all up.

Including him, Gonchev? Whose flat belly, legs still muscled by
mountain walking, and moderate hairiness, had passed muster with both
Malkoffs. Beach people anywhere like their friends to be stylish of body.
Bathers and strollers are scattered down the shoreline. Neighbors, all
geometrically striving together? Or is this a resort? A "second house,"
as Derek, who sorely wants a first one, would call it? He has really
learned a lot from that young man, and feels sorry for him.

Malkoff is watching his wife. Under his all-over-brown bodyskin, the
waistline is too clearly soft, but he is tall. Skinny, rather than slim. The
face, whiter than the rest, slumps toward the full mouth, the phiz of an
academic Pierrot. His black shorts bear a yellow insignia.

"Your university?" Gonchev asks, indicating it.

"Locker number, boat club." Malkoff, tense, doesn't turn. Daria is
sprinting toward the water. She dove. Dived? Which? Arching up and
then under the water in a curve like a nail paring. Or a slice of sickle
moon? No, she doesn't invite quite such a comparison.

Maybe she knows that. When she reappears, it is on the rock. Even
with the ocean sky behind her and her knee-clasped pose helping, she
is not quite what such a risky composition requires. She jumps. Reap-
pearing safely far out.

"Does it every time, dammit," her husband says.

"A good swimmer."

"Lifesaver's badge, like everybody out here. But nobody's good
enough for the Pacific."

But does she dive when nobody's looking? In this life out here, where
everybody has to be on view, that would be the test.

Would that be his test? To make a film when nobody's looking?

When she strides out, in the slow, waterlogged way swimmers do, her face is shy. He has to say something.

"Wow," he says. "Wow." That makes the two of them smile, in possession for the moment of their very own foreign clown, but he doesn't mind.

"My daughter and her boyfriend, they teach me to 'wow.' " Saluting them with dash, he runs down the beach on tiptoe and plunges into the sea.

Into this Pacific of theirs. Careful. Avoid the rock. No way you can swim will lead you back to where you want to be. Even though the world is round. Meanwhile, how this release from the earth's pull does cheer. Too bad he has no mask; he would like to visit the fish, to be temporarily in their calm. To be a fish was to be all fish; no pose was necessary. Even if always—on view.

Swimming water-easy, his own vehicle, he feels how exhausted he is by scrutiny. A platform is excused only by the work that feeds it. This talk-talk he's immersed in, isn't it changing his whole conduct of life? And he isn't alone in that, in this country of the platform. Where even the common laborer can listen to television, night and morning, so as to know where to stand and how to jog through the day. He hasn't met any laborers yet, though of course they have them. Peasants are what they don't have, Malkoff had told him, as they rode through the badlands of the West. "Even on the farms, all the blue collars are turning white." And banks would soon own the land, which would be worked on untouched by human hands.

Swim, swim. Raise the head, and plunge. As he rises, the horizon seems closer and grayer; cloud must be advancing. But he knows that rain comes seldom here. Is that why they exercise so much in these parts, to recover a natural stress? His own Elsinore had had to be approached across mountain wastes, and when he and his crew reached there, the water they drank from, even in his artificial city, was clear rill. "Oh, in a fascist country, yes," Malkov had said when he heard that. "Yes, of course. You won't find our water so pure. But still, you had to come, didn't you." In silence, while the train rumbled on, they had waited for the eagles. Gonchev had been glad beyond reason when a pair so identified by the conductor had appeared.

Swim, swim. Avoid their rock. They still have their badlands; is that comforting? But he must head back to shore now. This thud, thud must be his heart. Yet he is swimming strongly and advancing well. And nowhere near the rock. As he rises high to check for sure, the faraway cloud seems nearer the water. Or even part of the water's crest? Face the shore, Gonchev; the undertow is sending you there.

Rising high again, he sees only four people on the beach now, the Malkoffs and two of their servants, the old woman cook and the boy. All are waving him to come in. The surface of the water is maelstrom. Underneath, at the level of his ankles, a current of iron pushes him forward. Thud, thud. Not his heartbeat. He stops swimming. The thuds slap him to shore.

Or almost. The boy is hauling him, hauling him in.

"Knocked him out?" Malkoff says, above his head. "No. Just his wind. Okay, Luiz, you and your mother run on home—she has her car, yes? See you on Monday, if all's clear. Yes, both of you. You were right, Maria; your grandson is very quick."

Gonchev, trying to rise to thank him, is interrupted by her flood of Spanish to Malkoff. Who turns up his palms, saying, "Listen to your radio, Maria, same as us." And when the two of them trundle off, says in exasperation to Daria: "Four in help now. And on the back."

She is watching the horizon through the binoculars. "A very high sea. Not a tidal wave, they're saying, but we gotta git." The radio from the cabana chatters at her side. "Take it with you," her husband says. "In case the car one conks out."

Gonchev is instructed to dress as quickly as he can, bring with him any papers he values, and meet them at the car as soon as possible. "This is new to us," Malkoff says. "We're not directly on the fault. And the tremor's not that high on the scale. But they've ordered it." Daria has already vanished.

It occurs to him that "they" are the same anywhere on earth. Once he had been part of those in authority; is that his malaise now? He wouldn't have been one of those to order evacuation in time of earthquake. But he had been of their level. Their wives would have been on the phone to Vuksica.

He runs upstairs and comes down again with camera and duffel bag. Swim or ride, he is beating his way toward her. "Earthquake," he says to himself. Nothing that had yet happened to him would so qualify him in her eyes.

The car is packed full. His hosts must keep suitcases at the ready. Or else have an auctioneer's sense of what they value most. That would be Malkoff. And a secretary's efficiency with many small bags of obviously special function. That would be Daria. Years back Gonchev had been absolved of ordinary personal possessions. A library with the range of his was a treasure as good as laid up for him in heaven, since, in the event of some apocalypse, heaven might be the only likely place with enough space for it, barring the Vatican.

Still, he has brought his camera, viewed by his hosts with some doubt, when added to his duffel. "My portfolio," he says firmly, and sees to it that it is wedged in the trunk. They toss Gonchev an extra sweater, but would have installed him in the backseat with the luggage, if he hadn't stuck at the door. "Lucky we don't have bucket seats," Malkoff says as they pull him into the front. Still they are keeping their hostly obligation to him. Savages might not have done so. Or some other countries he knew of.

As they crawl up what could scarcely be called a driveway—more a garden path between shrubs that stood at attention—the house to the right of Gonchev, who is on the window side, shudders slightly and sheds one of its projections gently to the ground. So human a gesture, like a man shucking his T-shirt. Gonchev has seen a snowslide behave like that in his mountains, a peak tossing its tasseled cap, or wrapping an avalanche over a village the way Vuksica had toweled the children's heads.

Malkoff has to be appreciated as a driver. He's saying nothing about the slight ground shift to be felt each time they slow or pause. He has the good driver's welded trust in his car. When they come to the avenue out of their enclave he says, "Got the binoculars?" Daria has them. He focuses on what is up ahead. Daria has a look, then Gonchev.

The access to the highway is like an anthill the moment after it has been stepped on. Ant cars angle every which way. Only none are moving. All are jammed. Here and there, in a car swiveled backward by a wrong guess, one can see a face behind a windshield, jammed too.

"Can you pick up the highway, Dolly?" Malkoff is still inching the car. She can. They all have a look.

The highway, a raised one, is a glittering double necklace of car tops. Going both ways. Only not going. Some already have their lights on. As if warning the earth that hours are still in effect.

"Maria asked me whether to drive north or south," Malkoff says glumly.

Nature has stepped on the platform, Gonchev is thinking. When that happens the world doesn't work according to man's images anymore. Those people jamming up the highway have brought their immediate trouble on themselves. In a war, you may die according to a general's theorem. The people up there are trying to conduct an earthquake like a war.

The radio skitters on, issuing advice on routes and blockages, as if to commuters in the morning.

"Must be a recording," Malkoff says. "Computerized for changes— we hope. Or maybe it's come to a stop."

They sit in silence, thinking of what that could mean.

Silence must always be a sound during a natural disaster. That was the case in two Gonchev had encountered: the dead white absence in the ear after an avalanche; the pocket of vacuum when a hurricane paused for breath, while all those herded into the basement of a Florida college turned to each other, as in an airplane drop.

"Shall we take a vote? On where we'll go when we can?"

Malkoff, like any good leader, is trying to keep them on keel.

I should contribute, Gonchev thinks. But what? And would they welcome that?

"I wouldn't want to drive north," Daria says. "That's where the epicenters always are."

"Spoken like a true daughter of the Sunbelt. Gonchev, if we get you to the college—when we get you there, I should say—you should be briefed on the rival Californias. You'll have statewide status, of course.

But you won't hear too much about Berkeley down where we are. Northern California's a little like the East—to us here."

He's not a chatty man, really. Only trying to cheer.

"Oh, I wouldn't want San Francisco to burn," Daria says. "Besides, the band is there just now."

And by Gonchev's watch, only twenty minutes have passed since they left. Is that a movement in the car up ahead? No.

The car radio, blurting the name or names of towns reported to be at the quake's center, is speaking to them directly. Viaducts down. Emergency services. Water to be boiled. The mayor of one town speaks, a woman. Two families not yet found. "More than a nudge," the mayor says. A crack across Main Street in front of the Church of God has swallowed their mail truck, and an out-of-state moving van.

At the mention of the van, Gonchev stirs with recognition, as if someone has spoken his middle and secret name. The wastelands are rising. A truck in front of the Church of God might be only an emissary. The marshlands nobody noticed, those interstate wastes—will those be invading the towns?

The mayor is being interviewed by telephone. "Are you planning to evacuate? No? Why not?" The answer comes muffled, is repeated. "Can't choose your cracks."

A flush of blood begins to creep up Gonchev's ankles—the anti-boundaries flush. Will it overcome this sloth that the heat in the car is settling on his head? He hears the Malkoffs faintly, not distinguishing between her and him:

"Where are those towns?"

"Middle of the fault. Inland."

"A compromise, huh? Maybe the Lord took a vote."

They're talking English. United against him—or, in a sense, by him? He can't help squirming against the car door. The car's as heavy as a tank and has a tank's compressed eagerness. It eats ground, its owner had told him. Either desert or mountain. Taking its masters to Tahoe or Baja, with a three-year-old's zest. Teddy, the Malkoffs call it, in honor of a Roosevelt Gonchev hadn't heard of. "Because he too was a rover." Land Rover, this car is called. "Will go anywhere." And here it is.

"What's so funny, Gonchev?" Malkoff says. "Let us in on it."

Gonchev reaches for the binoculars, scanning the cars near them, the housed faces. Opening the window, he leans out, hearing the radios. Good cars here, most of them. An hour or two ago many of the people in them would have been in the sea, or immersed in their version of beach life. Now they are here, not a kilometer from their own homes, or in that gleaming mass of metal on the highway. It's hard to be an individual in this country. Very hard. Yet he is always being told that this is what one is here, and what he will be from now on. Maybe it's easier for a car.

"Got any advice, give it," Daria says. She has slumped toward her husband, maybe avoiding Gonchev's flesh.

Taking care not to touch her, he puts the binoculars in her lap. Malkoff waggles his eyebrows at him.

The lock on this Rover is a model of safety. And neutrality. A child could not open it by will. Or a Sahara wind. Or a passenger. He has seen how it operates—by driver control. Would these two oppose him?

He rouses himself. Remembering how it was to be personally angry. Not the anger that merely flails against the state. Or at those encroachments on the freedom of the air, the atmosphere, the atom, the gene, the laissez-faire of birth, that now invisibly wash the world. Nor the ever-ready anger of war, piped into the waiting armament of a country like stored blood.

A plain anger, felt in the fist. Against a man, a woman, and a lock.

"Get out and walk," Gonchev says.

He hears their shock.

"And leave the car?" the woman wails.

The man says, "Where to?"

Answer them, the monks of Gonchev's childhood say.

"You left your house," Gonchev says.

Their silence is smug, as with any who follow the custom of the country. They are making him submit argument.

Where would you walk, his monks say, except to where you are going?

"To our dinner party, no? You already told me where. And if I am late, I will have a good excuse."

And if the millionaire's house is no longer there, so will he, his monks say, clapping their hands in glee at their own riposte. From the perfect air of any man's primary school they reprove him, Why have you not applied to us before?

"Kindly to open the door," he says. "I wish to start out."

After due consideration, it seems, so do they.

"Very European of you." Malkoff is Malkoff once more. "I should have thought of it."

Luckily the car is almost on the road's shoulder. Malkoff leaves a note on the windshield, identifying himself and their destination. While they wait for Daria to change into flat shoes and to don a curious kind of belt she slides into like a harness, Gonchev asks to be let into the trunk, to get his camera. On reflection he opens his duffel also, to get the backpack stuffed with on-the-road necessities he has carried for years. His sandals are okay; his bathing trunks have long since dried.

Malkoff carries the radio, a flashlight, and a book-size packet he removes from the top suitcase in the back and tucks in the pouch his sweater makes above its waistband. "En avant!"

Daria echoes him, jutting her jaw at Gonchev; she won't forgive him for this. Malkoff has already appropriated the idea as his own. Gonchev is half sorry he didn't have to fight.

Threading their way toward the top of the hill, where the road joins the highway, they have to slide between the radiators of some cars and the rear ends of others. The cars have packed themselves close. One hood, brushed past, felt warmer than it should. Up above, it is still a perfect coastal afternoon in the Sunbelt.

Surreptitiously he bends to touch a wheel. The fender is hot, the tire also. Sidling along, he continues his research. Some cars are hotter to the touch than others of the same make and the same metal thickness. The earth must be hotter under them.

Dipping a knee, he manages to pat a side door from base to door handle. The door is definitely cooler, though still overwarm. Up ahead, the Malkoffs, taking their own path, are not observing him. Once they had decided to leave the car they had taken the lead, letting him follow. Our country, were they thinking? Our earthquake.

The last car he tries, a long Buick station wagon, is normal to the touch, like the three cars behind it, though its windows are closed. The sun is going down. His sweater feels delicious on his shoulders. The evening is dropping to dew-cool. Yet eight cars along the way to that last one are almost burning hot at the base. Their occupants, oblivious to the cause, have their windows rolled down.

Yet across the expanse not a motor can be heard running. No doubt about it, the heat is coming from the ground. Unevenly.

At the rear window of the station wagon he just tested, a small boy and girl kneel, their noses pugged against glass, watching him; too young to say what they see. In the front their parents sit, eyes glazed, not quite dozing. On the middle seat a Doberman rears, its head proudly arched, the way dogs do in vehicles. On second look, he sees that the dog, delicate ears up, nostrils winking, is shivering, not making a sound. As he passes, it rolls its eyes at him.

When he catches up with the Malkoffs, a big man is hauling himself out of his small car, a natty Japanese one that waits daintily for him to dislodge. "Civil defense." He flicks the badge on his breast pocket. "What you folks up to?"

"Our house is on the shore," Malkoff says. "We've all been told to leave."

"Yes, sir. In an orderly manner. So kindly return to your car."

"But are we against orders, sir?"

"Orders are to evacuate." The man says the word gently, the way one says a long but necessary word to a child.

"Yes, sir. We are doing that."

"Then get back in your car, that's a good fella." He spreads a hand toward the highway, inclining his head. "See? Like everybody else. We don't want any panic here."

"We are evacuating. Only we have decided to walk."

An exasperated pause. "You a visitor? Been renting a house here?"

"No, I own it. I'm a professor at Irvine. Have been, for the last fourteen years."

The man gives a big friendly laugh. "Then you should know by now, Professor. Out here we don't evacuate on foot."

How like our border guards he is, Gonchev thinks. Trained not to confront.

Malkoff is reaching into a hip pocket. As he does so, the article in his sweater falls forward and he restrains it with his left hand.

"No, Malkoff—" bursts from Gonchev.

All three turn to stare at him. Malkoff, squinting, has the same expression as the civil defense man. Exactly the same.

Malkoff had made a provocative gesture, a move that would be chancy anywhere in Eastern Europe. Possibly Malkoff actually has no gun. But even Klement would have known better. Correction. Klement would have known better than to reach for the gun he had.

He had best not say anything further. He is well aware of the effect an accent can still have in these hinterlands.

"I was searching for my own badge," Malkoff says. "But I'm afraid it's home on the dresser. My wife maybe has hers. We're both part of the CD for the neighborhood. Beach surveillance. That's why I forgot it, I guess."

"I never thought of mine. Everybody knows us," Daria says. "And in Berkeley."

The civil defense officer lifts his chin. "That where you're walking?" He turns slowly, enjoying his own wit, and focusing on Gonchev. "And who may you be, sir?"

He sees Malkoff mustering his explanations, as Gonchev had heard him do on the phone last night: Paul Gonchev, the director. We've simply got to have him, Provost. He's one of the movie kings of all time. Yes, the dissident, the one who films cities—ah, Provost, you're a Renaissance man, you know everything. Absolutely. We should have him. And he has his green card.

To overhear how your life sounds to others, and to think, Is that all? In his situation an earthquake is an encouragement. Along with what he now feels through the soles of his shoes. "Officer, will you please feel the sole of your shoe?"

"My . . . ?"

Is he going to drawl "Who is this character?," like in their films where one of the two fast friends, two men who caper through so much together, has to explain his sidekick to the cops?

But this man is no such fool. He kneels at once, pressing one hand on the ground, palmside down. Then the other. Then swears under his breath.

Gonchev nods. The warmth is at his ankles now, like at that hot springs in the Japanese prefecture where they believe arthritis to be a spiritual disease and bury one in a paste of copper mud mixed with the myth of the region. "The heat runs that way." He points. "This side is cooler."

The man goes flying down the line of cars, comes flying back, and slams into his little car. He leans out again, grasping an instrument he is alternately talking into and listening to, whose sound, as he holds it aloft, vies with the faint snarling of the walkie-talkie strapped to his chest. "How'd you know? What do you know about temblors?"

"I grew up in Japan."

"Oh, boy. Those Japs. This sweet car of mine almost talks. And want to know something? It coughed on the way out here. First time ever." He dives back in. Gonchev can hear his shouts to his instruments. "Get that frigging highway clear. We're hot. Two thousand people in my sector. I dunno—send copters. I don't have even a bullhorn."

Gonchev signals to the Malkoffs. The three of them creep off. He whispers to them to follow the cooler cars. Daria, slouching along using both hands, is the most adept. They pass the car with the dog in it; it is still shivering. As they turn at one angle they see the civil defense man darting in and out past cars packed every which way. Warning them? He hadn't listened to his own car—he is no wacko. Maybe he's a hero.

As they reach the crown of the embankment leading to the highway, Malkoff whispers, "If we're stopped again, let me handle it."

They are stopped, by a state trooper. Or rather, Malkoff boldly accosts him. "CD Officer Malkoff, Laguna. And team. Paul Gonchev, producer, and Dorothy Barno." He says that name as if the trooper would know it.

He does. "Seen you many times, Miss Barno. When you were on your own, and later too. People could always tell it was you. Your car down there? Wish I could help you. But I don't have a horse." He grins. "Or a tall building to swing from. So—sorry. But you'll have to go back." He chews his lip. "Or maybe not. Having a little problem down there."

"Oh, no, we can't go back." Malkoff hands the trooper a card. "Physics lab, the college. Carrying something out of there that—ummm—had better not be there at this time." He touches the bulge in his sweater. "Friend on Balboa has a plane. He'll fly it out for us."

The trooper studies the card. "We've done that detail before. Whyn't they send you an escort?" He snaps his fingers. "Don't tell me. They did. And it hasn't arrived."

"Right. So in view of the—problem, we're going shanks' mare."

"How's that again?"

"Walking."

"To Balboa?"

"It can be done," Malkoff says gravely. "If we two fade, Miss Barno is equipped to carry on."

"I'd pick your hitches, I was you. Carrying that thing. Wish I could spare you a—" Up on the highway a knot of troopers is engaged in trying to align cars free by pushing them.

Dorothy-Daria, head bent, stares at the ground. It isn't sullenness, then, but the withdrawal of someone too used to being looked at, a petulance that could spill over into private life. Film stars were especially vulnerable. Though some of the peasant extras Gonchev had used at home were just as bad. One of whom had said angrily to his wife at the public viewing, "Why clap the man up there. This is me."

"It's getting hotter," Gonchev says.

"Right," the trooper says. "Got any communication? Only a radio. What's that box?"

"A 1943 Kodak," Gonchev says. "No film."

"He's a director too," Malkoff says. "He uses it to—kind of look through its lens." He smiles at Gonchev.

The trooper scribbles them a pass. "And I'll wire ahead. What is that stuff you're carrying, Professor? Uranium?"

"Nothing—quite so stable, I'm afraid. Well protected, so far. But out of the lab, nobody should carry it around for long. That's why there're three of us."

"Oof. Put all your names down, I should. Mal-koff." He looks at Gonchev.

"Gonchev, Paul."

"And Miss Barno. . . . Say, Gonchev. Don't I have your name on a list from Washington?"

"What kind of list?"

"VIPs we're s'posed to take special care." He grins. "Half the state must be on that list, tell the truth."

"Oh, that would be my daughter, who requested," Gonchev says. "A worrier. Every time I go for a walk."

Does he go too far, aping the intimacy here? There's fantasy all around him; he's sure of that. Only he doesn't know the boundaries. Except for the earth below him, now doing what it pleases.

"Oh, yeah?" the trooper says. "Well, we are taking care, aren't we." The CB he is wearing crackles. He peers out over the field of car tops.

Has a kind of subservient dusk settled over those gleaming hoods? People wait for temblors, Gonchev thinks. For tremors they know.

"No, we don't want any panic," the trooper says to his walkie-talkie and, raising his head, to the three: "Better go. And God bless you, Dorothy Barno. If there was time, I'd ask for your autograph, for my kids." Another crackle. He tips his hat to the three of them. "Pass, you brave people."

Out on the double highway most cars are in line, in both directions. A few are scattered along the right-hand shoulder—cars whose drivers must have tried to shoot past the people ahead and been derailed offside. No one had let them in.

"There are children here," a man shouts from one of those cars. A second later they hear its motor rev up. Their trooper runs to it. Another on a cycle meets him. The car's motor dies.

"If one car starts out of line, they all will," Malkoff says softly. "And there might be a smog."

The three of them walk on, steadily. Gonchev resists looking into any of the cars as he goes by. He would be looking at victims. Passive ones, stared in on by a man still on his feet.

"Over here," Gonchev says suddenly. "There's a space. In among those trees."

"Yes, me too," Malkoff says.

Gonchev has to pee, but that isn't what he meant. When they are finished, he says: "Before we go on. Before any journey." He makes them squat down in the road and join hands. As the current of living flows through his hands from the man on his left, the woman on his right, he feels better. It doesn't matter with whom. Or what you are carrying.

"By God, we had this custom at home," Malkoff says. "On the road, wherever my father was singing. I'd forgotten." He takes off his spectacles to wipe them. "It makes you listen to who you are." His wife of two names says nothing. Maybe she listens all the time.

When the three resume walking, their relationship has gone up a rung. Gonchev sees it like that—the ladder of those who are walking. Who choose their crack. Or hope to.

"You have a stage name?" he asks the woman in the white jogging suit striding alongside him. Her metal-studded leather jacket is sleeveless but must be heavy, like the metal-studded belt, but she hasn't left them behind. Maybe she couldn't bear to, if they were for the band.

"The Barno is. But I was born Dorothy."

"Not in Russia."

"No. I was born in New York City. But I grew up in Hollywood, mostly."

"I knew it."

"You know her story?" Malkoff says.

"No."

"What, then?"

Gonchev is walking between them. "That she's like—excuse me, Daria—that you are like—many American women I meet."

"Why?" The first time she has looked at him directly since they left the house.

He attempts a laugh. Hard to, when walking. "Because you ask."

"Come on."

"I only meet the smart ones, college girls." Meet my consort, the men said. "Bankers, lawyers. My daughter's crowd." Such sullenness, yes, it could also come from a woman's being smart here.

"Old enough to have children?"

"They talk about nothing else. But they don't do it."

"I waited too long to have one."

"That's not so," her husband says. "You injured yourself. She's always—daring herself."

"Oh, I am so sorry," Gonchev says. "You tried suicide, Dorothy?" He says what Derek once had, to a man in the group. "Cheer up, then, eh? You didn't succeed."

Both husband and wife yelp in protest, Malkoff the louder.

"Shit, no. She is more involved with her life than anyone I know."

Except—should he say it? Why else were they walking, except to speak their minds. "Except you, Malkoff."

To his surprise they both laugh. "What are you?" she says. "A guru?"

"You two dizzy me, yes. Between you, I am spinning like one." But the ground is cooler. And we are covering ground. A fine idiom.

"No, that's what a lama does. Spin." She whistles between her teeth. "I've done it."

"She was a stunt girl, Gonchev. You're a moviemaker, you know what that is. At fourteen, she already was one. A father a director, a mother a star—you have to be different. A lot of her high school friends in the same boat, they went for kinky. My Daria chose muscle."

Hmm. That's maybe why Gonchev feels no urge to pinch her backside. "You still do it?"

"Not for film. I got so I stuck out, whatever I did. You have to be anonymous, for stunt."

"You acquired a style. You were too good not to."

Whatever she says, Malkoff inflates it, like a tout. Vuksica had never let Gonchev expand on her actress life, once it was over. It tires this girl too to hear it, but she doesn't leave Malkoff. Instead, she goes off for the night. Did Vuksica do that? Or for afternoons?

"I still practice," she says. "But I perform only for children. Crippled kids—our foundation, we give performances for them. Outdoors, my partner and I. He's a wonder."

"Ah, I see."

"No you don't," she says. "He's gay."

"Now let's not get down to the nitty-gritty," Malkoff says.

No, let's not, Gonchev thinks. Especially since that's where we are. "Oh yes, I see now. Why the officer said it. 'God bless you, Dorothy Barno.' What a tribute, eh? But why not 'Daria'?"

"His name for me," she says, not looking at Malkoff.

"It works for me," Malkoff interjects. "Our doctor suggested it. Our guru. She and I met there. She coming out of that office, me coming in. For six months. Then for another six months, me coming out from my appointment, she going in for hers. Finally—we spoke."

"He did."

"So long a time," Gonchev says. "You had an injury too, Malkoff?"

"We were in analysis."

"Ye-es?" Gonchev says absentmindedly. They have left the highway behind but are still on a crest of land. This lesser road must lead back to the sea, or in that direction. It has been well tended and must ordinarily be trafficked but is now deserted. "Oh yes, urine. Because of the drugs that had been used on me, I had to have that too, when I first arrived. Several times. But not for so long."

"No, no, no. Freudian analysis." Malkoff enunciates the two words as if tasting them. He sighs.

The patterns of three people walking together are difficult. And the answers intermittent. Here's Daria weaving behind her husband to insert herself between him and Gonchev. Now she's in the center, but still walking steadily, talking out of the side of her mouth in monosyllables, if at all. What a long stride she has, for a middle-sized woman—longer than Gonchev's. What is there about her—not clumsy, or not physically so, indeed crisply the reverse, and not naïve, at least not about what it is modish to know—that reminds him of a young man he used to see at the studio of a renowned potter in Tokyo. Placed there by family pressure, scion of a house that through him expected to earn merit as more than patrons of the arts, he had been without talent yet above menial tasks, and so was condemned to whatever mild limbo the studio could find for him—an ordinary young man trapped by the dogma that said he must not be ordinary.

"Border drugs—I had," Gonchev says. The phrase makes him shiver, coming to him out of the blue from a lore he had forgotten. Back where he had come from, if your conduct was in any way what was here called "freaky," you were said to be sniffing "border drugs." Can people over here ever understand nontravel? Or is that nihilism now beyond them—even as their own traffic jams?

"You don't know about analysis?"

"Of course he does, Dolly."

Here's yet another name for her; Gonchev isn't going to ask why. Some persons lightly accumulate names; others remain under only one. Personal force, or nullity, could equally be credited. Or here merely the habit of the addressor, a husband tuning his wife to his own concepts of her?

And still these two keep walking, heedless of what is behind them. He himself fears to look back. Wiser to keep looking ahead, to the causeway Malkoff has said they're aiming for. "Oh, I know of it. Until now I have not been in a country that uses psychology much. As much as here. Or only the government."

"Fascists!" Daria says.

"Oh? Not Japan, no. Conformists there, yes. Their cure would be different. From a cure here." Every afternoon Laura's boss went to a doctor who helped him with his fear that he was "dead from the neck up" because he was so good with stocks and bonds. Maybe the crash had helped him. And those girls who complained that they were "over-qualified" for love.

"It's got to be the same anywhere," she says. "You love the doctor temporarily. Then the doctor helps you love your life."

Oh, what depths are here, under that pursuit. Pfize had made him read the Declaration of Independence. Actually Pfize had read it to him. It sounded elegant in Japanese, like something out of a No play. "And, yes, we are committed to it still," Pfize had answered Gonchev's question. "Even in such numbers as we now are. And so had you better be, Gonchev. Ready for happiness."

Of a sudden Danilo is here to help him, strolling alongside them with one wicked eye screwed up to hold in that invisible monocle, his incurably shallow view of the world.

"I forgot my sister-in-law," Gonchev says. "When they are in Paris, she always wants my brother-in-law to be analyzed. Because he does not love her anymore."

"Haw," Malkoff says. "And does he go?"

"He goes to see the lady doctor Rémy chooses." Some of the new young French women medics are marvels, Danilo had told him and Vuksica. As pretty as marquises, with haircuts like young rogues just out of the hay. But not the one Rémy chose. "But she is not what he wants to spend that very special hour of the afternoon with."

Daria-Dolly is adjusting that harness of hers as she walks, shifting it to an easier hang. All silver metal and white leather, with double shoulder-straps, and a kind of cartridge belt loaded instead with clip-hooked retractable thongs, it must be part of her stunt apparatus. Squint at her out of one eye and she is a piece of modern sculpture, ambulating. Squint with the other and she is trussed in some instrument of torture or unnatural function. "I know how that feels," she says. "That's the hour I want to be with my band."

Malkoff is slightly in the lead at that moment, looming large on the empty road. He doesn't appear to be hurt by not having been chosen for company at that hour. Rather, does he appropriate these hurts as they come, to stow in his husbandly sack of them? "Or the hour when you want to meet somebody special," he says softly. "And you do. We did."

Is this the moment when a man should say to Malkoff in sympathy, "So did I"? Though at Pula, already burdened by his new migration, Gonchev hadn't been at all yearning for an affair. As at any festival, the dusks had been confetti hours in which one expected at most to find one's arm around a waist sliding against you on the carousel, or a papery kiss dissolving on the tongue. Not to meet a woman with a belly like an Ingres, a slow-motion smile, and a giggle like the carousel itself. A woman who did not plan to hurt.

They are now on a long, curved causeway whose end he cannot see. Land is still below them on all sides. Off to the right, the beginnings of a prettified, pastoral settlement. "Is that Balboa Island?" Gonchev says, seeing no water but yearning for a destination. From Vuksica's unknown whereabouts her voice echoes, sending a needle through his groin. Was her trouble that he no longer had had a destination?

"Oh no, not for hours yet," the Malkoffs assure him, in soothing tones similarly false. They are so relieved to be talking to him. Do they know where we are?

"It just looks like Balboa," Malkoff says. "Out here we have imitations of imitations. That's where all the energy comes from. Look at me, a classicist from MIT—excuse me, Gonchev, Massachusetts Institute of Technology. You'd never have convinced me that random research, even slapdash research, is better than rationale. Yet after eight years here—the prize. And look at us at La Jolla." He is still nursing the bulge under his sweater. If it's what Malkoff told the trooper it was, Gonchev hopes it isn't wrapped slapdash.

And look at us three, Gonchev thinks. Walking what may well be a death safari—in imitation friendship?

They slog on. They pause for what Daria calls pit stops. They drink from Gonchev's canteen, awed at his having remembered to fill it. They are nothing like the neat, dogmatic travelers he has known in his family, or on two continents. They applaud the amateur, but despise the real lore. In Daria's case, with almost anti-life rudeness.

Malkoff keeps going, Gonchev suspects, by sinking into his own brilliance as if into a cushion of moss, from which his greenish cat's-eyes peer in animal endurance fueled by intellect. He's wearing sandals of a design from the 1960s recommended to Gonchev, who may wish to order them, as Malkoff and his professor friends do, from an ad in a venerated left-wing weekly. The broad brown straps look naïve, hopeful—the liberal imagination dealing with the wilderness, on the principle that all men's feet are equal and deserve the same.

Gonchev is an urban walker, according to his children always looking down without realizing it. His feet have city radar, for the traps and cankers in pavement, and in potholed roads. Except for the miles of city park they've ankled along, they don't know green. But he is still a walker. The no-nonsense German footwear Pfize provided him with sports a bootmaker's stamp in the shape of a metatarsal arch—and is serving him well. Daria is wearing high pink sneakers studded with zodiac cutouts and with soles like corrugated flesh. Women, like ballerinas, work their stumps to a pulp and take the consequence.

For the first few miles he feels responsible for having made the other two do what they would never have done on their own. As he plods he hears the throb of his temples like evidence of some lone picklock beetle entombed in the pyramid of the world.

They must now have traveled at least five miles, maybe more. Conversation has shaken down to a silence he doesn't wish to break. Exactly how far in miles they have to go has never been said. When he asked to see a map at the outset, Malkoff said, "Home ground, fella. Driven it umpty-ump times." Now and then helicopters cackle overhead. Each time this happens Daria arches her head and chest toward them, as if she is about to fling up one of her hooks. A covey of three passes over. "They must see us," she said. After that, no one spoke.

That was an hour ago. Malkoff still trudges in the lead. Soon after they set out he had stopped dead and barked, "Hats."

From above one would now see three hats walking. A gentleman's motoring cap of white woven straw. A tennis visor like a bird's bill. And a floppy disc of rusty wool, in some circles still called a steamer cap, gift of the wearer's sardonic brother-in-law not too many birthdays ago and, in spite of the dig, instantly loved and incessantly worn, as on the day he was ambushed. The cap doesn't do for any part of America he has so far seen, but he will never discard it.

This bag, not as large as a real duffel, of a size perfect for the motorcycle, had also been with him when he was seized. Beat-up as it is, he continues to use it in gratitude—and rage. A new one, pressed on him by Laura and so cleverly expensive that one would not know it for unused, lies at home. No one has ever touched his old bag, not even his wife. He knows every article in it, from his silver razor in its snapcase down to the neglected jumble at the bottom: plastic soapbox, can opener, tin box that once held chocolate, money belt, match folders—a life-scurf that clings, waiting for the not-impossible need.

He thinks now of the box of crackers right at the top.

As a schoolboy he had been felled by what was there called the biscuit passion. In the great Mitsukushi department store in Tokyo, glass showcase counters higher than he were massed with small soya bits in shapes that taught the varieties of shape, from shrimp to flower tops to noodle string. One ate these ritually. One was eating the very shape, exerting the national passion for it. Children collected them like stamps. Telling his own children about that, he had mourned their having to grow up only "in pretzel and bun country." Laura's first month in New York, she had led him to the chips section in the supermarket. "Look, Papa. The Rockefeller collection."

Since then he'd eaten his way through the lot, he and Roko both, satisfying late-night cravings for which they wanted no analyst. Now, in his lonely motels, such packets console. They are personal choice. The crackle between the teeth takes the place of the hearth fire. The very name of them is an on-the-road whistle, an oboe solo of American yearning: junk-a-fo-od.

What he has with him now is mundane—saltines. If he offers, won't it be as with the canteen? He should not take the lead. He must move with tact. But not wait long, and not merely because of hunger. Tensions are shifting. After so much marching no soldier sees scenery. Dune, highway, town, more dune, highway again. Stop looking at your feet, Gonchev. Keep looking at your feet. Detail succors. Detail kills. Whatever's coming, let it come soon.

"Stop."

He's popped the balloon. Of silence. They sit. Three on a highway. Three people. On the good curbstone. Solid rock.

"I could pat it," Daria says. She does. She picks nervously at a thumbnail. The orange lacquer is peeling.

"Quit that," Malkoff says.

A laugh spurts. "We're lost, aren't we."

"I've only driven it. Everything—there's been a shift somewhere."

In us too, Gonchev thinks.

"Not a soul but us walking," she says. "Feels like we're shadows."

"The sky's walking with us," Malkoff says. "Been watching it?"

"It should be dark by now. Why isn't it dark?"

The sky's heavy, yes. Showing its molecules, instead of the powder-blue that should have been earlier, and the lanterned velvet it should be by now. But it's not smog. He'd better say what it is.

"Ash," Gonchev says.

Blood is soaking from Malkoff's right sandal. "As in Etna, yes," he says languidly.

"No volcano anywhere near. Nearer than Mexico," she says.

"Not a good day for bargaining. Can't stipulate." Malkoff's breath is short.

Daria hasn't seen the blood yet. Or has she? She is slipping off her shoulder bag, rummaging. A cry. "My bandages." Gone. She fondles the small empty cardboard. "I used them on Morton's cheek last week. Somebody in the audience swung a bolo at him."

Gonchev scrabbles for the first-aid kit required of all in his workshops. Home-rolled linen strips have long since supplanted the unobtainable gauze.

Malkoff's toes are a rubbed mess, purple-red.

"I have antiseptic," Daria says. "Vladi? May I?"

Malkoff nods. "Have the kindness, Paul. To hold my wrist."

She applies the brown stuff. Malkoff's clenched fist digs into Gonchev's thigh.

Vladi. His name day must be the feast of Saint Vladimir. But before you would know that intimacy from her, he has to bleed.

"Morton's the band's drummer." Malkoff is pale. The fist unclenches. Daria, her back to them, is a yard or two away, leaning over the curb. Is she retching or looking in a mirror?

"Paul?"

"Yes—Vladi?"

"Don't try to sort us out."

Daria is gesturing.

"Turn your back, Gonchev, would you? She wants to pee."

He squats to face Malkoff, who does not move.

"Stunt girls," Malkoff says. "They used to save their modesty up. To enjoy it." His voice is tender.

"They don't have those anymore? Stunt people?"

"Not much. Special effects take care of it."

He knows that phrase. Special effects—whole studios devoted to them. When you should just make occasional use of them. But maybe they will outmode his own work? What a time to be thinking that.

335

Daria's taking her time. Maybe she uses tampons. He feels his lack of women.

"She's delaying," Malkoff says. "I'm a—a bit diabetic. That's why the foot. She thinks I shouldn't walk on it. But I shall."

Gonchev sits on the curbstone. Man-made, it won't shift of itself. No wonder she patted it. No sway to the roadway, either, yet it doesn't look as it should. He is wondering how much Malkoff weighs.

"Dependency." Malkoff stares past him. "The kind a man and woman make together. 'S like cell structure, eh? Or didn't you ever go for long term?"

His eyes smart. He can't answer. He won't. But the man is injured, after all. "It is a film they make together."

"Sorry, Paul. What a pedant I am. I took it you were single, when you left. No? Sorry. Don't explain."

Three helicopters chug over them and disappear, going east. "That's odd. The last ones were going west." Malkoff wipes his glasses, which are rimmed with dust. Puts them on. "Oh, good God, she's fixing to carry me, if I'll let her. I won't." He wears a half smile. "She can, you know. Not far. Maybe to that little town over there. Off the track."

"I had lessons from a sumo wrestler once. What do you weigh?"

"One sixty-five. My father was huge. A real basso. But Mother was tiny. Typical." He is staring off to the east.

Is Malkoff wandering? When a body is failing, its mind may people the landscape with stories, in a last effort at control. At Keio University there had once been talk of a visiting abbot who, if you spent a week with him, would revise for you the stories of your life. Gonchev had applied to him—what a film that would make—but had been refused. You are too young, the intermediary had said, a jovial little monk with a dancing smile. You haven't lived the life. But at Gonchev's protest they had talked.

Now it occurs to him that the interviewer may have been the abbot himself. For shortly afterward, Gonchev, feeling his ignorance of people in their fixed dramas—of one house, in one culture, and living in a nation where such imprints were a religion—had had the idea for his cities. For films where he could see with the falcon stare of the émigré. Where people were seen in short takes, in vignettes. And in crowds.

And now you have the life, haven't you, the abbot's dancing smile says. So, in that spirit, receive this landscape.

The Other Coast, the East calls it. Or more often just the Coast. From the outset it would have seemed prime for the parade of gelatin visions that were to settle here. Desert just bleak enough to set off the human outline. Black-and-white film first, the two shades of folklore. Then the second stage: men and women, irritable with their own modest plumage and suitcases full of East Coast dolor, begin to copy the tropic butterfly and to lie back on the lurid wave. Even for daily living, the sand is as white as in Paradise.

Wait till you see California, the little agent said, her tucked eyes and freshly upbeat face-lines exalted. And now he has.

"Oil paintings look terrible out there," Malkoff had advised him, on the train. "Oil painting is for Europe. And antiques. All the tycoons had them at first. Got rid of them. So have I. All but one. Out there color has to be flat and loud. Summer stuff. Acrylic is best. Not too much depth."

To match the unease of the ground?

Oh, that's always there, Malkoff had said. Under the life-style. The cups shiver on the shelf, but you don't think about it. "What we have out there is a lot of life-style." If Gonchev will come with him, Malkoff will see to it he has use of the very office—left vacant by a prof on sabbatical—where one of Malkoff's favorite films was partly made. *"Planet of the Apes*—ah, that's my cookie. Yours too? Then it's a deal." They had settled it somewhere short of the Southwest, while staring out the windows for eagles no longer to be expected. "Passion of the convert," Malkoff had confessed then. "I admit that. But the East is sick with permanence."

"I'm one eighty-five," Gonchev says now. He ought to have more weight on him. According to the wrestlers at least three more stone, even with the fancy holds. "But Daria and I could manage. Maybe with a sling. There must be medical attention over there." Though it all looks deserted. No trucks.

"No, thanks." Malkoff gets to his feet, taking a tentative step. "Let's go."

Daria comes running, carrying the binoculars, pointing.

In the direction from which they've come a low-lying mass is visible through swathes of dust. As Gonchev watches, the mass appears to be moving very slightly toward them—is it land? Or optical illusion?

"Rescue." Part of her apparatus, coaxed now into a sling-seat, dangles behind her. She unhooks here, presses there, and the straps go back to plumb. "Sit down, Malkoff."

"Give me the binoculars." He takes off his glasses, glancing up briefly at the sky. When he shrugs the square object under his sweater shifts, falling forward as he lays the glasses on the curbstone.

Gonchev stares, fascinated. He had forgotten what is accompanying them.

"Give me that thing," she's saying. "I'll carry it."

Pressed to the binoculars, Malkoff ignores her. "Flight out of Egypt? Let's hope the Red Sea doesn't part for them." He hasn't sat.

There's nothing in the sky. What Malkoff must be seeing comes to him.

"Organization," Malkoff's muttering. "You have to admire them. Shit—they've even got a banner up, the blinkered fools." He hands the binoculars to Gonchev. "Don't seem to be gaining though. Gaining ground."

"They should have that bullhorn."

"You have such faith, Dolly. In megaphones."

They pass Gonchev the binoculars.

The cortege of cars coming straight at them must be eight or so abreast. In military order, no mavericks. Troopers on motorcycles at either side, herding them. They're under a mile away.

"I made you walk," Gonchev says. "And now here they are."

"Better so, pal. Even with banners. And my foot has caked."

The streamered banner says CIVIL DEFENSE ORANGE COUNTY. A middle section has flapped forward over the windshields of the center cars. Yet all seem to be moving. He's never before seen cars drill forward in such perfect phalanx—not even in old newsclips of Nazi parades.

Yet he can hear nothing from their gassy world.

Behind him those two are meanwhile hissing at each other in the presumed undercover of the married: Wish I never—You always do—

The car, where do you suppose the car—Who cares about the car—You should sit—I'll do as I—.

Connubial snakes. How often he and Vuksica had heard such pairs. His sister-in-law, Rémy, in particular hisses even in company, as if only Danilo can hear.

Catastrophe—some couples have a system to avoid it—their prattling talk.

Gonchev wipes his eyes and refocuses the binoculars.

What a singular fate—to be forced to see disaster as pure object. He has time to understand those Pompeians who homed it at the foot of Vesuvius under a threat coned on the horizon day after day. Or like the pair behind him—spatting away while the teacups shivered in the shoreline house? And spatting now—while Teddy, the car, waits like a child lost in a parking lot.

At the moment they're more human than he. He has time to hear them almost tenderly, like a god who also holds a spyglass. In its tiny circle the two end cars in the front line rise upward, spewed aloft like two contestants colliding in a drag race, and are sucked backward out of view.

One trooper, riding high on his machine, follows them as if on duty bound, backward also.

Another, falling sideways, vanishes.

A second row of cars, pushed forward, tumbles over those in the first.

Others from behind are already riding the sky. In what film do a man and a boy float over their city? Or a bicycle does. Or a Christ. He must know half a dozen films in which levitation makes its dream statement. He can't summon the name of one of them.

Behind him she says to Malkoff, "This damn bag. Where's my ID?"

"What the hell would you want that for?"

"Any transportation, it's better to be a VIP. How long coming do you think those cars'll be?"

"Hand me my glasses, Daria. They're on the curb."

In Gonchev's spyglass all the acronyms are tumbling. Behind him, those two are quiet overlong. He turns around. He can't find a voice to warn them with; he's too full of film. He doesn't have to. Both are crouched, their hands dug into their crotches.

The curbstone is moving.

As they all watch, the gold-rimmed eyeglasses slide to the ground—which cracks apart, not quite enough to swallow them.

Malkoff limps over to them, picks them up, stands over the crack, addressing it. "May I present my ID?"

"Malkoff—"

"I already saw, Paul. Minutes ago. Those cars' wheels aren't moving of themselves. The land is moving them."

Daria is screaming, wildly waving. A beehive of copters is passing over, west to east. Under where they hover he can see a looming density, shot with lights, obscured with dust.

"A portion of earth-mass must have shifted up. Or broken off," Malkoff says. "It's carrying them toward us."

Daria has the binoculars. "They're standing on the cars, some of the poor slobs, handing up the kids. There's no place to land. Oh, I could help."

A moment later she says quietly, "On its way to us. The whole shebang." She's already thrust the binoculars into Gonchev's hand and is releasing her straps, rehearsing them. Two fall in coils, retract to the belt. Elbows at her sides, she is making fishermen's casts, calling in the arced lines just before they fall. Slow motion, she repeats. She herself is quick—when had she put those gloves on? And has eyes in the back of her head. "Firemen's gloves," she says between her teeth. Onscreen, I couldn't wear them. Cut your hands to ribbons if you don't—one false move. Nylon's worse than steel."

There's a tranced peace in watching her rhythms, the same solace one gets from acrobats. Or from experts anywhere. Gonchev, watched like that once, had known that feeling of command. She's in her territory.

Who dares think that word here? The roadway is nudging the soles of his feet.

Malkoff is calling from behind. His voice is weak. They both turn.

He is waist high in a deep crack and already yards away from them. Their side is a cliff.

Running to its edge, ignoring his shouted "Don't! Stay where you are," Daria girds up, and casts. And casts again. The flung silver lines arc in vain and return, arc and return, over the widening chasm between her and Malkoff. Earth draining from under her is now piling at her ankles. At the last moment, Gonchev, who has held back in order not to fault her casts, tiptoes up, grabs her waist, and rolls the two of them head over heels to safety. On their side, measuring three quarters of the width of the road, the crumbling ebbs to a faint *sh-sh-sh.* Stops.

"You can't *do this to us, do this to us,*" she's whispering. The ditch that holds Malkoff rears like a vagina, in it a vulva of reddened earth. Eastward the sky is blown clean, and as stationary as he has ever seen a sky. The horizon itself is moving. He guesses this to be a second line of cars. "Back—back—" he wants to shout. Have their signals failed them? Or the ground is bringing them.

Under him and Daria the earth has quieted. As if he and she are now the illusion.

Malkoff, wedged to the armpits, is still erect. He's taken a package from his sweater. Brown wrapping paper, the size of a large book—a long hurl might get it across to them. For a minute he hesitates, then clasps it to him.

"I'm riding backwards," he cries. "But the walls are crumbling to-*waard* me."

The "toward" is a birdcall, high and clear.

"Tell them that at La Jolla. Tell them to check—" The last words drown with him. His spectacles sink in a yellow mane of earth rushing in from both sides. The crack closes. Has closed. A thumb of curbstone protrudes from it.

After a while Gonchev feels her begin to crawl toward the crack. She is still in the circle of his arms. He tightens them. "Don't. It may open again." After a time, it very slightly does. Or appears to.

"Oh, I won't"—she says in a child's voice—"fling myself over. I can't—I'm too physical." Although she's sitting and he's holding her, within his arms, she is still crawling.

When he's able to sneak a look at his watch an hour has passed. He hears no noise from that approaching island, to the naked eye still miles away. Perhaps he and she are now an island too. He doesn't stretch to see.

"He always wants to make his mark," she says then. "Could you get what he said?"

He thinks he has, but before he can tell her so, she nods off. A minute later, she wakes. "He's down there. With that look on his face like he's wearing a bow tie. Hundreds of tons falling on him. There's no hope, is there?"

None. But you and I, we'll continue to see him scrabbling there in the pouring dirt, nostrils filling with yellow. Saying to death: E-easy does it, I may have to walk on that foot.

"He did wear them, you know. Bow ties. To his classes."

There's a wind now. Their faces are grimed. Wind always reminds him of winter in the Kyoto temples—Zen blowing high in the winter eaves. "Did he have a religion?"

"He used to say that if he ever met God he'd be very kind to him."

On the instant Malkoff stands there printed on the air, talking it all down, his mouth full of lobster—or dirt.

"He made his mark," Gonchev says. "On me. From the first day. And what he said to that trooper, about my camera—that it was my lens. Even just to carry, he meant." He's not talking to her, really. In Japan he had had many male friends and now and then a confidant. In the sixteen years since, he has had none. Unless you included the spy.

"Where's your camera?"

He had dropped it when he pulled her back from the edge. This is not terrain in which one dare hunt for it. Any more than for a man.

Watching him come to that judgment, she pales. "Keep talking."

"And he carried that package," Gonchev says. "When he could have left it behind."

"Oh, he would never do that," she says absently. She has begun peeling her nails again, tensing to the task.

"He could have chanced throwing it to us. But he didn't."

"Oh no, he would never," she says. "It had his father's picture in it. The one painting he kept."

After a while, she says, "We're having a wake, aren't we?" So it's all right to be hungry. Or to want to fuck. People do. I could—somebody. Maybe that trooper. Not you."

He opens his duffel and brings out the saltines. "What is a wake?"

"When you sit around talking of the dead. But you don't cry."

"Oh yes. It is the opposite of sitting down in the road."

Munching, her cheeks wet, she peers into his bag. "Your bag is like a little home. Wish I could crawl in. And pull the zip."

"You—wouldn't?" he says.

"Do myself in? No. When the planet's trying to kill you, you don't lend it a helping hand."

"Not the whole planet," he can't help saying.

"No. Only this stinking—sneaky—part of it." She stands up, gathering her smeared cheeks, and spits. The cud flies back in her face. "See?" She drops to her knees, hunching over his bag. "Love to poke in other people's jewelry. Lemme poke."

While she does, he ponders what they can do. In the California Elsinore, the old location-town that he had copied, his antiquated pictures showed dolmens, natural ones, stationed like icons all the way up the side hills. Piled stone on stone, something a searching pilot might see? Now there is only the curbstone.

In his doze he sees the harbor of Fukuoka on Hakata Bay. A promontory bare except for one huge sign: SEX SHOP. Built for the American military trade once, and still active. The wrestler lived above the shop on the house's second floor, and for good reason—the floor beams, two-by-fours cadged from the American occupation forces, were strong enough to hold his weight, his mat battles, and his pupils' thumping pyramids. But he hated the sign. Worried that its legend, high over the bay, might taint, not him—he was five hundred or so pounds of wee-voiced modesty—but his ancient and holy trade. Always apologizing for the sign's presence to his more aristocratic pupils, of whom he considered Gonchev to be one.

Coming for a lesson, finding him at table in front of the fifteen or so assorted plates from which he stoked himself around the clock, one was always met by an apology suited to one's family and age.

The younger pupils collected these excuses and tallied their status. At the bottom there was the mild, "I have lived here fourteen years; I shall have to move." More serious were the various scripts for the sign's destruction: from wood-beetles trained to destroy only sexual allusion, to the squeaking apogee reserved for Gonchev, who is a man—the arrival of a tsunami, the great seismic wave. "Not a real tidal wave, Gonchev-san; these come from the earth itself. A ghost tsunami." Which one night would rise from the bay, destroy its target, and ebb, back into the world of ghosts. While he, the wrestler, luckily was away at a match. For any man who sees a ghost becomes one.

On the day Gonchev graduated from the course he was offered the chance to eat from the master's plates. He was about to choose from the mouth-watering fillet of fish with sesame, the minnows standing on their tails in gelatin, the winsome quail eggs in their orange sauce, when through the lattice he saw—rolling behind the master's hulking shoulder and up toward the sign in crescents higher than Fuji—the white wave.

"You were asleep."

He's famished. "I saw a ghost."

Her face is stolid. She is still poking. "Look at this. A straight razor. Where'd you find it?"

"A present from Sarajevo." Found in an old desk at the family forge and merrily thrust at him by Danilo at the stag dinner the night before Gonchev's wedding, with a "Here. Don't cut your throat."

He feels his stubble. "I should shave." He laughs.

"God," she's saying. "Here's chocolate."

"That's been empty for years. Can't get that kind anymore." He recalls the brown-and-gold wrapper it used to come in, the thin, bitter sheets. Schokolade für Reisende. Traveler's Chocolate. Maybe that's why he kept the box.

"We keep—kept—Cadbury's. In Teddy's dashboard." She's shaking the tin box, now almost black. "Something in there."

"A paper clip maybe. A collar button." How many years since he'd worn one of those?

"Something solid." She shakes the box at her ear with that blind look women have when they are teasing the past.

"Stop."

He wishes Malkoff were here, instead of her. Who might even understand such a deadly wish, who at times had said so quickly—Don't
Explain.

"Shut up."

He hears her rage. She's wishing the same as he wished, reversed.
Consigning Gonchev to the yellow maw. Her fingernail is blunt, but the
box's catch slips up easily, oily in the first rays of sun. "You must of
forgot," she's saying.

He's already guessed what's in the packet inside the box before she
unties it. Tan paper, gold cord, supplied to his house by his workshops—Director Gonchev's family insignia for wrapping small gifts.
The tin would have been pinched from his bag at some point—a wife's
opportunities are infinite. She would have waited then, months maybe,
until he announced a long ride. Telephoning ahead, perhaps when he
went to pick up the motorcycle from its shed. Sitting down then to wait
for ambush.

He sees her sitting there yet, at their window. Picking over what they
once were. Whether he would ever open the tin is her risk. Whether or
not, she is with him. Waiting for him to understand her betrayal. The
ultimate spy.

"Raisins," Daria says. "You must of forgot."

"Yellow muscats. My wife put them there." Just one of those ovals
would fill a navel.

"You have a wife? We wondered." Daria's dividing the booty. He
won't have any? "Well, I thank her. Why isn't she with you?"

"We had—an arrangement."

"Hah. One of those."

"No."

"Tell me." Her lashes are stiff with dust, like his. He can see the dust
between her lips. "Talk to me. It's almost as good as fucking."

He must tell somebody. It should be on record. "You have the custom
of the white feather in this country?"

"Never heard of it."

His grandmother had given his grandfather one during the 1917 revolution, when he was about to be the only one of his kind not to flee. "You waiting for another Tsar to make music for?" she had said.

"A woman gives a man one. For not defending—what he should defend."

"But you did! You're here!" She wipes her face, squinting over at the other island, quiet now, under empty air. "For what good it may do you. And us."

"But I wasn't." The dust grinds in his mouth. "I am not a real dissident."

She stares. "So?" Starts to shrug. Gouges her mouth with a forefinger, spits sand sideways. Gapes at him, grimalkin wide. "No woman does that just because a man . . ." The finger points at him. "She kicked you out." The thumb curves up. "And up. Upstairs." She clutches her chest, coughing. "Ow. Mustn't laugh. It hurts." Rolling over—"mustn't laugh, mustn't laugh"—she laughs until she gags, quiets. At last she sobs.

On what horizon they have, there's now nothing.

He is standing over the small abyss where Malkoff must be, watching its sealed lip tremble like the shiver of an irregular heart, when a pinwheel clatter approaches. Then overhead, the rotor hum of rescue, dipping and lifting over sand that was once water, water that was once rock, scouring the tumbled convexity of the earth for candidates. Choosing them. He doesn't look up, hasn't breath enough to shout. His arms have no more holds in store. Behind him a woman—what are her names?—has stopped sobbing. Is she alive? He has just enough force to drop to his knees, forehead on her shoulder. There is no territory anymore, no place to move. This is peace.

Above their heads that flicker of motion is noted. The copter's screws revolve horizontally, allowing it to rise and dip vertically. It has a simple hold on the universe, and a monkish sound—the sound of a single pair of castanets.

There's just enough room for it to land.

10

Danilo Unfrocked

IN THE PARIS APARTMENT Danilo is shaving off the beard he had begun to let grow about a week after he had switched places with his sister as an inmate of what was called the Waterworks Facility. His beard grows patchily at best. When full, as now, it is a bit carroty, but he has never been prouder of it, from his first days of adolescent fuzz. Once Vuksica was safe away—exchanged in a haste that allowed no coaching—he had spoken little in his masquerade, was seen to read a great deal, and generally imitated his sister's foibles with an artistry that perhaps over-reached, for several of the other inmates, all women, took counsel with each other and finally with him as to whether she, their sister prisoner Vuksica, was ill. "We think you've been too staunch to say," his nearest neighbor at mealtime whispered, and he had huskily agreed: "But nothing for the doctor. Just something female."

He had been discomfited by his own overacting. Casting agents knew him as a reliable second lead who would never be guilty of too much fire in the belly, or a handsome foreigner, capable of comedy. He had long since calculated that either role, perfected, would allow him a

347

certain leeway in life. He had grown accustomed, therefore, to acting out the kind of actor he was. But this role was life. And not only his life.

Conversely, once he had dared to stop shaving, eager to be discovered—in fact to be both Danilo again and Danilo in danger—he was so relaxed that none of the five women also sequestered here more than half noticed. Thanks to Klement, Vuksica had had a separate suite, and lights everywhere were dim. The staff, local women and girls, were far more cowed than their charges. The sense of prison was there in the food, in the daily workout in the rear courtyard, in the locks and bars and the male guards eating noisily in the kitchen.

But, maybe as planned, the place produced only a musty gloom of incarceration. Except for the bells that rang insanely every hour to remind an inmate that time was passing, though nothing was to be done with it, there were none of the exaggerations—torture, daily injustice, denial of human necessities—that brought political prisoners honor, and made them violent with hope.

The inmates were all highly connected women, not gross offenders, but in one way or another merely inconvenient. None were young enough to be warm sexual candidates even to one another, much less to him—which was lucky, considering his temperament.

Still, how Vuksica had managed to fend off the nunlike fondnesses the others had developed—"Sit by me at dinner." "In the courtyard maybe we can talk"—he couldn't imagine, until he saw that they might have been afraid of her, these aunties whose prime offense might be as heiresses to too much unconfiscated property, or a refusal to be socialistically modern or irreligious—or a loose tongue. No one else there had shot a son.

When his fuzzy skin began to be noticeable, he almost wished for Klement to appear—to be confronted at once. Only the lady with the most property had noticed, veteran as she was of expensive Italian and Romanian spas. "Vuksica, had you been taking hormones?" At his answer—'Not that I know of, unless they've been giving me something here"—the woman persisted in her parrot-beaked way. She wore earrings so large and pendulous they could have concealed tape recorders; possibly she was the house informer. "Or those under-the-bed pills," she'd said with a smirk. "I'm past it. But my daughters-in-law know Lola Trim. What a price she makes them pay." "Under the bed?" he had repeated, in the noncommittal tone in which one ran through one's lines in rehearsal, saving one's vim for the performance. "There's usually a man involved." She smiled cosily. How she missed them—men. Let her family do what they wanted with her acreage; she had had her fill of males in her time. "And not only at the spas."

What her sons were afraid of was that at almost eighty she might take a young lover and give their patrimony away. And they had reason. "Let me feel that fuzz," she'd said. "I can't see too well; I have cataract. But the rest of me's fine." Mmm, she'd said, smoothing Danilo's cheek. "How I remember." As for Vuksica, she would give her a depilatory. "Take heart, dear. The body will do anything when it's shut away." That hairiness was its protest at being moiled in politics. For which only men should pay the price. "Once you get out of here, it will disappear."

And so it is doing. There go the sideburns, there the cheeks, revealing the curved lips, a minim thinner than his sister's, that can mouth anything with grace, anything, and often have. And here goes the mustache, a silky variant of the several kinds he has worn onstage but has never permitted his own face. Angling to shave the left upper lip and staring at himself half denuded, he remembers what he said to Gonchev, the time Paul's razor slipped, no doubt intentionally: "We are both mountebanks—but at least I know." What with one man's travel being another man's prison—even including America—is it possible that Paul's comic lack of self-knowledge may no longer exist? What with his own new circumstance, he may never know.

Tenderly he gives the right side of his upper lip a last swipe. And here in the mirror once again is his familiar self. The face whose rescue, along with his neck and his future, he owes to Lola Trim.

When she came to see Vuksica he had been sent out to pace with her in the courtyard's covered walk. Any daily search for sun there was a sham, as their jailors well knew. In that leafy cloister light the orangey haze on his features might be taken to be a rash. For perhaps a minute and a half this ridiculously magnificent woman had done so, staring at him with eyes so round they might have been drawn with a compass.

Then—"In Allah's name, poor friend, is that what happens to us when we stop the pills?" Edging near, nearer, she'd scrutinized him, taking him in with a suction just short of touch.

Up that close—and veteran as he was of every kind of female configuration—he judged that any man embracing her would be holding a succession of pink balloons, not deflatable. And in sex perhaps slowly reddening. During which she must move the way she walked, like a powerfully activated mechanical drawing. But when a man got to those eyes he would realize how he was held—in a vise of calculation. Yet this woman breathing on him was surely in heat, if not for him, Danilo. Suddenly she'd burst out laughing. "No Muslim woman ever has to be told who is a woman, who is a man."

They had got along splendidly in her Italian, which she had learned from an old nurse, relic of the pre-Hoxha Italian occupation, and out of caution had always spoken with Vuksica. She knew his history. He didn't have to know hers. She came of that harem-hatched brand of politicos who down the ages had never needed the vote. This might be what gave her that authentic air of antiquity.

As they stalked the building's odd basilica of pipes, the staff and other inmates avoiding them out of deference, she and he had exchanged confidences.

"Prisons produce those intimacies," she'd said. "Even in visitors. That's why I like to come." If this was sadism, she was aware of it, unaffectedly. "And visiting prisons, one learns how to stay out of them." As for Gonchev: "He's like all the artists—a victim of the intangible. But I admire him for it."

Those in thrall to the tangible so often do, Danilo had dared to say. Getting what he learned to think of as "the stare," wielded like an extra feature.

"Grow that beard, signore. That's what'll get you out of here." With her intricate help. As for his sister, "I was drawn to her. She was my opposite. An artist's wife, almost totally." But prison would have changed all that by now.

"You have such faith in prisons, Lola." The Lola had been purposeful; he hadn't dared let himself be afraid of her.

"Doesn't the West?" she had said, honestly surprised. "You Christians especially. Or don't you admit to it?"

He had been careful. She had a pirate's naïveté. "Well, we don't admit to its being that much of an educational facility, Lola."

She had looked at him long. He had time to think of his brother-in-law, somewhere in the United States, and toiling away at the States' peculiar intangibles.

"Ah, but the—the *sedia elettrica* . . ." She had sighed then. She knew the English for it from Vuksica. "The electric chair. What a holy concept." To float a person away on a thrill that engaged the whole body. "Guilty or not guilty—what a death."

Wondering whether she had ever had an orgasm, he saw that she was not being satirical.

What she had really come to talk to Vuksica about was the man Demetrios, who would end up leaving both of them. "He's Greek. And will be starting a family. It's getting late for that, even for him." Up to now Lola and he had had only a business relationship, she intimated, though not detailing how far business might have gone. And now she, Lola, would not pursue him vulgarly—or like a woman at all. "These shipping-people, they are always moving their money." Right now with him it was airlines, but that too was very late in the day.

What she had in mind was to use her whole country to draw him back to her. "To draw him in." As she stretched, the hiked sleeves revealed forearms circled to the elbow with bracelets, which he fancied were trophies along the road to power. "And now I find you here. The logical man."

Now, just as he is patting aftershave on his regained face, the phone rings. He often notices this synchrony in his life. The stage has taken him over, though letting him come only as far as the nineteenth-century theater of coincidence. Perhaps he can improve on that, in time.

"Danilo?"

"Rémy."

"Renée."

This coyness was part of her willingness to come here, risking that careful Belgrade mechanism she called her career. "When we're in Paris," she would even say to her women friends, "Danilo and I have us a little *affaire* with each other. You know Danilo." So she aped the frivolity of the kind of woman she could never be and at the same time gave the authorities her alibi. Never understanding that you couldn't do both. Still it is sad, considering what life—and he—are about to do to her. Because just when you think that life can be completely controlled, things get done to you.

Some people fight that—like his sister? Some people swing along with it—like his brother-in-law? A hero and a heroine, each in their way? Or slightly more than life-size pawns? Not for him to say. The best thing to be is a character actor. In almost any kind of play there's a part for you. And you have time to ripen your roles.

"Yes, Renée. Where shall we meet, chérie?"

He never bothers to meet her plane at Orly, having persuaded her that this would be too husbandly. In fact, he is habitually late with women. He and she always meet in a café.

"Ah, Danilo, you choose." In the *affaire* she is all meekness, the opposite of her rigid university style at home. He already sees her disappearing around the new great bend in his own life—this once-star-faced young creature who had aspired, as wives do, to be a sun. Who would never understand that in an *affaire* a smart woman had better not be all anything.

"How about the Exile's Café?" She loves sauntering in there with her cool little overnight bag, a woman who has the best of two worlds, as one or two of those acquainted with her would be sure to say. Others—those who were permanently exiled—would not.

"Ah, Danilo," she squeals. "How sweet of you." She knows he hates it there.

On the bus he has time to reflect how little this woman knows of his so-episodic life, inner and outer. Maybe marriage is possible at best for only one half of a twinship. And at the start, how could one tell which?

What his sister and Gonchev would think of his new move is beyond conceiving—except that it is unlikely they would have a joint view of it. Which was why they had remained such a close couple, for so long. He has no doubt that if they were ever reunited, they could return to that. He can understand their mutual attraction, if not explain it. Nor would he mind admitting that their worldly concerns, and even their *affaires*, might have a more classical aura than his—are maybe even on the level of art. The kind of refugee art-lives that people like them drag around the world with them. There were some of those at the Exile's Café. Perhaps that is why he, Danilo, can't stand to be there.

What his brother-in-law would think of his television plans he can be sure of—as he had told Lola Trim.

"Betrayal? Don't be absurd. On that my conscience is clear. Gonchev would laugh at the idea. He is not copyable." He'd resisted saying that the only person who could possibly betray Gonchev would be his wife—and in her case one might call such an act something else, like cuckoldry. Meanwhile checking his own manner with Lola Trim.

To a woman as massive as she, phrases like "Don't be absurd" were almost endearments, and he had no intention of having a whirl with the Premier's wife. First off, he meant to keep his new mission pure, no matter what else outsiders might think of it. Second, even if her heart was already taken—and she'd confided it was—nothing involving Lola would ever be a mere whirl.

The café's door has no plaque, only a brass letter-slot. For many of the habitués, or their correspondents, it is a *poste restante*. Everybody who needs the place knows where it is, or is soon told. Rémy-Renée is already there, in her smart suit and shoulder bag and Italian haircut—still a pretty woman, even though the mouth had been tightened early by the Sorbonne schooling, and the nose since sharpened by too much testing of the way the academic winds would blow.

She has already seated herself at a table with others and looks as if the usual compliments have sleeked and rosied her. If he has kept her waiting, even though she came from the airport and he only from the rue de Bellechasse, she has been mollified by waiting here. And will make no scene in front of a crowd studded with her compatriots. Which is why he chose the place. Hoping to convince her that she must not wait for him for the rest of her life.

"Danilo." Her embrace is histrionic, too much that of a professor of drama. Still, he is sorry, and has to remind himself how unyieldingly she can cling—and that he has never been wilfully unkind. As a result, his own embrace is off-balance. The little tick-tock of his actor's body-sense records this. Still, he is sorry. Until, with the happiest air, she introduces him to the tables' two ongoing lines of argument.

On one side of the table they have been discussing the big brass doorhandle on the entrance to that library in East Berlin where Lenin had most certainly worked for a while, no doubt grasping the handle many a time. The question: Is the present one the original or a replica, there being evidence both ways. "And in either case," his wife says brightly, "what should be done with it?"

"What do you think, Renée?" Danilo says.

This is absolutely against protocol. These arguments, some of many years' standing, belong to the regulars here. After nodding to all, and particularly to those he recognized from sessions here, he should have allowed at least a few old hands to express themselves. But his wife, delighted at being asked her opinion by him—and before all these stars of the exile world—is already pondering.

"I think . . . that if it is original, it should be removed."

One of the several men whom one addressed as Miroslav—patronymics, though usually known, are avoided here—says, "Why?"

She has had her hair burnished especially, as her lifted profile wants him to see. He is about to be sorry again.

"As a sacred relic," she says.

Danilo takes a deep breath. He will bide his time and say nothing.

"And if it is a replica?" a man unknown to him says in a Russian accent.

"Then certainly . . . it should be removed."

A burst of laughter from a neighboring table known as "the Hungarians."

"That leaves the door without a handle," one says.

Danilo circles his wife's wrist with his fingers, allowing the tables to see that allegiance. "My wife has two names." But he can't resist testing the full savor of what he will be leaving behind him, not only in the café but in the rue de Bellechasse. To say nothing of Belgrade. "And what's the other argument?"

The other side of the table has been arguing the best definition of freedom. These were men and a few women who had been kicked out or been so badly displaced that it had seemed better to run for it—plus quite a few of the other kind, those who had arrived simply in search of brighter fields. One couldn't always distinguish between the two groups. Or between those who at one time or another had been prisoners of conscience, and those who had merely cannily jumped the gun. For different reasons both kinds tended not to talk about what had happened at home. In fact, the whole exile-émigré conception was very confused here, and what he is shortly going to do will no doubt add to it. He can hear next winter's arguments.

"What do you think, Danilo?"

Often, a person new to the room is finally applied to—his mind might be fresher. The asker is old Porly, whom Danilo knows. A partisan on whose head there had once long ago been a price, for years he has spoken only French or English as a matter of policy, and in his time off from his job as a museum guard, or maybe even on the job, has written sonnets the way some persons do crossword puzzles, never finishing them. "It's my definition they prefer tonight," he says shyly. "Or—over half of us."

As usual. And what is it?

"Freedom is a sonnet—whose sestet is never finished," Porly declaims, in both his languages.

"Sounds better in French," Danilo says, he thinks tactfully. "And what do you think, chérie?" I, too, he thinks, sound better in that language when I say "dear." At least to her.

Freedom is not a favorite word with her, or with her superiors. He sees the pedantry rise in her, as it does even in bed.

"All sonnets should be finished," she says.

In a corner there are tables for couples. More women arrive later in the evenings, along with students who want to dip into this eddy of history. "You will excuse us," Danilo says. "My wife has just arrived. And I have been away for weeks." He leads her to the farthest table.

"And where have you been?" she says, the minute the young Polish boy has left them their drinks—a beer for him, and for her, after some brooding on her part, a *pastis*. She is one of those irritating women who

355

always order something different. When she drank—never much—was when she let herself travel. "It was so embarrassing, Danilo. And risky. It was known you weren't working in Paris. And I couldn't say."

Should he tell her the whole story? He decides not.

"On location," he says.

"Of course. But where?"

He takes a deep, deepest breath. "I'm going back there. For a time. Maybe for a long time. To stay."

Her eyes widen. Her lips curve the way lips still do when the word is said in certain places—"A-merica." The one place, she has always said, for which she would leave her precious job, to go with him.

He shakes his head, mulling the best way to break it to her. And maybe get away. She isn't slow, but years of compromise have formalized her reactions; she's afraid of her own rage.

"No. A place that still has no television system to speak of. Oh, by now, a few sets here and there. For special people. And the programs—*faugh*. Where I was, I saw some. Pitiful. But the bigwigs want to open it up. In their own way." He leans forward like any actor telling his wife he has nabbed the role of the hero, the star part. "And I—I will be—the director."

Details to be settled later. Would he use Elsinore? When asked, he had shrugged, shying from specifics. He has no intention of using that mausoleum. He must use the present—knowing that the present, if used truthfully, always subverts. But in the premier's office in Tirana, whisked there from the Waterworks, how could he haggle? Freedom was an unfinished sonnet indeed. He had saved his pride by protesting loudly. No, under no circumstances would he accept the former director's house. "To see the ghosts there?" Lola had nodded over Danilo's shoulder. "No, comrade," which was what she called her husband, the Premier, when she was in his office. "No. And we women may have a good use for it."

In the end Danilo—and she for him—had bargained well.

"I'll show the world, Rémy. What such a system can be." When a government that doesn't know any better trusts it to a submerged journalist—who they think is only an actor with flair. What a status quo

356

he will appear to give them, from domestic reports to school orations—while all the time they will be traveling out.

His wife is very pale, with that hard line of white above the mouth.

"I'll be vilified of course, on the outside." Until they saw what he was doing. Which must go slowly and might take a long while. By which time would the country itself want to get rid of him? Or find him too useful to let go?

The one thing he hasn't decided is whether it would be better for him in the long run to make money for them or not. With the aid of the man Lola wanted to draw in, there was money to be made, a detail. On money he could trust himself to be pure. It had never been more than a detail.

"You won't want even to dip your toe in that, dear heart. But I'm going."

Where he can be rid of the double spirit that all his life has been dogging him. And perhaps return in time to that article on a subject he should not have deserted: what to be and what not to be in this mountebank world.

If Gonchev were here now, Danilo would no longer twit him on his long hibernation. For the self-development that some people insisted on calling art, there was nothing better than a good fat period of status quo. "Yes, Paul," he'd say. "I can see now how one could have wanted to imprison oneself. Let's get drunk on it. The way we did once." Except that he cannot for the life of him see Gonchev as a regular of the Exile's Café.

He'll be somewhere, dealing with his intangibles. So will Vuksica. Danilo feels removed from them, yet still linked. Today must be like the day one goes to be a monk or a nun—a day for muted sorrow, and a curious joy.

Across the table, his wife is sputtering. *Pastis* can be a sickening drink unless sipped, and she has downed it all at once. Or is she going to commit one of her enormous mistakes about him and his values. Like the time she accused him of sleeping with the married daughter of the landlord of their apartment here—that young sloven with kids at her skirts—when all the time he was having it on with that gorgeous surgeon, sister to the dreary woman psychiatrist Rémy herself had recommended.

"Twin!" she spits.

To let her think so? That this is why he is going back? He can't bear to. He's never been able to bear her great, thumping misconceptions. A pity. Some men expect stupidity from their wives, even love them for it.

"It's Gonchev who's in America. As for Vuksica, I don't yet know where."

"You'll find her. Or she you." Rémy's voice is that absolute guttural that an actor must admire for its rock-bottom lack of artifice but can't always respond to in kind.

He can try. "Want to know something, Renée?" A bad start. She doesn't. "I'm free of her. Of our . . ." He searches for a word, coins one. "Of our . . . itness. I no longer feel like a twin."

"Call me Rémy." She reaches for his untouched beer.

"You'll be sick." But she has already downed it. She's traveling.

"You'll be a twin in your stinking memory, then. All your stinking life. Else why go back there of all places?"

"A woman's memory is different. A man's actions cancel memory out." This was true, even if it came from one of the scripts for the Paris serial written by those two lesbians.

Is his wife going to vomit? He hopes not, not before he gets her a cab, presses a wallet in her hand, and gives the driver the number on Bellechasse. Where she will find the note on the mantel deeding her the apartment, his pension, and all their common possessions.

"At six, I have a job," he says. And a ticket on a plane.

Yet he still wants to leave her something of himself—what? Why does one always want to explain one's innermost being to the very person who will least understand it? But that is the case.

"Why do I hate this place?" he says, in a tranced voice. "Because I'm afraid I might someday end up here. Instead of where I should be." He looks across at the men gathered at the big table, nestled in their arguments. Two of them had been held in detention cells but had never been tried. More than one had left a family behind. "And I could never be sure of where that was."

He sees she thinks that what he's saying is dross, but he goes on. A lapsed twin has to tell somebody.

"I never should have given up the forge," Danilo says. "I'm not shallow enough."

11

Return of the Condors

SO HERE HE IS, SAVED, and out on his rescuer's patio, drinking alone. The Malkoffs' hosts-to-be had sent out scouts for them.

"When people are late for dinner, we always do," he and she said, not blinking, as their pilot shepherded Gonchev and Daria up the path from their heliport to the house steps where they stood—and before they had noticed that their guests numbered only two. The wide, fanshaped steps—how uncrumbled they were. At that point Gonchev had asked for a drink.

He's been drinking ever since, after what they tell him was a twelve-hour interval of sleep. He hasn't done this since certain days of his youth, in Japanese pothouses, but his capacity, untested during the severe socialist years, seems unimpaired. Before sleep he had drunk half a bottle of vodka-with-buffalo-grass, the last of what they serve Russians here, laid in for Malkoff on some previous visit.

During sleep he seemed to himself still to be with his old pothouse companions. One of these, a schoolteacher from the provinces, had spent eight years translating at night a book he had discovered on his own—Joyce's *Ulysses*—only to find, on completing it, that four other Japanese translations already existed. After which, choosing Dante for his new muse—"Since I too am now in the middle of life. And since, with Dante, nobody is counting"—he had resigned himself to merely trying out his *terza rima* on the other customers. All of whom, including Gonchev, had come to know "dear Alighieri, our go-between at the wedding of life and death," rather well—at least in rural dialect.

Gonchev is awake now, if weak-kneed, and willing to recuperate for a day under the wardship of those who have more money than they know what else to do with. The earthquake has relieved him of politics, perhaps permanently. An act of nature is an adversary that refuses talk.

He is mourning Malkoff, missing him. If Malkoff had been spared to be his guide and customs officer in this all-too-friendly enclave, what mightn't have been their dialogue? As it is, down there in the bowels of the earth, Malkoff may be with Dante now, bringing that other talkmaster up-to-date.

What Gonchev wants is to keep Malkoff talking, since he can't seem to bury him. And to toast him in his favorite vodka-with-buffalo-grass. And maybe listen in:

"There are dozens of such enclaves in the democracy, Signore Dante," he's saying. "Places where persons of more than average money, or energy—or even powers of mind, as in your case—can raise themselves above the common ruck.

"In my own field these tend to be institutes of higher-than-high learning. I myself have spent time at two. One right here on our Pacific Coast, where a physicist like me can study the aerodynamics of, say, the tumbleweed, while bronzing himself all over. Another at a university back East, where mathematicians may trot the upper bridle paths of theory, and perhaps tryst along the way with another scholar's spouse. Both places normally welcome dissidents of any order, especially if government sponsored.

"But, do you know, both refused Gonchev a visit. I'd thought he could use time out, you see. 'You're suffering from moral lumbago,' I said. 'From having to take too constant an anti-position.' But that West Coast think-tank suspected he might be using them as a leg-up to Hollywood. And the outfit in the East feels that any filmist is already there.

"So I cooked up a job at my own university. But Gonchev's never taught in a school, you know. He won't be going there now. Not without me."

Dear Malkoff. Who had consoled him for the turndown by laughing. "Well, you know, I have noticed even at La Jolla that the more one investigates the peculiar habits of matter, the more one's purely moral or political dissidence declines. Often confining itself to the wearing of eccentric socks, or letting hair grow in the nose. You mightn't have been happy there, Gonchev." But when Gonchev said "On the contrary," he hadn't been surprised.

"Moving vehicles reassure you, Paul, don't they," he'd said earlier, having noticed Gonchev's empathy for the vans in the depots, wherever the train paused. "Well, you've sure come to the right place, sonny-boy. But I shouldn't stay at the truck level, if I were you, except maybe for a dip in what's down under—ever seen the toilet in a regular truck-stop? Not always filthy. Scrubbed to the Dutch, rather, and fancy cathouse stuff in all the machines."

Malkoff's wife, a photographer, had done a study of these. This had been his only mention of Daria, and scarcely one to which a new friend would reply. They'd passed her by, as men friends can. "So you want to work?" his train companion had mused. "Need a backer?"

Now that Malkoff's dead, Gonchev can admit that he spoke émigré's Russian, the kind that said words like "backer" in English. "And will travel?" he'd said. "Hmm, kill two birds, maybe. Introduce you to a friend of mine." Malkoff had had a little notebook where he inscribed all his promises.

So here is Gonchev, saved by that small inscription. The steps leading up to the house behind him continue to fascinate him. Still so perfectly intact, even where they narrow to that exquisite point—one not leading to an untrustworthy sea but to a comforting strip where four helibirds normally perched. "My fleet's out helping the neighbors," his host had said solemnly. "And friends. So drink up, Paul, and rest easy. We're out of the slide area—I saw to it, long ago."

Gonchev had been unable to resist asking him how. "A study by two seismologists" had been the reply, followed by a *t-t-t.* Malkoff himself had introduced them to the right guys.

The table at Gonchev's side is certainly riding steady. Since waking at noon he has polished off most of the remaining vodka. On the table in reserve is a Swedish vodka, Absolut Peppar, containing pepper instead of grass—served him as properly sequential? Perhaps his hosts, vegetarian oriented, like so many in their state, believe pepper to be the proper specific, post-earthquake.

For they seem to have a specific—any that can be bought—for every emergency. Plus the formidable routines of those who indeed have everything but will not tolerate being bored by that condition. Daria is at present in mudpack, where she was put immediately on arrival, and after a nap, once again. This perhaps being their general curative for widowhood.

Such certainty, and a cheerful willingness to supply provender far beyond their own modest tastes, evidently brings the Minturns many guests, especially now, in what many are calling "thrill time." All, including several flown in for just that from regions not affected, have been arriving and departing by air—either in their own vehicles or their host's—and last night there were a lot of them. This is why the Minturns have run out of the other vodka. For although the estate, built by a long-ago opera star, is a fantasy of niches, caverns, and even minarets, where one might surely lay down a cellar, that's not the Minturn style. They love to run out of things, in order to fetch them by air.

> "This is Gonchev's first encounter with the small-private-plane civilization, signore," he can almost hear Malkoff say. "Let us see if he has got the hang of it."

New as this corner of the democracy is to him, Gonchev thinks he has. Lack of an acknowledged class system burdens everybody in the land, and the wealthy particularly; what can they do but fall into the separations that only money allows? Those imposed in the Sunbelt are like everything there—geared to light and air, and to the body's competence in sport-space. But since everybody now has a car, you no longer do that merely but fly even a short distance—just as you eat gourmet, which isn't always tastier—because this is your status in life.

"Gonchev is seeing this," Malkoff says. "He is seeing that we really don't pursue money here for money's sake, but in order to pursue money's obligations."

Minturn has apologized charmingly for the quake. Which is almost over, he says. When his copters are free again for his own service, he'll run out and get some more Absolut Peppar.

Or his "mate"—the pilot who found Gonchev and Daria—will pick it up for him. The pilot is a Los Angeles/San Francisco dentist who bought a plane to commute between his two practices, but succumbed to the higher bridgework of volunteer flying and now has the use of Minturn's airstrip, and others like it, in return for taking care of the family's teeth. Which explains his host's joyful greeting when they touched down—and before he saw that "old Malk" was missing— "Ahoy, y'all—and hope to Christ you also brought along that pesky inlay."

Now they are all gathered on the patio, in the sweet alcoholic haze around Gonchev's wicker settee. He can smell Michelle Minturn's scent. She has the mushroom pallor of the true brunette and an easy nature, troubled only by not having to know any longer where her next dollar is coming from. In that way she resembles Daria, who she says is her best friend. He suspects that Michelle's tunefully suitable first name, monogrammed on all the linen, may not be the one she was born with. Minturn, who is called Bill, he said, because his actual name is a string of patronymics that he was too abashed—and too smart—to use when he went away to school, can be heard clinking glasses at what they call the wet bar.

Minturn has a law degree he doesn't use either, except, as he said last night, "in a life-enhancing way." That may mean in a business way or it may not. Gonchev has learned not to underestimate the idealism of Americans, no matter how they act. And Minturn, all things considered, appears to act irreproachably.

The family names come from five generations of Californians. "Each of 'em hung one on me." The schools were a "Hotchkiss," which Gonchev at first took to be Yiddish, and Yale. All this Gonchev has acquired over a couple of drinks with Minturn himself.

"Let's just have a couple of prelims, eh?" he'd said after Daria had been sped away and Gonchev had emerged from the shower. "Eh? What? Oh. Nightcaps." He uses a jargon of his own, one piano key away from the ordinary, which he says comes from dyslexia, but makes him sound elite. "You're too tired to be shown round the property"—meaning with the other guests. So, in the pleasantly explicit way it is done here, his host had politely shown Gonchev around himself.

Both Minturns have now sensed that Gonchev is awake, but are gently cautioning others that he is still asleep, giving him leave to manifest himself when he is able, or wishes to. That's kindness. And they are not fools. As they move about their guests—once more reduced to a handful by the quick turnover here—Gonchev sees how people might take that kindness for granted, because it's so easily and socially exerted. Which, as Gonchev reminds himself, happens to poor and rich alike—except that the Minturns command their crowd.

Yet like so many who live their private lives out front, they lack full-bloodedness. They are traceries, through whom one can see their particular crowd. Top politicos are like that in the country he's from. And in Japan the whole nation had seemed to him so, though striving hard to achieve the personal psyches of the West.

His eyes are opening fully. It's good to be in the halfway house of the drunken, where one can see people as they almost are. The Minturns, gliding toward him again, have the slim characters common to those who live at leisure and keep thin at it. A gypsy might find their palms too uncomplicated.

"Who's this millionaire you are taking me to?" he'd asked the Malk-offs. "Not a millionaire," Daria had snapped. "Anybody these days can be that," and Gonchev had surmised she meant themselves. "Oh, a billionaire at least," Malkoff joked. "That's why they call him Bill. And only something of a do-gooder. But he knows it. That's the difference."

And here they are. He sees how any real sustenance they offer will appear more solid than they themselves seem to be—and is touched.

"Ho—Gonchev," Bill says. Smiling, he resembles his male children as much as they do him—a staircase of three blond boys, whose genes must have given up the Mendelian struggle to make them look like their mother. All three had been very manly yesterday with Gonchev over the earthquake, politely keeping him in his place as a grown-up, as had the two dark little girls who dipped the knee and were too mute for their gossipy eyes. All the Minturns' children are jointly theirs; no other marriages loom behind them. "Basic to our friendship," Malkoff had kidded: "We four are the most unmarried couples in California."

"No, don't get up," Michelle says now, adding, to the five or six people immediately near, "He has a bad leg."

Does he? He can't remember. Gonchev struggles to his feet anyway. Otherwise Malkoff's ghost will keep talking to him. He is introduced to assorted "neighbors" and wonders how far by air a neighbor would be. They are divisible at once into the stances he has become familiar with over here: husbands with their wives along, or women with their husbands in tow. He recognizes some singles who were here yesterday from Los Angeles: the girls with that pale-lipped makeup which makes the black-rimmed eyes seem to sprout on stalks; the brown young men. Also, a faculty nucleus from there.

Yesterday all had the air of refugees; today, garbed in their host's handouts, they have resumed their more usual roles. Most are leaving again tomorrow, or as they can. They have been told who he is and either are not interested or have forgotten, for which he is grateful.

Everybody is being exhaustedly trivial. Led by a bearded playwright named Buck, who is alone. No one's talking directly of the quake except two elderly ranchers in chaps, khaki hats, and string ties—members of the Sierra Club out checking the environment—who claim to be stricken about the coastwide water shortage to come, which they however see only in terms of horses and cows. "Death, death, death, nothing but death," one says robustly. Bill and the playwright, who knew the Malkoffs, are trying to head them off, for as Michelle whispers, Dorothy is coming down.

"Mr. Gonchev came in with Dorothy," Michelle says. "Came in" is the phrase being used. And she must be unique here for using "Mr.," which out here is a sign of age.

"You people commute like hell down here," Buck, the playwright, says. "It's your intellectual life."

"Saved yours, Basil," one of the young men says. He's a six-foot-six

366

beach god with hair salt-scorched or bleached—but, as Gonchev knows by now, is not necessarily a movie star.

"So it did. Wanna see me outside after class about it? And the name is Buck."

Gonchev is reminded that these people have been together for more than a night and a day.

"Eric's our champion surfer, Mr. Gonchev," Michelle says resonantly, smiling at the beach god. "Giving it all up. Been accepted by medical school next fall. In Scotland."

"Not every man who surfs is dumb," the dark one of the stalk-eyed girls says, taking the beach god's hand. "Or who's blond."

"Lots of water around Scotland," one of the ranchers says.

"Condors are back," the other one says. "Endangered species? Nonsense. We're seeing skeletons they've picked."

The dark girl gives a slight scream.

"Cattle, miss. Trapped in an arroyo, they'd been. Still, I was glad I was in a copter, not in a car."

"Talking of cars," the first string-tie says. "We saw the damnedest sight. Covey of cars down below, looked like empty. But in *V* formation. And on an island. But the geodesic map don't show any island there."

"Maps," the other rancher says. "To think I lived all these years with maps."

"Empty?" Gonchev says. "Then they got out maybe."

The rest on the patio are silent. The radios have been going all day. Michelle puts a finger to her lips. Up on a balcony a French window opens, swings shut again.

"Never met Barno, but saw her in action once," a girl breathes. "Fab."

"At one of her benefits, yeah," the beach god says. "She like surfs by air."

"Beautiful," the playwright says. "Can I have dibs on that?" Grinning, they shake on it.

"Basil?"

"Buck."

"Oh, we commute all right," Minturn says, suddenly loud. "Between sunsets, time zones, climates. Intellect I couldn't say it is. But I love it.

His glance sweeps them all in anxious plaint. "I couldn't be rich in the East anymore."

"Who could?" one of the ranchers says. "It's not clean enough." He rises. He has his own vehicle. "No need to show us out, Bill. I know your grounds." He tips them all a wink. "Used to visit when that gal who sang opera owned it." Both men shake hands all round, stopping at the playwright. "Spoke at Irvine, did you?" one says. "You know that college was once a ranch? Largest ranch in the state."

"Still is. Blow a whistle at night, all you raise is a team of campus guards—and a cat."

"It's where I'm not going," Gonchev says. But nobody hears.

"But nature must be telling us something good," the second string-tie says. "When a species like the condor comes back."

Once they've gone, Michelle says softly: "I'll go get her." She lays a hand on Gonchev's shoulder. "We call her Dorothy or Dot. Daria was *his* name for her."

Bowing their heads to that, several of the women follow Michelle.

"Everybody thinks California's still just physical." Buck speaks in the confidential voice men use when the women have gone. Though some remain, the patio is long. "But that's not true any longer; we're a philosophy now. Even the servants have it; that's why you can still get good ones here. Like in Victorian England—the servants and the masters share the same ideals."

Does Buck live down this way?

"No. Don't have a pilot's license yet."

"Dorothy has one," Gonchev says.

"Ah, poor Dorothy. Malkoff failed her."

"How can you say that? He was tops in his field."

"He died. To die is to fail."

"But we all do," Gonchev says. This time he is heard. He shuts his eyes again.

"Doesn't change it. Come on! Somebody you know, you see the obit. And that's what you think: *he* failed, *she* did; *I* haven't yet. That's why the young despise the old—they're on the way to it. To fail."

He is—what?—forty-five?

What about loving people? several voices say. Patio voices, inter-changeable.

"Oh, you do, you do. You love their life though. Not only them. Not them first of all, that is. Simple, really. You don't die for love. Except maybe for a weekend."

That mean not just lovers? Fathers, mothers, family?

Mothers have trouble with mother love out here. Yes they do.

Minturn's voice: "Have a cigar, gents."

"No, thanks," the playwright says. "I cut it out. I need to think gaudy though. That's why I come out here. Gaudy talk. Wipe your ass with a sunset towel."

"I feel like a parrot," Gonchev says, sitting up. "Being taught to talk."

"Want to be a parrot, better change your clothes," the playwright says. "Gray sweatshirt won't do. Whyn't you marry Dorothy?"

"Tomorrow?"

"In a week or two. Want to do it decent, a month."

But wasn't Malkoff a Nobel, somebody says.

Yes, something to do with cats and rats, that was going to help get us to Mars.

"Mice—the Mars mice," Gonchev says. From his yellow crevasse Malkoff smiles at him.

"So Dorothy has lost her love for Malkoff's life," the playwright continues relentlessly. "For their life together, that is. A widow is always a failure. I should know."

"But your wife is not a widow yet," Gonchev says. Nor is mine. He stares up at a minaret.

"Nah, n'ahm the widow. I was married to a guy."

Gonchev thinks a minute. What might a well-taught parrot say? "Tough tit."

"Hey," the playwright says. "Hey, Paul. Want to marry me?"

"Hold off," their host says. "He's a moviemaker. And my experience of them is they want to make movies before anything—they're always wanting to, the ones I meet. Right, Paul?"

Was this hopeful? "Right."

"Well, then," a chair in a corner says, "Dorothy runs a foundation. Money is movie."

"Right," Buck says gloomily.

"Has she got a plane?" Gonchev smirks into his drink. This parrot is doing rather well.

"They did have a couple," their host says. "Gave them up for the simple life. See what a mistake that was. What the simple life can do to you?"

"You fly, mister?" Buck says to Gonchev. "Come on. You can admit it if you don't. Now that we're not marrying."

"I used to ride a motorcycle."

"Ho. Ground surfers, they call those out here. But those wheels are just to keep a guy young. Don't get us anywhere great."

"To keep young, I used to hang-glide," Gonchev says. "But that was when I *was* young."

Dorothy enters, on Michelle's arm. The mud has drained her. She's neat, in shorts and shirt Michelle must have lent her. But there's no silver on her.

"What did I hear you say, Mr. Gonchev?" Michelle says.

He repeats it. "Used to hang-glide."

"Hear that, Dot. Cheer up."

She kicks a shoe across the patio. "He thinks I'm wrong for this territory. Or it's wrong for me."

Gonchev gets to his feet and puts his arms around her. "You're out of the mud."

"What's wrong with the territory?" Their host surveys his white leather, orange wicker, marble floor, and acres of watery blue domain.

"Malkoff and me—we handled it." Flinging off Gonchev, Daria begins to sob. "You lose a career, that's one thing. But Malkoff and me, we had a mystique."

"That's right, darling," Michelle says. "Grieve."

"This is grieving?" Gonchev is still too drunk not to say it.

Buck thrusts his chin forward. Under the chin-tuft, it isn't a weak one. "You don't like our kind of grieving, go back to where you came from."

"Buck," their host says reprovingly. "Shame on you. That Ellis Island stuff."

"Shed it," Dorothy Barno says. "All of you. I'll manage my own mystique. Billy, lend me a plane?"

"Sure, doll. Whatever we've got. But where to?"

She ignores that, turning to Gonchev. "Drop you on the way. So you can get back to Washington. And so home."

"Washington?" Minturn says, surprised. "That where you're from?"

A question he can never answer. "Where y' from?"—the automatic American hiccough. Frazzling him even when tossed at him by a porter. Say it to him and all the places he is from jam.

"Upstairs, I took a message from there for you," Daria is saying. "Michelle was in the sauna. 'Pfize calling,' the man said. He spelled it—'Agent Pfize.' He sounded like one. 'Agent Pfize calling Agent Go.' Calling *who?* I said. 'Go,' he said. 'Short for P. Gonchev. Kindly ask him to report in.' "

It's only a patio I'm on, Gonchev says to himself. Nothing so serious as a porch even, where your fate could follow you up the steps. Or a loggia, from which shots ring out in all the operas. But every face is listening.

"How does an agent sound, Daria?" Gonchev says.

Her face does crumple. Maybe she hears Malkoff too. Hears herself acting the silly widow before he's three days cold. She knows he trusted Gonchev.

Minturn is staring at him. No, they're exchanging stares—the static electricity that snaps between two who have underestimated each other. "Yes, Dolly, what's an agent sound like?"

"Like—gravel-voiced, you know? Like—'Hoo-hoo, I'm talking from underground.' "

Gonchev and Minturn burst out laughing. So does everybody else. Gonchev doesn't want her to be shamed. He takes her hands. "Pfize is attached to the State Department agency that deals with visiting foreigners like me. He brought me here. But he's an amateur really. He's . . ." How in the world can he explain Pfize? "He can't stop the drama. And he likes to joke."

And he can't drop me. I'm like a patient he's done well with.

"He said to tell you your camera's turned up."

"Turned up?" He can't help the squawk, or goggling at the ground under him. Everybody's quiet, suddenly conscious of the firm right angles of where they are. Trees rising unassailed. An untremoring house.

"I tell you what," Michelle cries. "What about you two taking off for one of the farms? Ours, I mean. Then you two can decide your—your route." She broods. "Not the Sonoma vineyard . . . no, I don't think. The Maine one—much too far. The one in the Ozarks—well, you could end up there. Not too bad a hop to Washington. But if you want to take off from the coast . . . I've got it. The San Juan Islands one. Just a hop to Seattle. Or Portland." She turns to Gonchev. "Billy and I are island nuts, you know. And that one is absolutely idyllic. The young people are like out of the *Whole Earth Catalogue*. Very helpful." She seems to think she is arranging a honeymoon. "And it's real near."

"Take me too," Buck says.

Others on the porch are staring into their laps. Flights may have to be arranged for them too.

"No dice, Buck," Dorothy Barno says. "You're not a celebrity. Not currently. With him on that list, they'll give me clearance."

"You're a celebrity," Michelle says loyally.

"Past tense. And only local. But okay, Puget Sound's a thought. Get me to a radio."

"The communications wall is right behind that panel," Minturn says. "Just press."

Michelle says, "We don't believe in decorative use of them."

"Coming?" Barno says to Gonchev.

"Of course. Only . . . put on your shoe."

"Listen to pretty Poll," Buck says.

In his office Minturn will help with the three calls Gonchev has said he must make. The office is bewilderingly appointed, under its modest paint—which is not paint. Gonchev touches all the surfaces, wondering. "Maybe not even plastic?"

Minturn's face screws in delight, ready to drop the secret. "It's all wood. Or slate. Or marble, crushed and mortared; we found that process in Greece. Almost any natural substance can be made to look like plastic. And that's what I did." He doesn't know why. Not because he's a nature bore. "It's just fun. Not to go along with . . . going along with things." That letter file over there though—not a success. Hardened wax. "But we're working on it."

No neon lights. There's reason to believe them unhealthy, as well as inhuman. "Some halogens. For after daylight." The room is a filtered glass box, the glass not clear but with the soft cloudy opaque of an amphora. "But the best electric is the old Mazda bulb—the ones in which you can see the curled filament?" He's having some imitations made. "And we're also working on the principle of the cruse—know what those are?"

Gonchev does. The oldest oil lamps, some only pots with a channel for the soaking rag. He himself once had two Chinese folding lamps for travel. Brass, and of the most appealing shape, an oval satisfying to the palm. "The top, where it lifted up, sat like a sconce. More probably a hollow for the wick." He's moved to tell Minturn more about Elsinore. "We had this burr pump, for instance."

Minturn doesn't know what that is.

"Made so the piston doesn't require a valve. A bilge pump, really. But imagine—we harnessed a waterfall to it." He too likes not to go along with what's being done.

Minturn hasn't seen his films. Minturn is "old Catalina," meaning old Californian, and not a movie buff. And although Gonchev might assume he has been to all those cities, he has not. "We're provincial by choice."

"But you have been to Paris."

Oh yes, he has been there. On honeymoon.

Gonchev is moved to tell him about the false film and the funeral parlor scene, where he had disposed of it. Though he and Minturn are drinking only soda water, they laugh and laugh. "I like scenes that are not all as they should be," Gonchev confides.

"We are surrounded by a hidden array of office components," Minturn tells him. "Secretaries have been all but banished here."

"All this electronic buggery." Gonchev uses the word in spite of Roko's having cautioned him. It means precisely what he intends. If he and the doctors had only known what a sustained drunk could do for him! All his languages are back, all his expertise at the ready. "For me, what's going on here in your office so silently should hiss and bubble and emit steam." And maybe dance along to the crackle of paper, and the *eek* of the typist as she's pinched. "But I'll learn it all. If I get the chance."

"That camera of yours—anything valuable in it?"

"All the pictures I am going to make."

"Got any in mind?"

"Oh, from time to time. In my travels. It's natural." They share a grin. "A few little documentaries: "The Short Beds of Mount Vernon"—you know, Thomas Jefferson's house? And how Americans no longer fit into them. Or a film on "The Rumpus Room," where they do. Or "A Steer Dinner in Cow Country." And how the husbands all die in the bedrooms, later. But those are all too clever. I want not to be clever about this country. In the beginning, every foreigner wants to be, and I am like the rest. But not anymore. Not after—"

"The quake? Any country can have them, almost," Minturn says lazily, as if he dispenses them.

"But this was yours."

"Ours maybe, Gonchev?" He lounges, quizzical. "Could that now be your case?"

"What are you asking me?"

Minturn smiles. Maybe his machines are meanwhile doing that for him. An electronic diagnosis.

"To come here by the Ellis Island door, Bill—that's one way. Every time I see a New York taxi driver I think, which diaspora are you? But me, I am given this country on a plate."

"In good company, I'm told."

Malkoff stands between them, saying that. As he would have.

"Too good. They served their time. At first I am jealous of them all, these dissidents. But now I watch, how they inch their words little by little toward the West. Then the feet. Then the heart. Maybe dragging one foot a little behind to keep in touch with home. Because to be an exile grand-style here, you have also to be a home expert. Else you are only a taxi driver."

"Those New York gypsy cabs," Minturn says. His chair is a rocker. "Turks, Russians, Poles. Koreans, Chinese. Always feel as if I'm traveling the world. And, when I see the pics of their American kids dangling over the dash, that I'm being punished. Because I got my country on a plate even before I was born."

"Oh, don't you worry, Minturn, you are being. By people like me. Who, if we are sick for the other place, can put it into pictures or poems, and meanwhile run around the platforms. Being a victim over there, a hero over here. So we don't have one country anymore, like you poor slobs. We have two."

Minturn continues to rock. One of the office machines, a long gray box with no keyboard on it, is very slightly exhaling, like an eraser tiredly going over words it has heard before.

Gonchev leans forward, wishing his chair could rock. "Tell you why Pfize follows me. He brought me here. I'm his responsibility. And he knows by now"—he looks over his shoulder nervously—"that I am not a dissident. Also what only a man like me can say about them. For it is a terrible thing to say. To see. And he wants to keep me from spilling the beans."

"Man like you? How do you mean? Somebody in the arts? Somebody world-class?"

"Fuck the arts," Gonchev says. "For the moment. I am émigré—born. That's what was given me. And though the word disgusts me, maybe 'world-class.' Not an exile—except by inheritance. Not a refugee— because no place was home. Not even a man without a country. After the first passport, all the others come. I travel because I am meant to. Even when I spend sixteen years in that place. Even when I suffer amnesia, from a language once stamped on my tongue. I had an Elsinore. It was in the cards that I wouldn't keep it. I made cities. The odds are I won't make those anymore. To begin again is what feeds me." He stops for breath. "I have no national honor, you see. I have had too many countries. But I know better than some what that honor would be if I had it."

The rocker goes creak, creak. "You tell Malkoff that?"

"I could have. I didn't need to. A scientist doesn't have a country, he said. Then he carried his inheritance into the earth with him."

Minturn lowers his feet to the floor. "Over here, when you have a terrible thing to say, you say it. Maybe even louder."

There's a flaw in the floor next to the rocker, a blotch where the wood hasn't accepted to be vinyl. Bending over, Gonchev smoothes the flaw with the flat of his hand. "If I were Japanese—in the bind I am in—I could jump. A suicide. Honor's all-important there. In some other places, maybe go to prison. But I only accept—to see."

Minturn bends over the blotch too. Their heads are close.

"You grow fat on dissidence from far away," Gonchev whispers. "You can't leave a country and have it too. Once you are safe, it's not honor anymore. Only talk. You can only be a dissident at home."

They straighten up. Gonchev wipes his eyes. "It's the soda water."

"Our quake shook you up." Minturn doesn't whisper. "Scared blue, aren't you. That the poor damaged old U.S.A. might be home?"

Then Minturn's hand is on his shoulder. Are they in comradeship? Or only in business? The transitions here are so quick. And the billionaires so educated. "I like to back people who spill the beans," Minturn is saying. "In that box camera of yours, maybe you have a biggie?"

"I had once—a Paris. See now why I never did make it. Shouldn't be about Paris itself. But about a small boy who grew up dreaming he had been there."

He sees in Minturn's glossy eyes how business can help push art toward sentiment. "And I have some ideas—no script yet—for a story about a man and a woman. Who betrays him for his own good."

"Aha. Aha . . . well, that's what they do. Have to have a new title for it though."

"Oh, that I have."

"Mind saying? Just for the contract, you know."

"I would call it *A Navel with a Raisin in It.*"

Business is such a safety valve. What was locked in, yearning, raveling away in the daily round, turns into live steam. Work steam.

"I'll have to see more of Europe," Minturn says, grinning. "By the way," he adds, leaning on the long gray box, "this records automatically. Would you like me to erase?"

"Oh, keep it. Maybe send a copy to Pfize."

He is left alone to make his three telephone calls.

Laura isn't in. He leaves a message on her answering machine, that he is safe and will be returning—who knows how? He had better say it all. "I have found maybe a backer, Laura. He gives me a free hand. You are to be the agent. You will hear from him." He muses, using up the tape's footage, then reminds himself that his extravagant daughter, his Americanized daughter, had invested in the nearest-to-perpetual tape. "We will get along with this backer. Won't be any bargaining. He's honorable."

He calls La Jolla. A web of secretaries meets his accent. For a bad spell he thinks he has returned to Japanese. But at last he is put on to a man who had worked directly with Malkoff. He knows who Gonchev is—Malkoff had told them he would be bringing Gonchev down to La Jolla. He sounds sad, measured, young.

"I know who you are too," Gonchev says. "He said you are the . . . eclectic one. I had to look it up. It means you choose such doctrines as please you."

"I know," the voice says, amused. "He and I kept getting beat for it. You say he left a message? But I thought it happened suddenly."

"A crack opened. He fell through. Not all the way. Not right away. I was on the edge across from him. His side was crumbling—slow. He called out something." Even while drunk Gonchev had rehearsed it, this small insight he might be bearing. "Malkoff said, 'Tell them that at La Jolla. Tell them to check . . .' I can't be sure of the rest." He hears that wail. "Two words. Could it be 'the balances'?"

" 'The balances.' " Is the voice disappointed? "Would you—repeat?" He does.

"Ah. But he said, 'Tell them *that*,' did he? Can you recall what he said before?"

He is shivering. He wouldn't have had to rehearse it after all. "The dirt is yellow. Red with blood too. But yellow. And he says . . . 'I'm riding backward. But it's crumbling *toward* me.' "

Has the line gone dead?

"And—to check the *balances*," the voice rings out. As if he and Gonchev are singing in plainsong.

"I am sorry to leave you with that picture," Gonchev says huskily.

"No, I can't say enough, how grateful I am to you," the voice says. "How grateful he would be. But come down to the lab sometime—and I'll hope to show you."

"Sometime, yes. When I make a movie."

He hangs up. He isn't shivering anymore. He sits. He would like to continue sitting. . . . Not to have to move. To sit in one's life, as he sees others do. That's what the quake has done to him. Not only shaken him up but annealed him. The way one fuses glass with the action of fire. In his own labs he had often caused it to be done.

He sees that young man bending over the encaustic in his La Jolla lab. He sees him dropping one small precious fact onto the navel of the world.

He has to phone Pfize.

He looks for a calendar. Pfize moves through a host of numbers, for days of the week. And one number to be used only in duress—his Sunday one. "The phone's next to the Jacuzzi in my bathroom," he'd said. "I've got one of those shockproof ones."

Gonchev knows a few of the numbers by heart, including that one. But what day is it? The only calendar visible is an ancient stand-up one, on what, from the family photos, must be Minturn's desk. He counts forward from the day of his arrival at Malkoff's. But the calendar has only numerals. In this room of marvels is there no little grocer's calendar that will show him the days of the week?

He is cursing the vodka, yet wistful for a final dose, when the phone rings.

Then, from a speaker at his elbow: "What cushy places you fall into, Agent Go. Answer please. They told me where you are."

Childish of him not to answer at once, although he's not sulking.

"Gonchev?"

"Gonchev here."

"Pfize."

"Ah. Are you in your bath?"

"No, I'm at State."

So it's Tuesday.

"If I got you in dutch with your host, I apologize."

"You are in dutch, Pfize. With me."

"Sorry. I brim over, sometimes."

With the truth maybe. "Why did you have to bill me as agent? That how your department sees it?"

"Every artist is an agent provocateur." Pfize sighs. "So enviable."

"I am not going to be labeled because of your envy."

"Paul—"

"I am not a spy. Except humanly. And in my work. Which is every person's right."

"Paul—"

"Don't Paul me." He is shouting now. "And I sever myself from the program." Sever. What a proud word. "I am he who is spied upon. I belong with those."

"Paul. Paul. Paul."

"It's over, you Shanghaier. You pimp."

"Paul—Vuksica is here."

Four hours later and after much use of the communications wall, he and Daria are getting out. "The bigger planes are off-island," Bill Minturn had said.

They took a launch to the mainland. The landing field there was quiet. All but two of the planes were up—still on emergency use. Walking over to those two with Gonchev, Bill says: "That navel? It isn't— Dorothy's?"

"No."

"That guy of yours sure got you and her the VIP path," Bill says. "Agent Go."

Gonchev smiles back.

Normally there were six planes, all in the family, Bill says. He pats the plane that will stay here, indicates the other. "One for you, one for us. Just in case." Buck has not come along.

"He gets sick in small ones," Michelle says. "But I understand his theater stuff is wonderful."

She's a nice person underneath, Gonchev thinks, and the surface is thin. "You're from the Middle West, I hear."

Her blush makes her look blowsy, and real. "Bill and I have a common ancestor. He came out here for the Gold Rush. We stayed in Minnesota. But that's how Bill and I met. My grandfather gave me his name."

"Told her, 'See how the Gold Rush is doing these days,' " Bill says. But he grins.

Two mechanics are giving the plane a final check. "Temblors are going down," Bill says. "Good luck, Dottie, and give me a buzz. Somebody will fly the bird back. Or you can keep it for a while."

"Might use it. Got things to do." She pecks both Minturns and climbs into the plane. The two attendants stand by.

"Thank you for California," Gonchev says to his hosts.

They look embarrassed, but hungry for praise.

"Time like this?" Bill says. "You must be crazy."

Gonchev embraces him. "I am crazy—for crazies."

"Malkoff and I had boats on Catalina. That's how we met." Bill's eyelids pinken. He blows his nose.

Americans are always telling each other how they met, Gonchev thinks. As if they are never sure that this big place will provide meetings.

Michelle says, "Now and then we have a little smog."

When the plane is well up in the ozone, its pilot says: "Creeps, aren't they, those two? But I love them."

He finds how fond of them he has got too.

"Stay in their shell," she says after a while. "Never see a real person, half the time. Never see anybody poor."

He is used to such statements from certain American mouths. And if he isn't careful, he could be just like them. He gazes out the window, but he is far too high up to see where trucks and railroad wasteland intersect the plump groves, if that division still holds. Or the bright lines of trailer wash.

"I have news for you," she says, maybe irritated because he is watching the clouds. "We're not for Portland. We're for San Francisco. Where my crippled children are."

He dozes.

When they are starting to descend she says: "The powers that be have a slot ready for you. All the way to New York. Where I gather you'll be met."

He nods, into the clouds.

They are circling, waiting for permission to touch down. Below, from what they can see, doesn't look bad.

"Touching down," he says. An idiom he knows only in this one language.

When they are angled in descent he says: "I love how you fly." And after a bit, "I love how so many of you fly."

He is not sure she has heard him.

And all this time, Dante has not said a word.

12

Naked Towns

WILL HE EVER AGAIN SLEEP as heavily—or as lightly—as on that plane from California? He slept a child's sleep on the night before the great day. At breakfast he was handed a message. Pfize—that name like a spurt of metal spray. How many times he'd wished the man had one of the thousands of neutral names that this country so comfortably provided. Asian names were the easiest, if a name had to tangle with one's life—almost impersonal. So that one might slowly fill in the syllables with the person in question.

The name wasn't solely to blame here. It was that the man in question was so chill yet so bluff about it. Nobody did that double act quite so well as the Americans. Your British chill—as evinced by embassy and business people Gonchev had had to do with in Tokyo and Osaka—was solid all the way through, like a snowman's. The French brand was almost absentminded—as if warmth, if ever it existed, had been mislaid. Neither exuded a heartiness like fake whipped cream.

Courier meets you at Kennedy, with ticket to D.C. There's been a hitch, fella. Keep your pecker up. Signed *Pfize*, and sent via the State Department.

The lissome steward who brought the typed message down the aisle had permitted himself a quip. "That's from the State Department?"

At Kennedy, the courier had known nothing further. "D.C.," he repeated. "D.C." In all the government time Gonchev had served here, they had never thought to send him there.

One gets to that ice cube, Pfize's office, on a chrome escalator like a snail's trail. In a corner there is a huge bottle-green flask the size of a barrel, with a ship's model in it. Not the usual three-masted schooner. A sleek barracuda of a yacht. He can't help looking for Vuksica on its albino-white deck. She isn't there.

Middle of the room, at a black plastic desk like an art moderne soapdish, he sits. You never have to look for Pfize. In jacket and tie instead of sports togs, he has somehow been taken down a peg. And the small room has no view. Only the ship in the bottle.

Gonchev is embraced—to a sharp smell of cologne—and retreated from. "I have earthquake still on me," he says.

Pfize shoots out that condescending smile of so many toward the foreigner who takes life so much harder than necessary. It's the attitude that counts here, fella. Optimism, no matter what. Save your exposé, your depression, for the newssheets—which then may be quoted avidly. Gonchev will never get the balance right.

To live each day for its qualities—and squeeze the picture from it? There's a word for that in this country: Bygone.

"Some bottle, Pfize. . . . And where is she?"

"My dear, dear Gonchev. What a mess. But at least we don't have to worry anymore. She's alive."

Pfize is all throat. No use squeezing it. Only words would spout.

"Of course she's alive. Where?"

"You mean you knew all along she was alive?" Pfize says. "How?"

He had spoken from the morass in him that was still Europe. Mirrors that took account of the past. A constant treading on history, as on old tile. Cords of feeling between people. Faces and features repeating, down genealogies older than monarchs with Hapsburg lips. Young brides with hook-noses out of ancient church murals. Women with the Etruscan single brow.

And a movie-star wife who wore noble Greek skirts to her weddings, and while they drank the toast to her and him, slipped her broad, sandal-reared foot, its straight toes as white as sugar, out of her three-inch-heeled shoe. The photographer had caught the foot and, in the war-buffeted faces of the guests—a half dozen or more, met in a boxy Socialist flat—the look of those still partisan to life. That cord which holds him to Vuksica more even than sex.

He stands transfixed, his own camera. "Knew she wasn't dead, that's all."

Pfize squints. What they mistrust here, they begin at once to dislike. "Then maybe you can tell us where she is now?"

"I thought . . . you brought me here to . . ." He had even checked to be sure he was still wearing his wedding ring.

"Your daughter said, 'Keep it dark. Until she's here for sure—my mother. She won't come otherwise.' So we did."

They had got her in legally enough. "As a prison person," Pfize says, his voice holy. "You know she was that?"

He scarcely hears the rest. How Danilo had for a year campaigned to visit her. How finally, being long-haired for a TV role, he had managed to confuse her guards, while she escaped into the city, where outside help was waiting to get her to Trieste—and so here. And how everyone—even Danilo?—had kept him, Gonchev, offside.

"Your own daughter arranged it all. Anytime she wants a job with Pfize, it's hers."

He remembers how Laura had got to this country. So this time, who has slept with whom? "Outside help?"

"Not me. I can't go anywhere twice. We think it was the same crowd that got you out. That big bruiser you punched—remember him?"

He is not surprised.

"Come to find, the rascal's an American citizen. Born here. Brought up in Greece. But the family—one of the big shipping clans—kept up the citizenship. We've reason to believe that the boy they sent back here at the proper age, for the period of residence then required, wasn't him—but who could prove it now?" Actually the man is now in the United States also. Or was. "Entered legally. On shipping business. At the moment we don't know where."

"And my wife?"

Pfize coughs, looking for another way to say it. But there is none. "We don't know where."

There's nobody to punch. He could kick in that bottle—and break his toe. "Why bring me here?"

"You'd have made it here while she was still around, hadn't been for the quake. She must have found out you were heading East. And skipped. You were in the papers. And then—so was she. This is a naked town."

"There's always a quake. And the towns are always naked. You people still romanticize them."

"And thank God for it, why don't you? Nobody here sniffing up your arse, is there, Gonchev. To see what you ate yesterday. Or thought."

"Nobody but you," Gonchev says. "You are my spy." And I suppose I should thank God for it?

"Hey, fella. You still concussed?" But Pfize slowly reaches for the hand slowly being offered him.

An unusual silence falls between them. In that glass bottle, lying on its side like a demi-universe, he thinks he can see—just possibly—a doll-size Vuksica, striding that sleek deck. Not in prison clothes any longer. But still a "prison person." Those words draw her backward and away from him, on her own black sail.

"What was she in prison for?"

Why does he feel Pfize has been expecting him to ask, yet doesn't want to say?

"Ah-rr—crimes against the state. The usual catchall."

"She's not being—held here somewhere? She left of her own free will? You swear?"

"Of her own free will . . . I swear." Pfize seems eager to echo anything he can.

"And—alone?"

He gets his answer. "Fella. Want to come out on the town? With some of my geishas?"

Getting no response, he follows Gonchev to the door.

"I'm leaving the program," Gonchev says then. "No, don't argue. I was never A-one."

But Pfize isn't arguing. Only agape, with the first honest amazement Gonchev has ever seen on him. "Why, fella. We're speaking English."

Outside, Gonchev feels enormously clearheaded—and about to fall. He makes it to a cab. Governmental Washington sifts past the window. Such a clean-looking town. No wonder there is so much corruption. Such vacant-eyed streets. All the official buildings look as if they sold stamps. He has been one of the stamps.

In the last motel they will ever book for him his festering clothes fall from him. He's afraid he's not going to make it to the tub. Below the neck he's all sponge and quiver, ankles gone. No one to phone, no one he wants to phone. Point of honor though, to make it to the bath.

Above the shower, a plastic clothesline stretches from wall to wall. Fixing it with his eyes from across the room, he hangs two words there, letter by letter. The letters swing there like a woman's undies, tattering behind bars. *P-R-I-S-O-N P-E-R-S-O-N . . .*

He makes it to the tub.

13

The Black Box

I LEAVE MY PLACE AT EVENING. The nearby boats in the Basin smell like garages that have learned to sail. The waves are the color of mice. This is not a river that any meadow would recognize. Yet the air is full of being. The streets are the consciousness of the people. There is no chatter. The only sound is the whine of a dog once he has deposited his load. Yet the age is upon us. I film in my mind.

Gonchev walks along Riverside Drive. Joggers sneak past him, their faces lifted toward the sky. One of them, the owner of the dog, a Chinese who works in the library at Columbia, is an acquaintance of Roko's. He is going to her wedding, although not in any important role. "Just as a guest."

"I also," Gonchev says.

They walk along together. The dog, a brown hound with a knowing muzzle, sniffs the ground like a lexicographer, occasionally looking up, as if there were matters the two of them ought to know. The owner now and then slips the dog a Chinese word. Whenever the animal stops of its own accord its master trots in place. The sight amuses Gonchev hugely. "What would happen if you lifted a leg?"

Mr. Wu, chortling, points to a passing police car.

They decide to go to the wedding together; Wu will leave the dog at his apartment. Although Roko had invited the dog to the reception, he says, since it was through her that he and Roko had met. "Roko is getting very American, isn't she? I am American too, as regards dogs. But the family would be insulted."

"Ah yes," Gonchev says. "In Asia a dog's a dog, mostly." He looks down. "Oh, yours is a female."

"Altered," Wu says stiffly. "It is best for apartment life." But in a minute his mood changes. "We are going to have marvelous food." The Chinese face is as mobile in merriment as any of ours, Gonchev reflects. It merely has different conventions.

During the Red Guard revolution in China, Wu says, his parents, both scholars, were sent to the country as laborers. He, then ten years old, and his younger brother were left in the family flat in Shanghai. Luckily a former servant who worked in a nearby hotel had fed them secretly, when she could. "It has left me a lifelong gourmet." He laughs, but has stopped jogging. The dog trots evenly now, bent for home; she's heard this story before.

"We were forbidden to go to school. Too risky. But luckily we had our parents' books. And—luckily—their subjects were different." So after the revolution, when they were rehabilitated, Wu had got a scholarship here. "In library science." His face closes. Gonchev suspects that this wouldn't have been his first choice, and that he's older than he appears.

"And your brother?" Probably a scholarship too. The meaner streets of the West Side are filled with such students, also the warrens behind the innumerable Chinese restaurants. And the best schools.

The dog stops but doesn't lift a leg.

"Our Shanghai flat was up high, a former attic. Luckily. That was in part why we went unnoticed. On the bridge down below we could see the old people stop every morning to do their Tai Chi. My brother—he rigged up a gym." He laughs again. "It was more dangerous than the Red Guards. Our ceiling was high too. And the ropes were throw-outs from the hotel laundry. One wire, though, very strong." He heaves a sigh. "I remember that wire. I prayed to it. And the rigged wire held. So now he is an acrobat. One of the most famous in China. But my parents do not approve."

The façades of Riverside Drive were just foreign enough to salve the hearts of refugees. Many had lived there, finding their level in the long-corridored, not-quite-august apartments, with their dull bathrooms and maybe a maid's room at the end, rentable in time of trouble. Or with the burst of river at the front and the candy dish, shining in the sun, if you had made the grade. Gonchev has visited all kinds.

"Students don't live here," Wu says. "Not since the Depression." When hundreds of families bunked here in furnished rooms.

Gonchev looks up at the grayish apartment houses they are passing, some of the older ones balconied, most of them low, as buildings go in this city; a few once-private dwellings are even turreted, as in Amsterdam, and up the hill there, a block of pillared eight-story buildings are very like slides he once had of the rue du Bac. Across from the marina, blocks below here, one front has a helmeted Athena in faded majolica over the front entrance. This is a part of New York he had never included in his research.

"These buildings suffered terribly," Wu says. "Like us. But it has all been papered over." If he can ever afford to marry, he would like to live in one. "Maybe in the back." His teeth shine. "Or in a depression. We do well, in those. Luckily." Meanwhile, he can walk his dog here.

"It's a street of aspirations, yes, I can see that," Gonchev says. "Streets with rivers always are."

And this Hudson River runs like an international scar, formed by the tissues of left-behind cities, and found after death in the hearts of those who have haunted these buildings. Leaking their stories to one another.

"And one can have all the children one wants," Wu says, cocking his head at two toddlers in bright overalls, one of them Chinese. "Not like in China."

"You can do that lots of places. India."

"But not places where you can do everything else, like here. Everything else." He flings up an arm, the leash tangling. The dog growls at his raised voice. He straightens the leash, quieting her in Chinese. "Luckily—I have her."

Meanwhile he lives up the hill with four other subacademics in the basement of a former tenement, now an office building owned by the university, and gets free rent for performing house services. He has two other jobs. One in the library as a nonunion nighttime guard, as long as he keeps his mouth shut about it. "And one serious job," he says. "For my career." And what is that one? "Ghosting term papers," he says, with the wraith of a smile. "And Ph.D. theses." For an agency that sells them. The theses pay especially well. He's saving money to marry. "And—in the basement I can keep her." The dog wags its tail.

"Ah, so you have a girl." In spite of Gonchev's own story, he's glad to hear of a better prospect for the unrelieved life walking beside him.

"No, but Roko's promised there'll be a girl for me at the wedding. I haven't met her yet." This time Wu doesn't add the magic word—"luckily"—that leads him through life. "And you, Mr. Gonchev?"

Should he tell Wu his story? Would Wu's dog—spayed, poor thing—understand it at once? Wu isn't up to it. Maybe one day he will be. Depending on the girl Roko finds for him.

Gonchev paces alongside Mr. Wu for some blocks. "I am sorry," he says then: "I never answered your question."

"Oh, that's all right. You were walking your dog."

They have reached Wu's building. Gonchev waits outside, on the stoop. In the six weeks since he's been alone on his boat the streets have fed him resolve. There are still many stoops in this neighborhood, gray and half-ruined, acid with animal urine and garbage-can seepage, their tops concave from human bottoms, their sides pocked from baby cariages and rubber balls. There's a luminous blur about them, the exact tone of a negative. The streets will be the stoops of his pictures. But this time his archive will wander more. Fields too are streets, and so are other terrains. He's learned a thing or two about terrain.

America's the concussion in his head. A clot of darkest blood, feeding on damage. But also a burst of silvery light, playing on the dustily indifferent air. That's the way he pictures what they call freedom here. Sometimes he walks the nearest West Side barrio, where the Puerto Ricans, who have been arriving since the nineteen-thirties, make parlors of the front steps. During the day, a straggle of the unemployed, the lame and the halt, whole families at dusk. Once in a while a window is smashed in the tenement above. Those below tread the crumbs of glass unconcernedly. The women retain a perfection of feature, luridly enhanced. The men—unshaven, liquored up—are still kings.

He sometimes frequents one of their bars. Except for the water pipes linking it to the city it might be a tavern these people had left behind in a simpler countryside. It has links with the warm haunt to which his motorcycle had known the way. Sitting in the golden Spanish chatter, he remembers the bovine creaking of that other bar. The sweaty silences, into which a bit of folklore now and then plopped like cow dung.

He'd once given Danilo a ride there. The only time he'd ever seen Danilo drunk—a pale face, holding its own above the murky waters of its central abyss. "There's a café in Paris," Danilo said, "I can't stand it there. The smell of roots." Hours later when they'd settled the bar bill to an amount that shook the solid proprietor, Danilo said, "Lucky Gonchev. Born without nostalgia. That's right, brother-in-law—you pay. Pay for mine."

That's what I could do for all here, Gonchev thinks. A migrant worker in my own way. Helping to pay for all the nostalgias gathered on a continent once home to the buffalo. Their old-world fields, hacked out of prairie—a pure patch of which he'd been taken to see, its tall grasses swaying like ghosts. "No phosphates," the tremulous old farmer said. "We drink our own water, good as beer." While back here in the city the new Borgias bought up at auction the landscapes of a century before. The farmer had known about that. Everybody knows everything the very next day—and doesn't know what to do about it. "Make your million, Laura," Derek had said. "Then we'll buy us an acre of pure dune."

Gonchev hasn't seen anything of Laura lately. She's lost her job and is looking for what she calls "a new in." Derek is long gone. Gonchev's own money in the bank is ebbing, but he will receive a monthly remittance until the grant runs out, plus what Pfize called "severance pay." "From us socialists," he'd said. "We don't admit that yet. Still, it ain't Scandinavia." Pfize keeps calling but has sent no more bulletins.

I could have kicked in that glass bottle of his, Gonchev sometimes broods. And him too. Maybe I will yet. In a film—about a spy who can't let go?

A girl pushing a baby buggy wheels it over Gonchev's outstretched foot. She has the insolence of the new mother. Her sweatered breasts are lush. His own sex isn't deadened, only lackluster. I'm on severance there too—but from whom?

And going to a wedding.

He watches the girl circle around the next stoop down. A body straight out of tsarist Russia lies at its base. The whole world is here, he thinks, excited. That's what they say they intended; why can't they get used to it? Instead of always sifting the stewpot for that little pearly white nation which must still be there, its eighteenth-century church spires pricking the North American blue. (And putting the Indians on the run.)

Yet sometimes, right here on a street corner, a burst of the free air here makes him catch his breath.

"Oh, Dad," Laura said when he broached some of this, "street life is your agitprop." A phrase that, when explained, enraged him.

"Life is the propaganda, you—you American. And since when do you call me Dad?"

Her eyes have a peculiar expression these days, almost hostile, when she looks at him. Or at herself in the mirror. As if she finds herself lacking too. "Some families stick together when they get here," she'd said. "For hundreds of years, even. Like the Kennedys. Or the Jews. And some break up."

He has never mentioned his trip to Washington. She in turn has never asked why his escape from the quake area—which she had indeed initiated—hadn't been straight to New York. Vuksica's name is not let fall. He cannot bear to. He thinks his daughter does not want to lie.

"I haven't heard from Danilo for a while" was all he'd said, the last time he saw her.

Danilo was expected back in Belgrade, she'd said. He'd been dropped from the Paris serial. For an unexplained absence of two weeks running—from which he hadn't yet turned up. "Probably some woman. You know him."

At the same time she'd put her hand on Gonchev's wrist. He'd been walking her up from the boat through the park strip, across the ramp and up the hill to Broadway, a route he wouldn't let her take alone. They were passing two women, both of whom proved to be black. From the rear there had been a queenly posture to one of them, a carriage of the head. "Oh, Papa. Stop looking." He hasn't seen Laura since.

When we come here we're all lost, he thinks. Waiting to be found again, no matter how proudly we come, or why. Maybe even the real prison person, as well as the fraud.

This morning he had three phone calls, two letters. One call from an unknown agent who wants to market Gonchev's version of the quake—which somebody else will "work up." One letter was from the lab at La Jolla, inviting him to a memorial for Malkoff, with a penciled note from the man he'd spoken with. *My God, Paul Gonchev, when we talked I didn't catch on it was you. Would you come someday, with or without camera, and meet the Mars mice?*

Everybody here wants a documentary of themselves—including a group of Jehovah's Witnesses who are building a new church center— "all by hand, as we volunteers always do"—on a very fine property on Route 22 in upstate New York. They want him to record the process, in return for the love he would gain—and the rescue, when Armageddon arrives.

The third call was from the florist shop that is sending his flowers to the wedding. Had they got his name right? "I am Russian," the woman said. Her voice was as soft as the Witness's but more shy. "We knew a couple, not quite the same name—Paul and Marina Bonchakov—they were to come over too. We have been here forty-two months. I thought maybe the order name could be wrong? No? No, you don't talk like our Bonchakov. Apologies." They'd had a chat. He thought that anyone who spoke her language and was a recent arrival here would have done.

In his pocket is a letter from Minturn's New York lawyers. Their client has turned up a warehouse in Long Island City. Minturn thinks the New York scene would be more to Gonchev's liking than Hollywood. If the old warehouse suits, it's Gonchev's to do what he wants there, all expenses paid, for a suggested period of five years. A postscript from Minturn himself: "Just want you to know I believe in navels."

What Gonchev would want to film just now is that rag-body on the sidewalk, its ratchety breath just audible—and beside it, a ghostly patch of waving prairie grass. With perhaps at their right, regarding that brief but historic collage just arrived upon—a man on a stoop. Who has been offered the privilege of citizenship.

His camera, returned to him, now suns itself at a windowpane in the houseboat, angling now and again with the wash from a passing barge. No scrubbing will ever remove the alluvial quake-deposit that has hardened on it. But its one eye is still open to experience.

Mr. Wu comes up the steps from his basement. He's changed clothes. The jacket is scarcely discernible from the one doffed, and the trousers, though sharply pressed, are summer ones, but a certain clarity of outline shows that he is in his best. The hairs that protruded from a nostril have been clipped. Two rosebuds, encased in a plastic tube, have been thrust through the buttonhole in the jacket's lapel.

"I can't go," Gonchev says. "I'm sorry. I can't see myself there."

Wu glances understandingly at Gonchev's brown turtleneck, scuffed blazer, and pants. "We are early. You would have time to change. A shirt and tie, maybe? I would lend you. But I do not have extra."

"Thank you. It's not the clothes."

"Ah. It is yourself."

How easily the East acknowledges the self. Without that psychological spittle the West sprays itself with. Gonchev nods. "I shouldn't have been invited, maybe."

"Not to the first ceremony, anyway. That was this morning."

"I sent flowers instead."

"To the Korean church, yes. I saw them. Brown orchids. Very rare."

"Are they? They reminded me of her." He thinks of the woman's call. "It's a very good florist."

"The best." Wu bows. "They all saw, at the church. Otherwise, I did not like the style. Of that occasion."

"You're not Buddhist?"

"But Chinese! Roko is my only Korean friend. But I can understand why you . . . still yearn for her?" Wu waits.

"I . . ."

"Ah."

"Only as one yearns for the past," Gonchev says.

Wu, risen on the balls of his feet, listens, head cocked. He's a graceful man. "I can see why she . . ." He smiles sadly.

"She what?" Gonchev says. "Yearns?" He dislikes the word.

"Why she—made herself translate Japanese for so long. A language she detests."

"I didn't know. She never let on."

"They hate the Japanese. From long suffering." He grins. "We Asians are not all of a piece you know. Some places, they hate us Chinese."

"She never let on."

"No. But now maybe you will come to the college chapel?" He glances at his watch.

As they set out, Wu says consolingly, "Your boots are after all very fine."

On the way, Gonchev says: "She did leave me, you know."

"We marry," Wu says.

In front of the university chapel he pauses, scrutinizing the dome. "Copied after St. Paul's, London, I assume? Anyway, very serviceable."

"Does the boy—the groom—belong to this religion?"

"Around here we are all of the—the university religion. And the groom sings in the choir. His friends are going to play."

Wu is removing one of the buds from his lapel. "Was for the girl I am to meet at the reception. But maybe too soon for a rose." He pokes the bud into the lapel in Gonchev's once-smart blazer. "The groom and his friends won't be dressed up," he whispers. "Only the girlfriends will do it, a little. And Roko's parents. If you are not in the wedding party they will all think you have been her lover. If you are with them, then you are only—the uncle. The patron uncle." He spreads his hands. "The American one."

Gonchev's head is awhirl with nationalities. No wonder the country is. He glances down at the stone steps, grasping at some solid base to things. "Wish you'd brought that dog."

Inside, the organ is playing; maybe they're too late. No, it's the introit. The light is dim, the full church not illuminated. The audience is small. A few older people sprinkle the front pews, a fair number of younger ones hug the rear. The chill is the same as in all churches, interdenominational.

A young usher, the only one, comes toward them, questioning.

"The bride's side," Wu says.

They are seated in a row sparsely occupied, well up front, but still audience, and near the aisle. He has time to note that the young choir are most of them in sweaters. A trio of music stands waits to one side. No extra altar flowers. But candles streaming nicely, as they always do in church.

Wu says: "Lucky you had a buttonhole."

Three young men take their places at the music stands. A cello, two violins. The violins wear turtlenecks. The cellist is in a dark suit.

"They are going to play from a wedding cantata," Wu whispers. "Bach." The cello to be played is a notable instrument; its story had been in the college magazine. "A rich person gave it to him. For his talent." Wu squints forward, his elegant mandarin nose riskily near the fur collar of a girl in the row ahead. Gonchev has recognized who Wu is smiling at. The cellist is the groom.

The choir rises to sing. There is as yet no minister. As the music vibrates in the checkered light, Gonchev is besieged by family thoughts, pulling these one by one from that lost center like twigs from a blown-down birdnest.

Could Laura be among the altos? She is not. Could he have somehow sent Klement an argyll sweater like the one that thick-necked blond young man singing too loud in the bass is wearing? Or got word to him through Pfize that if Klement could manage to bump a border for real, Gonchev would get him into uniform here—maybe the same one as that Haitian boy's?

In the choir a redhead is between two blacks, a couple of towheads flank a girl who may be from the barrio, and Asians are everywhere.

There's more than academic religion working here. Or that's what the religion is. Should he and Klement's mother not have stopped with Klement? Dwelt less on love in blue nightgowns and pills underneath the bed, and more on young ones to follow them—even if to sing in a choir of foreign choice? Or had that brown-and-white house of cards been his ultimate romance? What's happened to that house?

With the *Allegro vivace* he feels more hopeful. Or more bellicose, sometimes the same thing. She'll have to report in somewhere. Nobody's really on the loose here, no matter what's claimed. Certainly no newcomer. Papers to let you work, papers to say you can stay. Somewhere she'll have to surface. And a good Greek, even a brigand, will always return to Greece when he can. Most of all, Gonchev consoles himself, Vuksica once remarried a former husband. She and he are not divorced so far as he knows. Yet in the rhythm of marriage such a return might be the same.

The organ begins a wedding march. Not Wagner's. The Meyerbeer one his father hated equally. *Dah dah, duh dahdahdahdah, d'dah, d'dah, d'dah.* Just the thing for the joining of two Koreans in this sallow version of an Anglican oratory.

The minister now appears from the wing, robed. Sanctity will be observed. And from the wing opposite comes a monk. Gonchev blinks. The sight of a monk undoes him still.

Now the whole audience is turning. The bride must be coming down the aisle. Gonchev keeps his eyes on the four girls in front of him, all of whom have swiveled. All are wearing feathered earrings.

"Ecumenical ceremony," Wu breathes, with the first Chinese lilt Gonchev has heard from him. The girl in the fur collar looks sidelong at Wu. She too is Chinese. Not a beauty, but not bad. The earrings from Pipestone become her.

"What's 'ecu-men-i-cal' mean?" Gonchev whispers.

Wu's cheeks have turned orange. "The whole world."

"Ah, yes. Including the Indians." Gonchev doesn't want to turn. He turns.

The group appearing at the far end of the aisle is small. The mother, in brave red, is on the arm of the brother, who looks less gay than he used to. The father has the bride on his arm. Both men are wearing business suits.

Roko is wearing Gonchev's gift kimono. She has let her hair grow and swept it high. Various tinkling ornaments are disposed in it, and over her bunched figure. He recognizes the yellow sash. Her fingers, laced under her breast, carry his orchids, frugally used twice; the sleeves, elbowed out, help complete the shoulders' classic curve. His Roko of the winged hair and metal boots is gone. That big lacquer box whose power he had felt oozing into their tiny, chattering rooms—though she had proclaimed it empty—this is what was in it. Here is the bride who was in the black box, along with the grandchildren to come.

As they come nearer, he is sure all four have seen him. Although Roko keeps her eyes lowered he knows their clever corners. The mother, blinking rapidly behind the huge glasses, is digesting his presence for later legend. The brother glares. But it's the father, his mouth curled in anguished dignity, who gets to him. One row short of Gonchev's, he bows.

"They never let on," Gonchev breathes to Wu, and nodding quietly to others in his row, as if this is ritual, he slips past them into the aisle, in time to put the mother's free arm in his own.

The bride's squared-off sleeves dip for a moment only. Gonchev's flowers hold her hands fast. The father brings her forward. The groom deserts his music stand and comes to her side. The minister receives the couple with a smile. The monk, separating himself, stalks into the first pew. It all happens at once. As in any good script that has taken months to prepare.

Gonchev keeps his eyes lowered throughout. He's not asked to do anything. He was late; he is here. When the minister asks who will give away the bride, Roko's mother grips Gonchev fast, trembling violently, while the father accedes. The ritual is lengthy, involving an exchange of rings.

Gonchev stares at his own wedding ring, acquired in a ten-minute civil ceremony presided over by an official who wiped the lunch soup from his mustache after each response. During the wedding meal afterward, Danilo had mugged the whole act. That bitch Rémy meanwhile saying: "Not your fourth try, like hers, Paul." He answering: "No, only the first of four. If she'll have me each time." While the maestro waiter ground secret spices into the steak tartare.

Why does one's past, when looked back upon, always seem lived through by a blind person? Even while he can see the Danube moving far below the ramparts on which that restaurant was perched, and feel again the quiet release in the body that came of being with the right person.

Will he ever see Danilo again? Danilo's for decamping, no matter how hard his wife will pull on his coattails. But maybe the American arena is too vague for him. As the processional here starts up and their little wedding train reverses itself—that oh-so-Protestant academic robe and ministerial smile leading the way—Gonchev himself can mug what Danilo would if he were here: brother-in-law Gonchev caught by the coattails too, and dancing stiffly to the tune set out for him.

The organ, played by a young devotee, is going all-out holy on a simpering chorale: César Franck.

"Music you can paint a choir loft with," Gonchev's father says in his ear, "if you like to mix oil and pastel."

Gonchev's mother is watching Roko toss her bouquet straight at Wu, who passes it on to guess who?—causing feathery laughter among the other three girls. "Your Roko sewed so well," Gonchev's mother sighs. "A treasure. And look at that aim. She's Western now."

"But, Paul," both his parents add, their voices fading, "we were always a couple, your father and I, your mother and I—no matter what. We were refugees together. . . . Where's that other one?"

The procession's melting now, as processions always do. To a pattern no director can fully achieve, but along some theorem that goes to the core of human movement. Gonchev will kiss the bride on both cheeks, embrace the mother, shake hands with the father and brother—and escape in the wake of the monk. He'll direct himself well.

And carry with him the sight of that choir of faces, dotted in by a master of color . . . I won't be alone—I'll have the pictures to come, and all the crew . . . and a warehouse—big enough to build a new country in.

He has heard nothing further of the film that ended up in the undertaker's sink. As for Stepan himself, though it's said that two men with a passion for the same woman often become friendlier when cuckolded by a third, Gonchev feels no closer to him.

At the end of the aisle the monk stops, surrounded by the bridal party and their crowd. The minister, at the church door, regards them benevolently. He's taller than any of the Koreans, and this must be his church. Gonchev approaches the group to make his final gesture. Those at the fringe hang back to make a place for him. Yes, they know who he is. In their center the monk presses his lifted palms together and bows to him.

All Gonchev's planned script falls away. How well this eager crowd has learned to incline the cheekbone, press with the lips, and allow the small-boned fingers to be enfolded in larger ones. But the older people, not born here, are never comfortable at it. Even Roko, suavely carnal down to her toes, never liked to kiss. Not all these people would be Buddhists. Not all the monks he'd known had used the same greeting. But as Gonchev points his clasped palms upward and inclines his head, a sigh runs through them all—and through him a sagging relief. Yes, these people know who I am. We recognize each other. In all he's been through so far there, they are the first.

Gonchev bows. To the monk. To them all. To the bride.

Roko's not looking at him. Hands clasped to her chest as the kimono requires, head inclined sideways under its fetching but heavy gauds, she is straining to see across the aisle.

No one is any longer in the pews; all are clustered around the wedding pair.

No—one couple, facing all of them, is in the next to last pew.

His daughter is more dashingly dressed than he's ever seen her, a white saucer cocked over her forehead, her arm linked in her companion's. In a Mao jacket and trousers, he looks taller than he used to, though the baggy trousers look bizarre on him. His hair is short again, but in the rough-cut way of hair that might have been shaved. In those two weeks when he hadn't turned up in Paris, who had done what to him?

"Danilo—" Gonchev rushes forward, stops short.

His brother-in-law is staring at Roko. Under his deep tan—the kind he used to bring back from his love-forays to Istria, Capri, or the Greek islands—the impeccable profile is worn, to a beauty it never had before. He looks nobler, that's the change. He nods at Roko; he approves of her. She bows.

He turns, a hand ruffling the cropped hair. The eyes are as hazel as ever. Appraising Gonchev from head to foot.

The mouth indents.

Of course, of course, of course.

It is not Danilo.

14

Streets

GROCERY MOODS. If you want to get to the bottom of a country, you go food-shopping. Which may be why the men here shop so much more than they used to. "We Wasps never did," his friend and scourge Flaherty had informed him. "The foreigners and the Jews taught us."

Gonchev has come straight from the wedding. Back at the chapel, where he indeed would have knelt to Vuksica in the pew and made their reunion in the sight of God—where better?—that fiend in white silk, his daughter, hadn't allowed them a word. Nor, to tell the truth, had Vuksica.

"Where's she gone?" he said, champing forward, just in time to see her fade.

"To the ladies'," Laura said. "Always so hard to find one, in a church."

In his fury and relief he could only mutter, "Well, I hope she knows how to manage those pants."

Laura had had a right to be disgusted. Instead she said gently, "Papa, where she was, they wore worse. And over here she has got used to them."

They were on their way to the airport, she said. "To see a friend off."

"And how long has he been here, this friend? How long have the two of them?"

"Papa, don't roar. For Roko's sake."

But by then there was nobody in the church except Wu, waiting patiently at the door, his back to them.

A roar? He had almost no voice. "She's not decamped?"

"Oh, Papa." Laura's eyes brimmed. Her mother hadn't wanted to go to the airport. "But I persuaded her."

"Nobody ever persuaded your mother to do anything she didn't want to do."

Laura's eyes dried quite fast. "Some have." She put out a hand to stroke his cheek. "He's going for good, Papa. He plans to marry a younger woman and start a family." She gave a flip to her hat. "And I've never met him. I kind of want to."

"Why?" It's out before he can check it. What one should never ask Laura.

A stare, a smile, a shrug. "She could be at the boat, later, who knows? But she won't want to see you now. Give us two minutes' grace. So we can leave."

And he's willing. The rules of drama change. But still exist.

Outside on the church steps, Wu says: "Wow, was that a limo that just took off. Some people—how they do things."

"But you have two roses," Gonchev says, giving his back.

Now he is on upper Broadway, that avenue spilling with fruit, raring with shop bins pitched to every need or attitude, alongside which once an hour every type in the world will pass. A thoroughfare on which everything is straining to stay in the middle bracket, even the fruit. Except here, at this hub, the Fairway, where the herbivorous swarm down the lettuces for quality at a price, and even the homeless in their streetside sitting rooms stare at the parsnips as if these are cornucopias. Until guided toward the apples by some crone condescending from her riches of a furnished room with kitchen privileges: "This week the MacIntoshes are best." While at a counter where the great cheese wheels seem to roll in under their own steam, the real Broadway dowagers and fancy actor-men chat their travelogues to each other, free and clear.

The place is dense with actors, both the professionals and those amateurs condemned to dabble only in life; he feels comfortable here. In China once, on a winter evening in the provinces, where, if a chance blow had caught him out, he could have been expunged from the world's roster and no one would have known it, he had wandered into a corner market. Not one of the blackish or purple fruits or sage-green legumes had been identifiable, and even the boxed goods seemed more pharmacopeia than victuals. Then, at a far stall, he had found and bought a thin slab of chocolate, and personality was restored to him.

He often comes here twice a week, to tour the country, and to assess his past travels, now that those have stopped. In his English dictionary a "fairway" is defined as that part of the golf course between the tee and the putting green. But its prime meaning is "a navigable channel in a river, or between rocks." Or between the aisles of carrots offered him by the new world.

"Giving a party?" the girl at the bread counter says, surveying the pile in his basket. He doesn't know her, nor she him, but he nods, adding: "And I only came here to buy a box of raisins." She wags her head; people are always saying something like that. Actually he might call Derek and leave a message on his machine. "Call Derek," he's said to Laura now and then. "I miss that nut, even if you don't." In life you have to drop people, she always retorts. As if she knew all about life. And he replies, "And pick them up again." As if he'd learned nothing.

He would call Danilo if he knew where he was. Although he can hear Danilo's mocking riposte, in the only dialogue Gonchev would want from him: What, what can Gonchev tell Vuksica? To make her stay? . . . "My dear Paul, whatever did you do once? To make her follow you where she did?"

Outside, he wavers. He could cart his loot into a cab, and so home. Instead, he crosses the avenue to the gassed-out strip of benches on vanished grass that still divides Broadway. At Elsinore he'd had a nineteen-twenties postcard showing a sector of this same strip, the benches then filled with families and courting couples, bright as a Renoir café. Now it's called Needle Park. But mornings the aged come to swap Medicaid troubles he sometimes listens to; there's a suboffice nearby. The welfare cases emerge from it, blinking at what awaits.

He knows why he's lingering. These hours may be the last scene in his solitude.

Today a lively old white crone is reading from a printed form to a middle-aged black man who is blind. She's known here; it's her vocation. "I'm a pusher," she cackled the first time Gonchev sat down here. "Information. For free. I used to feed the birds." Today she lifts her chin at his armful. "Hoo—pineapple." He knows his full load is no ticket to these lower depths, but she awards him a vacant bench anyway. "Make yourself to home, we ain't doing no income tax." And to the blind man: "I know him. Just a kibitzer. He's safe. And so's your food check."

He's exhilarated at being known. Listen, Vuksica, how I am known. How familiar I already am with the country ahead of us.

In the beginning he had felt swollen with European culture, with no hope of discharging it. The Americans, so fond of the blank language of expertise, would call it alienation. But what he had felt wasn't anti where he was. Rather it was like some mild, cellular disease left over from an intense childhood. Like the fever called "undulant," which came from bad milk. Leaving the "cured" sufferer still subject to milky moods of remembrance that kept him heady and separate from others yet somehow more nostalgically alive. Or, like the cattle themselves, chewing his cud of phantom grasses.

They have motorcycles, God knows—why can't he see himself whiz-banging the streets of New York, or even those plains, on which one can really let go? Maybe because he now has nobody following him? Nor any of those "underground" ideas that in those days had to be lived with in compromise. As he had lived, kept up to the mark by a ham-handed yet somehow pure-minded spy. Until he himself had been imported here. Not as Paul Gonchev, but as their idea of him.

Short of war though, Danilo, can they really live with the idea of another country's pure idea? Or do they only take courses in foreign appreciation, where they grade themselves on their own tolerance? Like in their old shipboard musical films, where the stiffish rich widow learns to shake the hula skirt, though the boat stays in port and she returns to it each night. Coda: the boat sails on—bye-bye, whoopee-Tahiti—while the widow hangs over the rail, thinned by implied sex and "real" hot music, "shook," as they say, but still in funds.

Yet those old "hoofer" movies of theirs, Vuksica—where the true romance was all in the feet—how we and all Europe loved them.

Now even the young feet are all health, jogging. Like that boy there, dressed like a Hindu in headband and dhoti and weaving dangerously between the bicycles. Which are weaving dangerously between the trucks.

Oh, they feast on planned emotion here. And their sex lives can be more decadent than poor old non-Satanist Gonchev and his friends—and his wife—ever bothered with. They carry their own big ideas around with them like birthday cakes, even their idea of idleness. While the sweet-and-sour savors of an ordinary day seem lost to them.

So how to convince her that they must stay?

Gonchev bares his new watch. Bought at a stall on Canal, it spans his wrist like a manacle, numbering his days as well as his hours, all from a quartz heart oblivious to caress. His old watch is sulking in a drawer; its gold-whiskered Swiss face isn't up to clocking these people. This one has a thick red hand that jumps. In twenty jumps—while he monitors the passersby—it has counted as many differing Americans.

An intense people, whom he sometimes typecasts for hours—maybe they are too variegated for their own good? Texans are as full of Schwärmerei as the Germans and, he suspects, can dismember you like a Junker if you go against their code. Middle Western farmers are so polite they could be Japanese, yet their women show their huge blue-jeaned hams like choice cuts from the sty of a nineteenth-century Russian compound, and curl their huge yellow mops of hair à la Hollywood. It's an anthropological stunner, this country; no wonder it has trouble normalizing its parks.

What a documentary he could make for patron Minturn on the world's parks. In China the ancient tree-parks, pruned by philosophers, sculpture their own nearly immortal duration. In Deutschland the trees huddle to form ramparts so that children will obey orders, but shine most sweet-temperedly on Sundays.

The jolliest park in his collection had been Copenhagen's Tivoli. Food stalls that made the mouth water, and a poster of a girl whirling down a fun-fair chute, her bare legs wide open, and a pinwheel stuck in her ginger bush. In his version he would make the pinwheel whirl.

As for the only place where one could apparently make shots of couples fucking on the public slopes—surprise: London. A cartoon blurb said, "The younger socialists have at last stumbled on the outdoor pleasures of the landed aristocracy."

"In Europe," he had once explained to Flaherty, "the basic melancholy of life is taken for granted." So of course the surface gratifications, from dinner to sexual delight, are taken very seriously. Or, as in Japan, everything is prettified into order, while the shadows reign below.

"Oh, here the right to be happy is rampant," Flaherty said. "You expect to eat 'the quality of life' with the silver spoon you should have been born with."

Meanwhile, the very vastness of the American spaces, combined with the ethnic variations, does make for a randomness that even the natives, alas, aren't fully reconciled to. They see the grandeur, even puff it, but somehow can't be sated with mere inequality. "Our Constitution don't allow it."

So of course the newspapers, Flaherty's column included, are full of anger and accident, and you eat gloom with your rightful spoon. "I see you agree," Flaherty snarls—and "Yes," Gonchev dutifully answers: America—the States—is probably the gloomiest country he knows.

But since he still sounded doubtful, Flaherty, to continue the discussion, had hauled him off to his other bar—the one where nobody could find him, not even the barman, who lived in the back. "Unless I punch the bell."

Flaherty writes in the sawed-off front room, on a sofa spilling its guts, which reminds him handily of how he grew up. "If you live in a twelve-room house with five kids, and on Staten Island yet, that sofa's necessary. And if you're me."

Beer was on draft though, in a corner niche, supplied by a pump handle knobbed with the cast-iron head of a man, which Flaherty had taken the trouble to steal from McSorley's Ale House, a bar for men only, the night it went unisex. "As you will observe, the little man's cranium is cracked—I don't know from which side of the sentiment that evening." Flaherty liked best to be his own server and had done so with a flourish, several times over. "As you see, I am not averse to surface gratification."

"You mock," Gonchev said. "I don't mind."

"The shit you say. I simply speak from both sides of the mouth. A trick you're learning fast, now that the uses of our native tongue have returned to you. Any chance the citizenship might stick?"

That had been two months ago.

"I am—sort of waiting," he'd said. "To hear from my brother-in-law. I have written him, hoping he will join me. It would suit him. Maybe better than me. Danilo is sometimes a dissident. But doesn't always work at it."

"The best kind," Flaherty said. "Another beer?"

"Thank you."

"Welcome. Since I see our disappointments make you truly sorry for us."

The splashes on the floor had been sending up a fine malt. "Well, it's just so sad," Gonchev said. "To see people who aren't gladdened just by bread and wine and a little diddle before sleep." His elbow slid on the table, bringing his head closer to Flaherty's. What it was to have a friend who valued you enough to be your scourge! "Too many people say here, 'I hope I don't live until I'm ninety.' Maybe thinking of the terminal costs, yes? But elsewhere—we do hope it."

"Speaking from both sides of the mouth," Flaherty said, "all of us do. . . . By the way, there is no barman . . . but you might ring the bell."

Gonchev had searched the walls, under the table, the pint-size bar. "There is no bell."

"There you have it," Flaherty said. "Even with America having more of everything."

"Oh, but the saddest institutions here are the banks," Gonchev had told him. "Where the money misery forms in queue."

He was moved to describe how his mother had continued to go to the bank in Tokyo almost with pleasure, thanks to the politeness with which she was sat down on an elegant seat to discuss her debts. While at her side her young son had aped the grave posture of his schoolmates, whose every gesture was designed to convince the elders how well a child knew he was only a child.

"Oh, that's the way it is in the neater nations. Everything to human scale. Even the ennui." Flaherty sat up. "Tell you the truth, Goshuv, I live here. Mondays and Thursdays. With a Spanish girl."

So Gonchev too confessed. How, in spite of all he'd said, he can't help guiltily enjoying life here. How he is often dizzy with purely visual happiness. How the skyscrapers still rock him with their daring ugliness. How even the slums here have a visual coherence that somehow inspires him to hope. How he cannot—stop hoping. And how all this—and how to deal with it—troubles him.

"I'm s'happy to be drunk," Gonchev said.

The old woman rises from the bench by planting her feet wide, clapping a hand to a knee to fulcrum her weight and ending with the elbow of the other arm outstretched. She sees Gonchev watching and salutes. "T'ain't Tai Chi." He follows her progress across the avenue. Her companion remains.

Shortly, a young guy with one of those haircuts that make more of the head than the face is worth comes up to the black man. "Got anything, Daddy?"

"No sir."

"Ain't you a drop?"

"At one time. No more." The blind man speaks with a clerical sing-song.

"Ain't that risky?"

"Maybe."

The guy saws his right shoe on his left ankle, holds on to the back of the bench the man is sitting on, rocking it. "Maybe you ought to change your parking place, eh, Daddy? We kind of expect a drop to be here."

"Can't do that. She goes to pee across there." It is unsettling enough when a blind person doesn't shift his head. More so when he does, as now. "You want to listen in; we doing health insurance. She's handling my case."

"Good luck. I could use some of that. Like to tell me where there is a drop?"

"Might try the subway station, two blocks down."

"Thanks, Daddy." He inserts a bill in the man's fist, shuffles in place, brings out a huge curry-comb, frisks his hairdo, and sprints off.

"Look for a white man, blind like me," the black man calls after him. After a while he says, "Guess he didn't hear."

"Hear what?" the old woman says, returning.

"A little conversation."

When she brings out her papers again, Gonchev gets up. As he passes the two on their bench he hands the woman the pineapple. She grins at him. "Feeding the birds?"

On the west side of the avenue he lingers, not immediately hailing a cab. The curbstones were built worthily, old, gray city-muscles, still holding up. Down the side street to the river the sunset is as strict and sane as a diagram in Euclid. Up on this tawdry, brilliant, humbling avenue, people are scuffling along in all the terrors and comforts of laissez-faire. What picture will outdo it, this world that does and does not care? And lets you decide. Makes you decide.

Is this the way to deal with all the grim discards of nature and of the civilized? Vuksica, how can I answer? I am going to have to live here, here, here. I am beginning. I am beginning to feel part of this crowd.

In the cab it first occurs to him that prison may already have taught her any argument he is likely to need.

15

Exchanges

THE BELLY BENEATH HIS is like a face grown older.

"I don't mind so much what he did with you," he says. "But to know that he looked."

He didn't much, she would like to say. But it isn't true.

"I suppose you . . . learned things from him." Sexual things. He doesn't have to say.

"One always learns. And you?"

"She learned from me."

"Ah, for men your age, yes, better so."

Is she giggling? He smacks her. He had expected her to be shy. But the old coinage between them has survived.

"He left me with money. He insisted. I'm giving it to Laura, to invest." Flung up on the pillow, her hands move like a knitter's.

On elbow, he watches this domestic urge that has swept them on. "Laura and her Derek—didn't work out."

"No. Nothing that way will work out for a while. Too much else will. Then, maybe toward her thirties, she'll meet someone. Like I did you." She's looking at her body. An actress at fourteen, she had started

411

everything young. "Only—the children will be a little late. That's what they do now."

"Those smart girls," Gonchev says. "American women go into motherhood like into battle. And expect to be rewarded accordingly."

She buries her head in his chest. They are not only parents.

"The whole world will be controlling the coming of children," he says, nestling her. "What a film one could make."

"You have many pictures to do?"

"Many. And no Elsinore. I'm glad." He waits for her to be astonished. Her eyes are wide, but he isn't sure they are on him.

All this time they are smoothing each other's hips, stroking a shoulder, clasping it. Building up the old outlines. His body is recording the changes. Love relieves objectivity for a colliding moment, then revives it.

He kisses the navel. "I found that box you put in my bag."

"You were with me most of the time," she says. "Not always."

"Somebody's chucked me a warehouse to work in," he's saying. "Maybe we could also live out there."

"But keep the boat. Maybe let Laura. I don't think we should give up the boat."

The boat is rocking. So are they.

He's brought her coffee and biscuits on a tray. He draws a chair up close. This is their café.

"I still like to have a book," she says. "Before sleep. Even now. It was madness there, until they allowed us books. Even such books. East German tracts, Anglicized in the Soviet. They took away my mother's cookbook, the one from Novi Sad."

There isn't a book on board. He brings her the four city phone books he found. Even when old, these should be saved. "Soon this country won't need maps. These are their maps."

She's thumbing through the Manhattan book, then the Yellow Pages, where commerce is listed. "My God, what riches. You'll be able to map, and map."

"Oh, the Americans need us. Though they don't like admitting it." He thinks of Roko and her groom, those fresh shock troops of energy. And the student restaurant where, passing its window not long ago, he'd seen a line of cellos stacked and ready for performance, like brown concubines.

"Riverside Drive," she's saying. "Isn't that right up there, on the shore? Who lives there?"

"People like us once. From the Hitler time. Or before. Now they're long since rich, such families. Or gone to the suburbs. Or hanging on." Teaching people here about life. Or sometimes—becoming like them. Not without venality. That money she's brought will rankle.

"Laura wanted to move in there with Derek," she says. "But he couldn't decide between the East and the West sides. Why?"

"Who knows? Who knows what Derek was? Or if he knew."

"He was Czech."

"Oh?"

She's smirking a bit. What sessions she and her daughter must have had; he won't ask when or where. "On the mother's side. And on the father's, Australian."

A laugh bursts from him. "Then maybe Derek is really his name. Poor Derek." Whose answering machine now gives the number of a country place also. "Once he brought us a pizza pie so big it covered the table. No room for plates."

"It's a small table. For a dining table."

He recalls the big one she's remembering, the one he made. "It was a huge pizza—for pizzas."

"Laura wants for us to have apartments together up on the Drive. Maybe not on the same floor."

"Laura wants!" What new landscape are they already floundering in, he and Vuksica?

Her nightgown is pretty enough but short, as they are here. There are new veins in her ankles. "That place you were put in. I haven't asked you. Why?"

"Don't. I'll tell you. But not tonight."

She has shrunk back in the bunk. Small for a bed. He would like to scatter it with books. "Drink your coffee." He warms her ankle with his palm. "Politics. Some people live their whole lives without it. And without shame."

"Who? Where?" Her voice has all Europe in it. They took her cookbook away.

Where is there no politics? In workshops—hers and mine? Or on the green roads between the valonias? Worlds that can be killed, but spring up again, untouched. But who is he to say that to her. "Whatever you did do—we're not to have to call ourselves dissidents. That's only what they want of us. For themselves."

"So what are we?" The hair swept back from that brow hasn't a snowflake in it. He's always been happy that a woman as strong as she could still have artifices.

"We are whatever we are. For ourselves." He's almost upset the tray. He rights it. "Refugees. Visitors—begging for a green card. Exiles."

"Not me. Exiles live in the past. I don't bother with that."

He stares at her, this great blond beauty walking through life at a sleepwalker's pace but with the eyes seeing, the teeth chomping pleasures as she goes, and the rest of her not far behind at that duty.

She thrusts her jaw at him. "You don't have any past either; admit it. That's why I fell for you. That's why I—"

He says it for her. "Followed me?"

At her nod, a wide, tired smile stretches his face.

She leans nearer. "Over there all those years—one had to have a past. I had to. And with Danilo." She makes as if to spit. "Always asking him how people did, back home. And letting him lie to me. But here—there won't need to be a back home."

"How do you know? You are just this minute arrived."

Not quite. But neither of them is going to refer to that interim.

"The night after . . . you left, I began running all your films. In the studio. And the night after. And for nights after that."

"But you sent me away." All at once he is so furious he puts his fingers on her throat. But can't strangle her; she is giving him back his life. It is he who chokes. "What are we then? The two of us?"

She shrugs. "Yesterday, I was an immigrant. Tomorrow, I'm like everybody else. They mustn't need pasts here. Not like Europe. Maybe a little fuss, for the grandparents. Or they buy a past, you know? But it's not serious."

"How do you know all this?"

"I went through your library. Everything it had on the States. The minute I heard where they were taking you." She reaches for him. "Paul?"

The first time she has called him Paul. "What?"

"I meant it to be Paris, of course. For you to be there."

Too close an exchange can put one in awe of the gaps that can turn up. How long since he's thought of Paris? She had kept faith with it. "That—was generous."

He sips from her cup. "My library." The files he had kept at home had been only shards of a greater amber. A library is an amber holding thousands of files, like a memory—only for everybody. That was what had been wrong with his. It had not been for everybody.

"Still there. At—Elsinore." Her voice lifts on that last. Delicately questioning.

"No it isn't anymore. Not for me."

She spreads her hands. "See?"

He begins to laugh, deep vibrating chuckles. There's a shark down there inside him where those come from, black-finned, intent on itself, if from time to time forgettable. "I see."

"You told me—your films did—what this place is. A land for pictures, that's plain. You show it." She spreads her arms to an invisible audience. "Maybe they don't know at the time why they're looking, at your pictures, or at anybody's. Or why they love it so. But that's how you show them. Because, you know, you are the same."

She is standing now, her bare feet arched like marble on the boards. There had been a few rugs here—sailor's trove, Moroccan—but he had stowed them away, tokens for his landlords' safe return.

At Pula, where he and Vuksica first met, there had been a photo of her feet on a poster in front of the theater showing the film in which she played a barefoot girl; under it was the caption "Garbo? Or Trilby," from an English newspaper. Nobody at Pula had known who Trilby was. He had searched out the old tale and found a first edition with a drawing of the heroine's foot in it, but that has gone with the library too.

"I played all your films, Paul. Not only the ones about America. All. Until they came for me."

To the studio? Where the big screen would have been wooing her out of her own backstage shadow? Where he had built the cat-door, with its flap for the spy?

"Who? Your smuggler friend?"

"You didn't know? Truly?"

"What should I know?"

"I was in prison. Laura didn't say?"

"She said once. That you—might go."

But only once. Because he had then buried it. And Laura saw.

Outside, a boat chugs softly away, *putt-putt*, a sailboat maybe, using its accessory engine. There is no breeze. One is conscious of the breeze here only when there is nothing else to reach for. "Was it because of me?"

She's pacing, as they must do in prison, if they have room for it. Stopping in front of his chair, she shakes her head.

"Was it Klement?"

He's seen mother birds swooping down to alight next to a chick fallen too soon from the nest. She moves her head like that.

"He's alive?"

"Only an arm wound. He'll live. But in that country—maybe— nullified. Maybe—in any." She's rehearsed this; she doesn't stumble. But her head rears. That's the change in her. A prison person doesn't go blindly on. "After all, a son whose mother has shot him."

He would like to stand also, but doesn't. Who is worthy to stand next to her, next to that? All the shame of being here floods him. Here— while she was over there, dealing with what had to be dealt with.

Outside now, some boat is chugging toward the bay. On Ellis Island, was this how they felt, those lone immigrant fathers who came over ahead?

On his knees he clasps hers, asking pardon. Or some equality. "I was in an earthquake."

They rock.

. . .

River evenings sink gradually, aren't discontinuous with day. From the deck the apartments on shore are scarcely visible through the thickening barrier of trees. Lighted now, the shore buildings guard that obscure family current which doesn't peak or explode, but goes on.

She agrees with Laura. "You ought to be a citizen."

"You're used to the Danube," he says lazily, an arm around her waist. Or to those fierce mountain freshets that had never adopted the Gonchevs—the Goncharievs. "The Hudson's a more sluggish river. And a more subtle one."

"You'll be frozen into a position here otherwise. A living category. Just like you were back there."

Vuksica never draws herself up; she's too good an actress. She merely appears to be doing so. "A class." She hisses that like an epithet, through lips seemingly closed. "Refugee? Immigrant? Something."

"Dissident." He smiles. "Let them call me that. They still aren't sure from what." He stretches his arms. The stars weren't out, but on such a night they didn't have to be. "No, I can sink into bourgeois freedom on my own. Everybody who comes does, we can't help it. Neither can the citizens—it's their life. But I don't owe anybody here yet. So in the films I shall keep my shark's teeth."

"Oh, Paul. Who can keep the purity that we had over there? Not possible."

Prison makes their tongues so reasonable, he thinks. Even while their eyes still see the madness.

She slides a hand up his arm. "Look at you. Just now you were laughing. You never laughed, over there."

"Wait and see. Maybe it's temporary. Maybe I'll stop, eh? Oh, Vuksica, it's just that here I see what I was made for. Why I must have no country, don't need one. A native country colors one's every truth about the world. And"—he whispers it—"I have none."

"You have them one by one," she says. "And now you will have this one."

Suddenly her hand is on his chest, and her head. "That's your purity, yes. That you have no country. When everybody else does." She began to sob, he thought.

"And you mind that?"

Her lashes are thicker when wet. "Mind? I'll help. This time I'll help."

He is cautious. "Why?"

She nuzzles him. "I like this place. It's to my scale. Half the women have big feet. And loud voices. I won't do the voice of course."

"My God," he says. "You mean you'll act again? For me?"

"For anybody." Her eyes, cheeks, chin, all shine. "You know an actor has to do so. But for you first of all."

That had always been the bargain between them, of course.

"You always end up with the purity," he says.

He sees she is laughing, as well as crying. He begins to laugh too.

"I can't help it," she sobs. "Every time I say the word it makes me do this."

"What word?"

"American."

He's hunting out his old cap, tiptoeing round her asleep on the bed they have made on the floor. The bunk, big enough maybe for those two sailors, isn't wide enough for the two of them on this long, depthless night. A five-breasted bed, he thought, but didn't say, as they spread the bright blankets and pillows Laura had bought for him. They made love again at once. Nor did she speak of Danilo. Or he of Sefaru, or Malkoff. This one night was to hover over them, a sealed orb.

But now he's restless, and she has felt it. "Wear your cap out on deck, why don't you?" she murmurs, drowsy. "When you left, I know you had it in your bag." Over the ocean of all that has happened, this floats—and there in a corner under the night light is the old carryall. "I'll ride my motorcycle over the waves," he murmurs back, bending to kiss her, and goes out on deck to show the cap what it has yet to see.

Somewhere west and south of the Palisades, that movie director he had met, the one in a cap with a visor twice as long as Gonchev's, had lately become a father and, according to Flaherty's column, was about to make grist of that—and why not? Perhaps Gonchev and he should collaborate after all. Tossing coins for the preferred limo and driver? Or the contract to specify two drivers, in a car to be custom-made, like the baby carriages built for twins? With a jumpseat for the joint psychiatrist.

He's laughing all right. Is this because he's happy, or because he has the right to be? Or because, in the long, long ago, this is how she and he were taught to express the bitter as well as the sweet?

Or is he at last catching on to the weird ups and downs here? He's become overfond of the word "weirdo." Americans always suspect themselves to be at bottom a bunch of those. And are forever studying the extent of that, in a friendly delousing of each other's head.

Is it from the mess of having so many people, and so few common borders with foreigners, that they can't catch their national image of themselves anymore, just as they proclaim themselves no longer able to breed their native butterflies? Yet that image is forever lurking here. Like the band of swallowtails a geology professor had proudly taken Gonchev to a mountaintop to see. "The nation's romantics," he'd said. Or the beaver village Gonchev had seen in a field in Iowa, its dams industriously subverting the corn crop. The nation's radicals?

Is there any image that a weird-enough movie can't find? It won't be the kind of icon that a Haitian boy will find in the army, no matter how many icons an army always has. It'll be hiding, like one stocking or sock of an old pair you simply have to turn up again. He'd seen Vuksica hunt those. The women know; what do they know? Roko never could get used to saying "the United States," nor her family either. They wanted to keep on saying "Amer-i-ca" in devotional singsong.

But it's here—that corn-husk doll in the Indian-feather headdress, with the bisque or pickanninny face, and the one stocking. Down here, among the émigrés. And it will rise again. From the streets their dirty novels come from. And their popcorn movies. And those entrepreneurs the sweatshop boys, who come out of nowhere to found a garbage company that'll do illegal dumping—or a fortune standing on tiptoe like a statue of Mercury—on a computer chip. Whereupon in either case the fellow sets up some of his money in a foundation—or medical research, fellowships, museums—to remind people where he came from, the American nowhere. While those patrons descended from pioneers, the Bill Minturns, have to keep running in place?

Or if we remain failures, we émigrés—or maybe just nice middle-class steady-on-the-job workmen with union pensions to look forward to but no big visions behind the eyebrows—what then? Still they take the Staten Island ferry on Sunday; they're in that big weekend lineup, the husbands linking arms with the wives. The grown-up children live out on the Island, Queens, the choppy borough where you have to go when you have kids. They're all inside the States now; they call it the rat race, but they're here, citizens born. The older pair, stepping on the gray ferry dock as if it led to a cruise ship—they still have what they would call horizons. They're going to sail the harbor, see how the city looks from out at sea, maybe even point: "There's the old girl." But they won't get off the boat. Cheapest ride in town, maybe in the whole country, when you consider what you get for it. The ferry brings you back to where you were.

To where Gonchev is, in his marina.

If he is going to live in this country he will never be free of problems of conscience. Other countries have the same—in his wife's Balkans the Serbs and the Croats at each other's throats, in Romania, the proud Hungarians, who were an underclass, and Armenians fermenting everywhere. In Iran the Bahai, in India the Sikhs. Africans in London's Paddington, Algerians in France. He has documented such doings all over the globe, and perhaps that was his films' real attraction—that wandering, ever-homing lust for the national.

But this place, whatever you call it, is Babel to the left, Elysium to the right—cross on the red or green light as you can. You can scarcely walk down a street without bumping into an ethnic, which means Not Like You. Your skin color, no matter what color, is irreversible. If you have money, your duty is to flaunt it, by embracing outrageous luxury or costly simplicity, or by incorporating your good will. There is no escaping a public choice. If you have intellect, you are duty-bound not to keep it a private matter, although you may get no praise for this, may even meet resentment, and a scrutiny anticipating the worst. If you are poor you are a public charge—ergo, from birth a sinner against the state.

This is the class system here, all the more rigorous because it is underground, yet has to be constantly expressed. There are few acceptable labels, and you are given no instructions; people avoid both for fear of contaminating themselves with a revealed sense of class. If you have such a sense you conceal it, or else find some fanatic enclave. People do find ways of being ordinary, but have lost that fine edge that comes of being unaware of the social path one is following.

Yet the water slops on the boat side. The big river shakes its rhythm into the man. Who has such indelible pictures now. In the heart of the heartland, where freckles are still rampant and restaurant patrons seem as blood-related as their own dairy herds, he has been served by a former boat person and by a Bahai. In a crack in the earth, in movieland, a friend is sinking, is being his own burial urn. He is carrying his first-generation father in his arms.

One might have to work at daily living as a farmer works the ground. He could be a picture farmer. A dirty boat and a clean sky, what better recipe for living?

In the river, out toward its center, there is always a dark, shifting seam. Gonchev sometimes addresses it. "Malkoff," he says now. "Malkoff"—who was Malikovsky once—"I'm riding backward. But it's crumbling toward me." He doffs his cap.

In the bedroom they've made, she still sleeps, dreaming of jail maybe. Her legs have sprawled for freedom. The pose is shocking, like a body with its throat cut. Tucking the quilt around her again, he listens, heartened, to her breath. Leaving the one light burning, he slips into the bunk.

From there, her profile is hers; it will never be Danilo's again. As for Danilo, he'll surely be somewhere, acting. The long quarrel between art and fact won't be over, even for him.

From the bunk, Gonchev addresses his children. Laura, who no longer needs trees to stand under, but as citizen Laura may some day buy them.

Klement, whose photograph will be hard to look at but will never be turned to the wall. Whose father will not cease wooing him. Political hate has one virtue. Hate swerves.

It'll be harder than you think, for your mother and me. Without the borders we got away from. And looking at the world with one eye green, the other blue.

It is so hard for Americans to put the private dream and the public dream together. And he is now an American.

In the bunk itself a lens opens. As the boat rocks. There he is down there—the émigré child. As a child he could never be sick; that was his trouble. An émigré child could not afford to be, his mother said, shivering at what she saw, shoeless and scabbed, in the streets of Harbin. Even his careless father had assented—a piano pupil of his had lost the tips of both thumbs to frostbite. And Gonchev had obeyed. He was never ill.

But one night—after the ticket to Paris had long since come and he knew for sure they were not going to use it—he allowed himself to be ill. Even so, he didn't disobey them utterly. But that night, and for many nights after, tossing in a bed as narrow as a ship's bunk, he took them to Paris with him.

Staring now at what he had never before so focused on, Gonchev sees that the child on that train, going by rail from Kyoto to the Gare de Lyon in his Sunday shirt, wasn't truly alone. Flying behind him, through clouds painted by Chagall, his parents come on, winging steadily, and behind them, in a heaven tinted for each migrant by some local home draughtsman, the flying wedges of all the émigrés there are.

In the center of the lens is the place he took them to. Not a city of one name only. A site with curbstones as thin as the lips of pre-Renaissance Madonnas. Where healthy children could become angelically sick, and the sick ones angelically well. And broken-down pianists and seamstresses sent pillar-to-post had their rightful box seats, in a world that was wrong. Higher than Arles, it would be, or Mont-Saint-Michel, or any of the holy mounts from Athos to Fujiyama—that city the Gonchevs of this world were always trekking to, whether they had been kicked out from home by all the revolutions of evil, or were only gazing up at the masthead, under their own steerage steam. But he no longer wants to make a film of it.

When he has students again he will instruct them never to dream any city wholly, but to record wherever one is, while standing by the river of flux.

Vuksica's mouth is serenely closed, her breathing deep. He wants to be next to her. Even a few feet away isn't safe—though he knows this too is old habit. In the tiny quarters where he was reared his kind huddled even closer, over the smoking cups that were the only samovar.

Stowed in a chest here are two sleeping bags he's never exhumed, property again of the sailor girls—rounding what Cape are they now? He hauls one bag out, sniffs musty rubber but no bilge, and stretches out on top of it, next to her. What have he and she left behind that matters most—a son, a cookbook? The losses talked of around a samovar were always the same.

Beds cannot be trusted. Nor floors. After a while the deck between the two of them opens like a hatch. Agonies, purgatories, are stowed below as needed, maybe even to be coveted by a man like him. All sailing on with him, under whatever homeless skies. None too light or too heavy to escape that man's regard.

In their midst he sees the Salle Pleyel. He had never requested a slide of it, but had once seen a Pleyel piano. The dolly of his camera is now trained on it.

"What's that instrument you have there?" a voice in the row behind him says.

The child waits; he knows that such instruments as his are barred here. The man answers.

"It is called *le traveling*."

Seated at the keyboard, a figure hovers over the keys near middle C, its hands raised, humming to itself like an organ stop—as it had on a child's darkest night. There is no other music. The head, the wonderful skull of Rachmaninoff, rises and bends and rises—a grail entirely in the major key of light, a ticket to be used over and over again.

ABOUT THE AUTHOR

HORTENSE CALISHER's stories first appeared in *The New Yorker*. Born in New York, she worked, after Barnard, as a welfare investigator. She has since produced many volumes of stories, novels, novellas, and memoirs. *False Entry*, a novel, and *Herself*, a memoir, were nominated for the National Book Award. Her latest book, *The Small Bang*, was published under the pseudonym "Jack Fenno." *In the Palace of the Movie King* was begun after a State Department–sponsored tour of Hungary, Romania, and Yugoslavia. She has taught at universities and was awarded two Guggenheim fellowships and the Lifetime Achievement Award of the National Endowment for the Arts.

Ms. Calisher is a past president of American PEN and of the American Academy of Arts and Letters.

FIC
Calisher

Calisher, Hortense.

In the palace of the
movie king.

WITHDRAWN 25⁰⁰

DATE			